TYBEE RHAPSODY

REMEMBERING IRELAND SERIES

LEARA RHODES

Old Fort Press
Savannah, Georgia

*Dedicated to two women musicians
who have made this a better book*

*Rebekah Boles,
my piano teacher*

and

*Pam Asberry,
music composer*

"If you have built castles in the air,
your work need not be lost;
that is where they should be.
Now put the foundations under them."

Henry David Thoreau

1

Dublin, Ireland, September 1907

Gertrude rushes down the street. Every step puts her closer to her destination, but also makes her feel as though she is going nowhere. When she stops, her feet tremble on the sidewalk in the chill air as she waits for a tram. Umbrellas and cloaks are blown about in the gusty wind and sheets of rain.

As Gertrude waits, she looks about and finds no familiar faces. There is no one to say hello to or to gripe with about the weather. All she can do is stand in the rain and wait for the tram on its route to the National Concert Hall on Earlsfort Terrace near St. Stephen's Green. Her cloak hood is pulled low over her forehead, covering her hair. Fidgeting, she looks down the street to where the tram should be coming but then quickly glances down to make sure her shoes are not in the water puddles already forming on the foot path. Randolph would not be pleased with wet shoes.

A brisk wind and a moving carriage passing by push colder air into her face. Hair strands slip out of her bun. Her long blonde hair gets a lot of attention on the Dublin streets, so she is happy to have it tucked away. Finally, the tram arrives. As it stops, five people exit before she can ascend the steps. There is nowhere to sit. Not being tall enough to reach the straps at the top, she positions herself over by a wooden rod to hold. She cannot be late.

The tram does not move. She looks toward the front of the tram and sees a middle-aged man talking with the conductor. She cannot hear their conversation, but anxiety is building in Gertrude, who knows that time is ticking away. Finally, the man exits and the tram begins to move. The journey to get to her part-time job is as plodding as her life. Will it be this way forever? Will she always be running from one small job to another with no time to work on what makes her happy? Her dream, the reason she is in Dublin, is to play music and learn to compose. But making her dream come true is as slow-going as the tram.

Life would be easier in a big city, Gertrude had thought. There is a big difference between Dublin, Ireland, and Savannah, Georgia, where she is from. As a married woman looking to build her music career, her efforts seem fruitless. Just getting through a day is difficult. Her clothes and Randolph's must be cleaned and pressed. With him teaching violin at the Royal Irish Academy of Music, his jackets, shirts, trousers, gloves, and handkerchiefs must be pristine every day. Meals must be planned. Randolph teaches during the day and then often performs in the evening. With her part-time jobs, she has to keep track of their schedules to be prepared. Randolph doesn't like to wait for anything.

One of her jobs is with the Dublin Orchestral Society. Lateness is not accepted, and she is hurrying in the rain to get to the Concert Hall for a performance. At the tram stop nearest the Concert Hall, the rain is coming down in torrents. Cold and wet, she dashes into the building and shakes the rain from her cloak. As she passes through the lobby into the back hallway, there are numerous musicians and staff, but no one greets her. Invisible, she hangs her wet cloak on a peg in the hallway, pushes past the loaders, and makes her way into the back of the stage behind the rear curtain to pull the music from a bin and then wends her way over to the piano. She sorts through the music, checks the order, and places the music on the piano. Though she has done this many times, her fingers still shake a bit as they reach for the pages.

Musicians come onto the stage and find their seats. Gertrude steps behind the side curtain legs and stands back to let others enter. Peeking past the burgundy velvet curtains, she sees that the house is open. One of her favorite things to do is to look at the audience members when they enter. Their faces are full of anticipation for the promise of a good concert.

This has been billed as an important performance with a guest singer, the young John McCormack, a tenor from Athlone, County Westmeath, Ireland. The concert master had introduced McCormack to the orchestra members at rehearsal. As a young man, he had been singing in the choir of St. Mary's Pro-Cathedral in Dublin, where Vincent O'Brien recognized his talent, and in 1903, McCormack won the gold medal of the Dublin Feis Ceoil. Having trained in Italy, McCormack was on his way to America, but he was in Dublin visiting his family. The audience included his family, friends of James Joyce—a personal friend of McCormack's—and anyone who could snag a ticket. McCormack had a reputation for blending artistic music with more popular, accessible singing. His voice quality and charisma made him a new celebrity. At this concert, he is to sing "I Hear You Calling Me."

The concert master has emphasized the importance of getting the music right. Gertrude feels the pressure, especially since the piano has been instrumental in introducing this new work to an audience. Suddenly, she gasps. Coming down the aisle is Sharon Murphy, nee McGee. All the color drains out of her face. Her stomach tightens. She slides deeper into the curtain so that Sharon cannot see her, but the signal to be seated has been given and everyone has to be on stage, including her. The performance will start soon. Gertrude has to go in and sit now.

Somehow, in all that she has done within the last three months, she never thought that a previous friend from Savannah, Georgia, would be in the audience in Dublin, Ireland. Yes, Sharon married Connor and is now living in Wexford, Ireland, but this is Dublin, hours away from Wexford. Maybe Sharon will not spot her. Gertrude sees that the conductor is now standing on the other side of the stage. She has to go now. She moves onto the stage and sits on a stool beside the piano bench. The discordant sounds of the instruments stop as the first violin stands and cues the pitch from the oboe. Once everyone is on pitch, the conductor enters, the audience applauds, and the concert begins. She can only do what she is hired to do: turn pages for the pianist.

Rehearsals, though challenging, have prepared the musicians. However, when Gertrude stands to turn a page, she feels that Sharon is staring at her. Despite her fear of being recognized, Gertrude dutifully turns the pages. The concert is not long, and there is a reception for McCormack afterwards. Her mind wanders, and she hopes that the rain will be horrendous at the end of the concert so that everyone will run off quickly from the Concert Hall, including Sharon. Gertrude does not want to speak with Sharon, not now.

At the end of the concert, during the ovations when the musicians stand, she remains sitting. The pianist leaves without saying anything to Gertrude, who takes the music and places it in the bin, gets her cloak, and heads to the back door to exit through the garden instead of to the street. The rain has stopped. As she exits, she sees Sharon, who is dressed in the latest Dublin fashion, a lavender linen dress, her black hair braided and circled on the top of her head, and a purple tweed shawl draped over her shoulders.

"Gertrude," she calls out.

Gertrude wants to bolt and run. She had thought Sharon would never be able to find her in this big city, yet here she is. Gertrude stumbles but stops.

"Hello, Sharon. I didn't know you would be in Dublin."

"And I didn't know I would see you here as well. I wanted to hear McCormack and now I see you. How are you?

"Fine. Really, fine." Gertrude is standing still, but inside she is ready to flee.

Sharon looks at Gertrude, then softly speaks. "Everyone has been so concerned about you, Gertrude."

"Well, not to worry, you see I am fine." Her voice quavers at the end.

"I see you standing here in front of me, but I don't know that I see you as being fine. Why haven't you been in contact with anyone? Why did you just disappear from Brenau College and not tell a soul?"

"No one needed to know at the time," says Gertrude with a stronger voice.

"But so many wanted to know." Sharon crosses her shawl closer to her body. "Not hearing from you, your mother went to see Mrs. Schultz and the nuns at the hospital in Savannah to see if they had any news, thinking that since you had been a part of their nursing program, surely they would know where you were. The nuns had no idea you had even left Brenau. Mrs. Schultz contacted the Savannah Music Club, which sponsored you to study music at Brenau. No one there had heard from you, and no one at Brenau knew where you had gone. Mrs. Schultz wrote to me asking, since we are friends, if I had heard from you." Sharon pauses. "Why did you leave us all wondering what had happened to you?" Sharon moves closer to Gertrude, who backs away.

"I had my reasons." She looks away from Sharon. "I hope you will let them know that I am fine." Gertrude looks directly at Sharon. "I have another appointment and must go. Do take care."

Sharon is looking at her as though she were a stranger. Gertrude starts to move as Sharon takes a card from her purse.

"Please, call me if you need anything. You know Connor and I will be pleased to have you visit us in Wexford."

"Thank you," says Gertrude, taking the card, but then she pauses and looks at Sharon. "Why are you in Dublin?"

"I came on business for the shipping firm and wanted to hear the concert while I was in town." Hurriedly, she continues, "I am not leaving until tomorrow evening. Would you be able to meet me for tea tomorrow when we can visit better?"

"Sorry, I have a full day. I must hurry. Take care." Gertrude dashes toward the arches going into the garden behind the Concert Hall. As she reaches the stone wall, she glances over to where Sharon stands and sees Sharon watching as she leaves.

2

———

Gertrude has to hurry and change for her second part-time job. Inside the flat, Randolph is eating the dinner she had left for him and will be heading off for a performance. As she puts everything down and takes off her cloak, he looks up.

"I see you managed to get mud on the hem of your black satin skirt."

Gertrude looks down and sees the mud stains. They must have happened when she was caught in the rain waiting for the tram. Swallowing her retort, she asks, "How were your students today?"

Randolph doesn't answer. He wipes his fingers with his napkin and places it neatly beside the plate. "I know you will be out late; we'll talk later."

Gertrude hangs her cloak on the coat stand at the door. It is still damp from the rain. Her fingers gently touch the blue wool as though she has never touched it before, giving her time to think what to say. Turning, she sees that Randolph has pushed his plate away without eating much.

"You haven't finished," she says.

"I have eaten all I can." Randolph pauses. "You are not much of a cook, you know."

Gertrude reaches up and takes the pins out of her hair to let the blonde locks fall to her shoulders and dry out. Her damp hair strands stick to her face. Facing Randolph, she notices his long fingers are playing with his napkin beside the plate. His brown wavy hair has been shellacked and weighted down with gel to keep it tidy for his performance. His face is clean-shaven and lean. He shifts in his chair as though to get up, but he doesn't.

His awkwardness confirms to Gertrude that something must be happening that he doesn't want to talk about. She asks, "Randolph, why did you bring me here?"

Without looking at her, he stands up. "You needed to leave Brenau and see what else there was to see in the world."

"But I have seen nothing but a big city. I seldom see you with your schedule."

"Someone has to earn a living." He moves away from the table toward the sink to refill his glass with water.

"I wanted to write music. Couldn't I write music anywhere?"

"No, you needed more instruction in composition and theory. You could not write music anywhere without knowing these."

"But I am not able to study here. They will not admit me into the Academy. You had indicated that maybe I could get private lessons, but there has been no money for those."

He fills a glass with water from the pitcher on the shelf next to the sink. Without turning to her, he says, "What do you want me to do, Gertrude? I can't make them take you for free."

"But what about your connections? You said you had connections." Though she is still standing near her cloak, she raises a hand out to him.

"I do, but they have not worked out."

"Why not? Please tell me. Why not?"

Randolph sips his water and does not answer her.

"Why not, Randolph?" Gertrude raises her voice to a higher pitch.

"You want to know why?"

"Yes, because turning pages at the Dublin Orchestral Society is not getting me very far in learning to compose music."

Randolph slams his glass down on the side of the sink. "My connections heard you play."

"Where? Where did they hear me play? We don't even have a piano in the flat. Where did they hear me play?"

"At the pub."

"At the pub? The part-time job to help pay our expenses? The pub? Where we play traditional songs? They based my playing on that?"

"Yes, Gertrude, they think that a woman playing in a pub is not serious about learning to compose classical music."

"Really?" She stands with both hands on her hips. "And what do you think?"

"I agree. I don't think you have what it takes to write classical music."

Gertrude is struck silent. She looks at him and sees him for the first time. She thought she was getting a hand up the ladder to create music, but instead, there was something else. What is it that made him marry her and bring her to Dublin from Gainesville, Georgia? They met at Brenau College, where she was studying after being sponsored by the Savannah Music Club. He was a visiting instructor in violin. He flirted, he caressed, he said things she had never heard a man say to her before, and she was smitten.

Now, thousands of miles away from her Savannah family, from her friends in the nursing program at St. Joseph's Hospital, and from her music, she's here with a man she barely knows. He is talented and has a visiting fellowship with the

Royal Irish Academy of Music. That means something. And when he suggested that she come with him to Dublin at the end of his instructorship at Brenau in May, she did not even hesitate. She had hesitated too often growing up in Savannah, a child of Irish immigrants who were not able to give any financial support for a girl like Gertrude, who wanted to be a concert pianist. Her family saw her acceptance into the nursing program as a guarantee that she could earn a living. Nursing, however, was not her dream. Music was her dream. Randolph became a ticket to reach her dream. He promised.

Randolph crosses to her and attempts to take her in his arms. She pushes him away. "No, I can do nothing to please you. I can't cook. I can't write music. What can I do?"

He moves toward her yet again. "You could take me in your embrace and let me kiss you."

She glares at him, her eyes full of anger and disappointment. "That's it? If I let you embrace me and kiss me, then everything will be fine?"

Randolph backs up to the table. He turns and puts the chair under the table. "Gertrude, I can't give you the talent you lack. I can't even give you the lessons you so desire. There is nothing to do. You need to make the most of it." With that, he turns and gets his coat. As he puts it on, he reaches into his pocket. "My gloves. Did you clean them and not replace them in the coat?"

Gertrude walks over to the bureau, opens a drawer, and pulls out a pair of gloves. "Here are your gloves." She throws the gloves at Randolph, then pulls out other pairs of gloves and slings them at him. "Here are more gloves. Lots of gloves. Lots of clean gloves. Make your choice and pick them up, because I am not going to." With that, she goes into the bedroom and slams the door. As she changes out of her performance black gown and into a more casual dress for the pub, she hears Randolph leave the flat. Opening the door into the parlor, she sees Randolph has left the gloves on the floor.

3

___

The bandmates at the pub have a pint in front of them and are jostling with regulars and asking favors of the servers. There is a bay window in the front of the pub where the bandmates can sit or stand. The piano is against a side wall but angled so that more of the audience can be seen as well as the other bandmates. Gertrude greets the men and takes her seat on the wooden bench. She knows all the songs by heart, so no music is displayed.

The fiddle player, Ryan, calls the songs. He is the leader and the one who schedules the dates and makes decisions. All Gertrude has to do is follow along, relieved that she has another source of income. Growing up in Savannah, she learned the tunes from her mother, who had immigrated from County Wexford and brought along a memory of songs she had learned in Ireland. Ryan starts the tunes, and as Gertrude plays along, though the day has been a long one, the enthusiasm of the pub regulars is enough to keep her motivated. She plays and smiles and sings along. At one of their breaks, Ryan comes over and sits on the piano bench next to her before she has a chance to stand.

"Just wanted to let you know that the band has been asked to fill in for a couple of weeks at a hotel pub in Galway."

Gertrude says nothing.

Ryan looks at her, waiting for some response. "Well, what do you think?"

Clearing her throat, she says, "What should I say? Have a good time?"

Ryan laughs. "No, really, we want you to come with us."

Quickly, she responds, "Sorry, but no. I have other obligations…"

"I see, well, should those other obligations disappear, we'll leave from the Kingsbridge Station tomorrow at two in the afternoon."

Ryan smiles. Gertrude has left her hair down around her shoulders and feels his eyes looking over every strand of her hair. In an attempt to stand, Ryan realizes that he needs to move from the bench to allow her to exit. He stands and steps back. Crossing in front of him to the bar to get a glass of water, she can feel his eyes watching as she moves through the tables and chairs full of patrons. She does not look back.

The band plays another set. It is late. The last tram leaves shortly. She passes Ryan, who stops her and gives her a quick hug. His body is lean like Randolph's. She can feel the strength of his arms from all the fiddle practice. "We'll be in touch when we get back in a couple of weeks," he says as he hugs her again.

Gertrude smiles up at him, playfully hitting him on the shoulder. "You better." Calling to the other bandmates, she says, "Take care, guys. See you later." And she is out the door, dashing to the tram to go back to the flat for the evening.

The electric light causes Gertrude to blink her eyes in order to adjust from the darkness of the night to the inside of the flat. But as she takes off her cloak, she sees a large envelope on the table. Scrawled across the outside of the envelope is her name. Slowly stepping toward the table, she looks at her name and simply holds the envelope. Finally, she opens it to find another envelope, a handwritten letter, and cash. Frozen, she has no idea what this could mean. The letter is from Randolph. His handwriting is unmistakable, a script that is rigid and precise.

Dear Gertrude,

I had hoped that being in Dublin with me would be enough for you, but obviously it is not. I cannot give you all the things you desire. I did not want to be the one to tell you that you do not have what it takes to be a concert pianist, nor to be able to compose music. I can't give you talent. I planned to talk with you soon about our future, but I have been called back to Germany and must go immediately.

There are several things you need to know. First, I have a wife in Germany. Second, I talked you into coming with me because I thought you would be ready for adventure and would take any opportunity to leave Georgia and see the world. When you told me that you would not come unless we were married, I asked a colleague from Atlanta to come up to Gainesville to marry us. I completed all the forms, but to keep him from having to stay overnight in Gainesville, I offered to submit the forms the next day to the county office before we left for Ireland. I did not do that. The forms are in the envelope. Third, the cash is for a month's flat rent to give you time to decide what you need to do.

I have tendered my resignation at the Royal Irish Academy and have left for Germany. Know that I did have feelings for you and wish you well.

Randolph

Gertrude collapses on one of the chairs at the table. Her fingers, stiff and shaking, pull the flap to open the envelope. She finds the marriage form with both their signatures, as well as the signature of the Atlanta friend who performed the marriage ceremony. She feels hollow inside, like a gourd that has been emptied of its pulp and has no use other than to hang from a cord or be used as a vessel. She cannot think. She has no idea what her next move should be. The cash would pay the rent, but there are tram fees, food costs, and necessities that cannot be paid from the little money she earns from two part-time jobs, with one of them suspended for several weeks while the band travels. With no idea what to do, Gertrude tosses everything on the table and goes into the bedroom. Randolph's clothing is gone. His violins are gone. His toiletries are gone. She crosses back into the other room and opens up the bureau drawer. All of his gloves are gone.

In disbelief, Gertrude sits down at the table and rereads Randolph's letter. Staring at the marriage form makes her feel even emptier. Her dreams, her goals, and her future are all gone. She recounts the money, then quickly stands. She has to do something. She goes into the bedroom to get ready for bed, but instead pulls a suitcase out from under the bed and packs. Tomorrow, she plans on catching the train to Galway and posting a note to the Dublin Orchestral Society giving her resignation.

4
____

At the Kingsbridge Station, Gertrude sees Ryan and the other bandmates.

"So, I hear that you need a pianist."

The guys look her way and nod. "You have made a good choice," says Ryan, giving her another one of his strong hugs. He crosses over to the ticket window and purchases a ticket for Gertrude.

The train pulls into the station. Boarding takes longer than they expected, but as they settle into several seats in the train car, Gertrude chooses a window seat. Ryan sits next to her. The other bandmates find seats close by. As the train slowly pulls out of the station and leaves the center of Dublin, the Irish countryside changes from urban to rural with hills and farms, and with cows and sheep roaming between stone fences. There had not been any time to see anything of Ireland since they arrived in Dublin by ferry from Liverpool, where their ship from the United States had docked. The motion of the train is lulling, but instead of dozing off like the other bandmates, her thoughts turn to Sharon and her questions that Gertrude had not been able to sort through and answer. She did not respond to Sharon's questions because she does not fully understand why she made the decision to leave Georgia and come to Ireland. Randolph offered her a path to make her dreams come true, and she accepted him with no hesitation.

Arriving at Brenau College in Gainesville was the first time Gertrude had been away from home. She was excited to take classes with women from all over the country, so unlike the small group of Irish women in the nursing program in Savannah. Her spring classes were piano performance, teaching, and music history. While taking the classes, she continued her nursing education by working with Dr. Downey, who had plans to build a hospital in Gainesville. All of this had been arranged by the Savannah Music Club. The plan was for her to have both a music diploma and a nursing certificate, the latter to please her family, who did not encourage her to seek a music career.

After hours of being in class, practicing the piano, and working with Dr. Downey, she settled into a routine. Her studies included a lot of reading about music history, including the history of some women composers. There were not a lot of women nor a lot of information, but some. As she read, the information surprised her, and yet it didn't.

The class readings were mostly about music compositions, but there were brief biographies on each musician. As she made notes, she found that the information on women and their successes also included their difficulties. Women throughout the ages had been restricted from composing music by being denied music composition education. The texts didn't state that. They indicated that because men were more capable of composing and performing, women were not included. Yet Gertrude knew that elite music conservatory schools did not accept women; that is why she was at a women's college in the middle of Georgia.

Gertrude learned that women who had music composition training had learned from their fathers, husbands, family connections, or were from an affluent family who could provide private lessons. The women were few, like Louise Farrenc, a pianist who also married a musician; or Clara Schumann, whose father taught her to compose before she married musician Robert Schumann; or Francesca Caccini, whose father was a Renaissance composer.

Other notable women composers were nuns who had the luxury of time to compose and to work on their music. These women included Hildegard of Bingen, a Benedictine Abbess who composed seventy works and founded two monasteries, and Isabella Leonarda, who entered a convent at sixteen and produced many works but also taught music to the other nuns.

Gertrude does not have a family composer to teach her nor the money to hire private lessons, and though she is Catholic, she has no intention of becoming a nun. Additionally, those women who did compose music often had to publish their work under a male name, like Fanny Mendelssohn, who composed more than 460 works, many under her brother Felix's name and behind her father's back, or one of Brenau's graduates whose husband owned a print shop and published her work locally. Other works written by women were identified as anonymous, or by initials to mask their sex, or "By a Lady of Charleston." The professors lauded the fact that the women were protected by not being identified.

Additional social limitations on women composers resulted from their marriages. Amy Beach, an accomplished pianist who married, agreed to limit her piano performances to one charity recital a year. Her work and talent became popular only after her husband died. She was the first female composer to have a symphony performed in the United States in Boston in 1893. Gertrude knew of Beach's work and had actually played one of her pieces in the recital she gave in Savannah the previous fall.

Women composers and performers were also not paid the same as their male counterparts, according to the biographies of some of these women. Louise Farrenc was paid less for a decade until the success of her "Nonet in E flat Major, Op. 38" had her demand and receive equal pay. And though Farrenc may have succeeded, the social pressure was defeating for some women composers. Clara Schumann was quoted as saying that she lost her confidence in composing. "I once believed that I possessed creative talent, but I have given up this idea," she said. "A woman must not desire to compose—there has never yet been one able to do it. Should I expect to be the one?"

The fact that a talented woman like Clara Schumann realized she could not compose music was pointed out by the professors in class as proof that women were not meant to compose. Society wanted women to play for home recitals to entertain guests or to teach music. The course material made it clear that it is deemed inappropriate for women to play in a professional symphony orchestra or to compose a large-scale, complex work, such as a symphony.

Gertrude absorbs the lesson that what a woman needs to learn is how to teach someone else to play the piano. But she wonders why women can learn to teach males how to play the piano, but the women themselves are not seen as talented enough to perform or to compose. This does not make sense to her. What does make sense is that though she is now a better performer, thanks to attending Brenau, she wants to make her own music. The train keeps moving across the island. Exhausted, her thoughts stop, and sleep finally comes.

5

———

Galway is quiet when the train arrives just before dinnertime. The bandmates gather their belongings and make the short trek to the hotel near Eyre Park to stow their bags and instruments. They are playing in the hotel pub, so rooms are offered, but only two rooms. There is a discussion with management, and they add a small room at the back of the top floor for Gertrude. Not being on the same floor as the other band members is okay with her. The musicians are unknown to her. All she knows is that Ryan plays the fiddle and the others play a bodhrán, flute, mandolin, and concertina. At the Dublin pubs, by the time she arrived to play with them, the bandmates had already gotten a pint and were visiting with the regulars, so they never talked much with Gertrude, who always dashed away after the last tune. Even here now at the hotel in Galway, everyone goes their separate ways to store their bags with plans to meet at the pub to have something to eat before playing.

Gertrude walks up the three flights of steps with her cloak over her arm and her suitcase. The room on the top floor is indeed small. It includes a single bed, a small night table, and pegs on the wall to hang her clothes. The water closet is one floor down at the end of the hall. She puts her suitcase on the floor, hangs her cloak on a peg, and decides that her current dress is just fine for sitting on the piano bench out of sight of most of the audience. That's a skill learned from being a page turner, how to be invisible, a skill that worked for her until Sharon showed up in Dublin.

Returning to the pub, Gertrude finds the bandmates already at the bar with sandwiches and pints in front of them. There is an empty table nearby, but before she can sit, Ryan motions for her to come and sit next to him. He pats the seat of an empty stool. "This one is saved for you, Gertrude."

The stool is high, so she has to wiggle onto the seat and doesn't know where to put her feet. Being much shorter than the men in the band, Gertrude finds the stool uncomfortable and shifts from one side of the stool to the other. No one seems to notice. A sandwich is put in front of her and a pint is sloshed down on the bar counter next to the plate. There is no flatware or napkin.

"May I have a glass of water, please?" she says, not quite loud enough for the barkeep to hear her.

Ryan looks over at her and says loudly to the barkeep, "The lady would like a glass of water." Everyone stops eating and talking and turns to look at Gertrude, including the barkeep.

"Please," she says to him.

The barkeep leaves the bar but comes back shortly with a glass of water.

Traveling has made her hungry. The sandwich is ham and cheese with a dash of salad sauce on homemade bread. She takes a sip of water between every bite. With no one talking to her, Gertrude studies the different liquor bottles lining the back of the bar and looks at a mirror hanging over the back of the bar that shows an empty pub behind her. Ryan has been talking with the bandmate next to him. Gertrude finishes and is about to move away from the bar when Ryan turns to her.

"I saw you were nervous about eating down here at the bar with us guys, so I left you alone to finish. I wasn't ignoring you, is what I want to tell you."

For the first time in a while, Gertrude smiles. In his own way, Ryan is trying to be nice and gentle. "I appreciate your kindness. I am fine. I am no longer hungry, so that's good." She stands to move away from the bar.

"Where are you off to?"

"I thought I would go test out the piano and see which keys are missing."

Ryan laughs and wipes his face with his hands, then wipes his hands on his pants. "I totally understand."

Gertrude goes to the piano. There is no dust anywhere; that is a good sign. She sits down and runs a few scales. There is no one in the pub but the bandmates and the barkeep and they are busy talking. Seeing that everyone is preoccupied, she plays a piece she has been humming for days and had been practicing at Brenau. The dark opening notes start the piece, but it then comes alive with the dance tune that follows. At the end of the piece, after some four minutes of playing, she looks up and realizes that all the men in the pub have turned and are listening to every note played. Surprised by their attention, she says, "All the keys work." The men applaud. Her pale face is suddenly beet red. She stands and moves away from the piano, heading for the door, when Ryan catches up with her.

"What were you playing?"

"A piece written by Brahms, Johannes Brahms, a rhapsody."

"You play classical?"

"Yes, I have always wanted to be a concert pianist."

"And this rhapsody thing you played, I bet you know how it is written. Right?"

Gertrude pauses. This is the thought that she is not

supposed to have as a woman. She should not be able to know how a male wrote this piece, but she does. From her textbook reading, she recalls, "A rhapsody is a piece of music of indeterminate length, with no formal structure, comprised of a number of different musical ideas. A rhapsody is all about dynamics: light and shade, high and low, loud and soft, happy and sad. It is a story, a journey, and usually quite the musical ride."

She also remembers that Brahms wrote Rhapsody Op. 119 No. 4 toward the end of his life as an introspective piece. He sent the works to his friend Clara Schumann when her health was bad. Gertrude remembers reading a certain passage that Schumann wrote after playing Brahms' Rhapsodies. "In these pieces, I at last feel musical life stir once again in my soul." This quote resonated with Gertrude and became the guiding light for her to compose music, music that stirred her soul.

Gertrude chose this rhapsody for her spring performance piece. With a limited opportunity to produce her own work and now that Randolph has shared how others feel about her being able to compose, her self-esteem is shattered and her inability to create resonates within her body. All Gertrude feels she can do is play someone else's work.

After a deep breath, she says, "I have no idea. And I need to freshen up before we start." Turning, she walks out of the pub to locate a water closet.

This time, when Gertrude returns to the pub, there are people at the tables and drinks are being served. Quietly, she crosses over to the piano and sits. With no music to shuffle and nothing to do, she looks out at the people who are coming in to listen to music. It's the same behind-the-curtain look she had done at the orchestra, looking at the audience with their anticipation of having a fun evening. The patrons enter and order their drinks at the bar, then find a table to sit with friends and mates.

As the pub fills, each bandmate comes to the stage area and picks up his instrument. The concertina player sits in a straight-backed chair. The others stand about and make room for each other, shuffling around and tuning their instruments. Ryan comes to the floor with his violin and adjusts a few strings. Without any introduction, he nods to the bandmates and everyone begins with a soulful tune called "Galway Bay," suitable for their location. The list of tunes they play is geared to show off the talents of the bandmates. "The Rose of Tralee" highlights the concertina. "As I Roved Out One Morning" was for the piano and flute. Ryan's fiddle carries the "Billy Boy" tune and has the people in the pub singing along with the bandmates.

"Where have you been all the day,
Billy Boy, Billy Boy?
Where have you been all the day,
Me Billy Boy?

I've been out with Nancy Gray,
And she's stolen me heart away,
She's me Nancy, tickled me fancy,
Oh me charmin' Billy Boy.

"Is she fit to be a wife?
Billy Boy, Billy Boy?
Is she fit to be a wife?
me Billy Boy?

"She's as fit to be a wife,
As a fork fits to a knife.
She's me Nancy, tickled me fancy,
Oh me charmin' Billy Boy."

All the musicians play the faster drinking songs that have the people in the pub standing up, dancing, and singing along.

After the first set, the band takes a break. The men head to the bar for a pint. Gertrude stands and crosses the pub to exit. There is a courtyard off the lobby toward the back. The day has been hard with so many changes. She came on a whim without thinking about the next step. Pushing past one of the tables, the men, who have been drinking and singing loudly, all stand up to let her pass. An older man at the table grabs her arm to detain her.

"Pretty lady, please sit and share a pint with us."

Gertrude cannot move as he is holding tightly to her arm. "Thank you," she says, "but I cannot."

"Why not? We're good for a pint or two." He winks at the other men who are cheering him on.

"Please let go of my arm."

The man sits down and pulls her onto his lap. His strength and fierceness outweigh Gertrude.

"Sir, you must permit me to leave."

"Not until you have a drink with us, pretty lady. Waiter!" he shouts out, and the men echo, "Waiter, over here, waiter."

Gertrude attempts to stand, but she cannot. His whiskey breath permeates the air around her nose, along with the strong smell of cigar smoke oozing from his jacket and hair. He wraps his arms around her, enveloping her and making it impossible for her to even struggle. He pushes her blonde hair back and leans in to kiss her, when suddenly he is sprawling on the floor and Gertrude is being held up by Ryan's strong arms.

"What are you doing?" The man growls from the floor.

"Trying not to kill you," says Ryan, spitting the words out between his teeth. "You leave my bandmate alone."

Ryan, still holding on to Gertrude, takes her through the door and guides her out into the courtyard. "Are you okay?" he asks.

Shaking, not from cold, but from the tension of the moment and the violence, Gertrude puts her arms tightly around her body and holds herself together. "I'm not okay, but will be. I need a bit of time before I face that crowd again."

"I'll sit here with you and give you time." He gently puts his hand on her back and guides her over to a bench under a vine-covered arbor.

Gertrude stops shaking, sits, and places her hands in her lap. The sky above them is full of stars. There has not been time in Dublin to see the night sky with all the hurrying from one place to another. A scent of marigolds fills the air. Gertrude looks around to see large pots with these autumn flowers blooming in the courtyard. Ryan remains silent; he sits and looks at the sky with her.

"Do you know any of the stars?" she asks.

"I have studied them once upon a time. I'm better at the moon phases."

"Oh? Why is that?"

"My folks, we had a bit of land down in the Beara Peninsula and planted things based on the moon phases."

"Really? Why?"

"The cycles of the moon affect plant growth just like the gravitational pull causes the tides to rise and fall. Moisture in the soil is affected by the moon. Therefore, it is thought that seeds will absorb more water during a full moon and a new moon when more moisture is pulled to the soil surface, causing seeds to swell, resulting in better germination."

"So, nothing is done between a full moon and a new moon?"

"Okay, here's what I know. There are two periods of the lunar cycle. One period is the time between a new moon and a full moon. This is called the waxing of the moon. The second period is the time between a full moon and a new moon. This is called the waning of the moon. Certain plants are better to be put in the ground during each of these two periods."

"Which plants..." Gertrude begins to ask.

"...are planted in each period? Simple, plants that produce crops above ground, like corn, tomatoes, watermelon, and zucchini, are planted during the waxing of the moon. As the moonlight increases night by night, plants are encouraged to grow leaves and stems. Plants that produce crops below ground, like onions, carrots, and potatoes, are planted during the waning of the moon. As moonlight decreases night by night, plants are encouraged to grow roots, tubers, and bulbs."

Gertrude thinks about what Ryan says. It makes sense.

"You don't garden, do you?" asks Ryan.

"Is it obvious?"

A bandmate comes out into the courtyard. "Barkeep wants to know when we will start again."

"Now," says Ryan. He stands and offers Gertrude a hand. "Shall we face the dragons?"

They enter the pub and the table of rowdy men has left. Gertrude lets out her breath, not realizing that she was holding it until the cause of tension was gone. She crosses to the piano, and the second set goes as smoothly as the first. They end the set with "The Wearing of the Green." Ryan holds his fiddle and sings with the rest of the bandmates.

> "Oh, Paddy dear, did you hear the news that's going
>   'round?
> The shamrock is forbid by law to grow on Irish ground
> Saint Patrick's Day no more to keep, his color can't
>   be seen
> For there's a bloody law again' the Wearing of the
>   Green.
> I met with Napper Tandy and he took me by the hand

And he said, 'How's poor old Ireland and how does she
　　stand?'
"'She's the most distressful country that ever yet
　　was seen
For they're hanging men and women there for Wearing
　　of the Green.'"

At the end of the set, the men gather their instruments and
then head over to the bar for another pint before they go to
their rooms. Gertrude hesitates. The room with the possibility
of sleep after such a long day is more of a priority to her than
before, but after what happened with the "whiskey man," she
hesitates to climb the stairs alone. Ryan appears at her elbow.

"Are you going to socialize with us or leave?"

Her hesitation makes him continue. "I pay the band here on
a Saturday night since we have the day off tomorrow and don't
play until Monday night. Here's your pay. He hands her an
envelope.

"Thank you. I would stay if I could get a cup of tea."

Ryan laughs. "And here we thought you didn't like us. It's
the ale you don't like."

He leads her over to one of the tables and leaves her to sit as
he returns to the bar to ask for a cup of tea. He says something
to the bandmates because the men all turn and glance at her,
then they pick up their pints and come over to the table. As
they crowd around, she learns their names. Glen plays the
concertina. He prefers the accordion, but it's bigger and hard to
take traveling. Ellias plays the flute, tin whistle, and anything
else that he can blow. The bodhrán player can play almost any
percussion instrument but grew up playing this drum. His
name is Jake. Harry plays the mandolin. He prefers the guitar,
but the ballads they play are better with the mandolin.

As they end their round of introducing each other, Jake

says, "Ryan said we'd better introduce ourselves and get to know you."

Gertrude looks over at Ryan, who sheepishly grins. "So, I want to know about the music you played when we got here. That was classy music, not traditional. Where did you learn to play like that?"

Gertrude pauses. How can she tell these men that she had to learn? She felt in her core that she had to learn how to play the most difficult songs she could find. Would they understand? Does she understand? They are musicians, surely they will understand. Instead, she tells them the basics. "My mother taught me to play the piano. Then I had a neighbor who taught piano before leaving Ireland. He ate dinner with us in exchange for teaching me how to play."

"So, you're not from Ireland?"

"No, I was born in Savannah, Georgia, but my parents are from County Wexford."

The men relax but change the subject to talk about how they plan on spending their Sunday in Galway. There is a fair in Eyre Park next door in the afternoon. The talk goes late. After Gertrude finishes her tea and pushes the cup away from her on the table, she stands up to leave.

"I'm sorry, but I really need to go to bed."

"Will you be okay to go upstairs by yourself? We don't know where that group of rowdy guys went or even if they are staying at the hotel," says Ryan.

"Of course," she says quietly. "I am fine."

Gertrude stands and exits the pub through the door that leads to the lobby and the stairs. As she climbs each flight slowly, her insides are a mixture of feelings. Her eyes glance quickly around the landing and up and down the stairs. She wonders if there are eyes watching her. No one can be seen. She climbs another flight. Still no one. On the top floor, something moves quickly behind her. She dashes up the final steps, puts the key in the lock, and as the door swings open so does an arm that encircles her from behind and a hand covers her mouth.

"You thought your boyfriend would scare me away, didn't you?"

Gertrude did not have to hear the voice of the man who had grabbed her in the pub; she could smell him. She struggles with him as he pushes her inside the small room, kicks the door shut, and holds her against the wall. He stuffs a handkerchief in her mouth, turns her, and pushes her against the wall to tie the handkerchief so she cannot scream. As she continues to struggle with him, he brutally shoves her onto the bed. He pins her down with his knee and one arm as he begins to unfasten his belt. Before it is halfway unfastened, there is a knock at the door.

"Gertrude, it's Ryan. Just checking to make sure you got to the room okay."

The man pauses and looks at the door, which is just enough time for Gertrude to kick up and out at the man, who gasps loudly from the sharpness of the kick. Ryan bursts through the door and swings hard at the man, who falls back against the wall and slumps to the floor. Ryan grabs the man by his hair and his belt. As he moves through the door to toss him down the steps, the hotel manager appears on the landing.

"What is going on here? I heard a lot of ruckus."

"This man is trying to hurt one of my bandmates," says Ryan as he still holds the now-struggling man.

"Stop, I'll take him from here. I'll call the police and check with you when they come." The manager grabs the man's arms and half pushes him down the stairs. Gertrude watches from the doorway, leaning against the door jam. She takes one look at Ryan and bursts into tears. Long, deep sobs come from somewhere deep inside of her. Ryan reaches for her, takes her back into the room, and sits her on the bed. He kneels on the floor beside her.

"There, there," he says. "The danger is past. No need to worry."

"No, the danger is not past. I am the danger."

"What are you saying? You have done nothing wrong. He's a brute, is all."

"I have done many things wrong. Coming on this trip is just one of many things I have done wrong. I should not have come, but I had nowhere to go and needed time to figure out what to do."

"Are you running from someone?"

Her sobs do not stop. "From myself."

Gertrude does not tell Ryan her story. That story is close and personal. He finally agrees to leave and makes her lock the door behind him. He checks to see that the door is locked. Exhaustion overtakes Gertrude. She can't even manage to change for bed. She crawls under the covers fully clothed. Sometime in the middle of the night, sleep comes.

6

─────────

Gertrude is awake at dawn and frightened, not only of what awaits her but of herself. Her childhood fears reemerge. Her mother had warned her she wouldn't be able to care for herself. Being a nurse was a way Gertrude could have a career that could include a family and income without piece sewing or domestic work that most of the Irish women in her neighborhood in Savannah did to feed their children at the table. Yet here she is, so far from home and from family, with no one to talk with, no one to offer her a direction. Crying into the pillow with deep sobs does not make her feel better. She does not want a family, yet, but she so much wants to play the piano. For now, she is lost, terribly lost.

Suddenly, Gertrude sits up. In a moment of clarity, she asks herself, "What would my mother tell me to do?" Without changing, she grabs her cloak and goes down the flights of stairs to the lobby.

A young man is sweeping the floor. "Where is the nearest Catholic church?" she asks.

St. Nicholas, the oldest medieval Catholic church in town, is just down the lane. With her cloak's hood pulled over her head, she follows his directions. And though she has rushed to the church, at the entry gate, she slows down, remembering how long it has been since she has gone to Mass. But if she is to follow her mother's words to seek advice from the heavens, then Mass it is. She hopes it will lift the pain and stress within her. Plus, she needs to figure out how to deal with this guilt. She needs help and direction.

Gertrude enters through the medieval wooden doors that are painted red and propped wide open. Inside, candles burn at several prayer stations. She sits to wait for Mass to begin at the nearest empty pew toward the back and away from others. She hopes that the quiet moments in the church will enable her to reflect and maybe come to some conclusion as to what her next step should be. She is in Ireland, and surely, playing the piano somewhere is a possibility, but where and how can she find those places with no money and severed ties to family and friends? Never having had to ask for help, she is not sure how to do it. Abruptly, her thoughts are interrupted when the congregation stands and sings.

Throughout the first part of Mass, Gertrude stays silent, listening but not participating. A priest steps up to the podium. She feels she is wasting her time and there is no direction to be found here, but leaving would be too awkward.

"Good morning," he says. "I'm Fr. John and have just been given the opportunity to serve at St. Nicholas."

As Fr. John continues his opening comments, he introduces the topic of his sermon: "How to calm your mind." Gertrude raises her head and looks directly at Fr. John. Did he hear her thoughts?

"St. Patrick is someone we know well. We know that his feast day is March 17. We know that he preached Christianity to Ireland's people. We know that he was a humble man who thought he was too uneducated to be a teacher," says Fr. John.

"What we may not know is that he wrote two manuscripts:

the *Confessio*, his spiritual autobiography, and *Letter to Coroticus*, where he rallies against the British mistreatment of Irish Christians. Scholars have said that his Latin is rustic and his writings are incoherent in some instances. I want to suggest that his writings are about truth and offer a rare simplicity. St. Patrick bared his inmost soul in his writings. He spent forty days fasting and in prayer on Croagh Patrick, a mountain just up from us. There is a history of pilgrimages to there, first in pagan years and now for Christian penance as pilgrims walk the seven kilometers to the top, often in bare feet." Fr. John looks out at the church members, who are listening to the early Mass.

"St. Patrick set an example for us to follow in his footsteps," continues Fr. John. "To seek answers to our problems in silence and reflection as we walk the rocky terrain to the top and pray. With us today is Fr. Angelus Healy, a Capuchin friar, who will share with us the importance of the pilgrimage."

Fr. John turns to indicate a man who sits on the dais. Unlike Fr. John, whose liturgical vestments include a chasuble, an alb, a stole, and a cincture, Fr. Healy wears a tunic, a plain brown robe with a hood, fastened at the waist with a cord, and sandals. His long beard hangs straight to his chest. He stands and moves to replace Fr. John at the pulpit.

"I bring you blessings from the Capuchin community. Inspired by St. Francis of Assisi and founded in Italy in 1528, we live life with a passion for peace, honesty, and charity. As St. Francis sought to return to the way of life in solitude and penance, so do we. Fr. John has introduced St. Patrick, let me tell you more." He pauses and looks out at the people sitting below him.

"Because of a sin he committed when he was fifteen, men were saying St. Patrick was unworthy to teach. In utter despair, he went to the summit of the mountain, entreating God. He was at his greatest depression and asked to be forgiven of his frailties and for God to bless the work he was doing in Ireland," says Fr. Healy.

At this point, Fr. Healy looks over to Fr. John. "Fr. John has given me the opportunity today to let you know that the Capuchin community recognizes what St. Patrick started. We continue to encourage pilgrimages to seek solace, solitude, and forgiveness. In the past, the annual pilgrimage on the last Sunday in July has been supported by a local gathering. In 1903, though, a national demonstration of the Irish Catholic faith was supported by many Gaelic and Nationalist societies and Catholic organizations, and a thousand pilgrims walked to the summit. A new oratory was built, and it opened on July 30, 1905. And for the first time, a Mass was offered at the summit. The walk is not easy; it takes three to four hours to climb the 2,500-foot mountain with a level stretch about halfway up, and then a steeper climb over rocks and loose stones to the summit. I assure you, regardless of why you climb, the memory will be forever etched in your mind."

At the end of the Mass, Gertrude waits for Fr. John at the entrance to the church. She is not sure what to say, just that something needs to be said. When he comes to the door to shake hands with people leaving, Gertrude steps up to shake his hand.

"Fr. John, I need directions," says Gertrude.

"You found your way here. Where else do you need to go?" he asks.

"Life direction, but I also need directions to Croagh Patrick." Gertrude feels hot tears trailing down her cheeks.

Fr. John pauses. "Are you okay?"

"Fine," she says. "I just need to find my way."

Fr. John agrees to give her directions to find Croagh Patrick and tells her how far it is. "Take a train from Galway to Athenry, they run fairly frequently. From Athenry, transfer to the Great Southern & Western Railroad to Claremorris, and there you will need to change to the Midland Great Western Railroad to Westport. Lodging can be found at the Railway Hotel. If you are staying at a hotel here in Galway, ask the hotel clerk to telegraph them that you are coming. Then in the morning, the first thing, walk up Croagh Patrick."

Gertrude is overwhelmed. Spending money she should be keeping, leaving a two-week paying job, and traveling 112 kilometers away to walk up a mountain? This plan is crazy.

Fr. John continues, "There is a lot of history on that mountain. Many people come away changed after climbing to the summit. This has been deemed sacred ground."

Gertrude is silent. Thinking about what Fr. John has told her about how the mountain changes lives makes her want to climb. Her choices are slim. Her ties to friends and family are frayed. There is nothing left for her in the present, but if some direction is found at the top of that mountain, it would at least be something.

"Thank you, Fr. John."

"Bless you, my child. May you find a direction that will be good for your soul."

Gertrude leaves and makes her way back to the hotel. It is early. She goes up to her room and packs quickly. Returning to the lobby, she asks the clerk for a sheet of paper and an ink pen to write a note to Ryan.

Dear Ryan,

My day's plans may not allow me to be back by tomorrow night. Should you not see me, please know that I am trying to find my way. I am not sure which direction that will take me. I thank you for rescuing me many times in the past few days. I hope one day I might be able to repay you for the kindness you have shown me.

Yours truly in song,

Gertrude

After blowing on the ink to dry it faster, Gertrude folds the note and carries the ink pen back to the clerk. "Will you please give this note to Ryan, the band's fiddle player? And here is the key to my room on the top floor. I'm Gertrude Hamlin, no Kelly. Sorry, Gertrude Kelly. One more thing, would you please send a telegram to the Railway Hotel in Westport that I need a room for tonight? Thank you."

A decision has been made. The next step is to find the right train and climb that mountain.

7

———

The trains must have been blessed by Fr. John because there are only short waits for changes and no wrong trains. Gertrude is relieved. This is the first time she has gone on such a journey alone. Another positive at Westport is that the train station is just across from the Railway Hotel. She checks in to find her room arranged. She asks the clerk two things: Where is the hotel restaurant, and what are the directions to Croagh Patrick?

There is a quickness to Gertrude's step as she goes up to her room. Without someone else guiding her, she has found her way. She can do this. In the room, though, guilt overcomes her for letting yet another person down by not telling Ryan to his face about her trip. There would have been too much to explain. Her plan is to have an early dinner and go to bed. Sleep escaped her last night, with no sleep on the train in fear that the Westport stop would be missed. In the morning, she will make her way to the mountain, climb, come back down, and then take the next train back to Galway. Her mission, as suggested by Fr. John, would be complete. And maybe the information about St. Patrick will filter down to her and give direction for the next steps to take. She holds a schedule for the returning trains in her hands.

Gertrude is fine until bedtime. Her thoughts are spinning inside her head as replays of Randolph's criticism repeat over and over and over. Her frustration increases about how she had not picked up on his negative opinion of her music. She remembers his comments on her beauty, how her golden hair reminded him of an angel's hair, her fragrant smell, and how her petite stature allowed him to pick her up and swing her around. That's when she realizes he never said anything about her music.

There is a soft light coming into the room. Gertrude pulls up on her elbow to see out the window that the sun is rising. Changing into a thick skirt, blouse, and jacket, she also puts on a sturdy pair of leather shoes. Everything else is packed into the suitcase. She goes down to the lobby. After a simple breakfast of toast and fruit in the restaurant, she asks if there is something she can take along on the hike. The server returns with a cheese sandwich, an apple, and water in a mason jar. She retrieves a cloth bag from her suitcase, where various small items have been kept. These are transferred to a blouse, and the lunch is put in the cloth bag, which is easy to carry with a cord pulled over her shoulder. Next, she asks if the clerk will hold her suitcase behind the counter until she returns. All is set. Repeating the directions to the mountain, Gertrude takes a deep breath and heads out.

The first station is easy to recognize. There are candles, flowers, and memorabilia left by pilgrims who have passed by the station. She begins her journey on a path through the rocky landscape. No one else is in sight. All there is to see is the rocky slope and a few scraggly trees stunted by the lack of soil but growing in spite of the stones and rocks that cover the ground. The slope is not difficult for her to plod along. The morning is lit by a bright sun with no clouds in sight. Though it rains frequently in Ireland, Gertrude did not want to be burdened with a heavy cloak while walking the mountain terrain and left it at the hotel. Seeing no clouds buoys her spirits.

The walk has many rocks and stones, so the trek is not easy. As Gertrude ascends the mountain, the wind picks up. What starts as a simple breeze teasing her hair out of a thrown-together bun becomes stronger the higher she goes. At another one of the rock cairns, or stations, as Fr. John described them, there are fewer items left. There are scarves and gloves, containers that held liquids, things people discarded as the climb got harder. No time to stop here; it is not where she needs to be. She has to get to the top.

At a turn in the path with a steeper slope, Gertrude slides on loose rocks. With nothing to hold on to, she falls. Luckily, the bag with the jar of water did not hit the rocky ground. She sits up, takes the jar, and drinks some of the water. Adjusting her skirt and standing on the steep rocky slope takes a bit of balance. The wind is whistling off the crags and crevices of the bigger rocks. Clouds now cover the sky. Gertrude walks on, keeping her eyes on the rocks in front of her so as not to fall again.

The effort to pay attention to the rocks and the pathway empties her mind. None of her problems enters her thoughts as she focuses on walking and trying to maintain her balance. The walk is long as it is uphill and treacherous with the sliding rocks. The sun is hiding behind the clouds, but it is higher in the sky, so it must be midmorning at least. She stops and sits on a boulder beside the path.

Down in the valley below, the hillside is littered with small white specks that move around. Sheep are feeding on the green grass in the pasture. Sheep stay together and often follow one another. If one sheep goes to get water from the stream, all the sheep go and get water. They are flock animals and need the protection of the group. As Gertrude thinks about the sheep and how they live, her own life is so different. She has never been comfortable following others and learning a task just to be able to survive. There has to be more to life than that, than just making a living. Her desire to create causes her much consternation. Why can't she be satisfied with just playing the piano and being a nurse? What is wrong with her?

There are no answers out on the hillside. This adventure of climbing a mountain to figure out a direction for her life may be just folly. Gertrude stands, stretches her arms, picks up the bag, and proceeds to the mountain's summit. It takes her all morning to walk the steep paths. As the stones level off, on the far side of a clearing is a small white chapel, St. Patrick's Oratory. She has reached the top. Pausing to take in the surroundings, the bay is on one side while a lake is at the foot of the mountain on the far side. The wind has picked up on the top of the mountain and whips about, blowing her skirt and hair. Dark clouds blacken the sky and the air chills considerably. She regrets not having her cloak.

There are several large boulders nearby, so she sits down on the ground with a boulder supporting her back and eats her lunch, stretching her legs out. Muscles she has not used in a while are aching. The wind has increased, chilling her more. Then come the first drops of rain. Gathering her bag and water jar, she walks quickly to the chapel to see if it is locked. No one is around. The unlocked door opens to a small chapel that appears to be three times longer than it is wide. Additionally, the altar side looks wider than the entrance side, which Gertrude determines is about her height; should she lie down, it would be head to toe, five feet.

Gertrude closes the door behind her and shivers from the cold, but at least inside, the wind doesn't blast through her. The altar at the far end of the chapel has remnants of candles. She walks past the chapel windows, slowly. The narrow windows allow muted light from the now cloudy, rainy day. Instead of going directly to the altar, she chooses to sit on a bench along the wall under one of the windows. Listening to the rain, she sits and looks at the space.

Fr. John had shared with the parishioners at Mass that this is where St. Patrick spent forty days in prayer. Gertrude hears the rain coming down heavily on the roof and is relieved that, though cold, she is not wet. To get comfortable, she stretches out on the bench. After all the exertion of walking up the mountain, she falls into a deep sleep.

She does not sleep long as the bench is hard and narrow. Gertrude awakens and notices that the rain has gotten more aggressive and the wind slams the chapel's walls. Her body aches from the hard bench. She's weary but thinks about her task, one that Fr. John suggested and her reason for climbing Croagh Patrick: to find direction. There is nowhere to go in the storm, and when she can go, the only way is down. She sits silently and listens to the storm.

Listening, Gertrude begins to hear more than the storm. She sits up a little straighter to listen. The raindrops on the windows sound like soft chimes heard at the introduction of a hymn. Then the crescendo of the wind against the building off the north side of the chapel has an irregular beat that gives a rhythm to the storm. A swishing sound of the water falling from the eaves sounds like violins ebbing and flowing through a tune. Then a flute enters, offering another tonal quality to all the other sounds. The music echoes through the chapel with a calling out of an oboe or a clarinet that has a brief solo among the violins. Cellos and basses enter and create a loud symphonic sound that screams for her to pay attention.

To hear better, Gertrude stands and moves to the middle of the chapel. Pulled by the sounds, she turns all about in circles, listening to how each sound is coming from a different direction. The rhythms beat like drums from one corner of the chapel, the cellos and basses from another, the violins from the other far side, and the flute can be heard from the rafters. The energy of the music, an energy she has not felt in a long time, fills her body. There is life in the sound. There is despair calling out. There is pain shrieking as the flute returns to mourn the same feeling the storm arouses in her. She hears the power of the storm as it mimics all of her feelings.

As the storm diminishes, Gertrude crosses back to the bench and sits down. Instead of feeling exhausted, she is energized. What has she just heard? Music. She has experienced how a storm can turn into a musical composition. Yes, there is music everywhere if she can only capture it in her mind and write it down.

There is quiet. Gertrude goes to the door to look out. The storm has passed. Sunlight appears through the remaining clouds as the sun begins to sink toward the west. She has been in the chapel longer than planned. Now she needs to get down the mountain before dark. At this time of year, darkness comes early. She retrieves her bag and jar, and as she is about to close the door, she glances back into the space that has given her hope. Fr. John did say that the climb changes lives.

Though Gertrude would like to run down the mountain with the energy she has felt from the storm, the ground is wet and she needs to take her time on the rocky slope. She finds a stick that someone left behind and uses it to stabilize her steps as she descends the mountain.

The trip back down is a lot faster. Though careful, with renewed energy, Gertrude follows the path. In her mind, there is also a path that must be followed. She now knows what she needs to do next.

During the last stretch of the mountain path, before the evening shadows begin, there is a movement in the sky. Looking up, Gertrude sees a flock of birds. The birds come together and start to fly in patterns above the trees. They dance and float in and out. The birds are starlings, and in a brief time, hundreds of birds join the dance in the sky. Watching the murmuration, she admires the birds' abilities to create musical movements to end the day, like a curtain call after the brilliant sounds of the storm.

At the Railway Hotel, Gertrude asks for a room. It is too late to return on the train. She asks if she can send a telegram. With a yes from the receptionist, who offers pen, ink, and paper, Gertrude stands at the counter, pulls out Sharon's card, and copies the address. The message is brief.

Accepting offer. Arrive Wexford tomorrow on train from Athenry. Gertrude

Gertrude decides visiting Sharon is the most straightforward path since she is rapidly running out of money, has no job, and rejects returning to Galway and risking the "whiskey man" or someone like him. She needs help, a place to begin again, a friend who might accept her in spite of what she has done. Sharon is her only choice.

Dinner is in the restaurant before going to her room. It's the same room she had the night before. With an odor reeking from her clothes and hair, Gertrude desperately needs to freshen up. From her suitcase, she chooses toiletries and goes to find the water closet at the end of the hall. It's early in the evening, so the bath includes washing her hair. Wrapping her hair in a towel, she puts on a bathrobe and opens the door to look down the hall, hoping no one is between the water closet and her room. The bath rejuvenated her, and she is relieved that some of the stress built up over the last few months has washed away. In the suitcase is a notebook with a Cumberland pencil from the flat in Dublin. She tosses her hair free in order to dry and sits on the side of the bed to write. She writes the sounds heard on the mountain top, describing every sound in minute detail.

8

___

When the conductor comes through the train announcing Wexford, Gertrude is ready. She has powdered her nose and twisted her hair into a neat bun. She has put on her best jacket, a brown tweed, and her shoes are shiny clean. Her white gloves match the piping on her dark blue traveling dress. As the train begins to slow coming into the station, Gertrude strains to look out the window. The station is empty.

The train has arrived early in the afternoon. The telegram did not mention a time, just that she was on a train from Athenry. Gertrude leans back on the leather seat and takes a deep breath. From how she had treated Sharon when they talked in Dublin, she should not be surprised that Sharon might refuse to see her. She had been rude and definitely abrupt.

There is one more whistle from the front of the train and then all movement stops. She lifts the suitcase from the seat next to her and puts her cloak over her arm. It is autumn, but the air seems warmer on the southeast coast of Ireland. She steps down from the platform and looks about, confirming that no one is there to greet her. Crossing over to the ticket window, she asks, "Has a message been left for Gertrude Kelly?"

The ticket master moves items around on his desk as he looks for a message. "No, no message has been left."

Turning, Gertrude is stumped as to what her next move should be. Her cash is really low. She turns back to the ticket master. "Is there a boarding house nearby?"

He takes a sheet of paper and writes down an address. "This one is near. Cross the street in front of the station, and at Main Street, turn left. You will see it down on the left."

"Thank you." Gertrude holds the address in front of her, but before she can cross the street, she hears him call out to her, "Miss, oh Miss Kelly! There is a message for you. It had fallen on the floor."

She returns to the ticket master for the message.

Gertrude,

Thank goodness you are coming. I will be in the shipping office on the quay waiting for you. Turn left out of the train station and walk along the waterfront until you see our shipping sign. Come immediately. I can't wait to see you!

Sharon

Gertrude hurries down the waterfront on Paul Quay. She is relieved that Sharon is welcoming her. They had been close friends at the boarding house where they lived in Savannah. Though all the other women at the boarding house were in the nursing program at St. Joseph's Hospital, Sharon was provided room and board by her employer, a shipping firm in Ireland. Sharon married in November, and the couple left immediately for County Wexford. Gertrude had returned to her parents' home in Savannah since she was leaving for the music conservatory program at Brenau at the first of the year. Two friends, two different paths to follow, and both so hopeful that their futures would play out just as they dreamed.

Sharon's dream came through—a career with a great firm and a husband, but Gertrude's dream is just exactly that, only a dream—no hope for being a concert pianist or a composer. Her idea of having a partner came to an end when Randolph walked out the door. With so much going wrong for her, and even though she had not been gracious to Sharon when they met in Dublin, Gertrude has to admit that she is grateful that she ran into Sharon. Her only route going forward is to trust friends and see if she can start over and pick up her life's pieces.

The sign for the shipping firm is over a giant wooden door. Gertrude is at the right place. Just as she starts to go inside, she hears a voice coming from inside the office. Immediately, she steps back, turns, and hurriedly goes to the corner of the building. A stone wall that goes down the side of the building shields her from the man whose voice made her heart stop. The man steps out of the doorway and into the building's entrance, where Gertrude had been moments earlier. Sharon follows him out and they end their conversation. The man passes by Gertrude as she waits but does not look where she is leaning deep into the shadows of the stone wall. Gertrude hurries to the door and enters without knocking. Sharon turns around.

"Gertrude, you are here, you are actually here." Sharon moves toward Gertrude but stops. "What's wrong?"

"The man that was here, who is he?"

"He is a factor specializing in textiles. Why do you ask?"

"He was in Galway. I saw him in Galway."

Sharon takes Gertrude's arm and gently tries to persuade her to sit down. "Let me get you some water."

Gertrude trembles. Her hands shake. She puts down the suitcase but continues to hold her cloak. She sits but fastens her eyes on the door. When Sharon returns with a glass of water, Gertrude does not move her eyes from the entrance door.

"Gertrude, whatever has happened?" She kneels in front of Gertrude, offering her the water.

After a moment of silence, Gertrude looks at Sharon. "He... he tried to...", and Gertrude begins to cry, "...me in the hotel in Galway."

"Oh, my goodness!"

"I was playing the piano," she continues to cry, "with a band at the hotel near Eyre Park." Her tears do not stop. "And he tried to kiss me. A band member knocked him off his chair." Gertrude takes a break and is silent. "He later followed me to my room and stuffed a handkerchief." She breaks into loud sobs and cannot seem to control them.

Sharon hands her a handkerchief from her own pocket and reaches out to lay her hand on Gertrude's arm. "My dear friend, you have been through a lot."

"More than you think," Gertrude whispers through her tears. The door opens and Gertrude freezes. Sharon looks up and sees that it is another customer.

"Please, do come back in a while. We are on a break here." The man backs out of the door and closes it behind him. Sharon stands up, locks the door, and puts up a "closed" sign in the window. "Now, let's get you settled and see what can be done. You have traveled a long way and should rest."

"I cannot stay here!" Gertrude's voice is an octave higher than usual. "He is in town and I am sure to see him." She stands up and grabs the suitcase. "I must go."

"That is exactly what you should do," says Sharon, "but let's put together a plan that will guarantee your safety."

Gertrude stops and takes a deep breath. Sharon is right. Nothing good ever comes from haste in a moment of fear. She sits down.

Sharon pulls up a chair near her. "Now, tell me why you came and how I can help."

For the next hour, Gertrude pours her heart out to Sharon. She does not leave out any detail. If Sharon is to help her, then Sharon needs to know everything. Gertrude watches Sharon's face as she recites all that has happened in the last four months. When she reaches the Galway part of the story, she does not limit what happened and tells it all. Sharon's face shifts from listening to one of concern.

"Oh my, Gertrude," Sharon says. "I can't believe all of this has happened to you!"

"I can," says Gertrude.

"How so?"

"It has been wrong of me to think that I could be anything other than who I am." Gertrude breaks down again.

"And who are you? The woman I met in Savannah was a confident, talented musician. I see before me a woman who has been given unsurmountable challenges..."

"Who made choices that put her in harm's way, is a better way of saying it," interrupts Gertrude. "I should have listened to my parents and finished the nursing program. I did not need to go off and pretend to be someone who had a chance to be a concert pianist!"

"Gertrude, you have talent. You can do this. There has to be another way to make your dream come true."

"I should not dream," says Gertrude. She pauses and looks over to Sharon. "I do have to say, though, that the trek up Croagh Patrick gave me a feeling I haven't had in many a month."

Gertrude is silent. Sharon prompts her. "What kind of feeling?"

Gertrude stands up and walks over to the window. "I was caught in a storm on the top of the mountain. I sought cover inside the oratory. During the storm, I heard music. I heard the cellos, violins, basses, flutes, and percussion sounds. I heard them all in the midst of the storm. These sounds surrounded me and lifted me up with their music. The music of nature filled my soul. I could have listened to it for hours."

Sharon walks over and stands beside Gertrude. "That must have been magical."

"It was indeed."

The two women look out the window in silence. Slowly, Gertrude turns to Sharon. "I need to find a quiet place to put my life back together."

"I agree. Connor and I want you to stay with us for a while until you have time to figure it all out."

Gertrude reaches out at the same time Sharon does. The women hug and realize that their bond back in Savannah has not been broken; it was just in hibernation.

"I have some appointments coming soon, so I cannot leave the office just yet. My mother and father are at the cottage and are expecting you today. We all live in town in that wonderful little cottage Connor described to us back in Savannah before the wedding. Why don't you go and visit with them or take a nap before dinner while I finish up?"

Sharon gives directions. Gertrude is to go up Peters Street, turn right onto Main, and walk to Salzer. The cottage is distinctive, so Gertrude should not miss it. "Remember, the cottage has sky-blue shutters and a large bird bath in the front garden. An iron gate separates the cottage from the street and includes a tall hedge. The Murphy name is on the gate."

"I can find it, thank you." The women hug once more.

Sharon unlocks the door. "I'll be home just as soon as I can. Are you okay to walk alone? You can wait here until I am finished, but you seem tired."

"I am tired and I can find the way. The streets are few and narrow, with lots of people about. I will be fine. The 'whiskey man' does not know I am here."

Gertrude heads out the door with a quick step. Her renewed energy lessens how tired she is. She walks through the town with shops and businesses along the way. There on Main Street is the boarding house that the ticket master had suggested. As she passes, a man comes out of the front of the house. She almost freezes when she realizes who he is. She walks quickly and doesn't look his way. Her hood is up over her hair. Once away from the front of the boarding house, she does not slow down but must get to the cottage. Her pace quickens.

The streets do have a lot of people walking to shops or running errands. Her shoes slide on the cobblestones of the old streets. Then she feels more than hears someone walking directly behind her. Her pace quickens. The steps behind her quicken also. At the end of Main Street, with Salzer curving up a slight hill, Gertrude can see the cottage with the sky-blue shutters. She is close, almost there. The steps are even closer behind her. Suddenly, her arm is being pulled to one side, and the "whiskey man" leans down into her face, his breath as strong as ever.

"Did you not think I would recognize you in another town?"

Gertrude trembles.

"Ah, my pretty lady is trembling. So excited to see me after our last encounter, where I had to pay a small fortune to stay out of jail because of your boyfriend?"

Gertrude cannot even talk, scream, or move.

The "whiskey man" pulls her up the narrow street. "Shall we go and have another conversation? I know you have been wanting to have a conversation with me. I know a real quiet place where we can talk."

They are near Sharon's cottage. Gertrude can see the Murphy name on the gate. The "whiskey man" continues to hold Gertrude's arm tightly as he pulls her up the hill. His grip is hurting her arm. There is a shout. Gertrude looks and sees a woman standing at the cottage gate.

"Gertrude, is that you?" She rushes out and takes Gertrude's suitcase. "Thank you for showing her to the cottage," she says to the man. "I can take her from here." With a force not to be reckoned with, she snatches Gertrude's arm from the man's grip. He begins to hold Gertrude tighter and raises his other hand to strike the new woman attacking him.

"Stop! Or I will shoot," shouts a gruff voice from the gate. Gertrude recognizes Sharon's father, standing there with a rifle in his hands, cocked and ready. The man releases Gertrude's arm with such energy that it pushes both women into the hedge bordering the cottage. As Gertrude falls into the hedge, she hears him say, "This is not our last conversation," and he turns to walk away.

Sharon is not at all pleased with what she learns from her mother and father when she gets to the cottage much sooner than she had expected. Gertrude is shaken and is having a cup of tea at the dining room table. Sharon joins her.

"This is not going to work," says Gertrude. "I cannot stay here, but I do not know where to go."

"I know where you should go," says Sharon.

Gertrude looks at her friend and takes a deep breath. "Okay, where?"

"To Savannah. There is a ship leaving this evening. We will disguise your hair, take you in a covered carriage, and you will go home."

Gertrude had thought about going home, but facing her family, the other nurses, Mrs. Schultz, and the Savannah Music Club all seemed too much. She is silent.

Sharon speaks up again. "Let's have dinner with Connor. I'll go now and explain to him so that he can arrange the accommodations." Before Gertrude can say anything, Sharon grabs her shawl and goes out the door.

Gertrude asks where she can rest until dinner. She is shown the guest room, where she finds her suitcase. She takes her traveling shoes off and then lies down on the bed with a quilt over her and goes into such a deep sleep that Sharon has to rouse her by touching her arm. Gertrude yanks her arm back and lets out a sharp cry until she realizes that it is Sharon and not the "whiskey man."

"It's time to get you to the ship," says Sharon. "Mum made you a dinner basket to take aboard for later. We wanted to let you rest."

Gertrude sits up and immediately attempts to calm her hair.

"Not to worry. Here, put this on." Sharon hands her a large navy bonnet with a thick veil that hangs down below her chin. "This will work."

Standing up and straightening her skirt, Gertrude puts on the bonnet. Her face and hair are hidden behind the veil. A carriage awaits outside the house. Gertrude turns and faces Sharon.

"How can I thank you for all you are doing for me?"

"By staying in touch, my friend. Don't abandon me again."

Gertrude reaches out and hugs Sharon. "I promise." She takes the dinner basket and steps up into the carriage. The last light of the day is fading and darkness will soon envelop Gertrude's short ride to the ship and her farewell to Ireland. Though she may have made amends with Sharon, in Savannah, Gertrude will face even more people she had abandoned.

9

S avannah is a welcome sight after forty days rolling on the ocean waves. The ship is sturdy, but Gertrude has been sick from the first day of the voyage. She had not been seasick going over to Ireland, but this trip has been challenging for her stomach. She stayed in the cabin much of the voyage. Resting may have eased her sickness, but it did not help Gertrude prepare to face her family. Before Gertrude left Ireland, Sharon suggested sending a telegram to her family. When Gertrude hesitated, Sharon offered to send a telegram to Mrs. Schultz at the boarding house. Mrs. Schultz will know how to handle Gertrude's arrival.

In the stateroom, waiting for the all-clear from the captain that passengers could disembark, Gertrude is not sure if anyone will be at the dock to greet her. Again, Gertrude remembers that she has not treated her family, the nurses, and Mrs. Schultz decently with no communication. Her hope is that, like Sharon, they will forgive her and accept her back home. After Randolph's departure and how he described her music, and then with the threats from the "whiskey man," she needs people who know her. She is ready to be accepted for who she is: a woman who has dreams, one who has not been truthful with her family and friends, but one who will now work to mend her relationships and maybe, come up with some way to achieve her dreams. She has hope, not a lot, but enough to keep her going.

The clearance forms are in front of her, ready to present to the officials once the ship has docked. Passengers will be cleared on board before disembarking, so she waits in her cabin. No one will be on the dock when she arrives, so if she is the last passenger to disembark, that is fine.

A crew member walks past her door and raps gently. "Miss Kelly, you should go on deck and get cleared for departure now."

Gertrude gathers her few items. Traveling light is a benefit. With her suitcase and papers, she goes on deck and meets the officials at a raised stand-up desk on the ship's deck. The first question they ask is what her current legal status is in the United States. Randolph's note confirmed that she is single and still an American citizen. Had she been legally married, she would have forfeited her American citizenship. Silently, Gertrude is thankful that she didn't officially marry Randolf. She has never dreamed of beginning a family.

She is asked a few questions, like her Savannah address, her education, and employment status, which she answers as being a nursing student with family in Savannah rather than a musician. She is not certain what her employment status may be; therefore, being a nursing student can answer that question as well. Finally, she is free to disembark. Picking up her suitcase and crossing the ramp leading to the wharf, she hears a shout. "Gertrude!" Women standing together on the wharf are waving. Mrs. Schultz; Sister Mary Joyce, the nun leading the nursing program at St. Joseph's; a few other nuns from the hospital; and her mother are there, along with other family members. The group is cheering and shouting, "Welcome home, Gertrude."

At the end of the walk down the ramp, Gertrude is embraced by all the women waiting for her. Someone takes her suitcase. As she makes the rounds, hugging and greeting the women, she is finally face-to-face with her mother. They stand silently. The other women seem to sense the importance of this moment and quiet down to await what the two women will say to each other.

Gertrude starts. "Mum," she says, "I am so sorry I have not listened to your advice."

Her mother interrupts her. "Nonsense, I never listened to my Mum when she told me not to come to America. She wanted me to stay in Ireland and do the same things she did." She reaches out and hugs Gertrude.

The reunion moment stops when Gertrude dashes over to the side of the wharf and throws up in the river. It happens so fast that none of the women react; they all just freeze. All but one. Mrs. Shultz comes to Gertrude and holds onto her arm as she retches, then hands Gertrude a handkerchief.

"Thank you," she says to Mrs. Schultz. They walk back to join the women, who are all asking if she is okay. "I'm fine. The ocean voyage has been bad for me. I have been seasick from the day we left. I'll be fine; I just need to get my land legs."

The boisterous group of women finally dissolves into two groups: those women returning to St. Joseph's and those going over to the Yamacraw Irish community in Savannah. Gertrude promises Mrs. Schultz and Sister Mary Joyce that she will come by in the next few days.

Two days later, Gertrude knocks tentatively on the front door of the boarding house where all the nurses live as they work in the nursing program in St. Joseph's Hospital next door.

Mrs. Schultz opens the door. She wipes her hands on her

apron. "Hello, Gertrude, I'm just finishing up in the kitchen after lunch. Have you eaten? You know these women barely eat a thing at lunch; there is plenty left over."

"I'm fine, thank you. I can't eat a thing. I still have the seasickness."

"I see. Well, let's go into the parlor where we can talk. Can I get you a cup of tea at least?"

"A cup of tea would be good."

Mrs. Schultz goes to organize the tea, and Gertrude steps into the parlor. Though she has only been gone from the boarding house for seven months, it seems much longer. The brocades and velvets that cover the chairs, settees, and drapes are all the same. The writing desk in the corner where she first met Sharon, who had been constantly writing letters to her friends in New York to keep in touch, has not been moved. It reminds Gertrude that she did not learn anything from her friend about communicating with family and friends. To the right side of the front windows is the piano. How many afternoons and evenings had she played on that piano, getting ready for her recital at the Savannah Theatre for the music club? So many conversations were held in this room and around that piano. She walks over to the piano and touches the walnut finish. The keys are covered.

Mrs. Schultz enters with a tea tray that is placed on the table between the settees in front of the fireplace. "No one has played the piano since you left," she says.

Gertrude joins Mrs. Schultz at the table. As Mrs. Schultz pours their tea, Gertrude notices that the sharpness in Mrs. Schultz's face has gone. Though thin and still wearing dark-colored dresses, there is a softness to her facial features. "You look good, Mrs. Schultz."

Mrs. Schultz adjusts her high collar and pulls at her long sleeves. Her white hair is pulled back in a bun, just like

Gertrude remembers, showing the texture and waves, never lying flat.

"I feel good. The nurses have filled my heart with gladness. They are all about in the evenings in the parlor, planning their next fabric flower sale. Last fall's success selling the flowers to fund a nurse at the Fresh Air Home for the summer has inspired them to make even more flowers. They have a name for their endeavor: Fresh Air Fabric Flowers." Mrs. Schultz pauses to laugh. "They do have a rollicking good time here in the parlor. I have to thank you for giving them the incentive to make these elaborate fabric flowers for your recital."

"It was all Sharon," says Gertrude. "None of it would have been possible without Sharon's vision."

"Speaking of Sharon, I know you saw her in County Wexford. How are she and Connor?"

"I have to admit, though I did see her, there was such a rush to get me on that ship that we had no time to talk about what she is doing. She seems fine. Her mother and father live in the cottage with them, and that enables Sharon to work at the shipping office. Her mother runs the house, and her father takes care of the chores in the garden. I rested from my travels and did not even see Connor."

"I see," says Mrs. Schultz and stirs her tea with a deliberate pause. "Sharon's mother helped a great deal when they came down from New York. During the weeks before the wedding, Mrs. McGee insisted on following the housekeeper around and helping out. Sharon's father took on the gardening. So, I am not surprised at their new positions in Ireland."

Gertrude notices that Mrs. Schultz did not ask why she had been in such a hurry to leave Ireland and Gertrude has no intention of telling her right away. The time may come later when there is a need to share, but not now.

"No one plays the piano?" asks Gertrude.

"No, it has been silent, and our Wednesday prayer meetings

have the nurses sing without accompaniment. We do miss your playing."

"Perhaps that can be remedied should I be re-accepted into the nursing program. I have come to ask Sister Mary Joyce if that would be a possibility. I know I can't just pick up where I left off, but if there were any way I could reinstate, it would take the worry off my folks."

Gertrude sees Mrs. Schultz shake her head. "I don't know how. We have accepted the maximum women here at the boarding house. With you and Sharon gone, two more first-year women were added in August to the six they normally take. We have a full house."

There is silence between the women. They both pick up their teacups and sip their tea.

"Then maybe until there is an opening, you might permit me to use the parlor to give piano lessons. We have a piano at home, but the people who can pay do not want to come to our neighborhood for the lessons. Maybe we could make some arrangement where I could use the parlor several afternoons a week."

Mrs. Schultz puts down her teacup. "That sounds like a very workable solution to our lack of music in the house. I like that idea." She smiles so broadly that Gertrude is instantly cheered and sits up a little taller.

"I do need to visit with Sister Mary Joyce. I have many fences to mend."

"Yes, you do. You should also make a visit to Mrs. Lynch as a representative of the music club that supported your recital, the sale of the fabric flowers, and your sponsorship to Brenau."

"Yes, I know my shortcomings."

Mrs. Schultz is looking at her with tender eyes. Gertrude looks away, unsure whether the look is one of pity or caring. Then Mrs. Schultz says, "When you talk with Sister Mary Joyce, why don't you get her to examine you for why you have not been eating and are still sick from the sea voyage? I know you have been through a long trip, but there might be something she could suggest that will help."

"I will. I should go now. Sister Mary Joyce is often busy, and I have not told her that I am coming today." Gertrude puts down her teacup and stands. "Thank you for being so generous with the parlor. I will attempt to get students in on Wednesday afternoon. That way, I will be here for the Bible study and can play whatever songs you would like."

"That will be great. I look forward to seeing you on Wednesdays. The nurses are often here in the evenings working on their fabric flowers, so be sure to stop in and say hello to everyone."

"Yes, I will do that. Thank you for the tea."

As Gertrude picks up her handbag, Mrs. Schultz stops her. "Gertrude, whatever you have been through, know that there is always a safe place to be with the people you know and trust. We can help you put all the pieces together only if you talk with us and let us know what you need."

Tears fill Gertrude's eyes. Her vision is impaired and she stumbles on the carpet as she stands to reach over and give Mrs. Schultz a hug. "Thank you." She leaves quickly to go and find Sister Mary Joyce at the hospital.

Less than an hour later, Gertrude is again at the boarding house door. She knocks. When Mrs. Schultz answers, Gertrude is silent. If she speaks, she knows the tears will come. As she stands at the door, not entering, Mrs. Schultz takes her by the arm and guides her into the house and sits her down in the parlor. "My dear girl, whatever is the problem?"

Gertrude begins to cry. "Sister Mary Joyce..." but her tears are choking her throat and it is too hard to get the words out.

Mrs. Schultz sits beside her. Gertrude clears her throat and starts again, "Sister Mary Joyce says I am not seasick." Big sobs come out of Gertrude. "Sister Mary Joyce says I am pregnant."

Mrs. Schultz sits down next to Gertrude on the settee. "And pray tell, how did your travels make this happen?"

Through her tears, Gertrude whispers, "Randolph!" She reaches for her bag and pulls out a handkerchief and blows her nose.

Mrs. Schultz stands up and crosses to the door. "Come, let's go into the kitchen. We need a cup of tea to hear the full story."

Taking a deep breath, Gertrude follows Mrs. Schultz into the kitchen. The tea is made in silence. Gertrude sits at the table in the oversized kitchen. She has been to the door of the room before, but the rules of the boarding house restrict the nursing students from the kitchen area. Though her news is overwhelming at the moment, she is aware that she is in a new place.

Mrs. Schultz places a teacup, a small pitcher of milk, and a little bowl with sliced lemons. She reaches for the sugar dish off the top counter near the dining room door and brings it to the table as well. When the tea has brewed and each cup is poured with a small strainer to catch any tea leaves, Mrs. Schultz moves the other chair from the big work table over near Gertrude. "Now," she says, "let's start from the beginning."

10

S avannah, on a fall morning, is full of bird songs. Traffic moves rapidly on all the streets as people make their way to their jobs or are about town doing their business chores. Gertrude is walking from the Yamacraw neighborhood over to see Mrs. Schultz at the boarding house. Though she had taken this route many times during her apprenticeship in the nursing program, this is the hardest journey she has made.

Gertrude has told Mrs. Schultz most of the story. She left out the part about the note that Randolph left in the Dublin flat. Mrs. Schultz suggests that Gertrude needs to figure out what can be done and who might help. In the meantime, Mrs. Schultz will also try to figure out what kind of resolution might be possible. After two days, Gertrude has nothing.

Each time a conversation with her mother might happen, the talk turned to her mother thanking her for reaching out to the priest in Galway, which eventually led her to come back home. Discussion with her father is totally out of the question; he believes her husband needs to be contacted and forced to take care of her. Gertrude held back telling her parents about Randolph's confession.

Her main friend is Sharon, who might as well be a million miles away since she lives in County Wexford. Part of Gertrude thinks that staying in Ireland and living a life of abandonment would be better than facing the truth that Randolph had lied and left her with a serious dilemma. How is she to live? How will her family deal with her having a baby? She has no husband, no job, no nursing certificate, no education, nothing. How is she to have this baby? On top of having the baby, what are her choices once the baby is here?

Like her father, Sister Mary Joyce wants Gertrude to contact Randolph and have him commit to taking care of his wife and baby. She has no idea how to find Randolph somewhere in Germany. Brenau College may know how to find him, but then Gertrude would need to face the stigma of having fallen for a married man. The news would escape and her life would be over. Having an illegitimate birth was viewed in her Catholic upbringing and Irish family to be her problem, a problem that would include difficulty finding work or shelter. She has nothing. Not even her dreams can save her now.

After Gertrude reaches the boarding house and walks up the steps, she pauses. Instead of going inside, she sits on the porch. Soon, the door opens, and Mrs. Schultz looks out. "I thought I saw you coming up the street, but then you didn't come in or knock. Are you okay?"

Gertrude does not stand. "Please, Mrs. Schultz, there is more to the story."

Mrs. Schultz crosses to a nearby rocking chair lining the front porch and sits. "I'm ready, tell me the rest of the story."

Through tears and long pauses, Gertrude tells Mrs. Schultz about the note Randolph left in the Dublin flat.

"Oh, my dear Gertrude, you have been lied to and misused."

"How could I have been so duped?" cries Gertrude. "Was I so ego-bound and wanting a dream to come true of being a concert pianist and composer so much that I sold my soul to the devil? I have lost all!"

Mrs. Schultz reaches over and holds Gertrude's hand. "Maybe you did not make good decisions, but you have not lost all. You are giving life to another human being."

"Yes, but at what cost? I will be unable to get a job to take care of the baby. My family will reject me! What am I to do?"

Mrs. Schultz continues to hold Gertrude's hand, and then she says, after a long pause, "I have heard about the Florence Crittenton Services in Kansas City. It is a residential home where unwed women can live until they give birth. We could contact them and see if you could be placed there."

"And what happens to the baby?" Gertrude sniffs back more tears.

"The baby will be placed for adoption."

Gertrude is silent. "I have made a terrible mistake and must pay for it. Will you help me contact them and see if I can go? It seems like a better option than jumping into the sea."

"Yes, indeed, I will find out. I know the nuns at St. Joseph's have worked with them before. You are not the first Irish Catholic woman to have this dilemma." She moves her hand from Gertrude's. "Have you confided in Sister Mary Joyce about Randolph?"

Gertrude looks down at her hands now clutched in her lap. "No. I could not be readmitted to the nursing program if I told her about Randolph and our fake marriage. I could not live in the boarding house if I was married and cannot afford to live elsewhere without a job or some type of income. It is a conundrum. I am doomed if I was married and doomed now with the pregnancy because I am not married."

"I see." Mrs. Schultz stands. "Come, we must go in and have a cup of tea before I seek some answers to our questions."

11

———

Nervously, as they are having a second cup of tea, Gertrude asks Mrs. Schultz if she can wait at the boarding house for information on the residential program in Kansas.

"Yes, absolutely. And while you wait, there are flowers being trimmed in the parlor. I am sure the nurses would love for you to pitch in and help them with their fabric flowers."

"Thank you." As Mrs. Schultz leaves through the back door to the hospital next door, Gertrude goes into the parlor. Stacks of fabric pieces have been cut out and now need to be embroidered and stitched to form the flowers. She has sewn for others, made her own clothes, and is quite willing to sit for a while and create.

A single thread is held up and put through the eye of the needle. The process is second nature to Gertrude. Sewing is such an easy thing to do. But her mind is not easy. Her options are vague. If she goes to Kansas to have the baby, she could come back to Savannah and pick up her life's pieces, maybe return to the nursing program. Teaching piano could add some income. Mrs. Schultz already said students could be taught in the parlor. No piano has felt her fingers since returning to Savannah. Gertrude does not know why, other than that the piano makes her sad. Even the piano that she played many a day to prepare for her recital and to play for the nurses during the Bible reading did not entice her to cross over, sit down, and play. It is as though the piano is an instrument of torture to remind her of all the bad choices she has made.

Mrs. Schultz enters the parlor but is not alone. Sister Mary Joyce is with her. Gertrude looks up and remains silent. Sister Mary Joyce, a large nun in a white habit, sits down on the settee near the table close to Gertrude.

"I understand there is more to your story."

Gertrude nods.

"We do have contact with the residency program in Kansas. You need to know that most of the women in the program are a lot younger than you and come from backgrounds where they willingly sought opportunities that might result in pregnancy. The work habits and religious training are designed to change these women and make them into decent human beings, who can get domestic jobs after giving birth."

Gertrude looks at Sister Mary Joyce and surmises that the nun thinks she needs to be made into a decent human being, one without her baby. "Are all babies placed in adoption?"

"No, occasionally a woman leaves the program in a hurry with her baby, and a few create a life with a mate and the baby but never tell an employer about the conditions of her baby's birth."

Gertrude nods.

"However, I think there is another option. You will need to place the baby in adoption at the end, but here is what might work."

Mrs. Schultz sits in the matching settee across from Sister Mary Joyce. Gertrude listens to the other option. The Fresh Air Home in Tybee, run by the Froebel Society as a summer camp for impoverished children, needs a caretaker during the winter months. The last caretaker has taken a job in Atlanta and will be leaving shortly. There is a groundskeeper who does not live on the site. The caretaker will see to the big house, manage the mail and supplies to the house, and keep the house clean. Any maintenance needs will be reported to the society. As the summer approaches, linens for the beds will need to be sorted and all the things required for the camp will have to be organized. A list of supplies to be ordered in time for the children to arrive is in the house. The cook will arrive a week earlier to prepare the kitchen, but the caretaker will need to assist.

"Would I live in the big house?"

"No, there is a staff cottage. Just four rooms: a kitchen combined with a sitting room and three bedrooms. One is for the matron or caretaker, one for the assistant, and one for the nurse. The cook lives on Tybee and comes in to prepare the meals."

"Do we need to tell them, the society, my whole story?" She looks from Mrs. Schultz back to Sister Mary Joyce.

"I think that telling them you have been abandoned, which you have been, will suffice."

"What about the baby?"

"The adoption agency requires that the pregnant woman have regular checkups to assure the adoptive parents that care has been taken during the pregnancy. You will need to come into the hospital periodically. Once labor has started, several of the nuns are midwives and can assist with the childbirth. Should the adoption papers take more time after the baby is born, he or she will remain in the hospital and be cared for there until all the paperwork is complete."

Gertrude is silent. Mrs. Schultz speaks up. "There is one other problem we need to solve." She looks to Sister Mary Joyce. "Should I suggest some of the things we have talked about?"

"Yes, please do," answers Sister Mary Joyce.

"If you choose to go to Tybee, you will live rent-free in the staff cottage. Water is from a cistern at the house. The groundskeeper can keep you with wood for the stove and fireplace and oil for lanterns. However, there is no salary for food and essentials. The previous caretaker had family in the area and was able to take care of her own food and essentials."

Gertrude takes a deep breath. "I see."

"An idea we have includes your ability to sew. The children wear uniforms when they are at camp. The organizations around town have funded drives to raise money to pay for these uniforms, which are purchased from a mill. Sister Mary Joyce and I thought that we could talk with several of these organizations and see if they would split the money between the supplies and paying you piecework for sewing the uniforms."

Gertrude lets out her breath. This might actually work. Though she would be secluded on an island with few people during the winter, no one needs to know why she is there and what she does. Society folks will simply know that she is an abandoned woman. Surviving and finding a way to go forward once this is all over is up to her. If Croagh Patrick has given her any hope, it is in being patient and renewing her network with friends and family. This might be the way to do it. Telling her parents that she is pregnant is still not an option. If it is left up to her, they may never know.

"I accept. Please ask on my behalf about the sewing. I do know how to sew."

Sister Mary Joyce stands. "The caretaker is leaving soon, and the society wants a replacement right away. Can you be prepared to go to Tybee Island within the week?"

"Yes," says Gertrude, who stands with Sister Mary Joyce. "Thank you for helping me. I did not know how to do this on my own."

Sister Mary Joyce reaches out and touches Gertrude's arm.

"None of us do; that is why we have faith." She turns and leaves as quickly as she came. Mrs. Schultz stands, looks at Gertrude, and says, "I suggest that you go by the fabric store and get a pattern for the uniforms. Do you have money to pay for it?"

"Yes, I have some of the rent money Randolph left me. I can get it. Are you certain the organizations will agree to let me sew?"

"They will once Sister Mary Joyce asks. She's a force to be reckoned with."

Gertrude smiles for the first time. "Yes, that she is. I'm glad she's on my side."

"She believes that women often have to go it alone. She tries to right as many wrongs as she can."

Gertrude listens, then says, "I will go and purchase the pattern on the way back to Yamacraw. Thank you."

12

———

The week passes quickly. Gertrude's parents do not understand why she wants to be so isolated on Tybee Island for so many months. Gertrude assures them that it is her choice and a chance to be eligible for the nursing program next fall when there are openings. Helping out the Fresh Air Home will give her a place to be able to take care of herself. Finally, they stop asking questions and simply accept that she will come into Savannah to visit.

The traveling suitcase has stayed open on the floor in the bedroom Gertrude shares with several of her sisters. When something is washed, it is simply packed back in. The thought of leaving home yet again weighs heavily on her, so the tasks are minimized. Every evening after dinner, her mother asks if Gertrude will play the piano. There is a needlepoint cushion on the bench. The cushion had been made by one of the nurses in the boarding house and given to her when she left to go to Brenau. There was a going-away party and everyone shared something with her. The cushion is a memory of all that is lost. Inside, she feels as though she will throw up again. Gertrude finds excuse after excuse to say no to playing the piano. The thought of touching the keys again after all that has happened is too much to sort out. She just says no and bows out, complaining of a headache, tiredness, or seasickness.

On the day before Gertrude is to leave, Sister Mary Joyce meets her at the hospital for instructions. The groundskeeper has a set of keys for the house and the staff cottage. The society has left a list of instructions and contact information on the table in the cottage. Should there be any questions, there is a telegraph office on the island at the nearest train depot to the Fresh Air Home and she is to send a message. Sister Mary Joyce reminds her that monthly visits to the hospital for a checkup are required. She is given a train pass issued by the railroad office. The railroad gives free rides to the children who attend the Fresh Air Home and has agreed to extend that courtesy to her as caretaker of the home. It is good for two round trips to Savannah per month, should she need them.

"Any questions?" asks Sister Mary Joyce.

Gertrude shakes her head no.

"Then be prepared to make a go of this. It is a chance to help and be helped."

"I have every intention of staying the course," says Gertrude. In her thoughts, she adds, *I have no choice, and this may be my only lifeline.*

Gertrude stops in to say goodbye to Mrs. Schultz. The women's groups have approved the sewing venture. The cloth will arrive within two weeks.

"I put this together for you. I am not sure what will be at the cottage and I did not want you to fret over how to get these things." Mrs. Schultz hands Gertrude a sewing basket filled to the brim with scissors, measures, pins, cushions, thread, needles, thimbles, anything Mrs. Schultz thought Gertrude might need. Everything is covered with a folded lap cloth for the train ride.

For a minute, Gertrude cannot say anything. Cradling the

basket with both arms as though it is full of raw eggs, she says, "Thank you," then even quieter a second time, "Thank you." With the basket in one hand and the suitcase in the other, the journey to the railway station offers Gertrude a new direction in her life.

Following Sister Mary Joyce's instructions, Gertrude finds her way from the railway station to the Fresh Air Home, which is a short distance down a lane and then up a dirt path to several buildings. It is too short a walk to get a feel of the island, but there will be plenty of time to see what there is to see. Sister Mary Joyce predicts the baby will come in March. It is October; she has all of fall and then three more months to wait.

The Fresh Air grounds include a "big house," several storage sheds, and a small white cottage with a navy painted door that is locked. Placing both the sewing basket and suitcase on the wooden steps, Gertrude looks around the grounds to locate the groundskeeper, who is to have the keys. A young man is picking up branches and piling them in a small two-wheeled cart.

"Hello," she calls.

The young man stops loading the branches. He doesn't really walk over but lopes toward her. He is broomstick thin with a straw hat on his head and long wisps of hair flying about his shoulders.

"Do you know where I might find the groundskeeper?"

"Yes, ma'am. I'll get him right away." He goes to the back of the big house. Gertrude looks over the sandy yard with crab grass growing in patches. The big house is high off the ground, painted dark green with green lattice woodwork blocking the area under the house. Wide wooden steps with painted white railings lead up to a wrap-around porch. A path in front of the house and the staff cottage leads to a long boardwalk and the dunes. Though the dunes block her sight of the ocean, she hears the waves. The groundskeeper comes from behind the big house with the young man following him.

"Good day, miss," he says. "You must be Gertrude Kelly. The society folks told me to expect you today."

"Yes, I am."

He approaches her but does not get too close. "I have the key to the cottage." He hands the key to her, stretching out his arm. His gloved hands hold the key. "Sorry about the gloves, but some of these limbs have vines with thorns. The other keys to the house and cabinets are in the cottage. The society folks were here and left instructions inside as well."

"Thank you," Gertrude says as she takes the key. She sees a husky man her father's age with a reddish beard thickly covering his chin and halfway up his cheeks. "I know you do not live on the grounds. How do I get in touch with you should I need something?"

"Ah, good question. I'm Gerald, Gerald McMillan. You can find me across the first lane there," he points, "and four lanes over near the back river. I run a fishing camp there, the McMillan Fishing Camp. You will see the sign and can find me or the missus easily."

"Thank you, Mr. McMillan."

"Call me Captain, everybody does."

"Yes, okay, thank you, Captain." Gertrude takes the key and returns to the cottage. Aware that both Captain and the young man are standing and staring at her as she unlocks the door, she takes the suitcase and basket and goes inside, giving the men a slight wave with her hand.

The cottage is clean and orderly. The entryway is a little hall with a short wooden bench and pegs above to hang coats and hats. This hallway opens up into a bigger room. The kitchen is to the left and the parlor is to the right.

On the kitchen side, there is a long metal farm sink with a window looking out at the path and across to the big house. The window sashes are wide, almost like shelves. A wooden shelf, waist high and as wide as the sink, is along the side wall, a good place to prepare food. Above the shelf is a hanging dresser displaying a variety of plates, cups, and saucers. A wood-burning stove takes up a large portion of the side wall. Against the far wall in the corner of the room is a wooden pantry with shutter doors. The icebox is next to the pantry. In the middle of the floor in front of the stove is a rectangular pine table with four matching wooden chairs, simple but sturdy. A set of keys is on the table.

On the other side of the room is the parlor. A burgundy settee with an ottoman is near a side window. A round wooden table is in front of the window that faces the path next to the front door. Two large chairs, upholstered in navy with wooden arms and carved wooden legs, are positioned in front of a fire-place that dominates the room. It is a cooking type of fireplace. A door beside the fireplace leads to a hallway.

Gertrude puts the suitcase down and places the sewing basket on the table. She walks down the hallway, which is rather wide, to find a bedroom on the left side, simply furnished with a single bed, a chest, a table, a chair, and a wardrobe. Across the hallway is the water closet tucked behind the fireplace, which has access to an empty storage closet and a locked back door. Back in the hallway is another opening toward the end to the right. That opening leads to narrow stairs with a wooden wall going from floor to ceiling. The stairwell is like a tunnel leading up. She goes up the stairs to find two small garret bedrooms at the top. Both have a single bed, a chifferobe, and a small table with a single chair. A washstand with pitcher and bowl is near each door.

Gertrude returns to the main room. Hanging her cloak on a peg at the door, she retrieves the suitcase and begins to settle in. It's cold in the cottage, but Captain must have put wood in the fireplace as it is ready to light. She starts the fire. As the dry wood begins to burn and the flames leap about, the fire cheers up the plain room. That's when she realizes that she is quietly tiptoeing around the cottage even though no one can hear her. She is alone.

As the day ebbs, Gertrude grabs her blue cloak and goes out to the wooden walkway to the beach. It will be dark soon, so visiting the big house will be saved for tomorrow. The ocean is calling her. The dunes are busy places with birds flitting about, settling in for the night. Tiny crabs scurry around and a group of gulls huddle together in the sand. They move slightly, shifting in the sand and cooing.

Gertrude's attention is now on the waves slashing at the shore. Terns dip and splatter in the waves for their last meal of the day. The wind shifts as she walks along the boardwalk. Near the cottage, the breeze is brisk, but nearer the water, the wind increases and pushes her blonde hair out of the hood on her cloak to blow about her face. Cautiously walking out onto the sand, her shoes disappear in the softness, so she heads toward the water to find a harder surface.

During Gertrude's walk, the waves are moving closer and closer to the shoreline, indicating that the tide is coming in. She must learn more about the tides and the ocean, as her new life will be here for a while. The approaching evening and being in a new place have made her tired, a fatigue that has increased during these past few days. Returning to the cottage, the sky shows a sinking sun displaying a variety of colors. A deep golden sky is streaked with red, keeping the trees and land in black silhouettes. Grey and white clouds cover the rest of the sky. The wind is getting stronger. Crossing the sand to the walkway leading back to the compound and the cottage, she sees the groundskeeper. He seems to be waiting for her.

"Good evening, Captain," she greets him.

"Unlikely," he says. "There is a gale warning. I have put wood in the bin outside the cottage. If I was you, I would stay in tonight. I plan to also, but first I need to get to the fish camp and secure some of the boats. I will check tomorrow to see if there has been any damage here."

With that, Captain turns and leaves, going down the path and across the lane to the fishing camp on the back river.

Gertrude is not sure what having a gale means, but with the increased wind and Captain's warning, it cannot be good. She hurries to the cottage but stops at the wood bin to load her arms with more wood and goes into the cottage to fill the bin near the fireplace. She grabs two more armloads just in case the wood is needed. During the final load, the rain begins. Her rush to get inside the cottage and bolt the door leaves her out of breath. Leaning against the table after unloading the last of the wood, her stomach growls. A quick look through the pantry cabinet reveals two potatoes, an onion, a tin of tea, and a half-empty jar of honey. Inside the small icebox, there is a bowl of sea grapes. The former caretaker must have left them. The grapes quell her stomach temporarily. The potatoes are lifted with the log tongs and buried in the new coals below the burning logs. A kettle filled with water is hung on the cooking rod that swings over the roaring fire. She hopes that a cup of tea will calm her fears of what a gale might be like on her first night in the cottage.

While the potatoes bake, Gertrude pokes through the wardrobes in the bedrooms. Everything is clean and empty. She sorts through her clothes and puts them away in the bedroom. In the parlor, the sewing basket Mrs. Schultz put together is on the kitchen table. Gertrude takes the basket and begins to lay out the various items on the round table at the front window to get an idea of what she has. Mrs. Schultz has thought of everything, including knitting needles with two skeins of pale green yarn.

Aware of the increasing wind as she stands before the front window, she goes through the cottage and pulls the curtains closed so she can't see the wind movement. Just the roar of the wind is enough to make her fearful. The chill of the fall night increases and the rain begins. All the beds have quilts. She goes upstairs and collects the two quilts from the beds and brings them downstairs. All the doors to the hallway are shut behind her so that the fireplace heat will remain in the parlor and kitchen.

The tea water is ready. As the tea steeps in the pot, Gertrude looks about the room, a room that will be her living space until the spring. There is nothing on the walls, nothing to indicate who might have lived here before. All the quilts have duplicate patterns with no identity to tell a story of who might have made them. Gertrude is used to having quilts made from discarded clothing in the family so that the pattern of the quilt tells a story.

The "best" quilt in Gertrude's household growing up was a patchwork quilt made of many green cotton squares and triangles. Dress and shirt remnants were purchased by the bag from a shirt factory back in County Wexford. There were many patterns and colors: light green, dark green, stripes, flowers, dots, along with a few purple, brown, and light orange squares. The quilt had been made by her mother's female relatives before the family left for America. It was her mother's bottom drawer quilt for when she got married. That quilt, trimmed in royal blue and dark green, is the family's best quilt. Many stories had been shared when Gertrude and her brothers and sisters had crowded beneath the best quilt in the middle of a cold day in front of the fireplace.

Gertrude takes the potatoes out of the coals with the fire tongs and puts them on a tin pan. She retrieves a fork and a plate from the hanging dresser. The potatoes may be bland without any butter or seasonings, but she is still unable to eat much. The plain dinner will have to do. Sitting at the table, she hears the increasing force of the wind from outside. The cottage walls creak and moan as the wind from the ocean circles and strikes. A crash causes Gertrude to jump and to look through the cottage quickly, but she finds no obvious damage.

Back in the main room, she cleans up the table and then bundles up under the quilts on one of the chairs in front of the fire. The gale winds are a lot different from the storm she experienced on top of Croagh Patrick. The huge live oak trees surrounding the compound contribute their own type of sound to the gale. On top of the mantel is an oil lantern and a few candles. There does not appear to be any oil in the base of the lantern. She will need to ask Captain how to get the oil for the lantern. For now, the light from the fire is all Gertrude needs. She has no intention of going into the bedroom and trying to sleep. The wind may push a wall in or cause a tree limb to crash through a window. Though the curtains are drawn, the pounding of the rain on the glass is loud and occupies Gertrude's thoughts.

This is the first time she has been alone after the sea voyage back to Savannah from County Wexford. Though the visit with her family had been fine, there were too many secrets and the family members had too many questions for her to feel comfortable around them. She is better off here on Tybee Island, where there is time to sort through all the changes that will happen as a new life grows inside her. Suddenly, she feels a cold draft coming through the cottage. She looks into the rooms and sees nothing. Nothing is amiss upstairs and everything seems fine. There are no limbs through the roof, and no glass panes are missing from the windows. Back down the stairs, the air is still cold. That's when she sees a gap at the bottom of the front door where the age of the building has caused it to sag and change angles. Though the door closes and locks, it has a gap on the threshold. She stuffs a bed sheet from one of the beds upstairs around the gap to seal the wind out and keep the fire's heat in. Gertrude returns to huddle under the quilts.

The storm lasts most of the night. When the embers die down, she piles more wood on to keep the fire going. Somewhere in the early morning, Gertrude falls asleep slouching on the chair. Morning comes to her as the birds welcome a new day. A welcome is not forthcoming from Gertrude; every bone in her body aches from sleeping in the chair.

13

———

Changing clothes in the cold cottage takes Gertrude only a few minutes. There is no one to impress with her dress and hair, which is pulled back in a tight bun. Her tasks today are to find food and inspect the big house. Sister Mary Joyce had said there would be written instructions inside the cottage, but there are none. With her cloak and the keys that had been left on the table, Gertrude goes outside.

Limbs, twigs, and leaves are everywhere. Careful not to fall, she crosses to the big house and up the steps to the wide porch. The door key is easy to locate on the ring of keys; it is the biggest one. Inside is a big room with benches on the side under the front windows, probably used as a parlor. There is a plaque on the wall with the Bible verse from Matthew 25:40, "Inasmuch as ye have done it unto one of the least of these my brethren, ye have done it unto me."

A few small tables are grouped toward one side of the room with several wooden slatted chairs. The most noticeable items, though, are the vast number of pillows piled in bins along the far wall. A wide wooden stairwell is to the left. Across the room from the front door is another door. Through this door is a large room full of wooden tables and chairs. To the right, French doors lead out to a side porch facing the ocean. There is a long buffet-type table against the interior wall. And to the left in the opposite corner of the room, away from the windows, is a piano. Gertrude does not even go near the piano. It is covered with a white cloth, and as far as she is concerned, it will stay covered. Her desire to play the piano has led to her current problems. Until she has figured out how to go forward and how to have this baby, the piano will not be played.

Between the piano and the buffet table is another door. There is the kitchen. On the table in the center of the room is the list of instructions the society folks left for her. The back door leads to a porch. A large enclosed room on the porch has a Red Cross poster. One of the keys fits the lock. In the room, there are many locked cabinets, an examining table, charts on the wall, and all the necessary items for an infirmary. This is where one of the nurses from St. Joseph's will work in the summer.

Back inside the house, Gertrude climbs the stairs and finds large sleeping rooms with half a dozen bunk beds in each, where the children sleep, and several smaller rooms with three single beds where adults could sleep. Everything appears to be in place. The last caretaker left everything clean and ready.

Back downstairs in the kitchen, a look into the pantry results in finding several jars of beans, beets, and peas along with a bag of rice. She places them on the table in a basket, which is also found in the pantry. Pausing, she reads the instructions left by the society, which include how to contact the cook and where to get supplies. According to the notes left, Captain might have a young man who can run errands for her. That must have been the young man who had run to get Captain.

Everything is in place as described by Sister Mary Joyce. All that is left for her now is to figure out how to prepare food.

Growing up in a large household, her mother did all the cooking. Though she and her siblings helped in the kitchen, and they may have learned by watching, Gertrude never made the effort to really learn how to put an entire meal together. She simply allowed her mother to take control and she set the table. She knows how to heat things and put things like potatoes in hot coals to bake, but her cooking skills are limited. There is a lot to learn to keep her and this baby inside of her healthy.

Picking up the basket with the few items found in the pantry, she is ready to return to the cottage. In the dining room, she pauses. The light is good, and there are lots of tables where the fabric can be spread out and patterns placed to begin making the uniforms for the summer camp children. Some of the tables are too close together. Room is needed to move around them. Her hands grab one side of the table, but the heavy wooden table does not budge. She needs help to move these tables. She retrieves the basket of food items and leaves the house, locking the door behind her.

At the cottage, there are several large crates at the front door. The labels indicate that the fabric for the uniforms has arrived. Mrs. Schultz said two weeks, but here they are. Unlocking the cottage door and putting the basket of food on the table, she returns to move the crates.

Leaning down, Gertrude tries to pick up one of the crates, but it is too heavy. How can they be gotten into the cottage? A moment of inspiration comes. If she opens the crate's lid, the material can be moved piece by piece. She needs a tool to open the crate. She noticed no tool in the cottage in her earlier investigations, so she starts looking around the compound for Captain. Though he said he would be by to check on the grounds, he cannot be found. Returning to the cottage, she sees the young man pulling a cart full of broken limbs. He's outgrown the length of his trousers and his shirt is faded blue from too much sun and too many washes. A woven palmetto leaf hat covers his full head of lanky brown hair. Hair that needs a good trim, but from the looks of his clothes and his thin body, Gertrude doesn't think that will happen any time soon.

"Hello," she calls out to him.

He stops and comes over to where Gertrude is standing beside the crates of fabric. "Yes, ma'am?"

"Do you work with Captain?"

"Yes, ma'am, I do."

"I have been looking for him and cannot find him."

"That's because he isn't here."

The young man's nonchalant attitude amuses Gertrude. "I see. I need help moving these crates. Can you help?"

"Yes, ma'am." He immediately picks up one of the crates and goes up the steps to the cottage. Gertrude stops him. "On second thought, can they be put in the big house? That is where I will be using them." She hurries to unlock the door. Inside, the crates are put on the floor. "Can you open one of them for me?" He does so with a pocket knife he fishes out of his trouser pocket. Gertrude checks the fabric while the young man retrieves the other crates and opens them. The fabric is cotton muslin, which will need to be washed and ironed before being put on the tables and placing the pattern pieces.

"This is the last one," he says.

"Thank you. I'm Gertrude and will be keeping the house this winter."

"Yes, Captain told me after he handed the key over to you."

He turns to leave the room, but Gertrude stops him. "What's your name?"

"Michael," he says over his shoulder, and then he is gone.

Gertrude shakes her head at his behavior, but she is happy he came along when he did. Closing the crates, she leaves the big house, remembering to lock the doors behind her. Some food supplies are needed. Luckily, there is still some money left from Randolph's "rent" money. The market near the train depot may have limited goods, but it should have what is needed: rice, tea, flour, a tin of milk, and six eggs. This will have to do until she figures out how to eat on a meager budget.

Over the next few days, Gertrude cuts large lengths of the fabric, washes them, and hangs them out to dry. Then, two days are spent ironing the fabric. Once all the fabric is prepared, it is placed on the tables and covered with the pattern pieces to get the most out of the fabric. Just laying out the patterns will be difficult with the tables so close together. She should have asked Michael to move these when he was here, but she was checking the fabric and the amounts to see what she had and forgot to ask. Her attempt to find either Michael or Captain within the compound is not successful.

In the evening, Gertrude is bored and paces around the cottage. Light in the sky leaves early. The compound is dark, so Gertrude limits her walks to daylight and spends the evenings after dark inside the cottage. There is nothing to do. The cottage is quiet. She remembers the light green yarn and begins to knit in front of the fire in the evenings. Her imagination is limited, and there are only two skeins of yarn, so she decides to knit a scarf.

Food supplies are growing scarce. She must find a way to feed herself and the baby. Though not showing, Gertrude can feel her body changing as a baby grows inside of her. The last of the boiled eggs, along with cooked rice mixed with peas, is eaten. In front of the fire, Gertrude suddenly begins to talk to herself. "You are indeed a silly girl. You are living by the ocean. There are fish and seafood you can learn to catch and cook. You've seen your mother cook these things many times. Wake up, you can do this." Smiling at her own folly, she knits another row.

Early the next morning, walking out to the beach, she sees birds diving for fish. A few crabs dash back into the tidal basins. That's when Michael appears. He is in a small rowboat at one of the estuaries off the ocean.

"Hello," she calls loudly over the roar of the ocean.

Michael stops and turns toward her. "Good morning." He, too, has to speak loudly.

"You are up early," she shouts.

"Yes, this is a good time today to find crabs at high tide."

"I need to learn how to do this. Is it easy to learn?"

"I'll show you. But you need to have a boat or go to a dock to line a crab."

"Okay, I will watch from here and be better prepared later."

Michael talks to her about how to catch the crab. "Take a cord, tie some bait at the end. I use fish heads from when Captain and I clean the fish at the fish camp. The cord has a sinker tied onto it to make the string stay at the bottom." He shows her the baited string and the sinker. "Then you toss it into the water and wait." He says nothing and just sits in the rowboat. Gertrude watches and waits also.

After just a few minutes, he says, "I feel a pull-pull on the string." He stops talking and begins pulling the string up steadily and slowly. As the crab gets closer to the surface, Michael picks up a rectangular net framed in wood with a long pole attached. He pushes the net under the crab and lifts it out of the water. "Once the crab is up, put him in a bucket of ocean water."

Gertrude watches and figures she can do this, but she needs to invest in cord, sinker, bait, a wooden net, and a bucket. She waves to him and calls out, "Michael, I think I have the idea."

He speaks louder so she can hear. "It's important to put the crabs in ocean water until you head to the cottage," he tells her. "That way, the crabs will be fine until you cook them."

Gertrude nods and mentally notes the items she needs. "Thank you." She turns to walk back to the cottage when she remembers that she needs some tables moved. "Michael, when you are back on the compound, will you help me move a couple of tables in the dining room?"

"Yes, ma'am. I will finish here, take these home, and be back to help."

"Thank you." Gertrude returns to the cottage. She takes off her cloak and sits at the table. There is a lot to think about. Where would the items be found to catch the crabs? Where is the dock? Can a boat be borrowed? There are no fish heads, nor does she want any fish heads. Where does the money come from to buy these things when there is no money to buy food? Plus, she needs to learn how to cook crabs.

The food pantry in the cottage is bare. If crops were planted, there might be food later. Gertrude has never worked in a garden and really has no idea how long it takes crops to grow. A gardener would need to be consulted. When she goes into Savannah to see Sister Mary Joyce, she could ask Mrs. Schultz's gardener. But the Savannah trip is not for a few weeks. She needs food now and only has enough money to buy a bag of rice.

Doing something, anything, might relieve her worry. Gertrude stands, puts on her cloak, and goes outside to survey the land around the cottage. On the side away from the ocean is an arbor where a rose bush has been planted. Surely things can grow here. But what and when? Never having grown anything before, she needs a plan. The conversation with Ryan in Galway reminds her about how Ryan's family planted crops during the waning and waxing of the moon. Gertrude paces around the plot of land where crops might be planted when

Captain comes from behind the big house. Gertrude calls out to him.

"Captain, can you offer me your opinion?"

He approaches her with his boating gait. "How can I help?"

"There seems to have been a garden here before. Can I plant things here for food?"

"I would think so," he says. "There is a shed behind the big house that has all sorts of tools in it. I use some of them for the grounds, but there are others as well. Take a look and see what is there. But know that even though we are on the coast, winters can be quite chilly here. I wouldn't plant anything until February at the earliest. Now's a good time just to get the soil prepared." He pauses. "Do you know anything about growing crops?"

"Not a thing," says Gertrude. "But I am willing to try. Thank you." She looks about the grounds as Captain leaves. "Wait," she calls out to Captain. "How can I get oil for the lanterns in the cottage?"

"Just leave the lanterns on the kitchen table in the big house. I will fill them from the supply I keep at the fishing camp and return them to the table."

"Thank you." Gertrude looks at the plot of land where a garden might be. With no crops to plant until February, four months away, and the baby due in March, it would be futile to even think about planting anything. However, she is curious about what is in the shed. Behind the big house is the shed tucked behind a fence and a line of trees. The door is padlocked. She retreats to the cottage to get the keys to the compound, then finally gets back to the door and opens it. Inside are rakes, shovels, trowels, and other tools that Gertrude cannot identify. There are several crabbing nets with poles and reed baskets. The counselors must take the children crabbing when they are at camp. She now has the tools she needs to catch crabs.

On a shelf above the tools is a big, rectangular basket. Grabbing the side to pull it down, the heavy basket crashes to the wooden shed floor. Inside are lots of wader boots of different sizes. Sitting down on the floor, Gertrude tries on various boots. Many are too small. One is too large, but with some cloth pushed into the toes, it could work. There is another basket containing work gloves. Several pairs fit her small hands. There might be a need for these even if she doesn't plant a garden. Though there are no immediate food sources, there is a plan. She can catch crabs. Now she needs to figure out what to eat today.

On her return to the cottage, Michael appears. "Ma'am," he calls out, "I can help you move the tables now."

Gertrude has the keys in her hand and proceeds to the big house. "Good, I need to begin my project." They enter and go straight to the dining room. Together, they move several tables apart to give room for walking around each.

"Thank you," she says, but Michael is looking at the covered piano and not listening to her.

"I didn't know there is a piano here," he says.

"They must use it when the children are here in the summer."

"Do you play?"

Gertrude pauses. "Yes, I do play." Then she adds, "I have played."

Michael rushes over and takes the cloth off the piano. "Will you play something? Can you show me how to play?" He is looking at the piano and not Gertrude. He is so eager that it is hard to say no.

Gertrude pauses, then says, "No, I have chosen not to play." She turns away from him and begins to rearrange patterns on the table. She tilts her head to one side to see where Michael is, since he is not speaking.

Michael stands still in the middle of the room, just looking at her. There is confusion on his face. "You have chosen not to play when you know how?" Michael clenches his fists at his side and flexes his fingers.

"Yes," says Gertrude. "It is a long story, and I will not tire you with the details." Thinking that is the end of it, Gertrude glances back at Michael.

"Do you have dreams? You must have had dreams about playing if you know how to play."

Gertrude looks at Michael and sees a young man with determination, something she had once upon a time. "I have had dreams," she says. "I have had dreams that keep me up at night."

"Was playing the piano one of those dreams?"

"Yes."

"What happened? Why won't you play?"

Gertrude puts down the fabric she holds. "It's complicated, Michael."

He walks toward her. "My dream is to leave this island. Can I do that by catching crabs? By living off the land, day by day? I don't think so. I need to learn more. I would like to learn how to play the piano. I'm almost sixteen, and I would like to learn anything that will get me off this island." He looks at her with eyes that could plead. In a whisper, he says, "I want hope." He turns and leaves quickly, slamming the front door behind him.

Gertrude studies the spot where he had been standing. Out loud, she says, "I want hope, too, Michael. I want hope."

14

———

Two days later, Gertrude has no food in the cottage. The rice purchased at the market in the train depot has been used and so have the jars she had found in the pantry of the big house. She is pacing in the main room of the cottage when she hears a knock at the door. On the steps are two burly men with a large wooden crate on the back of a horse-drawn cart.

"Delivery for Miss Kelly," says one of the men.

"I'm Miss Kelly. "Can you bring it inside?"

"Yes, ma'am. It's heavy, so we'll put it where you want it."

"Do you know what it is?"

"Here's a note that is to be delivered with it," and he hands an envelope to Gertrude. She opens the note.

Dear Gertrude,

I hope this note finds you well. I had a conversation with Mrs. Lynch, and when she heard that you were making the uniforms for the Fresh Air Home campers, she found a used Singer sewing machine that might make your work easier. Sister Mary Joyce facilitated getting the machine and specified that we should get it to you soon. There are instructions on how to use the machine in a separate box that the delivery men should give you. I assured Mrs. Lynch that with your experience sewing, you probably already knew how to use it. Mrs. Lynch did ask if, when you were in Savannah next, you might drop by and say hello. I assured her that I would share her request with you. In the box with the instructions for the sewing machine are other items that I thought you might need. We are all looking forward to seeing you in a couple of weeks when you come for your check-up with Sister Mary Joyce.

Do take care, and let me know if there is anything you need.

Best Regards,

Mrs. Schultz

The men are standing by the door, waiting for Gertrude to tell them where to put the crate. "Please come in. Let's put it in front of the windows over against the wall to get good light."

The men place the crate and remove the wood so that the sewing machine is visible. It's a black Singer sewing machine with a treadle table. The "Singer" name stands out in large block gold letters against the black ebony finish of the machine. Other gold images outline the base of the machine. Though the table is wooden, the treadle is black iron.

She asks the men to move the burgundy settee in front of the fireplace to make room for the sewing machine. They also move one of the upholstered chairs to the front of the parlor near the round table at the window. The other chair is to the side of the fireplace and the ottoman is in front of the settee. As the men start to gather the pieces of the crate, she stops them. "I can do that, thank you." She walks over to the door and holds it open for them. "Thank you." The two men go outside.

Gertrude remembers that there should be a box. "Wait, is there a box that goes with this?"

"Oh, yes, ma'am. Sorry, we forgot to give it to you." They had placed the box on the floor of the cart under the front bench. One of the men wrestled it out from under the bench. It was a long, rather deep box.

"Please put it on the table inside. It appears heavy."

"Yes, ma'am." After placing the box on the table, one of the men uses his hammer to open the lid of the wooden box, then both men leave and drive the horse-drawn cart off the compound property.

Gertrude looks at the box and is grateful that Mrs. Schultz sent the sewing machine instructions. She has never used a machine before. Then, in the box, there are two other boxes. The first one has jars of beans, corn, tomatoes, and beets. The second box has bags of flour, sugar, salt and pepper, cornmeal, rice, a box of processed oats, and a tin full of tea. Gertrude sits down at the table in front of the food bounty. Tears sting her eyes and roll down her cheeks. She stifles a joyful laugh with a hand to her mouth and says out loud, almost in a prayer, "Thank you, Mrs. Schultz."

Her energy is renewed. The crate pieces and box are stored in the empty closet behind the water closet. Each food item is lifted and carefully placed on the pantry shelves. She plans to learn how to supplement all this food bounty from Mrs. Schultz with seafood. She needs to ask Michael.

Grabbing her cloak, Gertrude locks the cottage door behind her and heads over to the island's back river. She doesn't know where Michael lives, but she saw him head in this direction. There are few residents who live on the island during the fall and winter months, according to Sister Mary Joyce. People who do live here must know each other. The fishing camp is right where Captain said it would be. To the north of the camp appear to be new cottages being constructed, so she turns south on the lane behind the fishing camp. There are houses along the roadway, but no one seems to be about. The houses are diminishing in size and quality. Near a thicket, she sees a house set back from the roadway that is not on risers like the other houses along the back river. The house needs repairs. Various pots and pans are scattered around the yard. In the side yard, a big-boned woman with her brown hair braided down her back is washing clothes in an outside vat over a fire. Then Gertrude sees Michael come from the house with a basket that he puts down near the woman.

"Hello," calls out Gertrude.

Both Michael and the woman stop and stare. Michael steps forward quickly. When he is near Gertrude, he asks quietly, "What are you doing here?"

"I'm here to apologize for being so abrupt when we talked about the piano lessons."

Before Gertrude can say anything more, the woman walks toward her and wipes her wet hands on her dress, a cotton dress that was once a bright green but is now pastel colored with ragged sleeves and hem. She looks quite capable of lifting full baskets of wet clothes. "What piano lessons?" she asks. "He don't need no piano lessons. And who are you to come around here with such an offer?"

Gertrude addresses the woman but sees Michael's eyes begging her to be silent. "I'm Gertrude Kelly. I am the caretaker of the Fresh Air Home for the winter. Michael helps Captain and runs some errands." She glances at Michael.

Michael speaks up. "You know that I do work for Captain at the Home, Ma."

"I do know, but I don't know nothing about piano lessons."

Gertrude continues, "When Michael was helping move some tables in the dining area, we discussed the piano and the fact that I play. Michael thought he might like to learn, and I feel that I was too abrupt at saying no to Michael's request. I want to offer an exchange of maybe some seafood in exchange for the lessons."

"No was the right answer," says the woman. "We have no money and no time to be foolin' with such nonsense. You were right to say no. Any found seafood goes on our table, not yours. Now, go on, we have things we need to finish. If Michael learns anything, it must be in how he can earn a livin'." She stands her ground with her hands on her hips.

Gertrude hesitates but then sees a tall man leaning up against the doorframe of the house with a shotgun in his hands. He has his hat pulled down over his forehead and his shirt sleeves are rolled up to his elbows. The movement he makes forces Gertrude to look at his hands, which are weathered but clearly holding the shotgun with a finger on the trigger. "Thank you, ma'am, I just wanted to apologize. I don't mean to bother anyone." Gertrude turns and walks the way she came. Her steps are faster going than they were approaching the house. She wants to get as far away from these people as possible.

Back at the cottage and after taking a long breath, Gertrude knows there is work to do. She must cut out fabric for the uniforms. She needs to read the instructions on how to use the sewing machine. Since she is being paid by pieces, the sooner she gets some made, the sooner she will have cash to buy food for her and the baby.

Suddenly, Gertrude realizes that her sickness has disappeared. Sister Mary Joyce did say that after the first trimester, the throwing up might pass. Calculating in her head, that would mean that her baby would be due in six months. The baby should come in March. She needs to think about what to do after the baby arrives. Her thoughts are clouded by the fact that there are so few options and so few people to ask. First, what would happen to her if the baby is adopted? She could get a job and move on with her life. Can she live with that? Second, what would happen if she kept the baby? Could she raise a child by herself without a livelihood, without shelter, without a family willing to take her in? Her fake marriage labels her as a damaged woman unfit to marry. So her not wanting to be married earlier is a done deal now.

Next, her thoughts go in a different direction. Though she may have been given a chance to have the baby and survive by living on Tybee Island for the winter, is that all there is to life? Survival? Where are the dreams of being a concert pianist? Where is that hope she had when she went with Randolph to Dublin? Even the respite received from Croagh Patrick, that she could indeed compose music, seems so far removed from what she is facing now. She is going to have a baby, and that baby is changing her life forever.

15

———

In the daylight hours, Gertrude lays out the pattern pieces in the big house dining room. In the evening in front of the fire, she studies the instructions for the sewing machine.

Her first lesson is to learn how to treadle. The instructions guide her. Dragging a chair from the table in the kitchen area, she sits down in front of the machine. With the manual in front of her, she begins to read.

The most comfortable and effective position for treadling is with the ball of the left foot upon the upper left corner of the treadle and the heel of the right foot on the lower right corner. Treadling in this position takes very much less effort than when the feet are placed in any other position.

Having your feet side-by-side is easier at first, but quickly becomes very tiring. Start your practice session by removing the thread from the machine, removing the bobbin, and disconnecting the belt from the wheel. Move the presser bar to the up position.

Practice treadling smoothly with your feet, back and forth, until you can do it without looking at your feet.

Gertrude does what the instructions tell her to do. It is easier to keep her feet side-by-side, but she positions her feet according to the instructions and begins to treadle. She stops and reads more of the instructions.

Now, reconnect the belt. Undo the clutch on the handwheel. Pull the handwheel towards yourself and start to treadle with your feet. Your goal is smoothness and rhythm to your movements.

If you lose your rhythm, stop the handwheel with your hand and then pull the handwheel towards you and start to treadle again with your feet. Practice treadling for a few minutes. Practice starting and stopping.

The stopping and starting is not as easy as it sounds. Gertrude finds that her hand must be placed on the handwheel in time to have it in sync with the pace of her feet. That means that she will need to anticipate when to stop and hold the material with her left hand so the stitches will remain even. She continues to read.

Now tighten the clutch so that the needle moves up and down and practice treadling as before. Next, try feeding fabric under the lowered presser foot and treadling. Practice starting and stopping and sewing in a straight line.

She turns the pages to find a diagram of the machine to locate the clutch and studies the page as though someone will test her. What she has learned from having played the piano is that taking shortcuts may let one get through the music, but it does not let one know how to go through other music without thinking of new shortcuts. It is best to do it the way it is taught until the process is mastered, then make changes.

After you are comfortable with treadling, now you can thread the machine and put in the bobbin. Feed fabric under the presser foot and practice, practice, practice treadling. The faster you pump, the faster the machine runs. Use your hand to brake or slow down or stop the machine. Stop pedaling to stop sewing.

Be sure to thread your machine following the guide in your manual. Many problems with a machine can be resolved by simply threading it correctly. Make sure that the bobbin is wound and loaded correctly, too.

Adjust the tension until the stitches look even. The top tension needs to be adjusted depending on the fabric you're using. The bobbin or bottom tension needs to be adjusted by hanging the bobbin or shuttle by its thread and jerking it upward. The bobbin should drop slightly. If it drops too far, tighten it. If it doesn't drop, loosen it. After the bobbin is correctly adjusted, you shouldn't need to ever change it.

It's time to start sewing! Do you have your first project ready to go?

Yes, thinks Gertrude. There are quite a number of projects to make. Having the sewing machine will make the task easier. The sewing machine table is in front of the side window, but in order to have the fabric not be jammed against the wall, it needs to be positioned so that the side with the belt is against the wall. Tugging hard to get the sewing machine table moved, she is ready to practice treadling.

Gertrude's days become routine. A walk on the beach is the first thing in the morning. Next is a hot cup of tea. The kettle sits in the fireplace, so the water warms during her walk. Left-overs are put in a pot with water added to simmer as a soup for lunch. After a simple breakfast of cooked oats soaked during the day and simmered over the fire during the night, as well as tea, it is off to the big house to cut out fabric pieces. At lunchtime, she returns to the cottage for soup. Then there is another walk on the beach. The fresh salt air invigorates her. Without the walk, she is lethargic and wants to take a nap. She plans to ask Sister Mary Joyce about the fatigue.

She tours the big house to verify that everything is fine. The doors and windows are checked. She also inspects outside the house to make sure nothing is amiss. After the inspection tour, she returns to the dining room to cut out fabric. At the end of the day, her back aches. A tub bath might be just the thing to do this evening. She fills several buckets with water from the cistern. These buckets are put on the fireplace grate to warm the water for her bath.

After a dinner of rice and beans, she sews in front of the fire. Her body aches. She takes a lighted candle into the water closet, then retrieves the hot buckets of water to pour them into a tub. She must put a little more water into the tub to cool the hot water before she climbs in to soak. Her back continues to ache. The quiet in the cottage permeates her as well. She doesn't talk out loud, or sing, or make any sounds when alone. She is alone a lot. However, her established routine gets her through the week.

Saturday. Maybe something different should be done on Saturday. The day begins as usual, but just when she is ready to go out the door, she sits and puts on the pair of wader boots. The keys to the cottage are in her pocket. In the shed, the pole with a net attached and a reed basket is ready to use. The sun is barely up and the colors of the chilly fall morning are scattered across the sky.

Birds swoop and dive into the water with such freedom of movement. The tide is going out. Gertrude can't remember when Michael said the best crabbing is done. She'll have to take her chances. Though there is no dock, there are crabs scooting about at high tide. Maybe she can catch them in the shallows without a boat or dock. Hiking up her skirt and tucking it partly into her belt, she wades out into the cold waters. She looks down and sees movement, but whatever it is moves too fast to tell what it is. This is her first time ever being in the ocean. Feeling the water come and go around her feet is a new experience. She finds that her heartbeat, which was racing a few minutes ago with the idea of getting into the cold water, has slowed down and is in tandem with the ocean. The roar of the ocean has a cadence that fills the quiet. Only the birds screeching over their morning fish punctuate that quiet.

Gertrude refocuses on the water and her goal of finding crabs. There—she sees one. Almost tiptoeing, she moves the net closer, but the crab scoots away. She waits and walks a little more. There is another one. She moves faster this time, it's an allegro moment, not a lento one. The crab slips crookedly into the net. She jerks it out of the water. Looking at it for a moment, the crab is dumped into the reed basket she is trailing behind her. It takes her a while and many misses, but somehow she manages to capture three crabs. Exhausted but thrilled that she has found her own dinner, she emerges from the ocean waters and dumps the crabs from the reed basket into a bucket left on the beach. She sees Captain in front of her, moving stones to the path.

"Good morning," she calls out.

"And good morning to you," he says. "You've been crabbing this morning already?"

"Yes, Michael showed me how and I kind of created a way that I could do it. I found the items I needed in the shed."

"Enjoy."

But before he can turn away, Gertrude speaks up. "However, can you tell me how to cook them and how to get the crab meat out?"

Captain bursts into a laugh that could be heard at the train station, Gertrude is sure. "I'm headed back to the fish camp. Put some water on to boil. Wait for me to return before you put the crabs in. Keep the crabs in the sea water until then." He turns and walks down the lane, still chuckling.

Gertrude does not pause. Inside the cottage, she puts a pot of water on the stove to boil. Captain returns with some tools and a board that he lays on top of the wood bin. Gertrude steps outside and watches as he lays out the tools on the board. "Now, put the crabs in the boiling water. When they turn a vibrant orange and float to the top, after about five minutes, take them off the heat and bring them outside.

Gertrude does as instructed. She debates in her head for a full minute as to how to get the crabs out of the bucket and into the boiling water. Too embarrassed to go back out and ask Captain, she remembers the fire tongs. The tongs keep the crabs at a distance and soon all three are in the big pot of boiling water. After a few minutes, one of the crabs is orange and floating to the top. Again, using the tongs, she removes the crabs from the water and places them on another pan. When all three have floated, she takes the pan outside to Captain.

Nothing has prepared her for the work it takes to get the meat out of a crab. Cooking the crabs is easy. But to clean the crabs, strength, tools, and knowledge are needed. Before, others have done the crab work for her and never told her about the feathery cones of the crab's lungs, or the greenish liver, called the tomalley. She did not know that the bright orange part indicated that the crab is female and that it is the roe or eggs. Captain instructs her to keep the shells and boil them to make a soup. After sharing more knowledge with her about crabs than she thought she would ever have, Captain goes on his way. Gertrude puts the crab meat in the icebox and hopes for the best when it comes to preparing dinner. For now, she has fabric to cut.

16

Morning sunrises and evening sunsets are Gertrude's favorite times of the day. She plans her work activities in order to be on the beach for both; that is, unless there is a rain shower or storm that ruins these moments. Though in actuality, the rain does not always ruin the sunset or sunrise because sometimes there is a wonderful rainbow after the rain. One morning after a hard rain shower that delays her walk on the beach, she reaches the end of the beach and turns to retrace her steps. She looks up and sees a double rainbow. The twin has inverted colors with violet on top and red on the bottom. It is fainter and wider. She can see it during her entire walk back. To her, it is magical, like the murmuration of the starlings, a curtain call after a brilliant performance of a storm ending.

Gertrude returns from her morning walk, basking in the sight of the double rainbow, to find a small bucket of fish on the cottage steps with no one about. No one is waiting down below near the street. She takes the fish inside and plans a meal. The next day, she opens the door to find a bucket of clams. Again, they are taken inside for dinner. On the third day, she wakes up early, and as she stands at the sink and looks out the window, there is a shadow that moves quickly across the pathway in front of the cottage. Hurriedly, she goes to the door and opens it quickly. Michael is placing a bucket of seaweed on the step. He looks up and sees her.

"Michael, so it's you who is leaving food gifts on my step."

Michael doesn't answer; he just reaches out to hand her the bucket of seaweed.

"And pray tell, how do I use seaweed?" She is looking straight at him and not at the bucket.

"Fill a bucket with clean water and rinse the seaweed until all the sand has floated to the bottom. We make a broth using seaweed, potatoes, and onions cooked in water. If you want to save some of it, dry it on a string hanging up, but beware of flies. They love the seaweed. Once it is dried, store it in a glass jar and use it to thicken broths and make gravies or bake it into bread. When we find a lot, Ma dries it and we eat the seaweed that way."

"I see," says Gertrude. "Thank you for your food gifts, but why are you doing this?"

Michael looks away, down the path. "I am sorry for how my ma and pa treated you the day you came." Michael shuffles his feet on the rocks on the pathway.

Gertrude looks at his ill-kept hair and mud-stained clothes. His hands, hanging loosely at his side, are scratched with dirt under all of his fingernails. She looks back inside the bucket at the seaweed. "Is there a best time to pick seaweed?"

"At low tide on a calm day like today. I cut off only half the plant and leave the rest to form more seaweed."

Gertrude looks down at the seaweed in the bucket, then back at Michael. "If you are to learn how to play the piano, you must remove the dirt from under your fingernails. I will not have you play the piano with dirty hands." Gertrude turns to go into the cottage. Before stepping inside, she says, "We will have our first lesson today. Come into the dining room when you have the time to begin. I will be working there all morning." She goes into the cottage and hears Michael say, "Yes, ma'am," with an excitement that she has not felt in a long time.

Gertrude takes the time to rinse the seaweed. Cleaning it and feeling its silky fonds is a new sensation. There have been many new experiences since coming to Tybee Island, like cleaning fish and baking clams in the fireplace like her mum does. Both of these were done from memory. Cooking seaweed will be another new experience. The food gifts have made her feel better. Her energy has returned.

After the final rinse of the seaweed, there is no place to hang the seaweed to dry. Michael warned about the flies, and though it is chilly, it is a calm day, so there might be some around. Not sure how long seaweed needs to cook, she decides that rather than drying it, she will cook it. She puts water in the iron pot and places it over the embers with the seaweed inside to simmer while she cuts fabric. There is work to be done; she heads to the big house.

Midmorning, when it is time to ease her back and have a cup of tea, she hears the front door of the big house open and footsteps through the parlor. She should really latch the door when she is inside working and no one is around. Focusing on the door, she lets her breath out when Michael steps into the dining room.

"Good morning, I am about to have a cup of tea. I will get it and meet you at the piano. Please take the cover off."

When Gertrude returns, Michael is not sitting at the piano but standing beside it. She motions to the bench. "Sit there, I will pull a chair up beside you."

Michael sits on the bench with his feet tucked under. His hands are folded in his lap.

As she places the chair near the bench and sits, she observes how straight and tall Michael is sitting on the bench.

"Your posture is good, Michael. Now, put both feet flat on the floor and place your hands on the keyboard with your left hand here." She positions Michael's hand. "And the right one here." Again, she positions his hand. She smiles to herself when she sees how spotless Michael's hands are with no dirt under the nails. Gertrude begins with scales and takes Michael through the "C" scale, first with his right hand and then with his left, and then with both. He listens, not asking any questions, simply repeating exactly what he has been shown. His fingers are stiff on the keys, but she knows they will loosen as he learns.

"I know you may not have a lot of time to practice with all the jobs and errands you have to run, but I will be here every morning cutting out fabric and you can come in and practice for the few minutes you might have. We will have a formal lesson where I sit down with you and show you additional movements once a week."

Michael still says nothing and is just looking at the keyboard.

"Is that okay with you?"

He nods his head several times.

Gertrude stands and stretches her back. "I need to cut more fabric."

"Can I practice a little now? I don't want to forget what you have shown me."

Gertrude smiles broadly, remembering how often she practiced growing up and loving every minute of it. "Absolutely. I'll be right over here."

As the "C" scale is played over and over, Gertrude notices that the jerky movements of remembering which key is played next get smoother and smoother. Within a few minutes, Michael is running the scale smoothly with both hands. When he stops, he closes the lid to the piano and stands to leave. At the door, he turns to Gertrude. "Thank you, ma'am."

"You are welcome. Thank you for the food gifts. The trade is good with me if it is with you. But, please, whatever you bring, make sure it is something I can learn to cook."

Michael's grin is quick, and he is out the door.

Gertrude watches Michael leave. About to return to cutting the fabric, she sees the piano has not been covered and crosses the room, but instead of covering the piano, she sits down at the bench. Slowly, she opens the lid. The keys sit there, no sound, no movement, no music. She has to put her fingers to the keys for their sound to come alive. It is her spirit, her music that comes out of the instrument.

Gertrude plays the "C" scale, just as Michael learned, then she runs through all of the scales, and before long, she moves into playing Ludwig van Beethoven's "Für Elise." As the notes smooth and flow from her fingers, her mood moves into the music with the emotion she has always felt when playing this tune. Her hands fly over the keyboard. When she finishes, there is a smile. This is why she wanted to learn to play: the music fills her body, takes over her mind, and gives her peace with herself and with the world. When she stands to cover the piano, Captain is in the doorway with his hat in his hand.

"I didn't want to disturb you."

Gertrude quickly walks over to her fabric table. "How may I help you?" she says.

"I've never heard music played so beautifully. Why aren't you playing instead of cutting out fabric?"

"Long story, but cutting out fabric pays and music does not." She picks up her scissors. "How can I help you?"

"I was scheduled to take some folks out fishing this afternoon and they canceled. It's a calm day after the heavy rain we have had and the missus wants to go. She thought since you are new here on the island, you might like to go out and learn a little more about the island waters."

Gertrude pauses. An excursion might be nice. She has not been sick for a couple of weeks and thinks the movement of the boat would be fine. "I would like that very much. What time should I be at the fish camp?"

"Just after lunch, say two this afternoon?"

"That sounds good. Thank you for asking me."

"You're welcome. Just want you to feel at home here on Tybee. There might not be a lot of people around right now, but as the summer approaches, people come in droves."

Captain puts his hat on and leaves as silently as he came. Gertrude thinks about what it means to feel welcome. It is a small island. Though she feels safe to move around, as the baby grows and begins to show more, she will need to be careful with her secret and wear looser clothes and stay inside as much as possible. With fall and winter chilly weather, her cloak should help hide her fairly well.

17

———————

Gertrude changes into a heavier skirt with a jacket. A wool hat from Dublin will keep the wind out of her blonde hair. A wool scarf can be wrapped around her face should the chill of the day be too much for her. Though the weather is getting cooler, Gertrude finds she is often warm and skips putting on her cloak to go across to the big house. It must be due to her body changing with the baby growing inside of her. At the last minute, the wader boots are discarded. They are clunky and may cause her problems in getting in and out of the boat. A pair of worn gloves completes her wardrobe. She lifts her cloak off the hook at the front door; she may need it after all.

Walking across the island to the fish camp only takes a few minutes. Her arrival brings Captain's wife out to greet Gertrude at the dockside.

"Good afternoon. I'm Hazel. I'm happy to have you join us. I have been meanin' to come over and say a proper welcome, but things are always coming up over here and I have put it off. The boat is ready and we can go on board."

Gertrude notices how Hazel is able to step gingerly into the boat without holding on to anything. She takes her hand to hold her calico skirt and swings a long leg over into the boat, steadies herself, and moves quickly to the center of the bench. The tan on her face smooths some of the aging lines and accents others. A wide canvas hat covers her brown hair and ties with a cord under her chin.

The fishing boat is white with a red border painted near the upper edge. Made from white cedar, the bottom has curved frames with a high, square stern. There is no deck, but benches on the side and across the middle.

With her cloak wrapped around her, Gertrude steps from the dock into the boat, with Captain reaching out his hand to steady her. The fishing boat is bigger than expected, though it is a small boat. It is her first experience in a small boat. The boat holds steady in the water as she sits on one of the benches next to Hazel. Captain is on the back bench, untying the ropes holding the boat to the dock. At the bottom of the boat, Gertrude identifies clam and oyster rakes, a trident pole for flounder, a landing net like Michael had to catch crabs, and a shotgun. In the front of the boat is a wooden crate with ropes attached and several reed baskets with ropes.

As they move away from the dock, Gertrude says, "The water looks calm."

"For now," says Captain.

Gertrude looks about and realizes that she is too far from shore to step back out of the boat. "What do you mean?"

Captain is busy with the ropes and sail. "With the large mainsail and the jib, the round bottom and sturdy hull, this boat can maneuver in whatever unpredictable waters there are around here. And believe me, there is unpredictable water and weather."

The word "unpredictable" makes Gertrude a little nervous. She looks over the side of the boat into the back river. Captain and Hazel seem relaxed and fine. Hazel is shifting a basket around to find a good spot for it at the bottom of the boat.

Captain continues, "These boats are known for their stability and how easily one can manage them in shallow waters as well as steep, choppy waves out in the ocean, even when heavily loaded. So, not to worry."

Gertrude looks back into the hull of the boat. "Why the shotgun?" Her memory of Michael's pa with his shotgun in the doorway has stayed with her.

"In case there are waterfowl. If I have a slow fishing day, we still need to eat, so I look for birds and, if I am in the marsh, maybe raccoons or rabbits. A fisherman has to be prepared," he says.

Gertrude is not prepared. All these new experiences frighten her at times. The boat is out in the river, and Captain turns the boat using the rudder and sail to head up the river toward the marshes.

"Thought we'd see what the rest of the back river looks like." Captain has an oar in the water and Hazel picks up another. Together they row up the river using the sail to help zigzag across the river, using the wind when it is helpful and rowing when it is not. Gertrude offers, but both Hazel and Captain say they are fine and know how to work together. This relieves Gertrude because she has no idea how to paddle.

Holding her breath, Gertrude exhales and allows the sway of the boat and the smooth river to lull her into being calm. The riverbank has some large cottages sitting near the water with elaborate docks and walkways. Then the riverbank turns into more trees and fewer houses. As they continue, Gertrude notices the birds are different. Not so many sea birds screeching and diving. There are more tree birds and hawks. The river is quiet compared to the ocean waves and seabirds.

As they make their way up the river, Captain points out a low bank area. "Let's pull in and rest a bit." Hazel nods and together they ease the boat toward the bank. In the shallows, Captain leaps out of the boat and, with a rope, tugs it up onto the muddy bank. When it is secured to nearby trees, he reaches a hand to Gertrude, who steps out onto rocky land. Hazel follows her with the basket.

"I brought a little something for afternoon tea. We'll find a perfect spot to sit," she says. Gertrude goes behind her to let Hazel find that perfect spot. Hazel walks up to drier ground. She removes a faded green blanket from the basket and spreads it on the ground. Then she sits down, pulling her skirt around her knees, and sorts through the basket, bringing out egg salad sandwiches, ginger cookies, jars of tea, and small plates. Gertrude joins her on the blanket after taking off her cloak. Captain, however, gets a fishing pole from the hull of the boat and immediately begins to throw the line into the river, looking for fish. He wades out in the shallows. The two women watch Captain as he moves about the water. Hazel turns to Gertrude, "Where are you from that you should come out to the island during winter?"

Gertrude is prepared for questions. Mrs. Schultz had helped her practice answers to what people would be curious about. "I am in training to be a nurse, and the Fresh Air Home needed someone to oversee the house during the winter. This is just a good time to come over and take some time off the training, but still do a good service for the Sisters of Mercy at the hospital and for the Froebel Society at the Home."

"I see, but won't this take time away from your training?"

"Absolutely, but the nursing program at the hospital is hoping to place some of the graduates at the home during the summer months. This is good will, I suppose."

"Yes, I suppose," says Hazel.

Before Hazel can ask another question, Captain comes, yelling from the waters, "Go up higher. Go now, a river surge is coming."

Gertrude and Hazel are stunned. Gertrude stands and leans over to put things in the basket. Hazel gets the blanket and folds it. Gertrude picks up her cloak. Hazel takes the basket and puts the blanket inside. They can hear Captain yelling at them to hurry. He has taken another rope out of the boat and is trying to secure the boat to other trees, but the rope is too short. He drops the rope and runs toward the two women who are making their way through the thicket undergrowth.

Gertrude looks back and sees the boat pulling at the rope. The water height of the river has increased, and the boat is no longer sitting on the lowered rocks but bobbing in the river current. As the three get deeper in the thicket, Gertrude hears a roaring sound. She turns again to look at the river. Suddenly, there is a tremendous amount of water rushing down and overflowing the banks of the river. Where they had been sitting is completely covered in water. Tree limbs and debris from up the river are barreling down and crashing into the sides of the boat. Gertrude falls over a limb she has not seen since she is looking at the turbulence of the river. Captain and Hazel are quietly watching the same scene and do not notice Gertrude's fall.

"Do we need to get farther away?" Gertrude asks.

"I think we are fine in the thicket," says Captain. "But why don't you ladies go on ahead and find a place to rest. I'm just going to make sure the water isn't going to rise any higher."

Hazel trudges on ahead. Gertrude is getting stuck with the brambles on her skirt. She wads the skirt up, holding it with her hand, and pushes on to catch up with Hazel. The gnats are flying in her face, and attempts to bat them away are difficult while holding her cloak and skirt. Soon, she gives up and simply climbs over limbs and pushes around bushes. Gertrude is focused on getting far away from the raging river and pauses long enough to take the scarf around her neck and tie it over her face to protect her from the irritating gnats. The black gnats bite; the others only annoy. Glancing in the direction of where

Hazel has been going, Gertrude keeps pushing through the underbrush. She concentrates on getting as far away from the river as possible and finding Hazel, who should have stopped by now. There is no sign of Hazel. Gertrude stops and looks back toward where she thinks the river is. She is totally unsure of any direction, with no idea of how to return to where Hazel disappeared, or where the Captain may be waiting.

"Hello!" Gertrude calls out. "Captain! Hazel!" Listening, she only hears the wind in the trees and the birds. The chill of the October day is on her face. At a stump, Gertrude decides to sit and wait. It is only the afternoon, but daylight is getting shorter and shorter every day. The oncoming darkness makes her feel that she cannot just sit and wait. It is an island after all. The sun's position in the sky can be used to determine the direction to take. Remembering where the sun sets and rises is her starting point. The sun sets in the west, and that's opposite of the way she needs to walk. With the sun to her back, she heads east toward the shore where the sun rises and toward the cottage.

The woods thin out and there are gentle meadows. She crosses a few creeks and springs. After cupping some water in her hands to quench her thirst, she continues. In the quiet of the woods, there is a gunshot. Gertrude freezes. Is it Captain trying to tell her where they are? Or is it someone like Michael's pa, who is out hunting and would have no problem hunting her as well? She walks on but is constantly looking about her, watching for any movement.

There is another gunshot, but it is not from behind her, where Captain might be; it is to her left. A path in front of her is cleared of undergrowth and will make walking easier. The path takes her to a clearing where there is a plain white building. It has a door but no windows. Gertrude listens but cannot hear any sounds. Twilight is upon her. Near the door, there is yet another gunshot. She quickly enters. There are candles everywhere, and the little building has a dozen people in it. They are quietly kneeling but open their eyes and turn to stare at her when the door closes behind her. She backs up against the door and looks out at the people, all looking back at her.

"Good evening," says a woman nearest her. "We were hoping you would drop in and meet us," she says.

Gertrude does not know what to say and remains quiet.

"This is our praise house," the woman continues. "We come here in the evenings to sing, share, and pray. You are welcome to join us." The woman bows her head as do all the other people in the room.

A man at the far end of the building begins to speak. "Our Father, who art..." and then all the others join in to finish the prayer.

Gertrude stays still with her back to the door. Her fear and confusion have lessened and she begins to breathe normally again. As the prayer ends, there is a loud "Amen" from each participant. They stand and, as it seems to be their custom, go about the room shaking hands and telling each other that it is good to see them. As though she is in a receiving line, each person comes and shakes her hand and says the same thing to her. The people are both old and young. They have on their field clothes or work clothes. The women have their heads covered in cloths that are wound around and tied in front so that their hair is not visible.

The woman nearest Gertrude, who welcomed her, shakes her hand. She is far darker than the others in the room. Her plumpness gives her a mother-like image, especially when she smiles and her cheeks fill out. "I am Eley," she says. "I think I have seen you over at the Fresh Air Home."

Gertrude nods. "Yes, I am Gertrude, the winter caretaker."

"I thought as much. I take laundry to houses just down the lane from you." She pauses and looks about the room. "I guess you haven't been to a praise house before," says Eley.

"No, this is my first."

"What brings you out this far from the Home at this time of night?"

Gertrude explains the river trip, getting separated from Captain and Hazel, hearing the gunshots, and not knowing where to go as the darkness settled in.

"Ah, I heard the gunshots too. Kind'a unnerving if you don't know who's shooting."

Gertrude nods.

"Well, I guess I should get Mingo; we ought to get you back to the Home. Mingo's my husband. We'll walk you back." Eley lifts her chin up as a signal to a tall man with cinnamon-colored skin. He crosses over to them. "Mingo, this is Gertrude. We need to get her back to the Fresh Air Home."

Mingo nods, turns, and places a candle into a lantern. He motions for Gertrude to move away from the door, and he steps out into the evening air. Eley and Gertrude follow him.

The walk to the cottage takes longer than Gertrude had hoped. There is only moonlight and it is not fully up in the sky yet. Gertrude gets behind Mingo and follows his boots. He holds the lantern near his knees. Eley is behind them. They do not talk, just trudge down the path in the moonlight. Gertrude begins to see houses and recognizes the way when the path becomes part of a lane. The ocean can be heard as they reach the compound.

"I stay in the cottage," says Gertrude. At the steps, she turns to them. Mingo stops a few feet away, but Eley stays right with Gertrude. "Thank you for guiding me safely back."

"It's no problem. I wouldn't want a soon-to-be mother in any trouble out in the evening."

Gertrude is taken aback. "How do you know I am pregnant?" she asks.

"By looking at your face and your skin. Plus, I sort of know these things," Eley says. "You got to eat better, though. Your skin is telling me that you need more natural food."

Gertrude expels a little "huh" sound and then says, "I am only eating things from the sea with a few provisions bought at the depot market."

"Humph," says Eley, "You need to learn how to prepare some things, then, so you can eat better. I can teach you."

"I have no money to pay you."

"I didn't ask for nothing." She turns to go meet Mingo. Over her shoulder, she says, "I'll be back tomorrow afternoon and we'll see what you know." With that, she and Mingo disappear into the night. Gertrude lets herself into the cottage, takes off her cloak, and realizes how hungry and tired she is.

The fire embers come to life when Gertrude adds some wood. She fills a kettle with water and hangs it on the iron rod that swings over the fire. Seaweed soup made earlier is added to a pot over the fire to heat up. As the food and water heat, Gertrude takes a lantern and goes into the water closet to clean the long day off her skin. Holding her arm up, she looks at her skin and cannot understand how Eley could interpret her eating habits and her pregnancy by the texture of her skin. Yes, her skin is dry, and there are new blotches, but she attributed them to the island's salt air and sun.

Scrubbed with clean clothes, Gertrude sits in front of the fire to have a cup of tea and the leftover soup. There is a knock at the cottage door. Captain is standing on the steps.

"Thank goodness you are here," he begins. "Are you okay?"

"I am fine. How are you and Hazel?'

"Fine. After we got separated, Hazel returned to where I had been watching the boat. Miraculously, the rope held. We waited quite a while, hoping you might return. As it was getting towards evening, though, we took the boat and with the swift current were able to go back to the fishing camp at record speed. We were preparing to give a search for you at first light, but Hazel suggested that I come and see if maybe you had returned to the cottage."

"Thank you. I found a group of folks at a praise house and a couple walked me back to the cottage."

"You must have stumbled into the Gullah people. They have a praise house on the upper end of the island. That is quite a walk from here."

"Yes, it is," says Gertrude. "And, I am very tired. Thank you for checking on me."

"Sorry for the river surge. Glad you are okay." Captain turns and leaves.

Gertrude closes the door and returns to her tea and soup, relieved that the day has turned out fine for all, even though she is still frightened by the gunshots and remembers the look on the man's face during the short talk with Michael and his ma. Her fright makes her question if she can handle being alone all winter. Along with being afraid is the sadness that she feels every day. A new life is growing inside of her and will be given to someone else to raise. Why did Randolph lie to her? Why has she made such a mess of her life? Why could she not be satisfied with teaching others how to play the piano?

Teaching others is a noble career. There is nothing wrong with teaching. People taught her. What is her problem? She is tired and needs sleep. Her body aches. If Eley can tell she is pregnant, will others know? Can she hide on Tybee Island until her baby comes? *My baby*, she thinks. Sister Mary Joyce warned her not to name the baby. Not to think of the baby as hers. The separation will be so much easier for her. Easy, what's easy about having a baby all by yourself with no one to talk to? Gertrude falls asleep on the settee in front of the fire with a quilt tucked around her.

18

<hr>

Morning comes, but Gertrude's bones are weary. She aches all over. Even walking up Croagh Patrick had not made her hurt so badly. Holding the quilt around her, she puts more wood on the embers to get a fire up and roaring to warm the cottage. As she limps around the main room, getting things ready to go so she can cut more fabric in the big house, she hears a soft knock at the door. Standing on the step is Hazel.

"Good morning. Captain tells me he saw you last night and you are safe. Hearing about your long walk, and thinking you must be tired, I brought over some breakfast." She holds out a basket for Gertrude to take.

"Hazel, that's nice of you, but I am fine."

"I can see that, but we had hoped to have a nice time on the river and then the surge happened."

"I'm just glad that Captain knew what was happening and warned us. Thank you for the breakfast."

"All right, I'm going, but you tell Captain if you need me to do anything for you, you hear?"

"I will, thank you."

Unloading the gift basket at the kitchen table, Gertrude finds biscuits, slices of ham wrapped in butcher paper, a jar of raspberry jam, and two apples. She stuffs a slice of ham inside one of the biscuits and begins eating it without sitting down. She continues to eat standing up, but walks over to the fire and warms herself with her back to the flames. There is another soft knock on the door.

When she opens the door to find Michael, she realizes there are things to do at the big house besides cutting fabric. Michael needs his lesson if he is to learn how to play the piano.

"I'm coming," she says, grabbing her keys.

Inside the dining room, Gertrude has Michael run the "C" scale. Then she shows him how to number his fingers to move along the keyboard and introduces him to the music alphabet: C, D, E, F, G, A, B.

"Listening is a major component of playing the piano," she tells Michael. "Solfege syllables are a way to increase your ear training and learn to mentally hear music without having to play the notes with an instrument. This method helps you practice a song without sitting down at the piano. By listening to the notes, you will be able to sight read music, improvise, interpret sheet music, and recognize pitches."

Gertrude shares with Michael the history she learned at Breneau. An Italian monk, Guido di Arezzo, invented the solfege method back in the eleventh century. He used the "Hymn to St. John the Baptist" and gave spoken or sung syllables to each scale degree in the song. The syllables are the first two letters of the words in the lyrics: do, re, mi, fa, sol, la, ti, do. She demonstrates the sounds as she strikes the keys of the "C" scale. Then she asks Michael to strike any note and sing that note. His voice register is high, and he has to modulate it up or down a bit to get the right pitch.

"Good," she says. "Now practice going through the 'C' scale and singing the notes."

Michael slowly fingers the notes and sings out a quiet sound, so quiet that Gertrude has to lean in to hear him.

"Sing like you know the note. Let me hear you."

Michael strikes the E key and sings the "mi" note.

"Louder," she urges.

Michael sings louder.

"Good, keep on going over the notes until you feel you have each pitch right. I'm going to work on the fabric." Gertrude stands and moves over to the table to begin her work. As Michael negotiates the scale and vocalizes the pitches, she counts the number of pieces already cut out. Some of the uniforms must be finished for her to be paid. On her wellness visit to Savannah, she would like to be able to take a few to show that progress is being made. Halfway listening to Michael as he slowly picks his way through the "C" scale, when he finishes, Gertrude says, "Now, do it again."

Michael glances at her but then looks back down at his hands and starts with the "C" note.

Gertrude loses count of how many times Michael goes through the scale. She thinks about the pieces and what needs to be finished in order to begin sewing and have evidence of completing the uniforms. The pattern shows two front pieces with a tight row of buttons down the front, a collar, two sleeves, a back piece, a band that is below the waist with two buttons to adjust the size, and a little pleated skirt that finishes the top. Then there are the knickers: four pieces with a waistband and buttons to fasten. There were no buttons in the crates that arrived.

Staring at the pattern and seeing all the work it will entail, Gertrude alters the pattern. The top remains a tunic but with no collar and a wider neck hole so it can be pulled over a child's head. Sleeves are shortened, eliminating the cuffs but still long enough to keep the sun off a child's skin. Finally, the waistband for the knickers is adjusted so that a cloth ribbon can be pulled through to tie on either side of the waist. These uniforms will be functional, made out of the same cloth to look like uniforms, and yet be easier for the children to dress themselves and for the uniforms to be washed and ironed. Without knowing the children's sizes, these uniforms can easily be adjusted to fit many different body sizes. A large hem will be left on the sleeves, the bottom of the tunic, and the legs of the knickers.

There is silence in the room. Michael has stopped practicing and is standing next to Gertrude.

"Oh, Michael, sorry, I am busy planning the fabric pattern."

"I saw and didn't want to disturb you until you were ready. I need to go help Captain. We are going out on the boat today, so I will bring you some fish this afternoon." And without any other word, Michael is out the door.

Gertrude shivers a little in the cold room and decides to cover the piano to keep the instrument warm so that it will not have to be tuned right away. She knows that several of the keys need tuning. She will need to ask Mrs. Lynch how that might be done. In the meantime, more uniforms need to be cut out and sewn.

19

———

After a lunch of the last apple and a biscuit, Gertrude is eyeing the sewing machine. Finally, she gathers the cut-out pieces and pins them together. At the machine, she sits down and begins to sew. With the rhythm of the treadle and her concentration on keeping the seams even, she does not hear the knock at the door. A tap on the window startles her, but seeing that it is Eley, she motions to the door and hurries over to open it.

"I could hear you sewing, so I knew you were here," says Eley. She stands on the steps with a basket and bucket in her hands. The basket is covered, but the bucket is full of seawater.

"Come in, please." Gertrude makes room for Eley, who enters and crosses to the table to put down the basket and bucket.

"I came to teach you the basics of cooking seafood," she says. She pulls out an apron from the basket. "Do you have an apron?" she asks.

"Yes," says Gertrude, who takes it off the hook at the pantry cabinet.

"Let's get started."

Without even asking, Eley moves over to the stove and shuffles around, looking for a skillet. She lights the stove to get it hot and puts the skillet on the stovetop. "Measure out a cup of rice from the basket."

Gertrude looks in and sees a bag of rice, an onion, and something wrapped in butcher paper. She takes a teacup and pours in the rice.

"Good. Now take the rice over and rinse it good. Use another dish, a bigger bowl, to make sure you get it clean."

Gertrude has washed rice before, so she moves to the sink to put water in a bowl. She takes her fingers and moves the rice around at the bottom of the bowl.

Eley says over her shoulder. "You want to make sure any grit is gone and the starch is lessened."

Gertrude keeps moving the rice with her fingers. Tilting the bowl, she slowly pours the water out, keeping the rice in the bowl. She rinses the rice three times until the water runs clear and is not cloudy."

While Gertrude tends to the rice, Eley unwraps the butcher paper and lays the bacon on a flat pan on the table. When all the rice has been rinsed, Gertrude places the cup of rice near the stove.

"Now, take some of that bacon, cut it up, and put it in the skillet to cook."

Gertrude cuts off a thin piece with a kitchen knife, cuts that piece into smaller pieces, and puts them in the skillet.

"Make sure you turn the bacon until it gets crisp," she instructs. "Now, let's cut up the onion."

Again, Gertrude takes the kitchen knife, peels the onion skin off, and begins chopping it into smaller pieces. The onion makes her eyes water. She stops to wipe the water out of her eyes with a handkerchief from her pocket.

"Now, move the bacon onto a plate and put the onion in the skillet. You need to chop up the bacon and add it back in."

Gertrude does as she is told.

"While that is cooking, we need to clean these shrimp." Eley takes the bucket over to the sink and dumps the water but saves the shrimp. She begins to peel the shrimp and remove the tails, putting the raw shrimp into a bowl. Gertrude joins her. It doesn't take long before the dozen shrimp are peeled.

Eley pokes her head into the icebox. "Do you have any butter? There's no ice in the box."

Gertrude shakes her head. "Hmm," mutters Eley. "Well, we'll have to do with the grease from the bacon then. It'll help to put some cold water in if'n you put food in the icebox." Eley looks at the onion cooking in the skillet. "See how clear the onions are looking and browning at the edges? Now is when we put in two cups of water. Once that water boils, pour that cup of rice into the skillet."

Gertrude follows the instructions. As they wait for the water to boil, Eley washes up any of the dishes they have already used and puts them on a dish rag to dry. Gertrude simply stands in front of the stove watching the water.

When Eley sees Gertrude, she laughs. "Time passes slowly when someone is waiting for something to happen." Eley moves and sits at the table. "Pour in that rice and stir just a bit, turn the heat down low, put a lid on that skillet, and let's sit and visit. That rice will take about twenty minutes to soak up all that water."

"What do we do with the shrimp?"

"Don't take long for shrimp to cook, so we'll wait until the rice is about done and add it in with seasonings."

Wiping her hands on a dish rag, Gertrude crosses to the fireplace and removes the kettle of water she keeps hot on the coals. "Then let's have a cup of tea." She prepares the two teacups and then sits at the table with her hands folded in her lap. She looks up to see Eley studying her.

"Why don't we start with when the baby is due?" says Eley.

Startled at Eley's abrupt question, Gertrude simply says, "March."

"Humph, then you may be through the morning sickness after the first trimester."

"I haven't felt like throwing up in days. Even on the boat yesterday, I was fine."

"Good. What kind of food do you have as staples?"

"You mean canned or dried food, rice, flour, cornmeal, sugar, butter, those sorts of things?"

"Exactly."

"I was only able to buy some rice from the market."

Eley looks out the window, thinking.

Seeing Eley look away, Gertrude hurriedly says, "I do get fresh seafood from Michael. He brings me two or three small buckets of fish during the week and some seaweed he has harvested. He told me how to rinse the seaweed and then cook it. I don't find it very tasty, but it is at least filling."

"You got to put something in to give it flavor, like beef, mussels, shrimp, or fish. It needs some garlic and a little oil."

"Okay, that sounds like more than I have done. I just put it in some water and cook it."

"No wonder it's not tasty." Eley laughs and her open mouth shows some teeth are missing.

Gertrude looks back at her teacup and takes a sip. "I need to wait to buy some staples. I have to make some of these uniforms so that I can get money for the purchase."

Eley looks over at the sewing machine. "That's what you were working on when I got here?"

"Yes, I need to sew to earn money to buy food."

"From the looks of your larder, you haven't made too many of those uniforms."

Gertrude smiles for the first time. "No, I haven't, but I will. I'm going to Savannah next week. Hopefully, I will have some of them finished and can get paid."

"Good. Well, this is what you need to buy and bring back with you, if'n we are going to get you cookin' and eatin' right." Eley rattles off a list.

Gertrude stops her and gets a pencil and paper from her bedroom. "Now tell me again what I need to have?"

Once the list is made, Eley suggests they go foraging for some greens to go with her seafood and any meat Mingo might be able to hunt down. "There is still some kale and turnips in our garden. Wild onions, garlic, and chives can still be found. In the meadow near the praise house, I have seen patches of mint as well."

"Thank you. I will be happy to go with you and learn."

"I will bring some healing herbs with me when I come again."

"Why would I need healing herbs? I'm not sick."

"Look at your skin. And I figure you ain't sleeping very well and get tired during the day."

Gertrude looks at the blotches and dry skin that Eley had pointed out. Plus, she is always tired. "Thank you."

While the food is cooking, Gertrude asks Eley, "Captain says the praise house where I met you is part of the Gullah here on Tybee. Is that right?"

"That's right," says Eley.

"Who are the Gullah?

"I'm Gullah. My people came from West and Central Africa. They were enslaved and brought to North Carolina, South Carolina, Florida, and Georgia to work on the coastal rice, Sea Island cotton, and indigo plantations. Our isolation helped us keep many of our African traditions, such as food, crafts, and spiritual traditions."

"Like the praise house?"

"Yes, like the praise house. My people also created a new language, Gullah, spoken nowhere else in the world," says Eley. She stands up. "I have to be getting on home. I got a ton of laundry drying and need to get it ironed. Put that shrimp in 'bout a few minutes before you eat and be sure to add some salt and pepper for flavor." She gathers her basket and the bucket she brought. "Mingo is out hunting. Whatever he gets, after he cleans it up, I'll get him to drop something off for you."

"Thank you, Eley." Gertrude follows her to the door. "How can I pay you?"

"I ain't askin' for nothing. We got to make sure you are strong to deliver that baby of yourn by March, is all." With that, she is out the door and sashaying down the pathway to the lane.

Gertrude closes the door. She smells the dish simmering on the stove and her stomach rumbles. She is looking forward to a good hot meal. She goes over to the stove and lifts the lid. The rice is swelling and filling the skillet. Her hot meal may last several days. There are a lot of onions and rice in that skillet, and the shrimp are ready to add.

20

Michael comes more often to practice the piano than Gertrude expects. She has introduced all of the keys, as well as the basic scales for each key, and how to listen to the notes. Now they are beginning simple tunes. Gertrude sits at the piano, and Michael sits in a chair next to her. The easiest tunes for Gertrude are Irish tunes she learned at home when she was beginning to play. The first tune is "Wee Falorie Man." She plays the song, then slows it down, and plays it again. Michael is concentrating on her hands.

"Here, let's change places and you try."

Michael plays the first four notes, but then he does not remember where to go next.

"Good, I can't believe you remembered the first four notes!" Gertrude smiles, but Michael does not. His eyes are glued to the keyboard. After several other tries, Michael casts his eyes down and moves his hands to his lap.

"Michael, you are just learning. It is fine not to remember everything the first time you try. What is important is that you keep on trying." Gertrude is looking at Michael, but inside, she is thinking about what she just said and must apply the same advice to herself. "Look, the song has lyrics. Maybe that will help you learn the notes."

Gertrude places her hands on the upper keyboard and has Michael move down to the lower notes.

"Okay, let's just do the right hand first. Here are the lyrics:

"I am the wee falorie man, A, A, A, A, B, A, F, D.
    A rattlin' rovin' Irishman, E, F, F, F, G, F, D, and
hold the D.
    I can do all that ever you can, A, A, A, A, B, A,
F, D.
    For I am the wee falorie man. E, F, F, F, F, E, E,
D, D.

"Now, let's put the left hand with the right. There is a second verse. Ready?

"I am a good old workin' man, D, F/A, D, F/A
Each day I carry my wee tin can, D, F/A, D, F/A
A large, penny bap and a clipe of ham, D, F/A, D, F/A
I am a good old workin' man. D, F/A, G/A, F/A

"Now, let's do it one more time together."

They play the tune with Gertrude singing the lyrics. Michael hears the pattern and stays up with her until the last line, when the G/A makes him pause to look at Gertrude's hands. Then he plays the last note after she plays.

"Great listening," she says.

"Thanks, but there are a couple of questions."

"Yes, what are they?"

"First, you must be Irish."

"That I am," says Gertrude.

"So, tell me what *bap*, *clipe*, and *wee falorie man* mean?"

"Ah, easy. A bap is a small loaf of bread. Clipe is a large hunk, in this case a large hunk of ham, and the wee falorie man is an interesting fellow." Gertrude moves her chair back from the piano. "Now, play it by yourself."

Michael moves over to the middle of the keyboard and begins to play the song. He is slow and methodical, thinking about every note and how long he should hold that note.

Gertrude is confident that he can remember the tune, so she turns to go back to cutting fabric and thinking. Last summer, the home housed two hundred and seventy children. The number was frighteningly large, but then she was told that many of the uniforms were used by many of the children since they did not all come at the same time. In her estimates, only twenty-five uniforms will be needed for the first week, but maybe they will need twice that number to have different sizes and in case of accidents that may ruin a uniform.

With only six months to make fifty uniforms, Gertrude wants to have them all cut out before she begins to sew. If one uniform is sewn every evening and all the uniform pieces are cut out by the first of November, the uniforms should be finished by the beginning of the new year. That is, if she can keep up that pace. The plan allows for several missed days when she has to go to Savannah for her checkups.

The quiet in the room makes Gertrude notice that Michael is not playing. She looks up and sees he is not there. He is gone. Usually, he says something to her before he leaves. She is not sure what to make of it. She hears the front door open. Michael probably had to leave for just a minute but will return. She stands up ready to admonish him for leaving without telling her, but instead of Michael, she sees another man, someone she does not know, standing in the doorway. He doesn't say anything. He looks at everything in the room. He is tall and lanky. His hat is squarely on the top of his head, but the rim of it is wide and keeps his face in shadow so that Gertrude cannot see his eyes. His brown hair is long and drapes unevenly over his ears. He is holding a bag, actually two bags, both in the same hand. One looks like a carpet-type traveling bag, and the other is a smaller leather bag, a work-type bag.

"What can I do for you?" says Gertrude.

The man continues to look around the room. "I heard music and had no idea a pretty lady like you was playing."

Gertrude has not put her hair in a bun and it is hanging in golden locks around her shoulders. She straightens her back and raises her chin to look at him. "I was not playing. So, how can I help you?"

He moves slowly toward Gertrude, who remains steadfast. She is still holding a pair of scissors in her hand and raises them so that they can be seen.

"I heard the playin' but I also heard the bad keys. I travel about tuning pianos, and when I heard the sad way yourn sounded, I decided to poke my head in and see if I could be of service."

Relieved but not settled, Gertrude answers, "I know it needs tuning, but there is no money to pay for tuning at this time. Thank you."

The man moves closer to her from across the room. "I'm not asking for money," he says.

"Who are you and who do you work for?"

"I'm Richard Turner, the tuner. Clever, ain't it? I don't work for no one; I am my own man and can do the work."

"I'm sure you can, Mr. Turner, but as I said, there is no money for tuning it at this time."

Richard looks about the dining room. "In this big ol' house, there has to be sleeping rooms."

"Yes, when the house is occupied in the summer, there are sleeping rooms upstairs."

Richard moves another step closer to Gertrude. "I see. So, no one else is here at the time being?"

Gertrude could bite her tongue for having let him know that she is alone. What a fool she is! "Captain and Michael are here. It was Michael you heard playing. He'll be right back."

At this time, Richard is within several feet of Gertrude. "Doesn't that bad sound from the piano hurt your feminine ears?"

"I agree that the piano needs tuning, but as I have told you, there is no money to pay you." She takes a step back.

"Then let's you and me make a deal." Richard stops moving toward her and walks over to the piano. "I will tune the piano, and in return, I get to stay in one of the sleeping rooms for a week while I am tuning other pianos on the island. I come this time of year to get pianos tuned for those who come over for the holidays. You know how it is with people who own pianos, they want to use them for entertainment and for family get-togethers, so they want them tuned to sound pretty, as pretty as you are," Richard says, turning to face Gertrude.

Gertrude has heard the compliments before. She remembers the man in the Galway pub and then seeing him again in County Wexford. She is not going to be nice, not after what Randolph did. "I can't make any such arrangements for you. You will need to speak with someone in the Froebel Society, who manages the Home. And none of them are available to accept your request. So, thank you very much, but you need to leave now."

Richard looks at her. He shoves his hat back on his head so that she can now see his eyes. They are brown, and the skin around them is weathered and leathery-looking. He smiles at her. "I hear what you are sayin', pretty lady, but I need a place to stay and you need this piano tuned. I don't see no harm in my staying in a sleeping room for a short while as I do the work I need to do in the area."

He crosses over to the piano, puts both bags down, and lifts the lid. He takes the leather bag and opens it to display various tools that look legitimate for a piano tuner to have.

Gertrude is silent. She has used all of the persuasive skills in her toolbox, yet he has not left. Instead, he is adjusting the strings on the piano. She decides she should leave. With the scissors still in hand, she exits through the kitchen and out the back door. On the porch, she races down the steps and quickly crosses behind the house and looks about for Captain or Michael. Neither can be seen. She passes the windows of the dining room and hears the pinging of the piano tuner on the keys. At the path in front of the big house, her speed increases. At the lane, she sees Captain coming up from his fishing camp.

"Captain!" she calls out.

He crosses to her. "I see you have your scissors at the ready. What's wrong?"

Gertrude is out of breath from having raced to find Captain but steadies herself. "There is a man, Richard Turner, who says he is a piano tuner. He is tuning the piano in exchange for sleeping in the house for a week while he does other jobs around the island. I can't seem to get him to leave."

Captain says nothing but walks past Gertrude and goes up the steps into the big house. Gertrude stops at the steps and waits for Captain and Richard to come out of the house. After what seems like a long time and they do not appear, she climbs the steps and goes through the parlor into the dining room. No one is in the dining room. Hearing footsteps coming down the stairs from the sleeping rooms, she returns to the parlor. Both men appear and stop briefly when they see Gertrude.

"It's all settled," says Captain. "Richard will stay the week, tune the piano, and must get one of us to let him in and out of the house."

Gertrude cannot believe Captain. "Are you sure?"

"Yes, pretty lady," says Richard, "He's sure."

21

The work Gertrude has planned must get done. Richard is up early and out of the house all day. Gertrude has cut out fabric and piled the pieces on one of the tables to take over to the cottage. Rather than leave the pieces in the dining room, she takes them over to the cottage and stores them in one of the upstairs bedrooms. The light from the lantern is small, so she wants to avoid leaving the cottage after dark and entering the big house when Richard is about.

Midday after lunch, her routine has Gertrude returning to the big house to lay out more pattern pieces when Michael comes into the dining room. She looks up at him. "You didn't say you were leaving after the lesson yesterday."

Michael ducks his head. "I know. I'm sorry, ma'am."

"You left me alone and a man, a piano tuner, came, and now he is staying in the house after talking with Captain."

When Michael doesn't reply, Gertrude asks him directly. "Why did you leave so quickly without saying anything?"

He shuffles his feet. "I needed to leave, is all."

Gertrude looks at him. "Why so quickly, Michael?"

He looks up at Gertrude. "I saw someone coming into the house. A reflection on the window glass. He was tall and thin, like my pa. I thought it was my pa."

Gertrude walks over to Michael. "You haven't told your folks that you are learning to play the piano, have you?"

"No, ma'am."

She walks over to where Michael is standing and looks closely at his downturned face. She sighs long and deep. "Okay then, we have a secret." She pats him on the arm. "Let's hear you play your scales and then 'Wee Falorie Man,' shall we?"

Quickly crossing to the piano, Michael sits and begins his scales. As Gertrude returns to her cutting table, she listens to Michael's playing. The keys sound no different after Richard tuned them than they did before, no difference at all.

The time goes quickly and Michael interrupts her cutting. "Ma'am," he says. She notices that he does not call her by either her first name or her last. He just refers to her as ma'am.

"Yes?"

"Is there another tune I can learn? I know I need to practice this one until I know it good, but I want to think about yet another one while I am not at the piano."

Gertrude remembers her passion for playing and learning everything she could as quickly as possible and smiles. "I do remember one that I think is appropriate for this time of year."

Gertrude crosses to the piano and sits down on the bench that Michael has vacated. He stands beside her to watch her hands. First, she runs through a scale to loosen her fingers from all the fabric cutting. "My hands get stiff using the scissors; it's good to loosen them up a bit," she says. "This is called 'The Last Rose of Summer.'" Her soprano voice, soft and gentle like the words, accompanies the music.

"Tis the last rose of summer,
Left blooming alone;

All her lovely companions
Are faded and gone;
No flower of her kindred,
No rose-bud is nigh,
To reflect back her blushes
Or give sigh for sigh!

"I'll not leave thee, thou lone one.
To pine on the stem;
Since the lovely are sleeping,
Go, sleep thou with them;
Thus kindly I scatter
Thy leaves o'er the bed,
Where thy mates of the garden
Lie scentless and dead.

"So soon may I follow,
When friendships decay,
And from love's shining circle
The gems drop away!
"When true hearts lie withered,
And fond ones are flown,
Oh! who would inhabit
This bleak world alone?"

At the end of the song, Michael is silent. Gertrude looks at him and sees a solemn look on his face. "What's wrong?"

"Pretty bleak, isn't it?"

Gertrude thinks about the words and has to agree with Michael. It is pretty bleak. "So, you want something with more lift to it, then?"

"Yes, please."

Gertrude stops for just a moment to think and then moves into a traditional jig. "This is 'Morrison's Jig.' You will like it because it is fast and there are no words." She plays it lively two times through. Michael is smiling when she looks over at him.

"Yes, that's what I need," he says. "But for now, I have work to do with Captain. I will leave you some fish. We are going out to sea." He pulls his cap tightly over his shaggy hair and is out the door.

Fish, she thinks, *more fish*. She's so bored with eating fish. Her visit to see Sister Mary Joyce next week has gotten new meaning as she is looking forward to eating at Mrs. Schultz's boarding house with the nurses. She may even see if she can spend the night. There has got to be a cot somewhere in that house. If she plans the trip for Friday, surely some of the nurses will be going over to their families' homes for the weekend. A change bag and some toiletries are all that is needed.

Gertrude glances over at the piano and thinks about the tune played for Michael, "The Last Rose of Summer." What was she thinking? No almost-sixteen-year-old boy would like to learn to play a song about withering roses and death. It was a quick choice for her. For the past week, her low energy has her feeling like not doing much of anything. Just coming over to the big house to cut out the fabric has been an effort. Even eating has to be planned, and so does an occasional tea break. Sitting down and sewing in the evening has to be forced. What she wants to do is to cuddle up under the quilts and stare for hours at the fire leaping in the fireplace. Out loud, she says, "I need to take a walk."

As Gertrude clears the dunes and sees the water, her head lifts to watch the birds circle and swirl over the waves coming into shore. The tide is turning and will be high tide in a couple of hours. Turning to the left, she walks with the wind blowing off the water. The air is chilly. Her hood is pulled up and her hair is tucked under, out of the way. Spray from the waves rolling into shore bounces off the sand as Gertrude walks near the water's edge.

She does not welcome the solitude. Though Gertrude was alone on the ship coming over from Ireland, there were people in the dining room and crew members who greeted her. People were confined to the ship, so one could always find someone to have a brief chat with about the weather, how long they had been at sea, and where they were going when they got to Savannah. But in the cottage, there are no guests, no visitors. Michael leaves the fish on the steps. Daily, he comes to practice, but the minute he is finished playing, he is up and gone. Captain is seldom about. Eley said she would be coming, but Gertrude has not seen her. Her solitude has turned into loneliness.

Gertrude walks with the wind pushing her along the beach. Clouds fill the sky and hang overhead like ominous beacons of her sadness, reminding her that life is not always sunny. Her energy is gone. Holding up her arm to the sky, she sees more blotches and more dry skin. Suddenly, she stops. Something is happening in her stomach. Standing still, she clutches her lower stomach and waits on the sand with the wind snagging at her cloak. There it is again. It is like a churn, a tiny adjustment inside of her. Though the wait until March seems so long, with all her work and the routine established, the idea that she is going to have a baby has been pushed to the back of her mind. But a life is forming inside of her and the movement proves that the baby exists.

Turning about, facing the wind, Gertrude returns to the cottage. Her steps are slower. Her feet adjust to allow her to walk steadily on the sandy beach. As the boardwalk comes into view, Richard is there, between her and the cottage on the boardwalk. She continues, trying to keep him in sight, but there is a big dune that blocks her view. As she walks down the boardwalk, he has moved to sit on the cottage steps. He looks up and watches her approach.

"Good day, pretty lady. I saw you on the beach and thought I would wait here for you."

"How may I help you?"

"I would like to finish tuning the piano in the big house since I am back from looking for jobs today. I didn't find any."

Gertrude knows the fabric pieces must be finished and did not expect to be delayed. She does not feel comfortable in the house with him, especially in the same room, plus hearing the noise from the tuning would change her beginning headache into a more blistering one. Sister Mary Joyce must be asked about the fatigue and the headaches.

"I see. Let me get the keys and I will open the door for you."

Richard does not stand, and Gertrude finds it impossible to step around him. "Please let me get into the cottage," she says.

The grin on Richard's face sends shivers down her back. He stands and takes one step away. She pushes past him, opens the cottage door with her key, goes inside, and gets the master key ring off a hook near the door. During this process of getting the key, Richard has stepped back onto the cottage steps, blocking her exit.

"You must move out of my way if I am to get to the house to unlock the door."

"Just give me the keys and I'll unlock the door and return the keys to you," says Richard.

"You heard Captain. Either one of us can open the door for you, but you do not get a key."

"Pretty lady, you can trust me." Richard steps in closer to Gertrude, limiting any movement except backing up into the cottage.

"She has a name," comes a loud voice with a tinge of menace from the side of the cottage. Michael steps around and walks straight onto the steps, surprising Richard, who loses his balance and falls sideways off the steps. He has to catch his balance by grabbing the side of the cottage. Michael is now standing in front of Gertrude. He looks up at her. "I came to see if I can practice some on the piano."

"Richard intends to tune the piano," says Gertrude. "That is why he is here, so I can open the door for him."

Richard is standing with his feet far apart and his fists curled by his side. "Do you intend to knock me about and then let it go?" he asks Michael.

Michael looks past Richard into the trees beyond. "I have no intention of doing anything with you," he says.

Gertrude sees a side of Michael she has never seen. He always is courteous, shy, and almost invisible. Yet, here he is facing down a stranger and not backing away from him. His stance is solid but not fierce, almost like he knows that Richard will not do anything if challenged. Where did he learn that? Gertrude wonders.

Michael glares at Richard. "If you plan on tuning pianos, where are your tools?"

Gertrude looks about and realizes that Richard did not have his tool bag when he was on the cottage steps.

"I left them in the sleeping room."

This time, Gertrude speaks up, "You said you were out looking for tuning jobs to do and did not find any. How could you do those jobs if you did not have your tools?"

Richard ignores her question. "Why don't you let the boy practice and I'll tune the piano later." He turns and quickly walks down the path toward the lane.

Michael shrugs and looks at Gertrude. "Okay?"

Gertrude shakes her head in confusion. She does not know what is going on, but she is relieved that Michael seems to be on her side. They go into the big house, and this time Gertrude locks the door behind them. As Michael goes to the piano, Gertrude asks, "I thought you were going fishing with Captain."

Michael sits on the piano bench. "Yeah, I was." He begins playing his scales.

Knowing that Michael will not say more, Gertrude goes to find a pair of scissors she has left in the kitchen. Just to be sure, she checks the back door. The door is unlocked. It had been locked the previous day. She locks it again. Michael finishes his scales. As Gertrude enters the dining room, Michael starts playing the "Wee Falorie Man." *The pacing is good*, she thinks as she listens.

Michael stops playing and says, "I think I can remember 'Morrison's Jig' if we do the key letters like we did on 'Wee Falorie Man.' Do you have time to do that with me?"

For a moment, Gertrude is transported back to when she was learning to play the piano. Memorizing the tunes helped her pay the rent in Dublin by playing at the pubs. Knowing the old traditional tunes provided her with a way to earn a living. People love them. "Yes, of course." The fabric cutting can wait. She has a student.

22

Gertrude decides to go to Savannah on Friday. She has avoided Richard all week. There have been no additional confrontations with him, which pleases her. A few items are in her bag just in case there is a place to sleep overnight. She told Michael of her plans and asked him to share the information with Captain.

Moving through the cottage to make sure everything is clean and put away, Gertrude develops another headache. She pauses a moment to catch her breath, then locks up the cottage and walks down to the depot to catch the train to Savannah. The train pass is indeed helpful since there is no money in her purse. Two samples of the finished uniforms are packed in her bag, one for a boy and another for a girl. Of the fifty uniforms needed, the fabric has been cut for ten more. Learning how to prepare and cook new food has delayed her. Her fatigue is also a hindrance. And though no seams have had to be let out of her current skirts, she feels bloated and knows it is only a matter of time before none of them can be fastened. Fortunately, she knows how to sew, if there is fabric.

Savannah is bustling. Gertrude has to take a moment to

adjust to the street sounds, the large number of people on the sidewalks, and the chimes of the hour strike. These startle her since she has not heard them for weeks on Tybee Island. The wind down Bull Street is fierce. October is here with a fury. She wrestles a pair of gloves from her cloak pocket and adjusts her carry bags. The walk to Mrs. Schultz's boarding house is only about fifteen minutes. The route is familiar; she has walked it many times.

Approaching the boarding house, Gertrude stops and looks at the tall three-story house on the block near Taylor and Habersham Streets. The grey exterior, with its dark green shutters, has a wide porch in front and a half dozen rocking chairs. For the year and a half she lived in the house, she never once sat on the porch. Only during her last visit did she sit on the porch to calm her confusion and make a decision on what needed to happen.

The time on Tybee Island has slowed her down. She never really looked at the house before. The house was where the nurses lived next door to where they worked in the hospital in the nursing program. She now sees the house in a new way. The front steps are steep, but shrubs and small trees border the porch, leaving just a small patch of grass made even smaller by the number of flowers that line the stones leading to the front steps and bordering the shrubs. A magnolia tree is in one corner of the yard. The camellia bushes are in bloom in October. Gertrude loves the smell they offer at this time of year when other plants are going dormant. Slowly, she walks up the steps and knocks.

Mrs. Schultz opens the door. An apron covers her navy blue house dress. Her hair is pulled back in a neat and tidy bun, though her wavy hair creates a casual look rather than a formal one.

"Come in, Gertrude," says Mrs. Schultz. "Come in. I'm about to have a cup of tea. Let's go into the kitchen, shall we?"

Gertrude enters. In the foyer, she takes off her cloak and hangs it on the coat rack along with her outside traveling hat. She places her bag on the floor beneath her cloak. Mrs. Schultz has already gone into the kitchen. Gertrude follows her.

"Sit down, the water is nearly hot."

As Gertrude sits, Mrs. Schultz scurries about the kitchen gathering the cups and saucers, spoons, sugar, and lemon slices in a covered bowl. Finally, with the tea kettle in hand, she sits and pours both of them a cup of tea.

"How has the time been on Tybee Island?" she asks.

Gertrude tells her about her walks on the beach, her progress at cutting out the uniforms, the people she has met: Captain, Michael, Hazel, and Eley. She pauses.

"And who else? It seems as though there is more to the story," says Mrs. Schultz.

Gertrude looks up at Mrs. Schultz, knowing that she has not always told the entire story. "Richard is the more. Richard Turner, the piano tuner." And Gertrude shares her opinion about Richard with Mrs. Schultz.

"My, my, he sounds like a person I would stay away from," says Mrs. Schultz.

"My intentions as well. I am hoping that he will be gone when I return to the cottage."

"And if he isn't and there is a problem, we can certainly get the Froebel Society folks involved."

"I really don't want to do that. I am enough of a problem as it is. I don't want them to think that it is not good to have me there. I need the position. It just seems that trouble follows me."

"Why do you think that?"

"There was Randolph, the man in the Galway pub, Michael's pa, and now Richard. All have frightened me."

"Michael's pa?" asks Mrs. Schultz. "You did not mention him. What has he done?"

Gertrude puts the teacup she has been cradling back onto the saucer. "I went to find Michael at his house to invite him to play the piano in the dining room. His pa stood at the doorway of their house with his hand positioned on the trigger of his shotgun. I am afraid of him."

"As I would be," says Mrs. Schultz, "especially under the circumstances. But you have done nothing to encourage or antagonize these men, right?"

Gertrude looks squarely at Mrs. Schultz. "No. I have not. In fact, I avoided Randolph for quite a while, but my desire to be successful with my music made me accept him, thinking he really did care for me and he really could help me succeed. I was such a fool."

Mrs. Schultz is quiet. She sips her tea and then pours another cup for both of them.

As the women drink their tea, Gertrude realizes that she has not shown Mrs. Schultz the uniforms. She also needs information on who might pay her. Excusing herself, she goes to her bag in the foyer to retrieve them. Returning to the kitchen, she lays out the two uniforms on the kitchen table. "I adjusted the pattern to make each piece adaptable."

Mrs. Shults picks up each garment and inspects the stitches and the style. "These are nice," says Mrs. Schultz. "Your adjustments to the pattern are exactly what is needed for the children to be comfortable and for the uniforms to be used on more children. These are great."

Gertrude lets out her breath. "Good. I'm happy you approve. Now, I just need to know how the organizations sponsoring the piecework are prepared to pay me. I did not ask before. Who do I request payment from?"

"Ah, that would be Mrs. Lynch."

Gertrude stops looking at Mrs. Schultz and looks out the window over the sink. She feels Mrs. Shultz must know her reluctance to see Mrs. Lynch.

Mrs. Shultz speaks up. "I think maybe now you must go by and see Mrs. Lynch. She has been asking about you. I think regular reports would be a good thing."

Gertrude looks down into her teacup. She knows she should see Mrs. Lynch. The Savannah Music Club has been so supportive of her piano playing. They were the ones who sponsored her to Brenau. "I guess I need to face the music."

Mrs. Schultz smiles. "Yes, I think you do. Why don't we send a note to her and ask if you can see her this afternoon? I can get the gardener to deliver it if you like. You can meet with Sister Mary Joyce, and if you get a timely response from Mrs. Lynch, you will have time to go by there and mend another fence."

Gertrude agrees. "I know where the paper and pens are in the parlor. I will write the request now." Her steps into the parlor are driven by the need to right her wrongs. Mrs. Lynch cannot be avoided any longer if Gertrude has any desire to stay in Savannah once the baby is born.

The request is dispatched, and Gertrude goes to the hospital to see Sister Mary Joyce. Her walk through the hallways reminds her of all the hours spent working in the hospital. She rounds the corner and sees Olivia, one of the nurses Gertrude knows.

"My goodness," says Olivia. "I can't believe it is the one and only Gertrude Kelly. What brings you back to Savannah this time of the year? Is the music program not in session?"

Gertrude offers a weak smile. "I am not at Brenau this semester. Just checking in with Sister Mary Joyce. I hope you have been fine."

Olivia looks at Gertrude with a puzzled expression on her face. "Yes, as well as one can be. I am soon going to finish the program and would like to stay in Savannah to be near my family."

"Of course," says Gertrude. "I know you are busy, and I must meet up with Sister Mary Joyce. Take care."

"And you," says Olivia.

Gertrude can feel Olivia still watching her walk down the hallway to Sister Mary Joyce's office. Gently, she knocks on the door.

"It's open," says a voice from inside.

As Gertrude opens the door, she looks back at Olivia, who is still standing in the hallway looking towards Gertrude.

The checkup goes smoothly. Gertrude learns that her pregnancy is proceeding normally. The headaches are part of the changes in her body and are nothing to worry about. To handle the fatigue, she needs to increase her exercise and find ways to sleep better all night long. She is thinking about how she is to do that when all the things to think about are keeping her up late and waking her in the middle of the night. When leaving the hospital, she goes through the hospital garden and around to the front door of the boarding house and knocks again on the door.

The door opens and Mrs. Schultz announces that Mrs. Lynch is prepared to see Gertrude if she comes right away. Mrs. Lynch has an evening engagement and must have an early supper and prepare for the event. Without going inside, Gertrude bids Mrs. Schultz goodbye and begins walking down the steps to the street.

Mrs. Schultz steps out onto the porch. "Gertrude," she calls.

Gertrude pauses, turns, and looks back at Mrs. Schultz.

"Why don't you return for dinner at five o'clock? The women would love to see you. I am sure there could be a place for you to sleep here tonight. Several women mentioned that they were going to see their families since it is Friday night."

A sigh escapes from Gertrude. "That sounds lovely. I will plan on returning."

"Good, I'll set another place. By the way, you can simply come into the house. You do not have to knock."

"Thank you." Gertrude turns to continue her walk to see Mrs. Lynch, relieved that after what is sure to be a difficult talk, there is a sanctuary of sorts to return to. She does not think she will want to take the train in the dark and return to Tybee in the night after this next conversation.

23

———

Gertrude steadily walks to Mrs. Lynch's house in the Old Fort area of Savannah. Her walk was brisk and carefree when going to Mrs. Lynch's for meetings in preparation for her recital, but now she goes to tell a truth she would prefer to remain secret, and her walk is slow.

Gently, she knocks on the door. The housekeeper opens it and invites her into the parlor, where Mrs. Lynch is waiting for her.

"There you are, Gertrude. Many folks have been wanting to know where you have been, me included." Mrs. Lynch is not in the mood for polite greetings. Her hair is swept up in rolls across her forehead, and her deep, wood-bark brown dress is trimmed in beige lace across the bodice and on the sleeves near the cuffs. Everything about her indicates her station in society, including her tone, which displays a dissatisfaction with Gertrude.

"I thank you for agreeing to see me on such short notice."

"How could I not? You might disappear on us yet again." Mrs. Lynch moves over to a purple velvet chair and sits down. "Why not take your cloak off, sit down, and in as concise language as possible, explain your whereabouts for the last five months?"

Gertrude expects Mrs. Lynch to be forthright, but does not expect the terseness of her words. Gertrude removes her cloak and hands it to the maid who has been hovering at the doorway to see what might be expected of her. Gertrude turns and crosses to a chair near Mrs. Lynch. "May I?" she asks.

"Yes, please do."

Gertrude sits and looks directly at Mrs. Lynch. The walk over allowed her to get her nerves calm and prepare how she would start the conversation. "I have made choices that I am not proud of," she begins. "I will be as direct as you have asked. At Brenau, I discovered my passion for composing and playing professionally. Brenau offers education, excellent education, I might add, for the student who will pursue teaching piano and music to others. Mr. Randolph Hamlin, an instructor there, convinced me that with my talent and desire to perform, I would benefit from going to Dublin to work with the Royal Symphony there. He was so convincing that I lost all sense of who I was and agreed to marry him and go to Dublin."

Gertrude pauses. Mrs. Lynch is silent and sits, watching Gertrude with a stony face. Gertrude clears her throat and continues. "My youth and inexperience did not allow me to know how to tell my parents, nor any of the people at Brenau, nor those of you in the Savannah Music Club, that my plans were changing. I think I was somewhat embarrassed that I may let you all down and wanted to see if I could be successful and make you proud despite my lack of consideration for others."

This time, when she pauses, she does not look at Mrs. Lynch but looks down at her hands in her lap. "In Dublin, I discovered some truths that shattered me. Randolph abandoned me. I had burned so many bridges that I had no one to reach out to. I ran into Sharon. You remember Sharon from the boarding house, the accountant for the shipping firm?"

Mrs. Lynch nods. "Of course."

"I ran into Sharon in Dublin, who invited me to County Wexford. At this time, I had no way to make a living and made the choice, with Sharon's help, to return to Savannah and possibly be reinstated into the nursing program. Sharon arranged my trip back to Savannah. I visited Sister Mary Joyce at St. Joseph's in hopes of returning to the nursing program, but I discovered there were no openings. However, there was a need to have a housekeeper on the grounds of the Fresh Air Home on Tybee. The request was made and accepted, and I have been taking care of the house and sewing uniforms for the children."

Mrs. Lynch shifts in her chair. "You haven't contacted any of us at the Music Club."

"I know. I am so ashamed that I have let everyone down. I did not know what to say or when to say it. So, I postponed coming to give you any reason at all. I come today to tell you the truth and to say I am sorry. I have behaved badly."

"Yes, you have," says Mrs. Lynch finally. "We had such faith in you and what a disappointment you have been. Now that I have learned that you are married and didn't tell us either, the disappointment is even greater." She sits silently, looking at Gertrude.

Uneasy with the scrutiny, Gertrude begins talking again. "I don't think you can be any more disappointed in me than I am in myself. I have stopped playing the piano. It has been my downfall. I am teaching a young man on the island to play and that may be my saving grace."

Mrs. Lynch sits up straight in her chair. "You have stopped playing? You think your piano playing influenced you to make these bad choices? If that is what you think, you are more ignorant than I had given you credit for."

Gertrude is stunned. "I'm sorry, I do not understand what you are saying."

Mrs. Lynch folds her hands in her lap and looks directly at

Gertrude. "You have tremendous talent. Your bad decisions cannot, should not, be blamed on your talent. No, your bad decisions came from not being prepared for the limelight that your looks and talent may bring. No one schooled you properly on how people outside of your family and close friends may present choices to you that seem almost irresistible. Who would not want to go to Dublin and be famous?"

Silently, Gertrude listens to Mrs. Lynch.

"Now comes the true test of your apology. How do you propose to rectify the situation? The Savannah Music Club's reputation has been tarnished by your actions. What do you propose to do that may make our reputation regain respectability?"

"I have no idea," Gertrude answers. "Can anything be done to rectify the situation?"

Without pausing, Mrs. Lynch answers. "First, you need to address a letter to the faculty of Brenau stating that the reason you left at the end of the term and did not return was based on your marrying and needing to leave with your husband for his next teaching assignment in Dublin. Second, you need to address a letter to the board of directors of the Savannah Music Club telling them the same thing. What comes next will remain a test of time." Mrs. Lynch stood up.

Gertrude sat silently in the chair.

"Well?" asks Mrs. Lynch, looking at Gertrude with a detachment rather than an interest.

"I cannot write that letter."

Mrs. Lynch remains standing. "And why not?"

Gertrude begins to cry.

"Come on, Gertrude, no tears. This is an adult conversation between women."

Choking back her tears, she looks up at Mrs. Lynch. "Okay, I will have this conversation, but it must be a conversation just between us, or I will walk out of here and you will never see me again."

"Don't be so dramatic. Tell me what you need to say."

Gertrude takes a long pause. "I married Randolph. However, the marriage is not legal. He left me a note and departed without saying goodbye or explaining. He did not file the marriage papers in Gainesville before we left for Dublin. Thus, we are not legally married." She takes another pause. "Additionally, he told me he was already married to a woman in Germany." Gertrude looks down at the floor. "And, after being seasick the entire voyage to Savannah from Wexford, I discovered that I am pregnant."

Mrs. Lynch nearly collapses back into her chair.

Gertrude again waits quietly.

"Goodness," Mrs. Lynch says in a whisper.

"Now, do you see why I can't write those letters? The faculty at Brenau surely knows that Randolph is married. The information I just relayed to you makes my situation bleaker and bleaker."

"Who knows this?"

"Just Sister Mary Joyce and Mrs. Schultz. They are helping me go through the pregnancy by assisting me in getting the position on Tybee Island. My parents and the Froebel Society only know that Randolph abandoned me and that I have no idea how to contact him. They do not know I am pregnant."

"Goodness."

"And that brings me to another point. I came today not just to offer my apology, but I have no money. The Froebel Society offered me the cottage to live in, but I must provide for my food and expenses. Sister Mary Joyce talked with you as the liaison between the Froebel Society and the other women's organizations, which have paid for the uniforms for the children attending the summer camps. The agreement, as explained to me, was that I would sew the uniforms and be paid for that work. What had not been explained was who I would contact to make that happen and how often I would be paid."

Mrs. Lynch leans forward. "How have you been eating?"

"The young man I am teaching brings fish and shrimp by the cottage as payment. I forage for other foods like seaweed. I am learning to catch and clean crabs."

"I had no idea," Mrs. Lynch says, and then is quiet.

Gertrude stands up from where she has been sitting. "Thank you for listening to my saga and woes. I truly am sorry for all the discomfort I have caused in making the decisions I have made."

"Okay, now that you have opened your heart to me, tell me what you intend to do with the baby."

"I have little choice. Sister Mary Joyce says they will keep the baby at the hospital until he or she is adopted. Part of why I am here today is that Sister Mary Joyce says I must come monthly for checkups so they can verify the health of the mother and the baby for the adoption."

"Okay," says Mrs. Lynch, yet again. There is a long pause. "Well, we have a piece rate established for the uniforms. How many do you expect to have finished before next month's checkup?"

"I have two now. I wanted to show Mrs. Schultz both the girls' and boys' styles since I adjusted the patterns. My target is fifty uniforms, and I believe I can finish at least fifteen a month. My other duties at the house require making sure everything is functioning and kept clean and handling any mail or deliveries. Once the summer approaches, there will be more duties like preparing the linens and helping with supplies in the kitchen, house, and infirmary. That sort of thing. But yes, I feel I can finish fifteen before next month's checkup."

"Okay. I will pay you for the two you have completed and will send a cashier's check to the depot on Tybee for next month's work. Look for the check next week. We don't want you or the baby to be hungry."

"Thank you."

'Wait here and let me get the money for the two you have completed."

Mrs. Lynch leaves and Gertrude is left to study the oriental rug pattern in front of the fireplace in the parlor. Gertrude's perception of Mrs. Lynch was one of a woman married to money. Mrs. Lynch wore feathers, lots of feathers, at Gertrude's recital in the Savannah Theatre. Now that Gertrude needs people who do what they say they will do, she needs to reevaluate her opinion of Mrs. Lynch.

On her walk back to the house, she replays the conversation with Mrs. Lynch over and over in her head. Gertrude doesn't want everyone in Savannah to know her dire circumstances, but she has reached the conclusion that though Mrs. Lynch needed to believe in her, Gertrude also needs to believe in herself. Asking herself over and over if that can happen, Gertrude wants to think that it can.

24

Gertrude arrives at Mrs. Schultz's boarding house just as the chimes ring five o'clock. She enters without knocking, leaves her cloak and hat in the foyer, and joins the women in the dining room. There are many questions, comments, hugs, and return hugs. Everyone wants to know if she will play the piano in the parlor after dinner. As Mrs. Schultz brings in the last platter of food for the Friday night dinner, Gertrude sees that it is fish.

"Of course," she says, "of course I will play." Some days, there are few choices, she says to herself, as she chooses a fish she has not had to cook.

After dinner, several of the women need to return to the hospital, but the others, especially the women who are the second-year nurses and who remember how beautifully Gertrude could play, crowd into the parlor, chatting and sharing information with the first-year nurses. Mrs. Schultz puts the food away. Everyone waits for her to come and sit in her favorite chair, the gold brocade one with its mate on the other side of a small lamp table at the parlor door. Gertrude is at the piano and drops the keyboard lid in her nervousness to open up the piano and get everything set. With no idea what the women would like to hear, her choices are all over the place. As they wait, Gertrude runs some scales to loosen her fingers and stretches her small hands so that she can reach the chords needed in the songs. Mrs. Schultz dashes in and sits down quickly. The women stop chattering and all look toward Gertrude.

Gertrude nods to the women. "This first tune is a traditional Christian hymn of Irish origin. The words are based on a Middle Irish poem by Dallán Forgaill. In Old Irish, it is called 'Rop tú mo baile' or in English, 'Be Thou My Vision.'"

She plays through the song. Then she sings a few of the lyrics.

"Be Thou my vision, O Lord of my heart
Naught be all else to me, save that Thou art
Thou my best thought, by day or by night
Waking or sleeping, Thy presence my light."

The women applaud, and as Gertrude nods a bow, she sees the second-year nurses look at the first-years with a look that says, "We told you she was good." Gertrude glances at Mrs. Schultz and sees her smiling, leaning back in her chair with her hands folded in her lap.

"Next," says Gertrude, "I would like to play 'Araberque No. 1, Op. 61' by Cécile Chaminade. I learned about her at Brenau. She was French but has played all over Europe and the Americas. Salons have developed called Chaminades where women play her pieces. Here's 'Araberque.'"

Gertrude does not see the women's reactions until she has finished and looks about the room. The women listening smile and applaud. Gertrude feels that the lilting movement and repetitious tune speak to them in ways that Gertrude has heard these songs.

"One more," says Gertrude. "This is a little tune that I am teaching a young man to play." She plays "Wee Falorie Man." The women clap along with the tune. At the end, Gertrude stands and, as the women continue to applaud, makes a little curtsy.

The women who know Gertrude crowd around her to ask many questions. Gertrude avoids direct answers and simply says she has been adjusting to being back in Savannah. As the women continue to talk, now among themselves, Gertrude moves away from them and crosses the room to where Mrs. Schultz is sitting.

"Have a seat, Gertrude," says Mrs. Schultz. "I, too, have been wanting to ask you a few questions."

Gertrude sits in the matching chair next to Mrs. Schultz.

"You met with Mrs. Lynch today?"

"I did."

"And how did that go?" Mrs. Schultz asks.

"Better than I expected. I was honest with her and told her the entire ghastly story. She seemed to be appalled but did not throw me out. She paid me for the two finished uniforms and is forwarding a check for the next ones that I hope to finish this month. She made it quite clear that she was disappointed in my lack of communication over the past few months. And, I don't blame her. I am disappointed in myself."

"Is that why you played 'Be Thou My Vision' tonight?"

"Yes, I am hoping for some peace of mind."

"And, are you finding it on Tybee Island?"

"No." Gertrude pauses to think carefully as to how to explain to Mrs. Schultz that the solitude has turned into loneliness, that the guilt of her actions has turned into a weight that tires her every day, that the people she has contact with are not always going to be her friends, and that some of the men who come into her life frighten her.

"Please explain," says Mrs. Schultz.

Gertrude pauses, then says, "I walk in the morning and evening on the beach seeking answers. I watch how the birds dash into the water every day and must do it every day to survive. Over and over and over they dive. When they do rest, it is with a watchful eye. There are predators, there are sharks, and there are waves too big to make it through, yet they keep on diving and foraging to find food to survive. I see no end to their plight. I feel much like these birds. I am foraging for food every day. I work to cut out the patterns so that I can get paid to buy food. I am constantly running into men who accost me and scare me. I carry the weight of all I have done and see no end to my plight. March is a long way from now, and even when March comes, there is no guarantee that my worries will be over. I see new problems on the horizon. I am sad and want to sleep more than work. For me, the future is not bright." Gertrude stops and looks down at her hands in her lap. "I fear I have lost all hope." She does not look at Mrs. Schultz.

After a lengthy wait, Mrs. Schultz says, "Gertrude, you are a bird, a songbird, not one to just forage for food. You are one who offers music to the world. With your gift, you offer songs of hope, songs of visions, songs of encouragement."

Mrs. Schultz looks out at the women in the parlor. "You were playing and maybe did not notice how the women absorbed your music tonight. I watched their faces. They were relaxed, enjoying the music. Every day in their hospital work, they see suffering, pain, and death. You have worked in the hospital. You know the kind of misery these women see every day. So, when someone offers them a moment to enjoy something that allows them to forget those miseries, even for a little while, that is a gift." Mrs. Schultz turns her full gaze on Gertrude. "You should not take your musical gift lightly. You must use that gift."

"And how can I do that when I am so isolated on Tybee Island?"

"Be patient, Gertrude. Healing takes time."

They are interrupted by one of the women holding two fabric flowers. "Mrs. Schultz, which do you prefer, the violet or the spiderwort flower?"

As the focus is turned to the fabric flowers. Gertrude thinks about what Mrs. Schultz has said. Healing. She has to heal. But every day, a new wound seems to appear. Does she need to learn how to heal every day?

Mrs. Schultz finishes with the flowers and turns to Gertrude. "I know you must be tired. The bed available tonight is the one you had when you lived here. Please feel free to go and rest."

"Thank you. I think I would like to sit and listen to the women for a little while longer."

"Good," says Mrs. Schultz. "So do I."

The two women sit side by side. Gertrude notices that though there is a lot of talking and frequent movement of the women around the room, both she and Mrs. Schultz remain on the sidelines.

25

———————

In the morning, when Gertrude is preparing to leave after breakfast, Mrs. Schultz stops her at the front door. All the women have scattered to the hospital or upstairs; it is just the two of them.

"Gertrude, it was good to hear you play last night. I am relieved that you can now sit down at the keyboard and share your talent with the rest of us. Thank you."

Gertrude doesn't know how to respond. Though she played last evening, she has not fully committed to playing again.

Her silence has Mrs. Schultz pause, but then she says, "And, if you have any problem, any at all, telegraph me immediately. You know that there is always someone here who can help or listen."

"Thank you." Gertrude looks out the door instead of at Mrs. Schultz. "The care I have received from you and Sister Mary Joyce is more than I deserve. Thank you."

Mrs. Schultz puts her hand on Gertrude's arm. Gertrude has to turn and look at her. That's when Mrs. Schultz hands her a basket. "Just a few things I thought you might enjoy. Look it over when you get to the cottage."

Gertrude leans in and hugs Mrs. Schultz. "Thank you." She doesn't have to look back to know that Mrs. Schultz is still standing at the door watching her walk away. At the corner, she glances back and sees the door just then closing.

Gertrude's trip back to Tybee Island is uneventful. Feeling enriched with a good night's sleep, two full meals, even though she ate more fish, and now a basket full of something for her to enjoy nestled on the seat beside her, makes her more peaceful. She thinks long and hard about Mrs. Schultz's conversation on her piano playing. Teaching Michael has been a pleasure. She enjoys seeing how quickly he is grasping the tunes and how much he wants to practice to be good. Though her trip back to Tybee Island had been uneventful, as she walks up the path from the train depot, she sees Richard sitting on the steps of the big house.

"Good morning, pretty lady. I was hoping you would be along."

"Why is that, Richard?"

"I need to get my tools. I have a job lined up and need to take care of it."

"And where is Captain?"

"It's Saturday and he's off fishing out in the sea. He met me here earlier and locked the door when I left."

"And you didn't bring your tools with you?"

Richard is standing up now. She can tell he is not pleased with her asking him questions. He makes no response. His hands are at his side, but they are clenched in a fist.

"I see," says Gertrude. "If you will wait here, I will get the keys and let you get your tools."

Richard does not wait as asked. He comes down the steps and follows Gertrude to the cottage door. Before unlocking the door, Gertrude half turns to Richard. "Please wait."

"Just give me the keys and be done with it," says Richard.

Gertrude turns and unlocks the door. As she steps inside,

she quickly closes the door and locks it behind her. There is a moment of quiet, then Richard pounds on the door. "Just give me the keys!" he roars as he hits the door.

Gertrude puts the basket on the table and her bag on a chair. Removing her cloak, gloves, and hat, she hangs them on the pegs at the door. Though Richard has stopped taking his anger out on the door, he is still on the other side of it. She crosses to the window at the sink and sees Richard looking into the kitchen through the glass. She hurriedly pulls the curtains together. Her heart is pounding much like his fists on the door. He has made her a prisoner in the cottage. As long as he is outside, Gertrude must stay inside. How can she get word to Captain when he is out to sea? How long will it take for Richard to get tired of this and leave?

She needs a fire. Richard is still shouting at her from the front of the cottage. As the fire starts and the cottage begins to heat up, she goes over to the basket Mrs. Schultz gave her and lifts the cloth off the top.

Richard continues to shout, "You will be sorry you did this!"

Gertrude hears what he says, but then there is a long pause. She waits and listens. There are no sounds. She returns to the basket with no intention of leaving the cottage yet. Under the cloth are herbs from the garden stored in small glass jars, a bag of sugar, a container of baking powder, and one of salt. There are garden peppers wrapped in butcher paper, a mess of kale from the fall garden, potatoes, and a large bag of rice. Tucked in the side is a jar of raspberry jam. She stands to put the supplies on the pantry shelves when there is another knock at the door.

Gertrude tries to see out the window curtains but cannot see who it might be. On the second knock, she goes to the door and calls out, "Who is there?"

"It's me. Eley."

Gertrude opens the door and pulls Eley in quickly and locks the door behind her. Eley is staring at her.

"What's the matter?"

"Please, come in and have a cup of tea. The water is hot in the kettle." Gertrude does not answer Eley and moves over to the hanging dresser to get the cups and saucers.

Eley goes to the kitchen table and sits down. "Are you going to tell me what's going on, or not?"

Gertrude brings the cups over to the table but still doesn't answer. Eley goes and gets the kettle out of the fireplace. She puts the tea leaves into the kettle and puts it on a cloth on the table for the tea to steep.

"There is a piano tuner, Richard Turner, who has made remarks that scare me. He came to the cottage wanting me to unlock the big house for him to get his tools, but he is too aggressive and demanding, so I locked the door when I came into the cottage. He has been shouting and banging on the door. I think he left just before you arrived."

"Why were his tools in the big house?"

"Captain has allowed him to stay in one of the sleeping rooms upstairs for the week in exchange for tuning the piano in the dining room."

"Hmmm, well, we can remedy this." Eley stands up and crosses to the door. "Come on, get your keys. We're going to put his stuff out on the porch. He won't need keys to get them now."

Gertrude gets her keys and follows Eley out the door, locking the cottage door. They go into the big house and lock the front door behind them. Before starting up the stairs, Gertrude says, "I want to check the other doors to make sure they are locked; they have been left unlocked several times." She checks the French doors in the dining room and then the back door in the kitchen. All are locked. She joins Eley and they go up to the sleeping rooms. They find the room Richard has been using. Eley gathers his clothes and stuffs them in his carpet bag. Gertrude finds the toolbag.

"Here, while we are up here, let's get the bed stripped and take these downstairs to be washed."

Quickly, the sheets and quilt are removed and bundled. Eley takes the sheet bundle while Gertrude picks up the carpet bag and the toolbag. They go down the stairs. Eley takes the sheets into the kitchen and puts the bundle on a chair. Together they go out the front door, making sure to lock the door and place the carpet bag and toolbag on the porch near the door.

Eley follows Gertrude back to the cottage. Inside, they remember the tea has been steeping.

"I think it is ready," says Gertrude.

As Eley sits at the table, her eyes evaluate the pantry items Gertrude has removed from the basket. "I see you got some herbs."

"Thanks to Mrs. Schultz," says Gertrude. "I stayed overnight in Savannah last night, and she surprised me with this basket of goods."

"I want to ask how you are feeling," says Eley.

"I'm tired a lot and want to sleep."

"That's pretty normal for being pregnant. You do need more meat to fatten you up and more exercise."

"I'm already fattening up," says Gertrude. "I need to make a couple of loose-fitting dresses because my regular skirts are too snug."

"I know you can sew. Why don't you make something?"

"I have no material."

"I saw lots of material on the dining room table in the big house."

"That's for the children's uniforms. I can't use that material."

"Why not?"

"That material is for the children."

Eley's face shows her question. "What about your child? Isn't covering up and taking care of your baby important, too?"

"Yes, but I can't use something I didn't pay for," says Gertrude.

"Then what else can you use?" She appears to be thinking. "Are there curtains on the windows upstairs?"

There are curtains on the windows upstairs. Nice thick cotton curtains that reach to the floor. "Yes, but they belong to the cottage."

"Couldn't you borrow them, make them into dresses, and then turn them back into window coverings later?"

Immediately, both women stand and go upstairs. They take down the curtains. "They need washin', but they are fine," says Eley. She piles the curtains she has on the floor near the sink.

"Yes, they are fine. I am not excited about wearing white curtains, but they are fine."

"You could get some berry juice and dye them to make them brighter."

"That would be great."

"We need to go foraging soon anyway. We'll go up where I know there are some beautyberries. You probably need to walk some since you just got back. I got some time. Let's head out. I can go with you in case that Richard fellow returns."

Gertrude puts on her cloak. Eley ties her striped shawl, faded from the primary colors it once was, tighter around her shoulders. Taking a basket with them, they leave the cottage to walk toward the ocean. When the walkway ends, Eley turns left to head up to the north shore. There is no sign of Richard.

The walk does make Gertrude feel better. The two women do not talk. They just walk along the beach until they find a bush of beautyberries growing in the sand. Eley explains that the berries are good for the birds in the late fall and winter for food and that though folks can eat them, mostly they are used for wine or jams. She leaves the beautyberries for the birds since she has made jams all summer from blueberries, black-berries, raspberries, and elderberries. She has enough jam.

They pick a half-basket full of berries.

"That should be enough for the material," says Eley. She brushes the berry juice off her skirt.

On the walk back, Gertrude asks how the dye is made.

"First, put a big pot on the stove to boil. Add salt. When the water is hot, put the material in. Let it sit in the hot salt water for a while. Second, in another pot, you put the berries and some water. Heat the berries until they pop and color the water. Once they have all popped, remove the berries with a spoon. Third, put the fabric into the colored water and let it sit. It may take overnight. Finally, using sturdy sticks, remove the fabric from the colored water and rinse in the sink until the dye does not run off the fabric. By then it's okay to wring out the fabric and not discolor your hands. If you do get some dye on your hands, it'll wear off, not to worry. Dry, iron, and use the material to make your dress."

Gertrude nods. Eley's instructions sound easy enough.

"But for now," says Eley, "we have to cook some venison. Mingo has been huntin'."

Raising her eyebrows, Gertrude is not sure if she is ready to cook venison.

Eley sees the look. "It'll be fine, I'll show you how."

With that, they walk quickly back to the cottage. Eley looks up at the big house porch. "Well, we don't have to worry 'bout Richard. His stuff is gone."

Thank goodness, Gertrude says to herself. She opens the door to the cottage but locks it back once they are inside.

Eley tells her what to do. Put a cast iron skillet on the stovetop and get it hot, then baste the pan with grease or butter. Eley cuts off two small slices of the hunk of venison wrapped in butcher paper and tells Gertrude to put both pieces into the hot skillet with sprigs of rosemary, parsley, and thyme. The herbs are on the table given by Mrs. Schultz. The meat needs to be seasoned with salt, pepper, and a piece of garlic. "Sear both sides until it's done enough for you," she says.

Gertrude follows Eley's instructions but also watches as Eley gets a big pot and rubs some grease in the bottom and sides. Eley adds the same seasonings and several cups of water and moves the pot to the hook over the fire. "Need to get the water hot before putting in the meat. Then it can simmer all day. That's all there is to it. You can add some root vegetables to the fireplace pot about a couple of hours before you want to eat, or make some rice on the stove and serve some of the meat and juice over the rice. Once you take your slices out of the skillet, put them in the fireplace pot. That way you'll keep the juices inside the meat."

Gertrude looks about the kitchen and takes a deep breath to smell the aromas filling up her small living space. The meat sizzles in the skillet and sends its flavors to her nose. She can definitely distinguish the rosemary and thyme, but she can't smell the parsley since the other spices overpower it.

Eley is fastening her shawl about her shoulders. "I need to go. Saturdays, I have to pick up laundry from houses nearby and get it washed and dried for Monday morning."

"I haven't been down the lane. I know there is a hotel down toward the south beach. How many people are on the island during the winter?"

"I don't rightfully know, I just see a maid that stays in the house when residents are gone."

Eley describes how there are two sections to Tybee Island designated as summer homes. "There's a row of private summer cottages along the oceanfront next to Hotel Tybee. Each has a setback from the dunes, much like this property, which provides a grassy expanse, or strand, between the homes and the beach. This section is called the Strand. The second area being developed is the Back River area. I get less work during the winter from the Back River area, called Colony Row.

Most of the houses were destroyed on the Back River during the hurricanes of 1893 and 1898. These cottages are still being built up towards the mouth of the Back River. They have separate servants' quarters on the back of the property, so the maids who live year-round often do their own laundry during the winter months."

Gertrude had thought she might walk south and see the rest of the island, but after hearing Eley describe it, she thinks she needs to stay on the beach near her and not risk being seen out by others. "Do folks come during the holidays?"

"Yes, many of the folks who live in Savannah and have cottages on the Back River spend their holidays on Tybee Island."

Walking to the door with Eley, Gertrude unlocks the door to let Eley out.

"I would keep the door locked until you know for sure that that Richard fellow is gone."

"Thank you. I will indeed do that. And thank you for the meat. I am so tired of fish since I can only cook it in certain ways."

"You'll learn," says Eley, and she is sashaying down the path to the lane.

Inside the cottage with the door secured, she removes the venison from the pan. The rest of the meat is seared. Once the meat is ready and the water is hot in the pot over the fire, the meat is added along with the seasonings, as Eley told her to.

The next hour is spent making the berry dye and washing the cloth as Eley suggested. The cloth needs to be covered in the berry juice for a while. Now that Richard has gone, Gertrude goes over to the big house. The sheets and towels Richard used need to be washed. She puts water on the stovetop to get it hot. She pulls out other big pots that the cook must use to make the large amounts of food needed for the children. As the water heats, Gertrude goes into the dining room to assess her progress with the uniforms. Her progress has been slow. More needs to be cut out, but first, the linens Richard used must be washed.

With all the shrubbing and wringing out of linens, her morning turns into early afternoon. Gertrude hears a knock on the front door of the big house. Cautiously, she peeks around the doorway to see Michael at the door. Quickly, she gets the keys and unlocks the door.

"I went to the cottage first. I'd like to practice a bit if I could. Captain has gone off in the boat to take that piano tuner up the river to the nearest place with houses and pianos."

"That's good to know. Yes, come in. I am cutting out fabric."

The afternoon passes with Gertrude listening to scales, "Wee Falorie Man," and "Morrison's Jig," over and over and over. If Michael is anything, he is persistent. She goes outside to get the linens off the line and back into the house. They are not quite dry, even with the ocean breeze, so she spreads them out on the kitchen chairs and makes sure the back door is locked before going upstairs to remake the bed with other linens. Michael repeats "Morrison's Jig" yet another time. Back downstairs, Michael is standing near the piano, waiting for her.

"I need to go now," he says. She gets her keys and lets him out the front door. As he exits the door, he runs back to face Gertrude. "I just want to say something." He looks away from her and says, "It's good you are here." With that, he is off the porch and jogging down the path to the lane.

As Gertrude watches him leave, there is a new feeling inside of her. There are things she can do to survive this winter on Tybee Island. Eley's visit, where she learned how to dye cloth and how to cook venison, made her realize that she can take care of herself, that is, with some learning along the way. She is taking care of the big house by cleaning the linens and the room Richard used. Now, having Michael come and practice provides her with another accomplishment: she can teach piano. It has been a full day. Gathering the cut-out fabric pieces, Gertrude returns to the cottage. With Richard gone, her twice-daily walks on the beach can resume. She hurries to get her cloak and secure the cottage door. The afternoon will soon be gone now that the days are so much shorter.

The walk on the beach has all the usual sounds and smells: the birds hawking, the salty smell of the ocean water, and the crunching sound of her shoes on the sand. The sky is full of clouds and the smell of rain fills her nose. She walks farther than in previous walks, but when she turns, her steps quicken. The clouds have darkened. There will be more washing and drying if the rain soaks her on the way back to the cottage.

26

———

S unday comes and Gertrude is restless. Her cooking, sewing, and washing have all been accomplished, but now her mind needs something. More rain is coming, so another walk is out. The knitted scarf is finished and hangs on a peg at the front door, so there is no sitting in front of the fire and knitting. Then she knows what to do. It comes like a flash and she can't believe she has not thought of it sooner. Retrieving her notebook and pencil, grabbing her cloak, she locks the cottage door and goes to the big house.

Inside, the dampness of the coming rain, along with the chill of early November, leads her to go to the kitchen and see that there is wood in the bin. There is a lot of wood. Captain has been good about keeping the bins supplied. There is a fireplace in the dining room, but the room is so large that it is difficult to heat quickly. However, the kitchen is smaller and with the wood-burning stove, she can at least heat that room to cut the chill. She prepares the fire in the wood stove and closes the door to the kitchen.

Returning to the dining room, she removes her cloak but leaves her gloves on. These are her sewing gloves where the fingers have been cut out so she can sew but keep her hands warm. She removes the cloth covering the piano, sits down, and runs the scales. The piano still needs tuning. Mrs. Lynch may know where to find a legitimate piano tuner who could tune the piano.

Gertrude opens her notebook and turns to the page where she has written everything down that she heard that day on Croagh Patrick. What had been heard?

First, there was the quiet, then the coming of the storm, the sounds made by the storm, the vastness of the sound, and the fact that it came from many different directions, similar to the sounds of the wind and rain the first night she was on Tybee during the gale. Her fingers play some notes that make her think of the rain.

Second, she remembers her discomfort in trying to sleep on the bench, being hungry and thirsty, and not knowing how long the storm would last. All the bad choices she made were replayed that day, along with her guilt of not contacting family and friends.

Third, she was out of patience with herself and the choices she made left her in despair. During the storm, she realized that she had nothing, no one, no money, no job, no talent, nothing. This left her distraught with nowhere to go. Whatever was she to do?

Fourth, the wait in the chapel that day allowed the storm to give her answers. She heard the music of the storm. Her hope to find a direction was fulfilled. Once she heard the music in nature, she knew she could create her own music. That's when she had hope of having friends who would help her if she swallowed her pride and asked. That's when she contacted Sharon, who indeed came through.

Gertrude begins to play. Her idea is to write about the storm as significant to her life. Mrs. Schultz has said that she has a gift. What is that gift? Being able to compose and play would be ideal. If music can be about that feeling, that excitement of having an idea and then making it work, wouldn't that be grand?

In the next section, the feeling should include how an idea falls flat, like the storm raging and offering nothing but lightning and thunder and sheets and sheets of rain. There is no productivity. She is void.

But the following section has her crying out and asking, "Where is my creativity?" It is somewhere. Why are people saying a woman can't write music? And specifically, why have people in her life steered her away from her creative impulses?

Finally, what is heard in the storm makes her know that music is all around her. The sounds of nature are loud and clear. And, for the first time, she has hope: hope to compose, hope to play, and the hope of sharing her music with others.

Writing the music means playing notes on the piano, working out various parts, and jotting down notes and sequences. She works on the music until her hands are too cold to go on. The kitchen should be warm by now. As she pushes through the swinging door, she stops abruptly. Sitting around the table are Michael, Captain, and Eley. They stand up quickly.

"What are you doing here?" she asks. There is silence. Gertrude looks from one of them to the next. "What is going on?"

Captain speaks up. "Eley came by the fish camp to let us know that Richard's stuff was moved from the porch and wanted me to check in on you to make sure things were okay. I ran into Michael when I returned from taking Richard up the river, so he and I came back to see how things are."

Eley nods. "And since I had laundry to deliver along the lane, I came over to check as well."

"I see." Gertrude remains standing and looking over them all. "And are you satisfied that everything is fine?"

"Yes, ma'am," says Michael. "Things are mighty fine. When we heard you playing the piano, we came around to the back so as not to surprise you from the front of the house. And we didn't want to disturb you."

Captain interrupts. "We were waiting for you to take a break."

"I see," says Gertrude, moving over to warm her hands in front of the wood stove. The kitchen is comfortable after being in the drafty dining room.

"Ma'am, if I can say so, that's a beautiful thing you were playing in there."

"I say 'amen' to that," says Eley.

"How long have you been listening?" asks Gertrude.

The three of them look at each other and, in a variety of ways, all say, "Not long, no, just a short time."

Gertrude sees the empty cups on the table in front of them and the kettle sitting on the stove. She picks the kettle up to pour herself a cup of tea, but the kettle is empty.

Eley takes the kettle and quickly goes to the sink to refill it. "Here you go. The water will be hot shortly. Here's a cup and saucer." She picks up the other teacups and takes them to the sink to wash them.

Captain and Michael cross over to the door. They have their hats ready to put on, but are awkward in leaving. "Guess we should be going since you are fine and everything." Captain unlocks the back door and they leave, including Eley, who dashes in behind them but shouts back, "I'll be by later in the week and we'll go foraging."

Gertrude locks the door behind them and smiles at how funny people can be when they are caught doing something they think they should not be doing. She thinks she should invite them to come back the next Sunday to listen to her practice playing.

The tea warms her up a bit. Upon returning to the dining

room, Gertrude realizes how late in the day it is and how hungry she is. After tamping down the fire in the wood stove and gathering her notebook and pencil, she returns to the cottage to have venison and rice. And if she hurries, she can take another walk on the beach before the light of day is gone.

Eley comes by early one morning before Gertrude can cross over to the big house. "We are going shopping in the meadow and woods. Come on," she says. "And bring a basket."

Quickly, Gertrude grabs one of the baskets off the shelf and locks up the cottage. For a stout woman, Eley knows how to make tracks. Gertrude has to step up her pace to keep up. There's no small talk between them. They head up the lane, but before they get to the back river, they turn up another lane and head north.

Eley turns her head slightly and talks downwind to Gertrude. "We came this way from the praise house, but it was dark and you were tired, so I reckon' you don't remember this a'tall."

"No, nothing looks familiar."

They push on up the lane and turn off to the right on a path. Soon, there is a meadow.

"This is what we need to look for. In meadows we can find prickly pears, lion's mane mushrooms, wild onions and garlic, chickweed, and hickory nuts."

Gertrude looks over the meadow. She sees grasses, bushes, and some trees edging the sides of the meadows. She doesn't see anything she could eat. As Gertrude stands there, Eley walks over to a flat area.

"Here's some onions and garlic. Let's dig."

Eley kneels down on the grassy area and pulls a trowel from the waistband of her skirt. She begins to dig out the bulbs and stops to hold them up, then passes them over to Gertrude to put in the basket. Eley stands up and moves through the meadow grasses. Gertrude follows. When Eley stops and points to their left, Gertrude sees a cactus-like plant with spikes.

"Those are prickly pears." Eley moves toward the plants. "We want to choose the fattest, darkest purple-red fruit." She takes a cloth out of her pocket, folds it four times, and holds onto the fruit pods with the fabric. "Got to be careful 'cause those spinely things hurt." She hands the fruit to Gertrude to put in the basket. Gertrude hesitates to take the fruit because it is covered in bristles and long spines. A corner of her skirt becomes a pot holder and the fruit is put into the basket. Gertrude makes a mental note to remember to bring a trowel, knife, and cloth or work gloves for the next foraging adventure.

Before Gertrude can ask, Eley says, "To cook them, put a stick in the fruit and roast it over the fire. This burns off the spines. When the outer skin is darkened and slightly blistered purple, let it cool. Then, squeeze the fruits out and put the pulp through a strainer until there is just syrup. Use it to cook with or as a sauce for fish. Or, you can peel, chop, and fry them. Some people think they taste similar to green beans."

Gertrude nods but is overwhelmed with trying to remember everything Eley is telling her. Before she can ask another question, Eley is moving over to the edge of the meadow where the trees begin. Stepping over a fallen tree trunk, Eley looks down. "There, see those? Those are lion's mane mushrooms. They grow on dying hardwood trees like oak, maple, and beech. This is a beech tree. They mostly appear after a good rainfall."

The mushrooms are single, large, white, globular masses resembling a pom-pom or a lion's mane. The name certainly fit their description. "How do I use these?"

"Slice them, fry them in a dry skillet, and then add just a

little oil to finish crisping them up. The flesh is firm and has a slightly sweet flavor. Good with beef or vegetables."

Eley is moving through the trees along the edge of the meadow. "There's a hickory tree; might still be some nuts the squirrels and animals haven't gotten yet." She moves toward the hickory tree but stops suddenly. "There, see that little vine with the white flowers?"

Gertrude stops beside Eley and looks down at the nondescript little vine growing under other bushes. Such a little vine could have easily been missed. She bends down to look closer. "The one with the ten petals?"

"Actually, if you look closely, there are only five petals, but each is split so that it appears to be ten. And yes, that is chickweed. You can add it to salads and soups and eat it raw or cook it."

Together, they pinch off a mess of chickweed. Eley picks up a palmetto leaf nearby and wraps it around the chickweed to protect it from being bruised in the basket with everything else. When they get to the hickory tree and poke around on the ground, there are no nuts that the animals have not cracked open and nibbled on.

"You might have to come back and check this tree. There are still nuts on the branches. You just need to get here before the animals do." Eley wipes the dirt off the trowel and cleans the knife with the edge of her apron. "Next time, we'll head over to the marsh and look for palmettos. The dwarf ones have edible hearts underground like a long potato. I shred the root and cook it in bacon grease. We might even find some persimmons."

They both stand. Gertrude looks over the meadow and sees it differently from her first introduction. There are many things around that will help her survive the winter. She has learned how to crab, harvest mussels, and pick up sea lettuce that is often washed up on the beach. There is enough dulce seaweed in the cottage now to season her food with its peppery taste. Though feeling a bit flushed from all the bending over and kneeling they had been doing, she also feels a sense of pride in learning how to take care of herself. Eley has given her an understanding of how her food supply can be supplemented for survival.

27

———————

Gertrude plans on going to Savannah early on Tuesday and does not plan to spend the night this time. The trip is early enough that she doesn't even stop by to see Mrs. Schultz first. Instead, she goes straight to see Sister Mary Joyce. Her checkup is fine. After all that Mrs. Schultz has done for her, she knows she has to at least drop in to say hello. She opens the front door and enters. She calls out to Mrs. Schultz, who emerges on the landing above. "Hello, I am in my office planning menus. Now I can take a break and not do that." She joins Gertrude in the foyer. "How about a cup of tea?"

"Actually, I want to ask if I can take a minute and write Mrs. Lynch a short note?"

"Of course, you know where to find what you need."

"Thank you." Gertrude goes into the parlor and sits at the desk to ask Mrs. Lynch how to get the piano tuned. Now that she is playing, she desires a better sound. Tucking the note and envelope in her purse, she intends to drop it off at Mrs. Lynch's house on her way to the train depot. She does not find Mrs. Schultz in the kitchen. Gertrude does not feel comfortable going up to Mrs. Schultz's office to find her, having never been in that office even during the time she lived in the house. As Gertrude stands in the foyer and tries to decide what to do, Mrs. Schultz emerges and comes down the stairs.

"Now are you ready for a cup of tea?"

"Thank you, but I need to return to Tybee Island. I have a lot to get done."

"I see," says Mrs. Schultz. "Do tell me, though, how things are going?"

"Good, I have finished several uniforms and am keeping my schedule. I continue to teach a young man on the island how to play the piano, and actually, I am playing some of my own compositions. Some people I have met on the island come by on Sunday afternoons to hear me practice. "

Mrs. Schultz has joined Gertrude in the foyer. "That all sounds promising. And you are feeling okay?"

"Yes, I got a clean bill of health from Sister Mary Joyce. Though she wants me to walk a bit more since I am sitting so often to sew."

"I agree. The salt air should do you wonders."

"Well, I must go. Thank you for all you have done." As she turns to go out the front door, Mrs. Schultz speaks up.

"Wait, I have a basket prepared for you, just in case you came and left quickly." She rushes into the kitchen but returns right away with the basket. "Just some goodies you might not have time to make for yourself."

"Thank you." Gertrude holds the basket near her face. "Is that bread I am smelling?"

"Yes, Edwidge made an extra loaf this morning, and not being one to waste food, I added it to the basket. I thought you might like it."

"I will, thank you." Gertrude has her hand on the door.

"Oh, and one more thing, Thanksgiving is coming. The nurses will be here since they must work in the hospital. Please come and dine with us. Edwidge is planning a wonderful dinner. We'll have a cot ready for you as well. Since all the nurses will be here, we can set the cot up in my office. You can have some privacy there, I assure you."

Gertrude stops and turns, "Thank you, Mrs. Schultz. The invitation is accepted. I would love to come and celebrate Thanksgiving with the nurses."

"Good. We'll see you then."

Gertrude leaves with the feeling that a place is being made for her back in Savannah. Her friends have not forsaken her, even with all that has happened. She must remember how good it feels to have people care about her. In the meantime, she must drop the note off at Mrs. Lynch's, take the train back to Tybee Island, and find time to work on her music before her evening walk.

The cottage is beginning to feel like home. She uses the key to open the door to the little hallway where she hangs her cloak. The basket from Mrs. Shultz is on the table. Material and uniforms are strewn all over the chairs and furniture, except for the settee. Moving the settee over in front of the fireplace when the sewing machine was delivered was a good idea and gives Gertrude a place to stretch out her aching legs.

Gertrude has set up staging areas in the parlor to produce the uniforms. The upholstered chair near the fireplace is for the pinning stage. Cut-out pieces are placed there to be pinned. The first window on the far side of the room is where the sewing machine was placed to get light. Once the uniform pieces are pinned together, they are placed on a chair at the sewing machine. The other upholstered chair is in front of the window at the front of the cottage, where the final handwork on the uniforms can be done. The round table has a lantern if she needs it at night to work. There are no small tables in the cottage, so two chairs were moved from the upstairs bedrooms down into the parlor area to hold items needed at the staging areas. Mrs. Schultz's basket provided ample scissors, needles, thread, and pins that can be kept at each stage to save looking for the items when they are needed. One of the bedrooms upstairs is where the cut-out pieces of fabric are moved from the big house, and the other one is for the finished uniforms. Everything has a place, though it may look cluttered.

Over the top of the fireplace is a needlepoint that had been given to Gertrude at the party thrown by the nurses to celebrate her leaving Mrs. Schultz's boarding house to go to Brenau. One of the nurses had stitched the Lord's Prayer. The handmade banner reminds Gertrude of her Savannah home. Her mum was always making needlepoint gifts for family and friends. Three enamel candle holders, each with a candle, are on the mantel. Two are white with a circular holder to catch the candle wax, while the other is blue. All have finger holders to make them easier to carry. Gertrude had found a rather large box of candles stored in the water closet.

Baskets from Mrs. Schultz and Eley are displayed on the wide shelf near the sink. Herbs in clear jars get light on the wide windowsill above the sink. Eley showed her how to pot and then tend them for continued growth. The peppermint and thyme are to be used for bloating and stomach aches. Garlic is to be in most dishes. Chamomile is to be dried for a tea to relax and help with sleep. Just a little rosemary should be used in her cooking. Eley prepared St. John's wort oil for Gertrude to use on her dry and blotchy skin. The oil is kept in the water closet to use after bathing.

On the wooden table in front of the stove are sea oats in a tall, clear jar. Gertrude had found a simple white cloth in the pantry, and with colored thread she got during one of her excursions into Savannah, she had embroidered a floral design around the edges one evening when sitting in front of the fire. The cloth is under the jar on the table. The cottage has become a home.

Unpacking the new basket from Mrs. Schultz, Gertrude finds a loaf of bread, a jar of blueberry jam, and three medium canvas bags; one with dried peas, one with rice, and the other with tea leaves. As the items are placed on the pantry shelf, she says out loud, "I need to go shopping on the beach and find some sea lettuce for a salad tonight." At the moment, though, she wants to feel her music.

Crossing over to the big house, Gertrude finds that Captain has built a fire in the fireplace, ready to be lit. In the kitchen, the wood stove is also prepared, and so she lights the stove and sets the kettle on top with water for tea. While the water heats, she returns to the dining room to assess the status of the uniforms. It is November. If the uniforms are to be cut out and ready to sew before Thanksgiving to meet her deadline, there is plenty of work left to do.

The tea has steeped. Gertrude pours it into a cup and sips it in front of the fire. Ready to play, she moves over to sit on the piano bench. After she plays her warm-up scales and a few tunes played in the pubs with the band in Ireland, she is ready to tackle her music. She is working on developing the second part. This part should demonstrate how the creative idea has fallen flat. There must be despair. There must be abandonment. There must be guilt. Yes, she lives with the guilt every day. Guilt makes her feel unworthy, scared of the past, and unable to understand why things happened. She struggles to forgive, acts defensive and distant, and is afraid to try again. Yes, the guilt part is familiar. What she does not know is how to make the music show guilt.

Gertrude sits for a long time and watches the fire, seeing how the flames leap and change colors, how the wood chars, catches fire, sags, crackles, and crumbles into the ashes. She watches until another log is needed to feed the fire. Then, slowly, the music comes through her fingers onto the piano keys. She plays the music with notes sagging, then surging with new vigor, to finally be reduced to ashes. The notations Gertrude makes in her notebook indicate the articulation and dynamics used. The music is to be played first with a fermata. The notes are to be sustained longer than written. The feelings last longer and so should the notes be. Then the notes gradually increase in volume, crescendo, until they are extremely loud, fortississimo, but are then reduced to being very soft, pianissimo. She pauses and reaches for her handkerchief that is stuffed in her sleeve. The emotion and energy to create this music pulls the heat from her body and she wipes the perspiration from her brow. She banks the fire in the dining room, picks up several pieces of fabric cut out for the uniforms, and heads to the cottage. She needs a walk and wants to grab a basket to hold the sea lettuce.

28

—————

The week goes by quickly with the cutting, sewing, cooking, cleaning, and playing. Michael comes in and out to practice. Captain waves from the grounds when she goes down the boardwalk to take her beach walk in the morning and late afternoon. Eley does not visit. Gertrude is alone, but for the first time, she is not lonely; in fact, she relishes the solitude.

On Friday, when Michael comes in for his lesson, Gertrude finishes but then says, "I will be playing new music on Sunday afternoon." She moves quickly away to the cutting tables.

Michael stands up to leave, but Gertrude stops him, "Please let Captain and Eley know should you see them."

"Yes, ma'am," he says and then dashes out the door and down the steps.

Gertrude allows a little smile to ease out of her lips. Then she realizes she must practice if there might be an audience on Sunday. Her routine for piano practice is to run a few scales, then play the first part of her composition. She cringes a bit. The piano badly needs tuning. Next is the second part of the composition, which she hesitates to play. The mood created when she wrote it kept her up late into the night. All the old feelings of despair and depression enveloped her and made her toss and turn half the night. She positions her hands above the keyboard, ready to start, but that's when she hears a knock at the front door. At the door is a woman. Gertrude asks, "Hello, how can I help you?" The woman is facing her but not really seeing her.

"Good day, miss. I am to ask for Miss Gertrude Kelly."

"I'm Gertrude Kelly."

"Mrs. Lynch contacted me to tune the piano here."

Gertrude studies the woman's face. She is acutely aware that the woman cannot see her. She hesitates, but the woman speaks up.

"Yes, I am blind, but I apprenticed at Wing & Son Piano in New York. I have a cousin who lives up there, but I am from Savannah, and my family has a home here on Tybee Island. I can tune your piano as well as I tune the piano for the De Soto Hotel Orchestra in Savannah."

Gertrude immediately says, "Please, come in." Gertrude holds the door for her as she uses her cane to cross the threshold. "What's your name?"

The woman pauses and waits for Gertrude to close the front door. "Frances Lynch."

"The piano is in the dining room. Shall I walk ahead of you to lead the way?"

"Yes, and take my elbow, that way we can go quickly."

Gertrude leads Frances to the piano. "I was just playing, so the cover is off."

"I heard the playing from outside. I also heard why you need a piano tuner."

Frances sits down on the piano bench. "This will take a while."

"Okay, I have work to do. I will be here in the room with you, cutting out fabric, should you need anything." Gertrude watches as Frances opens her leather bag and props open the top of the piano. She is tall and has long arms. She slips off her black jacket and puts it on the floor behind the bench. She is wearing a black skirt with black shiny shoes. Her white blouse is trimmed with black lace. Under a smallish black hat, she has twisted her brown hair into a trendy bun. Gertrude thinks she is at least thirty. Then Frances pulls out a pair of gloves from her bag and prepares to tune the piano. Before she goes to her cutting table, Gertrude asks, "Are you related to Mrs. Lynch in Savannah?"

"If you mean Susan Lynch, the program chair of the Savannah Music Club, yes, I am her cousin."

The pinging of the piano keys distracts Gertrude from her cutting. She goes into the kitchen to prepare a cup of tea. As the water heats, she stands looking out the kitchen window into the side yard of the big house. A previous garden had been created with a thick, stick border wall built around it to reduce wind damage to the plants. Raised garden beds have been augmented with soil, not sand. This site would be perfect for the children to plant and maintain crops while they are at the Home in the summer. Another project to think about. She takes a cup of tea into the dining room, where the pings from the piano continue.

Nearly two hours later, Gertrude hears a tune and not the pings. Frances is playing. At the end of the piece, Gertrude asks, "I haven't heard that song, what is it?"

"'Alice, Where Art Thou Going?' Words by Will A. Heelan and music by Albert Gumble. It was just released by Jerome H. Remick & Company in New York. My cousin sent it to me."

"It's quite a lively tune and sounds great, now that the piano is tuned."

"Yes, it is a lively tune, and yes, the piano needed quite an overhaul." Francis stands up and puts her tools in the bag.

Gertrude watches the precision Francis uses to place the

tools in their proper place where she can find everything. When Francis finishes, Gertrude asks, "Would you like a cup of tea? The water is hot."

"That would be lovely."

"Join me in the kitchen, then. I will guide you."

"Thank you." Frances picks up her jacket behind the bench and puts it on. Then she stands with her cane in front of her. Gertrude takes her elbow and the two women walk into the kitchen for their tea.

As they talk at the kitchen table, Gertrude learns that Frances has been playing the piano since a little girl. She lost her eyesight when she had scarlet fever at fourteen. The family in Savannah was close to the family in New York, so to keep Frances from being bored, they sent her to live with her cousins in New York. It was there that her five-year apprenticeship began as a piano tuner with a piano factory. When she returned home, she continued to play, but her ability to hear pitches allowed her to be a good piano tuner. She regularly tunes the De Soto Orchestra piano and the Savannah Music Club's piano when her cousin, Susan Lynch, asks her.

"As you heard, the piano did need to be tuned," says Gertrude.

"Yesterday, it needed to be tuned yesterday."

Both women laugh. Then Frances asks, "What were you playing when I arrived? I don't think I have heard it."

"It's nothing, just something I am working on."

"You compose?"

"Hardly, but I am trying."

"Like Fanny Mendelssohn," Frances says.

"She composed many pieces but had to publish them under her brother's name."

"Yes, she was always hesitant about telling people she composed. It is difficult being a woman composer."

Gertrude says, "I'm hardly at the level of Fanny

Mendelssohn; I have only started composing." She pauses. Because Frances plays and seems to know about women composers, Gertrude decides to ask, "What if you feel you have no choice but to compose?"

"Then that is what you need to do." Frances stands to leave. "Before I go, will you play the piece you are working on so I can hear if the pitch is good on the piano?"

"Could I play another tune? Something from my childhood?"

"I would really like to hear your piece, if you don't mind."

Together, they walk back into the dining room. Gertrude pulls a chair out from the nearest table and Frances sits. Gertrude prepares to play by running a few scales. Then she plays the second part of the piece, the one full of despair. At the end of the section, she turns to find Frances sitting with a handkerchief wiping her eyes.

"Moving, very moving," she says. "Now, I can go. The piano is tuned."

"How do I pay you?"

"You just did."

Gertrude leads Frances to the front door. "How will you get home?"

"I know the way. Not a problem. Remember, I grew up in Savannah and on Tybee Island. The house is just down the lane toward the hotel." As Frances moves down the steps and onto the path leading to the lane, she stops and turns back. "Gertrude?"

"Yes?"

"Will you be playing your new compositions anytime soon?"

With a smile in her voice, Gertrude says, "I play on Sunday afternoon after lunch for a few Tybee Island folks who sit in the kitchen and listen. You are welcome to come. They sit around the table drinking tea."

"Thank you. I will be here on Sunday, then. Have a good day." And with her cane waving the path in front of her, she moves on down the path.

Locking the front door, Gertrude goes to the cottage and gets her cloak. There is time for a late afternoon walk on the beach. She has a lot to think about, like how to write the next part of her composition.

29

———

The third part of her composition is on how it feels to be at the edge of a cliff, so to speak, when there is nowhere to go, no one to talk with, and no choices to make. The decisions already made are crashing in and causing major distress. As she walks down the beach, she remembers the storm on Croagh Patrick, the wind's crescendo against the building, the rainwater falling from the eaves of the building with whistle sounds and surges that changed with the weight of the storm. There were thunder crashes that screamed and could be heard from different corners of the building. She remembers hearing the mournful sounds of having lost everything. There had been sounds of violins, flutes, oboes, drums, and cellos. All she has is a piano. Can that feeling be created with just a piano? As she walks and thinks about how to compose this section, her pace gets faster and faster. At the end of the beach, she is winded and has to pause to catch her breath.

Gertrude's return walk is gentler. Birds are diving for dinner. There is a shrimping boat out on the sea. Shrimp season has ended, so the boat must be looking for eels, which can be caught all year if the eels are at least nine inches long. She listens whenever Captain says anything about sea life. The evening is getting cold with a chilly breeze coming off the water. This makes her steps fast again to get to the cottage, heat water for tea, and plan dinner.

Inside with a cup of hot tea, she restrains her temptation to go back over to the big house and work on her composition. She must sew and work to finish the uniforms. She counts the number of pieces already cut. There are twenty for boys and twenty for girls. Ten more need to be cut out to make her goal of fifty. Where has the time gone? It is the first week of November, and fifteen uniforms need to be finished by Thanksgiving. She picks up one set of fabric pieces, goes back downstairs, and puts it on the chair by the fireplace. Two more logs are put into the fire. Dinner will be beef Eley brought by. Gertrude removes the small slab of beef from the icebox and places it in a skillet on the stove, ready to be seared. She adds water to the pot on the hanging hook over the fire and chooses herbs growing in pots on the windowsill. She tosses thyme and rosemary into the water.

Now it is time to pin the fabric pieces together to be sewn. The chair near the fireplace is the staging area for pinning the fabric. Pins from the sewing basket and fabric pieces ready to be pinned are on the wooden chair, which is being used as a table. When the fabric is pinned. Gertrude moves the pieces to the sewing machine and returns to check if the water over the fire is hot. After searing the beef, she puts it into the water to cook while she sews.

Gertrude sits at the sewing machine and runs the treadle a few times to get her rhythm and then sews the seams. Each sewn uniform is placed on the chair by the front window, which is the hand-sewing area. A pin cushion that holds the sewing needles—Mrs. Schultz had thought of everything, a spool of thread, and a small pair of snipping scissors are on the round table, ready to be used to finish the uniform.

Smells from the beef simmering over the fire lead her to check on the meal. She sees that the beef needs more time to cook. In a basket on the kitchen shelf are vegetables, and Gertrude chooses a palmetto root. Eley had taken her to the marsh to dig up some dwarf palmetto roots. Rather than grate them and fry in a skillet, as Eley suggested, Gertrude cuts up the root into small pieces and tosses them into the pot with the beef. If they are sort of like potatoes, as Eley said, they'll cook this way, too. Her life in the cottage has taken on a new routine.

On the weekend, Gertrude adds to this routine. After her late afternoon walk on the beach, she returns to the cottage to prepare dinner and sew. During the day, she needs to forage for extra food. Though Mrs. Lynch has been true to her word and sent money for the monthly quota for the piecework, Gertrude wants to be careful about what is spent. Her purchases have included staples like flour, baking soda, salt, butter, milk, rice, eggs, and tea. Though she almost doesn't need the tea since Eley has taught her how to make lavender, chamomile, and mint tea. All of the ingredients are growing on the windowsill.

Everything else is foraged from land or sea. Crabs are getting easier to catch. Mussels are easy to harvest once the colonies are located. Michael leaves her fish and shrimp. Mingo has been consistently providing some sort of meat from either his hunting or trapping. The sea lettuce, mushrooms, and prickly pears are still in abundance. Her food has certainly increased and improved with her learning how to cook them and how to find them. Eley has taught her a lot.

Sunday afternoon is the time to play music. Gertrude has to smile at the fact that Frances has been invited to her growing kitchen audience. To prepare, she goes early to the big house to heat the rooms. Captain has prepared the logs in the dining room and in the kitchen's wood stove, which is ready to light.

The kettle is filled with water and put on the stovetop to heat. She gathers cups from the dresser and puts them on the table. Finally, she goes into the dining room and loosens her fingers by playing scales. The back door opens. In the kitchen are Captain and his wife, Hazel.

"I thought I'd join in and give a listen," Hazel says. Gertrude gets another cup out of the pantry. They hear a knock on the front door. Gertrude goes to answer. Frances has arrived. Gertrude leads her to the kitchen and introduces her to Captain and Hazel. They knew each other from having lived on the island for so many years. Everyone chooses a place to sit and prepares their cups for tea. Michael comes in the back door. Gertrude gets another cup from the pantry. Before she can put it down, Eley comes in with Mingo.

"Mingo wanted to come too," she says. Gertrude gets another cup and refills the kettle with water. The kitchen is full of talk. Frances knows Eley, who does washing for Frances' family, but has not met Mingo. Gertrude disappears into the dining room and shuts the door. She crosses over to the piano and sits, but she doesn't play, not yet. She prepares in her head to play. She then begins her warmup by playing a few scales and a couple of Irish tunes she had played with the band back in the Irish pubs. Then, she starts to play her music.

Near the end of the first section of the composition, Gertrude realizes that there is no transition to the second section. Anticipating the transition both mentally and then physically, she fixes it and plays the new part, making the music flow better and connecting the two sections. The second section begins with the despair, tumult, and loss of hope. That's all that has been written so far. Her goal is to write two more sections.

Silently, Gertrude sits on the piano bench after playing, but after a few seconds, she realizes that there are no voices coming from the kitchen. Maybe they all left. She goes to the kitchen door and opens it. All six people are sitting around the table. Hazel, Eley, and Frances are dabbing their eyes with handkerchiefs. Michael stands abruptly with his back to Gertrude and crosses to the sink. Captain and Mingo both stare at their hands, gently placed on the tabletop in front of them.

"Well?" Gertrude asks.

Frances is the first to speak. "Better than you played the other day. There is a transition that wasn't there before."

"My, oh my," says Eley. "I had no idea that music could make me cry. You pulled out my heart and crumpled it." Her handkerchief is balled up in her hand.

Michael turns and faces her. The look on his face emphasizes his words. "See why I have to learn to play?"

Gertrude understands, totally understands. Her need to learn has caused her to do some outrageous things that have gotten her in a lot of trouble. And part of those outrageous things just kicked her in her stomach. She instinctively reaches down to touch where the baby is kicking.

"I didn't know you were pregnant," Hazel says.

Gertrude sees that all eyes are on her. She looks directly at Hazel. "Yes, well, I am." So much for keeping a low profile and keeping her pregnancy a secret.

30

─────

Eley rushes the men out of the kitchen. "We're ready to have another cup of tea." She goes to the pantry and gets a cup for Gertrude. Frances and Hazel sit silently at the table. Eley bustles about refilling cups. "Let's have a cup of tea and talk."

Gertrude sits at the table across from Frances. The women are unusually quiet. Eley speaks first. "How are you feeling?"

"You knew she is pregnant?" asks Hazel.

"Why yes, when I first saw her. I looked at dry skin with blotches. That's a sign of pregnancy," explains Eley.

Frances sips her tea. "I never noticed."

Gertrude almost spills her tea. "Frances has a sense of humor."

"Frances has to in order to survive what life has tossed me," she says.

The other women look first at Frances, then at Gertrude. Frances continues, "I didn't want to be blind. I got sick and the blindness came. I came to the conclusion that I could either stay in my room and become a hermit, or I could learn to live with being blind."

"Is it hard to do?" asks Hazel. She stares at Frances with her mouth slightly ajar.

"Not so much anymore. The first year was disastrous. I threw temper tantrums, got angry quickly, and refused to listen to anyone about what I needed to do. I was difficult. I was fourteen."

"Then what happened?" asks Hazel, caught up in the upheaval that Frances must have faced.

"I heard a song written by John Newton, an Englishman who experienced a violent storm off the shore of County Donegal, Ireland in 1748. He later came to believe in God and wrote this song." Frances sings.

"Amazing grace, how sweet the sound
That saved a wretch like me
I once was lost, but now I'm found
Was blind, but now I see."

"My goodness," says Eley. "That's a powerful song and one that motivates."

Gertrude speaks up, "I can see how that song motivated you to find other ways of living, but can music, any music, motivate people who weren't looking to be motivated?"

Eley interrupts Gertrude. "I think so. I have a song too. My people came from slavery. We lost many who were sold, killed, or died. Folks I knew were often beaten and punished for nothing. I was always asking questions, and my mama would say, 'We are the Gullahs and will cheer each other up by singing.' Then, just a few years ago, a visiting minister came to the praise house and shared a new song with us. This song speaks to me like your song speaks to you, Frances. I don't know who wrote it, but we sing it all the time in the praise house." Eley sings.

"Lift every voice and sing,

'Til earth and heaven ring,
Ring with the harmonies of Liberty;
Let our rejoicing rise
High as the list'ning skies,
Let it resound loud as the rolling sea.
Sing a song full of the faith that the dark past has
 taught us,
Sing a song full of the hope that the present has brought
 us;
Facing the rising sun of our new day begun,
Let us march on 'til victory is won."

The women sit and listen. Gertrude hears these two songs and sees that what she is going through is different from what Frances and Eley have faced, yet there is a sameness. They have all gone through a crisis, become angry and despondent, but then found a way forward. The women are all silently sipping their tea.

Hazel stands. "I better be gettin' on off. I got dinner to prepare and things at the fish camp to clean."

Gertrude stands with her. "Thank you for listening to my music today."

"My pleasure," Hazel says, "but I was hopin' you'd explain how you got pregnant and got no husband about."

Gertrude is silent. Hazel remains standing at the door, waiting. "I guess I may be waiting a lot longer." She turns to go out the back door.

"Hazel," calls Gertrude, "it's a long story."

"When you have time, let me know." Hazel goes out the door.

Eley is picking up the cups and saucers and washing them in the sink. Frances stands. "I should be going as well. The music has been wonderful to hear. Thank you. Will there be more?"

"I plan on writing another section this week."

"Will you be playing it next Sunday?"

"Yes, I can do that."

"Good, until then. Oh, and I can let myself out. I know the lay of the land now through the house."

After Frances leaves, Eley and Gertrude finish in the kitchen, close everything down in the wood stove, and bank the embers in the fireplace in the dining room with cold ashes held in a bucket to the side. The fire screen is placed securely in front of the fireplace. Gertrude knows that the Captain will clean the fireplace and put everything ready for next Sunday. She will use the wood stove when she comes to work in the big house during the week, plus she only has a few more uniforms to cut out, and then she can clean up all the tables and not have to spend time in the big house each morning. Both women leave through the front door. As Gertrude locks up, she sees Eley sitting on the top step. Gertrude sits next to her.

"You didn't tell me how you were doing with the baby," she says.

"Fine. I got a checkup from Sister Mary Joyce at St. Joseph's Hospital just last week. Everything seems to be going as planned. I'm fine. The baby is fine."

"You got a name picked out?"

Gertrude sits down next to her. "Eley, the story is long."

"I got time."

Gertrude takes a deep breath and then a long sigh to gain the fortitude to tell most of the story to Eley. Having spent time with Eley and knowing how helpful she has been, Gertrude thinks Eley will understand far better than Hazel would. However, as much as Eley seems to be trustworthy, Gertrude leaves out the "not being married" part.

Eley sits and looks down the boardwalk to where the ocean is. "Okay, so your husband abandoned you and people who are helping you tell you that you need to give the baby up for adoption. And to make it easier for you to give that baby up, the sisters tell you not to name the chil' so you won't be attached." Eley sits a moment and looks down at her hands, then she looks at Gertrude. "Aren't you attached already? It's growing inside of you."

Gertrude can no longer hold her tears. "When I don't think about her. When I go about my day and don't have time to think about her, it is fine. When she kicks, or when I realize I am getting bigger, then it is right in front of my face."

"I don't mean to pry or nothin', but isn't it unusual for the sisters to find a place like this to put a pregnant woman with no one looking in or helpin' when needed?"

"My family doesn't know that I am pregnant."

"How come? Aren't they in Savannah?"

"Yes, they are."

"Don't they care about you and their grandchil'?"

"Again, they don't know."

"How come?"

"It's complicated."

"I'm listening."

Gertrude chews on her finger, a habit she started back in Ireland. "Eley, I made some really bad decisions when I had choices. I decided that my music was more important than my family and friends. When I left for Ireland, I did not tell any family, friends, or the sisters."

"I get that, but I have a feelin' that it's not the whole story."

"Why are you asking me?" Gertrude spits the words out before she thinks.

Eley cuts her eyes over and looks at her. "Well, you need to tell me because as you get more along with this chil' you will need somebody's help, and I don't see nobody outside the cottage standing in line to help."

There is quiet between the women. Gertrude looks out toward the ocean. Silent tears cascade down her cheeks.

Eley reaches out and takes Gertrude's hand. Startled, Gertrude turns and looks at the two entwined hands, the white one and the black one. "I haven't been able to have a chil'," she says quietly. "We've tried, Mingo and me, but no chil' seems to be growing inside of me."

Gertrude squeezes Eley's hand with compassion.

Eley continues. "Life's got its ups and downs, that's for sure. But one must have links with others in order to be safe and to get through all these ups and downs. I got my people, my praise house. Just wanted to tell you that you don't have to do this all by yourself."

The hug is spontaneous. Gertrude laughs a little through her tears and wipes her eyes with the back of her hand. "Thank you."

Eley stands. "I'm off. I'll see you when I see you."

"Yes, you will," says Gertrude and watches Eley sashay down the path to the lane.

31

For the next few Sundays in November, Gertrude plays her music. Hazel does not come since that first Sunday when Gertrude's pregnancy was discovered, but Captain, Michael, Eley, and Frances come. Mingo comes when he is not out hunting. Gertrude has written more of the music and plays all that she has written so far. The first section is built on nature and its connection with music. The second part is how one is in deep despair. The third part is full of rage and is heard through the sounds of a storm. But the fourth part is where a direction is found and hope is alive.

All the pattern pieces have been cut from the fabric and the dining room has been cleaned. The process for the uniforms in the cottage has expanded. The cut-out pieces are in one bedroom, and the finished uniforms are stored in the other bedroom. There are ten uniforms on the chair that need to be hand-sewn. When her body is bigger with the baby inside and she has to sit more often, the hand sewing can be done. In the meantime, Thanksgiving is approaching, and there are more uniforms at the "to be pinned" stage. Progress is being made.

Gertrude is also making progress identifying nature in her

walks. She starts each beach walk earlier and walks for longer. During these walks, her thoughts sort out as she tunes into nature and feels the different types of breezes. In the morning, there are land breezes that push out from the land to the sea. These breezes are dry. In the afternoon and evening, there are sea breezes that push in from the ocean onto the land. These breezes tend to be wetter. If the breeze blows her hair softly, that's a gentle breeze; should the speed pick up, it becomes a wind, and her hair is whipped about and cannot be controlled even under her cloak's hood. The speed and direction are determined by whether or not the breeze is forming over the ocean or the land, as well as what the temperatures of both land and water may be. There are many types of breezes she has experienced on her walks, and all of them add to how she sorts through her music.

Along with the breeze identification, shells catch her eye on her beach walks with a growing collection of clam, oyster, and mussel shells. She also collects sand dollars if they are white or light gray. Michael has explained that the brown ones with hair-like spines are alive. She also has found several knobbed whelk shells. According to Michael, the search for shells is best an hour before or after a low tide and during a full moon or new moon period. She finds the knobbed whelk shells after a storm.

She views birds differently, too. Whereas only the terns were seen when Gertrude got on Tybee Island, feeding both morning and evening. Now the terns perch on rocks, posts, rails, or boats. They seem to have territories and will run or fly at any intruder. On the other hand, Gertrude notices that the gulls are not nice birds. They harass and rob other birds of their catches. And once a gull picked up a hard-shelled mollusk and dropped it onto rocks to break it open. The wading birds, like the egrets, walk about in the shallows of the ocean searching for food. As she learns about the seacoast's natural habitat, her curiosity extends to what is below the surface of the water. She knows there are huge fish and whales, but what else? What lives down under?

The ocean is vast and has a life all its own. But since the river surge, Gertrude has not asked Captain to take her out to sea. Though he seems to take safety seriously, Gertrude cannot swim, and being in a small boat with unpredictable weather and sea movements makes her nervous. Would it be safe for the baby if anything were to happen and she went overboard? Probably not. She may wade out to catch crabs and to find mollusks, but she has no desire to go out on another boat.

Every day, Gertrude is working, sewing, cooking, and walking. Her energy levels have allowed her to get everything done, and by the Sunday before Thanksgiving, she has drafted out her full musical composition. The last section buoyed her up for days after finishing. She is hopeful and the music is a part of that hope. As her new friends gather in the kitchen to hear her play, her nervous energy has her straightening the chairs in the dining room, aligning every chair in the room.

A quick look into the kitchen confirms that all have gathered and are chattering away and sipping their tea. Gertrude closes the door and goes to the piano. This time she runs through her scales twice, then pauses. Her mind is on the music, but the room is warm. Rather than bank the fire, she goes and opens the French doors leading out onto the porch and notices that clouds have formed. There is a scent of rain coming in the air.

Gertrude returns to the piano and begins to play. Again, there are tunes she plays to relax. Her hands are ready. She plays the first section and, using the new transition, moves directly into the second section. After another brief pause, the notes move the music into the third section. Her entire body leans into the music. She hears thunder, but the music goes on. The storm is building outside, but so is the storm from the music. Finally, it is the last section. Her body is erect on the bench. The music flows from her fingers, from her heart, from the deepest part of her soul. She can hear the rain falling from the eaves of the big house. At the end of the composition, Gertrude shivers from the chill in the room. When she crosses the room to close the French doors, she sees the people. Strangers are sitting on the porch floor. Lots of people are crowded onto the porch with their blankets and quilts.

Gertrude backs into the dining room but leaves the doors open. Walking quickly to the kitchen, she opens the door and the first thing out of her mouth is, "Why are there people on the porch?"

Michael grins. "Thought you'd never notice. People have been sitting out on the lawn on Sundays to hear you play. Word must have spread."

"What?"

"I think you have an audience," says Captain.

Eley is looking out the kitchen window. "The rain is still coming down really hard. Why don't you play some more?"

Gertrude stares at Eley. "Go on," Eley says. "People want to hear."

Stunned, Gertrude silently returns to the dining room, not glancing at the people on the porch. At the piano, she improvises and starts to play songs that make her spirit bright, a melody of songs from long ago. She plays one after another for more than an hour. At the end, she plays "Clair de lune," by Debussy, the last song she played at her recital a year ago at the Savannah Theatre. The storm has passed. Going over to the French doors to close them, she looks out at the people still gathered on the porch. These people, her audience, break into applause. Bowing her head gently to thank them, she retreats into the dining room.

Before Gertrude can get the doors closed, a man steps up and puts his foot in the doorway to stop the door from being shut. Gertrude looks up and sees a tall, lanky, young man in a suit. He is wearing a hat with a "press" card in the brim. She knows who he is, but she does not know why he should be on Tybee Island with the audience on the porch listening to her music.

"Gertrude?"

"Yes, you are Lucas."

"Right you are. I'm Lucas Laurent. You are the pianist who has been giving the Sunday concerts?"

"I have been playing on Sunday afternoons for some friends who happen to be in the kitchen."

Lucas moves into the dining room and shuts the French doors behind him. Gertrude sees the man her friend, Sharon, had known and introduced to the nurses at the boarding house. She remembers that he and Sharon had walked all over Savannah.

"What can I do for you?" asks Gertrude.

"I'm on assignment for the *Savannah Morning News*, writing a story about the Tybee Island concerts on Sunday afternoon."

Holding up her hands, she says, "No, there is no story. There are no concerts." Gertrude looks quickly at the people who are leaving the porch.

"I heard music. I saw a rather large gathering on the porch, listening. What do you call it then?"

"Practice. I am practicing."

"I covered your recital last year. If I remember correctly, you left to go to Brenau. You were sponsored by the Savannah Music Club, right?"

"A lot has happened in a year, Mr. Laurent. But there is no story here."

At that moment, Eley pushes the kitchen door open. "Folks here are about to leave, just wanted to say bye."

Gertrude is facing Lucas but glances at Eley, who motions

for Captain and Michael to step up to the door. The men step around Eley and move into the dining room near Gertrude.

"How can we help you?" asks Captain.

"Just talking with Gertrude. I'm on assignment from the *Savannah Morning News.* You have been listening to the concerts from the beginning?" Lucas pulls a notebook from his jacket pocket and a pencil.

"I told you there is no concert and no story," says Gertrude. By this time, Eley has moved into the dining room, and Frances has joined them.

"Then why are you all here?"

"They are friends, that's all," says Gertrude.

Lucas turns to Captain. "Don't you supervise the grounds here at the Fresh Air Home?"

"I do," says Captain.

"And who are you?" asks Lucas, pointing to Michael. "Haven't we met?"

And before Michael can say anything, Captain says, "He works with me."

"And you?" Lucas asks, looking directly at Eley.

"A friend," she answers, putting both hands on her hips.

"And you?" Lucas points to Frances, who does not answer him. He speaks up loudly. "Ma'am, why are you here at the 'no' concert?"

"Frances, he's asking you," says Eley.

"I'm the piano tuner," says Frances. "I may not see you, but I can hear you. Please don't shout."

Lucas begins scribbling in his notebook. Gertrude motions with her hands to her friends that she is okay. "Thank you for being here to hear me practice," she says to the group. "I have met Mr. Laurent before in Savannah. I know you have many things to do today. I'll take care of things in the house." She turns quickly to Lucas. "Will you wait for a minute? I have something I want to say."

Lucas nods. Gertrude goes to the back door and thanks her friends for coming. She locks the door when they leave. Frances has gone out the front door. Lucas remains in the dining room. Gertrude crosses to the piano, closes the lid, and covers the top. She turns to Lucas. "Please, sit."

They sit at one of the dining room tables. Gertrude folds her hands on the tabletop in front of her. "It's good to see you, but I must ask that you not print a story about me. Please."

She sees that Lucas has put his notebook and pencil down on the tabletop. He, too, has folded his hands in front of him.

"Why?"

"It's a long story."

"I have time."

"I don't, I have projects I must get to."

"Gertrude, there is a story here. Many people have crowded onto the porch to hear music. The music is really powerful. I know, I listened. Why don't you want people to know about it?"

Gertrude sits for a minute to think about how best to answer Lucas's question. Finally, she says, "It is not so much a story about music as it is about survival. I have learned that I need to play in order to live. I made many decisions I should not have since June. Five months of bad decisions. However, my sanctuary is here for now, and I must retain the quiet and peacefulness that Tybee Island offers me. There are things that I feel are private and cannot be shared with others."

Lucas is quiet.

Gertrude pauses but continues. "Lucas, I know you cared about my friend, Sharon. She shared with me the adventures the two of you had a year ago. Sharon and I are still friends, thank goodness. And if you had cared about Sharon, maybe, as her friend, you will honor my request to not write about my piano playing on Tybee Island."

"Sharon knows you are here?" asks Lucas.

"Yes, and she supports me in these decisions."

Quietly, he asks, "Is she happy in Ireland?"

"I saw her in County Wexford with her parents, all tucked into a lovely cottage with a birdbath in the front yard. She's happy."

"Of course, she has a birdbath in the front yard. Good. That's good."

The silence is tense between the two. Gertrude shifts in her chair. "Well?" she asks.

"I'm after a good story," says Lucas.

Without thinking, she says, "What about writing about Frances? She is a local person. She is related to Mrs. Leo Lynch, the program chair for the Savannah Music Club. She is a blind piano tuner. You don't have to write anything about me or the people listening to me play."

Lucas seems to be thinking about her suggestion. "Hmm, that's not a bad idea."

"Their summer home is just down the lane, but she has been staying there this fall and comes regularly to my Sunday afternoon practice sessions."

"Are you practicing next Sunday?"

"Are you writing the article?"

"I haven't decided yet. So, are you practicing next Sunday?"

"Probably. I want to finish this composition. I will not have as much time this week. Mrs. Schultz has invited me to Thanksgiving dinner at the boarding house."

"Do you visit your family and stay over when you go into Savannah?"

"I have stayed at Mrs. Schultz's once, but I only go in monthly. There are frequent trains, so I usually come back to the cottage the same day."

"You don't see your family? I remember meeting them at the recital."

"I need to be here," Gertrude says. "I prefer the solitude.

Plus, communing with nature is doing wonders for my cooking skills."

Lucas laughs. "How so?"

"I am learning to cook seafood that Michael leaves for me and meat from animals that Eley's husband, Mingo, has hunted and shared with me."

"My, oh my," he says, "I came to write a story you don't want me to write and here you are surprising me with everything you say."

Gertrude chooses to be silent. She watches as Lucas puts his notebook and pencil in his coat pocket.

Lucas stands to leave. "Okay. If I do not write about you, will you tell me the whole story?"

"Why should I tell you?"

"Because I am good at keeping secrets?"

"Right, you are a newspaper reporter who wants front-page stories."

Lucas laughs. "Yes, that is true, but I also want my friends to know I am loyal. Please let Sharon know I asked about her."

"You cared a lot about Sharon, didn't you?"

Lucas is heading toward the door but turns back to face Gertrude. "I asked her to marry me."

"She never shared that with me."

"I guess we all have secrets."

"Yes, we do."

"When you are ready to tell me yours, I will listen."

Gertrude looks at his face and thinks that he may mean what he says.

32

Monday begins like most weeks since Gertrude has been on Tybee Island. She walks on the beach, gathers sea lettuce, harvests some mussels, sews uniforms, and in the evening in front of the fire, sews by hand. The handsewing station has been moved over to the chair by the settee since there is no more pinning to do. Additionally, with the baby growing inside of her, it is more comfortable to sit on the settee and stretch her legs out. She has added pillows from the big house parlor to the settee.

Thanksgiving morning, Gertrude prepares for her morning walk. Her beach gear is under the bench at the front door, which includes a canvas bag, a reed basket to put in the water, and a small bucket that holds seawater should any food be found for the table. Because of her travels today, however, she only takes the canvas bag for shells, should there be any she doesn't have.

The sun is just coming up over the water. The colors are a rich burgundy, orange, yellow, and grey. Terns and gulls appear to be greeting her as she comes onto the beach from the walkway. Her skirt is tied in a knot and tucked into her waistband.

To keep her skirts drier and to be able to walk closer to the water, she has learned to tie up her skirts by watching Eley. It works. There is no one on the beach this early. There is a section of the beach with a lot of shells. Only the ones that look different from those already collected are put into the canvas bag. It is getting harder and harder for her to bend over. Should she stoop, standing back up is challenging.

Gertrude brushes sand off some of the shells, stands up, and continues her walk. However, the minute the ocean waves fill her head, her brain begins going over the music. She rehearses each note on the beach. To finish the composition, she must walk a little farther, then she turns and heads back toward the cottage. There are more shells and an idea. She has nothing to contribute to the Thanksgiving dinner, which has been bothering her for several days. However, if the shells are washed and put in a glass jar, they could be shared with the nurses, who always want natural items to decorate their clothes or hats. She picks up more shells now that there is a reason for them.

After she is back at the cottage and the shells are washed, she sees how the sunlight shining through the jar highlights the shells' iridescent colors. A cloth ribbon made from the uniform fabric leftovers ties a sea oats stalk onto the jar. She will carry the jar rather than put it in her satchel.

Several loud whistles announce the train's arrival in Savannah. As the train pulls into the station, Gertrude puts on her cloak as the day is cold. Her feet hurt. She needs larger shoes since her regular boots, which keep her feet warm and dry, have begun to hurt her feet. As the train stops, she gathers her satchel and the jar of shells. Exiting the train and going down the platform steps to make her way to the boarding house, she sees a man leaning up against one of the posts at the edge of the platform: Lucas.

He greets her. "Good morning."

"Good morning, Lucas." Gertrude looks about. Lucas does not appear to be moving toward the train to board, and there is no one getting off the train but her. "Why are you here?"

"I came to escort you to the boarding house."

"That's sweet, but you don't need to do that."

"I know."

Lucas is silent. Gertrude is confused as to why he might be here. He takes her satchel and offers his arm. As she puts her hand on his arm, she asks, "By meeting me here, do you think I will give you more of my story?"

His laugh is contagious and she smiles. "No," he says, "I believe you are a woman of your word. No story is no story. I will wait for Sunday and interview the blind piano tuner."

They walk briskly toward the boarding house. After keeping that pace for a couple of blocks, Gertrude speaks up. "Do you think we could slow the pace just a little?"

"I'm sorry. I always had to walk quickly with Sharon. She blamed it on being from New York."

"I'm from here, from Savannah, so let's go at a reasonable Southern pace."

"Yes, of course," Lucas says as he tamps down his strides.

Gertrude glances at him. "I walk twice a day on the beach, but I don't have to watch my feet like I do on the city streets."

"Why do you watch where you are going? Don't you know the way to the boarding house?"

"I do, but my feet are killing me and I don't walk in shoes on the beach."

"Ah, now you're the island girl, barefoot and fancy-free."

Gertrude lets out a small giggle. "Unlikely. It is chilly on the beach with the sea wind crossing the cold water, so I wear the rubber boots I use when I go after crabs or mussels. My feet are just a bit swollen now, so the shoes I have on hurt my feet."

"You go crabbing?" Lucas almost stops in the path.

"I do if I want to eat. I also forage for sea lettuce, mushrooms, hickory nuts, chickweed, wild onions and garlic, prickly pears, palmetto hearts, persimmons, and dulce seaweed to season some of the food."

"My, my, you are a regular John Muir."

"John Muir? I don't know who he is."

"He was a naturalist who walked seven hundred miles in thirty-eight days to reach Savannah back in 1867. As the story goes, he had little money left by the time he got to Savannah on his way to the end of the continent. He checked with the bank every day for six days for money being wired to him from his brother, to no avail. So, he climbed a fence and slept in the Bonaventure graveyard, eating off the land whatever he could find. It has been said that his environmental, ethical, and philosophical beliefs solidified during his time at Bonaventure. He is the "father" of our national parks, cofounder of the Sierra Club, and defender of all things wild."

"Well, then, since I am living off the land, I guess I am a bit like John Muir. I have had no goal to be..." and she stops talking suddenly. She was going to say "mother" of anything, but since she will be...she continues, "But I do live in solitude. I should read up on him."

"And Thoreau."

"I have heard of Henry David Thoreau. He wrote a book called *Walden*."

"Yes, have you read his book?"

"I have not, but it seems as though I should since I am living a life similar to his."

Arriving at the boarding house, Gertrude pauses to thank Lucas for meeting her at the train and walking her there. As she reaches for her satchel, she says, "Thank you, Lucas. This is sweet, but not necessary."

"No problem, but I can take it in. Mrs. Schultz invited me to Thanksgiving dinner as well."

Gertrude raises her eyebrows to look at Lucas more carefully. "She did?"

"Yes, and there will be a few other gents in attendance, I believe, maybe boyfriends of some of the nurses."

"Now I am the one who is surprised. You did not share any of this with me."

"Did I need to?"

The front door opens and Mrs. Schultz walks onto the porch. "Welcome, Lucas and Gertrude, please come in."

33

———

As the nurses and guests gather around the dining room table for Thanksgiving dinner, Mrs. Schultz looks out over the assembled people. Next to Mrs. Schultz are Gertrude and Lucas. At the table are two maintenance men from the hospital who are former ship workers, Sister Mary Joyce, and the gardener with his wife. With the extra guests, the table is crowded with chairs added from the upstairs bedrooms. But even with the crowd, there are three vacant chairs.

Gertrude looks at the food displayed on the table. It is a bounty that has not been seen on her table. There are oysters on the half-shell, celery, turkey stuffed with oysters, cranberry jelly, mashed potatoes, baked squash, boiled onions with cream sauce, peach pickles, Waldorf salad, and hot yeast rolls. Gertrude's stomach rumbles and Lucas glances at her. "I did not eat breakfast," she whispers.

Everything is on the table when the cook, Edwidge, with her two children, who have helped with the dinner preparation, come into the dining room and sit in the vacant chairs. Mrs. Schultz smiles at them, then turns to Sister Mary Joyce. "Will you say grace?"

As every head bows, Sister Mary Joyce stands at her place. She folds her hands in front of her. She begins the Thanksgiving Prayer, which has been taught to all the nuns in the Sisters of Mercy order and deemed appropriate for the Thanksgiving celebration. "Lord God, maker of all those we encounter in our world, we are struggling to reach our home in you. We are traveling on a path filled with the holes of temptation and the bumps of hardship and loneliness."

Gertrude glances up at Sister Mary Joyce, thinking that she is talking directly to her, even though Sister Mary Joyce is looking up at the ceiling.

Sister Mary Joyce continues, "May those who help us begin the journey be blessed with a final destination in you. May those who share their wisdom with us be blessed with knowledge beyond all understanding."

Though she is listening, Gertrude looks at Mrs. Schultz. The older woman has her head bowed and her hands in her lap. The look on her face is one of contentment. Gertrude wants to duplicate that look. How does one reach that stage?

Gertrude listens as Sister Mary Joyce prays for resources, encouragement, strength, and courage for those on their own journeys. She talks about the rough stretches. Gertrude knows something about those rough stretches, like being in Ireland with Randolph and then being abandoned. As her mind wanders to Randolph and those final days, Sister Mary Joyce begins to talk about those who guard our safety. Gertrude remembers Ryan's gallantry in protecting her from the "whiskey man," and Sharon's ability to hide her and ship her off to Savannah. Her thoughts shift to the Sisters of Mercy and how they are providing her with resources to survive the recent bad decisions. The baby chooses that time to kick and shift. Gertrude instinctively reaches for her stomach to calm the movement and sees Lucas looking at her. Quickly, Gertrude glances back down at her empty plate.

Sister Mary Joyce concludes her prayer. "Our efforts will not go unrewarded. Our way will be made easier by the many companions you send. May our prayers of thanksgiving for their hearts centered in your compassion be heard. Amen."

"Amen," echo the people at the table.

Gertrude is silent. Being thankful should be at the forefront of her thoughts, but she first needs to mend the disconnect between her and her family, friends, and associates like Mrs. Lynch. Her decisions have created many problems. People like Mrs. Schultz, Sister Mary Joyce, and Eley are trying to find solutions for some of her problems. Michael and Captain are ready to jump in and help, and now Lucas seems to be a part of her support, maybe. Lucas has been true to his word and not written about her practice sessions on Tybee Island, at least not yet.

Mrs. Schultz stands up and moves the turkey in front of Lucas. "Will you kindly carve the turkey?"

Widening his eyes, Lucas looks first at Mrs. Schultz and then at Gertrude. "I will be pleased to do so." He stands and picks up the carving knife and fork. He holds the carving utensils with confident hands. First, he removes the legs and thighs, then cuts off the wings. Mrs. Schultz places an empty serving platter next to the turkey for him to lay out the sliced turkey as he carves. Next, he removes the turkey breasts and slices the white meat. He carves the dark meat last. When he finishes, he crosses the carving utensils on the platter with the wings. Mrs. Schultz removes that platter and puts it over on the buffet. Lucas sits down, picks up the platter, and passes it to Gertrude.

The food on the table is passed and shared. There are too many people for conversation to be shared with the whole table. Gertrude turns to Lucas. "You carve a turkey like a professional."

Handing her the boiled onions with cream sauce, he says, "I come from a long line of French chefs."

"Now, I am surprised," says Gertrude, "I did not know you could cook."

"Oh, I can't, or I should say, I don't. I live in a boarding house and must take my meals with them or out at cafés or saloons. I just know the basics since I grew up in a house where the men did the cooking."

"My mother, the Irish matron that she is, insists on doing all the cooking at home. My sisters and I were there to assist, not to do. I may have picked up things along the way, but I need practice to be able to say I can cook. But with your family so heavily involved in cooking, why don't you want to cook?"

Lucas reaches for a roll and hands one to Gertrude. "The family believes that all members should work in the restaurants they own. I learned to do many things in the restaurant, like washing the dishes, waiting on the customers, cleaning the tables, and taking out the refuse. But I needed to be outside, to be around many different people. I did not want to be inside four walls day after day and long into the night with only family members. It became suffocating."

"Is that why you came to America?"

"Yes, to find my way by doing something different."

"And are you happy with being a reporter?"

"Happy? No, I am not happy being a reporter. The pay is low. The hours are long. The owners are forever setting deadlines that are hard to keep."

"Then why do you stay?"

She sees Lucas's face grimace and his eyes narrow as he pauses before answering. "I guess I want to prove to my family that I can make it on my own. And, I do like the freedom of moving about the city, finding stories. That is, if I can find stories. Some stories remain secret."

Gertrude looks down at her plate. Almost every bite has been devoured. She has no intention of sharing her secrets with

Lucas. Just at the right time, Mrs. Schultz gets her attention and asks about the uniforms, allowing her to avoid Lucas.

As the talk decreases and stomachs are full, one of the nurses suggests that they clean off the table and let Mrs. Schultz relax. With a smile, Mrs. Schultz invites everyone into the parlor. They are welcome to choose desserts from the buffet in the dining room. She has set up coffee and tea in the parlor. And as she starts to stand, Gertrude interrupts.

"I almost forgot. I brought something for all of you." Leaving the room quickly, Gertrude returns with the jar of shells. "I know how much the nurses in the house love to accessorize, so I brought a variety of shells for you to find ways to use them." The nurses giggle as Gertrude opens the jar and passes it to the first nurse near her. "And, Mrs. Schultz," Gertrude continues, "my Irish ancestors would say that we need a toast." She raises her water glass. Others around the table raise theirs. Gertrude begins, "May the road rise up to meet you."

And then all the nurses who come from an Irish heritage chime in, "May the wind be always at your back. May the sun shine warm upon your face; the rains fall soft upon your fields. And until we meet again, may God hold you in the palm of His hand."

The chatter among the nurses increases as everyone stands and begins to move about. The guests go to the buffet for dessert, and the nurses clean the table. The lunch has been long. Gertrude ignores the desserts and goes into the parlor for a cup of tea. She has not eaten so much at one time in many a month. Feeling sluggish, she sits and begins drinking her tea. Mrs. Schultz enters the parlor and also gets a cup of tea. The two women are the only ones in the parlor. They sit quietly.

"How are you feeling?" asks Mrs. Schultz.

Gertrude looks down at her teacup. "I'm fine. I think I'm fine. I have swollen feet and they hurt in these shoes."

"I have heard that the feet do swell during pregnancy. You

seem to still be in your regular clothes, though it is your fifth month."

"Ah, I have let out some of the skirts and have confiscated the upstairs curtains, dying them a light purple to make a couple of duster-type dresses. I need to breathe during the day."

"The curtains?"

"I have no money for fabric and will remake the dresses into different curtains once the baby has come."

"I see." Mrs. Schultz sips her tea.

Gertrude notices that Mrs. Schultz's eyes have not stopped looking at her. Gertrude fidgets under the scrutiny. "Have you heard from Sharon?" She abruptly changes the subject.

"No, I was planning on asking you the same."

"Lucas explained that he had asked Sharon to marry him."

"Yes, I believe that happened."

"I did not know. Sharon only talked about Connor."

"Exactly, she was in love with Connor from the beginning."

There is silence between the two. Several of the guests come into the parlor and find a place to sit as well as to get a cup of coffee. The conversation between Gertrude and Mrs. Schultz ends, much to Gertrude's relief. As others filter in, Gertrude stands. She reaches out to Mrs. Schultz to thank her for inviting her.

"You are not leaving, are you?" Mrs. Schultz asks.

"Yes, I want to get back before it is too late."

"It'll be dark in an hour."

"I know. But the path is easy to follow from the train depot on the island and I am sure the train will be as deserted as it was when I came." She crosses to the front door. Mrs. Schultz follows her.

"I know you will come the first week in December for your check-up, but many of the nurses will be away for Christmas.

Please come and spend Christmas here. Or do you have plans to be with your family?"

"I have no plans yet." Gertrude looks at the closed door in front of her. "I have not seen my family since I arrived in Savannah."

"I'm sure they would be eager to see you."

"No, I don't think so. They are not yet apprised of my situation."

"You have not told them?"

"No. And I do not plan to." Gertrude turns and looks directly at Mrs. Schultz. She realizes that her tone is a bit terse. "I'm sorry, Mrs. Schultz. You have been so wonderful in helping me in so many ways, but I know my parents. They will never accept me if they know, so I am trying to keep it from them."

"If they see you, they will know soon enough."

"Exactly, that is why I do not go to visit. Thank you. I will think about your kind offer of Christmas and let you know." With that, Gertrude is out the door and down the steps. She walks quickly toward the train depot, thankful that the cottage is waiting for her on Tybee Island, a peaceful cottage where no questions are asked.

The conductor tells her the train schedule has changed due to the holiday when she arrives at the depot. It will leave in fifteen minutes. Gertrude walks to the far end of the platform and sits on a bench. There had been a time when there was no time to sit on a bench and wait. The nursing program took a lot of time: working in the hospital, cleaning the uniforms and especially the collars and cuffs, running errands, visiting family, and running errands for them. Piano practice had to be squeezed in whenever there was time in the evenings or on the weekends. Now there are whole days to fill, and she fills them with sewing, foraging, cooking, playing the piano, and resting. She seems to need a great deal of rest with the baby growing.

The train whistle blows and Gertrude takes the first seat in

the first car of the train. There are only two cars and no one else
has been waiting to board. She has a private train to Tybee
Island.

Daylight is gone by the time the train arrives on Tybee
Island. Even the twilight is gone. Though there is no lantern,
the path is wide and lined with rocks that take on a bit of the
moonlight, but the moon is not high in the sky yet. Gertrude
clutches her satchel and heads in the direction of the cottage.
Just as she crosses the lane and comes to the path leading up to
the cottage, there is a noise off to her right. The trees block her
sight. It's probably an animal. She walks on, feeling her feet
hurt in the shoes. Then a twig breaks. She thinks it was a twig.
It is dark. Listening more acutely than before, she hears footsteps. Whoever it is in the dark does not care if she should hear
them, and that relaxes her a little. The cottage is near; the white
outline can be seen against the dark sky.

The footsteps seem closer, and Gertrude doesn't want to
stop and try to figure out if it is a friend, animal, or foe. There
have been too many foes in her life, which cannot be stopped,
as evident from the encounter at Galway. Her small body is
light and she is too sluggish after the huge meal at Mrs.
Schultz's for her to be able to defend herself and her baby. Just
getting into the cottage is all that is on her mind. The door is
right ahead, and with the key in her hand, she steps up on the
stoop, puts the key in, and opens the door. As she turns to close
and lock the door, a foot is wedged in the corner, stopping her
from closing the door. She jams the foot with the door, and it
disappears. She slams the door shut and bolts it.

Frozen at the door, Gertrude does not attempt to move.
Outside, there is a thrashing about and a shout. Something is
slammed against the side of the cottage that makes her jump.
She can hear voices, but cannot understand what is being said.
There is a growling sound. Her pounding heart is louder than
the noise outside and echoes in her ears. The outside sounds

motivate her to pick up one of the kitchen knives and crouch behind the settee. It is dark. The noise stops. Something or someone can be heard moving quickly down the lane. There is a sickening quiet. Gertrude is still. There is no movement but her labored breathing. She holds the knife in front of her like a shield. There is a soft knock on the door, and a voice says, "Gertrude?" She doesn't move. Her heart is pounding so hard, she does not know if it all may be a ruse. She waits longer.

"Gertrude, it is Lucas. Let me know that you are okay. If you don't want to open the door, I understand. Just tell me so I can hear you that you are okay."

Gertrude stands and crosses to the door. Standing in front of the door without unlocking and opening it, she asks, "If it is Lucas, tell me what I should be reading?"

There is a soft laugh. "Thoreau, you should be reading Thoreau."

Gertrude opens the door. "Come in."

Lucas steps through the door and into the cottage. Gertrude shuts the door with a bang and bolts it.

"Are you okay?"

"Yes, I think I am," Gertrude says.

"Then can you put the knife away?"

Gertrude had forgotten that she was holding one of her largest kitchen knives. Quickly, she crosses to the hanging dresser and puts the knife down.

"Why are you here?" She turns and asks.

"Mrs. Schultz told me that you were catching the train back to Tybee Island and that she thought it was too late to go alone. So, I decided to get the train and make sure you arrived at the cottage safely. I arrived just as it was about to leave, so I boarded in the last car. I was not sure you would like it that I followed you, so I did not come through to let you know I was on the train too."

Gertrude is listening but also glancing out the windows.

She is pacing around the room with unspent energy. "Who was following me?"

"I didn't bother asking his name before he ran off."

"Did you assault him?"

"You mean, did I throw him up against the side of the cottage and threaten to tear his arms off? Yes, I did."

"What did he look like?"

"It is dark. He is tall and slender, wearing dark clothes and a floppy hat pulled over his face. I have no idea what he looks like."

Gertrude slows down. She stops and looks at Lucas. "Who would want to scare me so?"

Lucas moves toward her. "I don't know. All I know is he is gone for now." He moves even closer to her. "Are you going to be okay here in this cottage by yourself?"

Gertrude looks around at what has been her sanctuary, a place where she could heal and think, a peaceful place that is growing on her, one that is making her feel she belongs as she practices her music and sews the uniforms. And now there is an intruder in her life. Will she ever be safe?

"I am sure that whoever it was intended to just scare me. People drink on holidays. Probably a tipsy guy with nothing to do."

"Right, but I saw him following you from the train."

"From the depot?"

"Yes, that is why I did not turn around and leave with the train."

"Is there another train tonight?"

"No."

"My, my, we are in quite a pickle."

Lucas laughs again. "A pickle?"

"Yes, a difficult situation. I can't let you stay here in the cottage with me. What in the world would people say?"

"I get that, but do we have options? I really don't want to sleep on the porch with a lunatic running free."

"I thought you said the person was gone."

"Yes, but I could be wrong."

Gertrude doesn't know what to do. The entire event has startled her, and thinking logically has never been her strong point. The cottage is cold, so she goes to the fireplace to build a fire.

"Here, let me do that while you figure out our options." Lucas kneels and begins with the kindling and then the logs.

Gertrude's mind is still racing, rehashing the confrontation at her door. She needs to calm down. There is a hotel down the lane, but the expense might be too great for a reporter and she has no money. The logs are catching fire and soon the cottage will be warmer. A cup of tea would calm her a bit. Lucas pushes another log onto the flames.

"Okay, this might work. I have the keys to the big house. There are sleeping rooms upstairs. I know it is cold, but there are tons of quilts and a wood stove in the kitchen to warm up in the morning."

"Will anyone mind?"

"I am in charge of keeping the house clean. Captain, who is in charge of the groundskeeping, is the only other person with keys. Captain agreed for a piano tuner to stay in one of the sleeping rooms for a week, so it should be fine."

"How will I know how you are?" He steps closer to Gertrude.

Gertrude pauses before answering. "Some of the sleeping rooms upstairs in the big house face the same lane as the cottage door. You can see the kitchen window where I have herbs growing. I will put a lighted lantern on the shelf. If there is a problem, I will move the lantern."

Lucas now stands right in front of Gertrude. "If that is our only option, let's do it." He is close enough now to touch her. "But first, I would like a cup of tea."

"Right, you are. Let me get the kettle on." The kettle is pulled off the hook in the fireplace and is filled with water from the pitcher kept next to the sink.

Lucas looks about the room. "You have a working factory here, don't you?"

Glancing up at him as she hooks the kettle and moves it over the flames, Gertrude says, "Yes, I have to get the children's uniforms finished before March."

"Before March? I thought the children did not come to the camp until June?"

Stumbling over some material that has dropped on the floor, Gertrude quickly says, "But there are other things that need to be done before they arrive. Last-minute things like supplies for the house, kitchen, and infirmary. I need to work with the cook to plan the menus and get the house set up to receive the first children."

"I see." Lucas moves over to the kitchen table, where there are empty chairs. "May I sit here?"

'Yes, of course," says Gertrude and bustles about getting cups and saucers, sugar, and spoons. She takes tea out of the pantry and places everything on the table, then she sits down at the table across from Lucas. "I'm sorry that I have little to offer. I need to go foraging tomorrow."

"You live from day to day here, it seems," says Lucas.

"Indeed. I hesitate to tell you what I consume." Gertrude rearranges the teacup and spoon without looking up at Lucas. With his hat off, she notices that his brown hair is full and wavy on the top, combed back on the sides. The top-heavy hair gives his face a long look that matches his height. Most men wear their hair rather short and combed off the forehead. Lucas's hair could easily curl on his forehead if he did not wear a hat all the time. Gertrude thinks she would like to see it curl on his forehead. She focuses on the kettle, hoping the water is hot but knowing it has not had time to get hot over the fire.

Lucas, however, is focused on all the herbs on the windowsill. "You must be cooking a lot," he says. "Few kitchens have the variety of herbs to choose from as you do."

"It's all Eley. These are her ideas. Some of the herbs I have no idea how to use, so I just toss them into the pot to see what happens."

"We were taught from an early age how to pair herbs with foods," says Lucas. "Herbs can be sweet, savory, spicy, or bitter, and these flavors can complement or contrast with the flavors of foods."

Steam comes from the kettle. Gertrude stands to get the kettle off the hook. Measuring out the tea leaves into the kettle, she sets it aside on a trivet at the table for the tea to steep. She takes a big breath and says what has been on her mind. "Tell me what you thought you would accomplish by following me here?"

"Ah, I see you are skeptical of my intentions."

"Remind me as to what you do?"

"Do not let my job hinder any frank and honest discussions between us."

"On the contrary, there will be no frank and honest discussions between us that you can write about."

"I get that loud and clear." Lucas looks up at Gertrude. "My only intentions were to guarantee your safety and be able to report back to Mrs. Schultz that all is fine. How did I do?"

"Good. I think. The intruder left. Did he hurt you? I should have asked."

"A few punches and a body grab, but no, he did not hurt me."

Silence sits between them as they sip their tea. Gertrude thinks about how long it has been since she has sat with a man sipping tea and talking. Randolph did not drink tea. Maybe this is her first time besides her papa. She is aware that they are alone and that is not good for appearances. Hazel has already made it clear that she does not like Gertrude being pregnant without a husband around. Suddenly, Gertrude stands and gets her cloak. "We should head over to the big house and get you settled; it is getting late." There are three lanterns on the mantle. She lights them, puts one on the shelf with the herbs, and holds the other two, one for her and one for Lucas.

Lucas swallows the last of his tea, stands up, and takes the cup and saucer over to the sink. He meets Gertrude at the door. "As you say."

Gertrude hands a lantern to Lucas and locks the door behind them. Into the big house they go, remembering to lock the door behind them. "There is no electricity in the house," she says as she leads Lucas up the steps to the sleeping rooms on the second floor. She chooses the room facing the lane and looks out the window. "There," she says as she points across the lane. "I can see the lantern."

Lucas comes to stand beside her and looks out the window. "You are right, I can see it as well."

There are three single beds in the room. Gertrude removes the quilts from two of the beds and puts them on the bed nearest the window. "I think the window will make this bed colder, but it is the one where you can see out to the lane."

"Yes, I prefer to see out." He stands still, looking out the window. "This might solve tonight's problem, but what about other nights?"

"You are returning to Savannah," says Gertrude.

"Not me, how will you be?"

"I will be fine. Please do not worry."

Lucas turns to look at her closely. "I tend to worry about people I am getting to know."

Gertrude picks up her lantern. "I hope you will be warm enough. Captain keeps the bin full in the kitchen for the wood stove, should you want to get a bit warmer." She looks at him but then glances back at the bed. "I hope you are comfortable and will have a good night's sleep. The water closet is at the end of the hallway." She looks about, checking the room. "I must go."

"I'll walk back to the front door with you and you can lock me in."

Gertrude smiles. "That's right, I have the keys. However, you can open the French doors off the dining room to exit in an emergency without a key. The bolt is on the inside and cannot be locked from the outside."

"Good to know."

They walk side by side down the stairway to the front door. Gertrude passes through the front door, but before Lucas closes the door, he reaches out as if to touch her arm. He doesn't, though. Instead, he simply says, "Good night, Gertrude."

The way he says good night makes Gertrude feel as though he wants to say something more, but the night is dark and she needs to cross over to the cottage and get some rest. It has been a long day. "Good night, Lucas." At the cottage door, she turns and sees that he is standing at a window watching her. She goes in and bolts the door behind her.

34

———

The morning is overcast. Gertrude decides not to go on her morning walk. The kettle is heating over the fire. She chooses to make griddle cakes for breakfast like Sharon had made at the boarding house, and she takes the ingredients from the pantry and puts them on the shelf by the sink. The recipe seems simple enough: dump the cornmeal in a bowl, add salt, baking powder, an egg, and then water to make a batter. For flavor, she adds hickory nuts that she had shelled earlier. She puts a jar of beautyberry jam made with Eley's help on the table.

The baby has been active during the night and this morning. Gertrude has to stop and massage her stomach to lessen the movement. She hesitates when she hears the knock at the door and asks, "Who's there?"

"Thoreau," says Lucas through the door.

Gertrude opens the door quickly.

"I left through the French doors. If you trust me with the keys, I will return and lock those and lock the front."

"Thank you."

Even though Lucas will return shortly, Gertrude shuts the

door and bolts it. At the stove, she puts a little grease leftover from frying up some beef that Mingo brought into the skillet to heat. She sets the table with plates and cups and saucers for the tea. She adds some dried seaweed stored in a large crock with a cork lid to the table.

There is another knock on the door. As Gertrude waits, a voice on the other side says, "Thoreau, it's Thoreau." Lucas enters and knowingly puts the keys on the hook and closes and bolts the door.

Gertrude thinks he seems comfortable in the cottage. She has been comfortable in the cottage, but with the intruder from the night before, will she be comfortable again? Can she ever let her guard down? She moves over to the stove. "I am making griddle cakes. Sharon shared the recipe with the nurses on how to make these."

"Yes, I have had them. Mrs. Schultz served them with a stew once."

Pausing with the spatula in midair above the skillet, Gertrude has to remember that he knew Sharon better than he knows her. And that he had asked Sharon to marry him. Not that it matters anymore with Sharon being married to Connor, but she needs to remember that Lucas once cared for Sharon. *I shouldn't be concerned*, Gertrude thinks. Marriage is not in the books for her anymore. "I did not know that. These can't possibly be as good, but they may be warming on this overcast, November day."

Lucas crosses to the fireplace and adds a log to the fire. He rubs his hands together in front of the flames. He had left his coat on, but now he removes it and hangs it at the front door next to Gertrude's cloak. Watching Lucas out of the corner of her eye, Gertrude has to admit that it is nice that he is so at ease in her space and does not need to be entertained every minute. Randolph insisted on her attention when they were together, that is, until that last conversation.

Lucas returns to the fireplace and gets the kettle. He measures the tea leaves from the pantry and puts them into the kettle to steep.

Gertrude finishes frying the griddle cakes and places the platter on the table between them. Gesturing to Lucas, she says, "Please sit down and have something warm to fill your stomach."

Lucas smells the cakes as he sits and moves one of them to his plate. "What's in the griddle cakes?"

"Hickory nuts."

"Goodness, you are quite the forager." He puts several more cakes on his plate.

Gertrude passes him the jam. "I made beautyberry jam. Correction: I helped Eley make the jam after we picked the beautyberries."

Lucas looks at the jar and takes a spoonful to spread over one of the griddle cakes. Gertrude watches. He notices that she is looking at him and stops chewing midway. He looks down and continues to chew. She does not move. Finally, he finishes and swallows.

"The jam is spicy with just a hint of sweetness. It goes well with the nuts and cornmeal."

Gertrude smiles. "I'm happy you like it. Are you showing off your culinary knowledge?"

"Yes, ma'am. I know about food."

Lucas continues to eat and takes another griddle cake and another spoonful of jam.

There's a knock on the door. Gertrude freezes at the table. Lucas stands and looks out the window. "It's Captain."

Gertrude goes to the door and opens it. "Good morning, Captain."

"Good morning, Gertrude. I came by to see how you are and to see if you had a visitor last evening."

"I'm fine, and yes, there was a visitor last night who scared me."

"He scared Hazel as well. But I wanted to let you know that I found him hiding out in one of my boats this morning and have had the police take him to the military jail at the fort."

"Who is he?"

"Richard, the piano tuner we thought we got rid of."

"Oh, no. He came back?"

"Said he had some unfinished business. That may end my generosity in letting people stay in the big house," says Captain.

Lucas steps around in sight of Captain. Gertrude is silent. Lucas says, "Good morning, Captain. I met you last Sunday at the piano...practice."

"I remember you," says Captain. He looks away toward the sky as though unsure of what to say next. "Were you here when Richard came?" he asks.

Gertrude interrupts before Lucas can answer. "Captain, come in and have a cup of tea. There is more to the story."

Captain comes inside the cottage. Lucas gets the kettle from the fireplace and Gertrude puts another cup and saucer on the table. She moves some uniforms off a chair, but before she can move the chair, Lucas grabs it and places it at the table. "Please sit down," she says.

Removing his hat and putting it on the bench at the door, Captain crosses to the table and sits down. "So, what happened?"

"I was late yesterday leaving Mrs. Schultz's in Savannah after Thanksgiving dinner, but wanted to get back to the cottage," says Gertrude.

Lucas jumps into the explanation. "Unknown to Gertrude, I thought it was too late for her to return, so at Mrs. Schultz's suggestion, I followed her on the train to the Tybee Island depot. I had every intention to turn around and go back to Savannah once I saw that Gertrude was across the lane and onto the path to the cottage. However, I saw a male figure come out of the shadows and follow Gertrude."

"On the path to the cottage, I heard something," says Gertrude. "I thought it was an animal and kept walking. When I got to the cottage door and got inside, as I tried to shut the door, a foot became jammed between the door and the threshold. I could not see who it was. He didn't say anything."

"That's when I came up and slammed the guy up against the side of the cottage."

"I locked the door."

"There was a skirmish between us on the path, and he ran off. I did not see him clearly; it was dark."

"So, you stayed the night here in the cottage?" asks Captain.

"No, no," say Gertrude and Lucas at the same time.

"I slept upstairs in the big house and Gertrude stayed in the cottage," says Lucas.

"Since you agreed to let Richard stay in the big house, and the last train had left, I thought it would be fine," says Gertrude.

Captain looks at Gertrude and then at Lucas. "I need to rethink my hospitality," says Captain. He puts down his teacup. "Richard is being held at the fort and should not be a problem to you."

"What happens if they release him?" asks Gertrude.

"The commander told me that they would hold him overnight and then escort him to Savannah. If you file charges, they will hold him in Savannah for the judge to decide."

Lucas speaks up first. "She will file charges. He had every intent to harm by following her and attempting to push his way into the cottage. If I had not been here, I doubt if Gertrude could have held him off." He looks over at Gertrude. "Though she did have one big knife in front of her when she opened the door for me."

Gertrude looks away as Captain gives a little humph sound.

"I guess she could have handled it without us, but it was good that you were here, Lucas."

Gertrude looks at Lucas. "I think so, too."

Captain stands. "Thanks for the tea. I need to be off."

"So must I," says Lucas. "There is work for me in Savannah today. I'll get my coat and walk with you, Captain, as far as the depot. I think the first train of the day will arrive soon."

As the two men leave, Gertrude remains sitting at the table. Lucas looks back. "Are you okay, Gertrude?"

"I'm fine," she says, but she does not get up.

"Okay, I will see you Sunday," says Lucas, leaving with Captain.

After they leave, Gertrude stands, goes over to get her cloak, and exits the cottage, locking the door behind her. She needs a walk on the beach this morning. There is too much to think about. She needs the sound of the ocean to process all these new emotions. Fear has surfaced again.

35

Gertrude's walk on the beach on Sunday morning is slow. Over and over, her mind repeats the scenario of what happened with Richard, Lucas, and then Captain. Her solitude has been broken, or maybe she just fooled herself into thinking there was peace and solitude when her life has shown her that there is no peace for her. During her walk, her stomach feels bloated and her feet hurt, even though she is wearing the wader boots found in the shed. Eley would tell her to have some peppermint tea, but even though the leaves can be used fresh, she has no energy to make the tea.

Today, Gertrude smells everything: the salt in the air, the fetid water in the sand-logged pools left by the outgoing tide, the birds flying over her attempting to scare the human from their territory. She can actually smell their wet feathers. Shells on the beach do not interest her. They are fragile and will break and chip before returning to the cottage. The canvas bag was left behind. But of all the smells, the one she remembers the most is the smell of her fear last night when a foot kept her from closing the door. The smell of fear is familiar to her.

Gertrude first smelled fear after Randolph left and there

was no real job to sustain her. The second time was after the "whiskey man" accosted her first in the pub and then in the hotel room. The same smell, a musty smell, emerged when the "whiskey man" was seen in County Wexford. There was even a strong smell when Sister Mary Joyce told her she was pregnant and there was no safety net in place.

And now, Gertrude thinks that the security that Sister Mary Joyce and Mrs. Schultz have offered her with this caretaker's position has made her careless. A scuffle with Richard and a knife in the cottage may not have ended well. The baby in her womb could have been hurt or killed. Taking care of herself is one thing, but now she is taking care of another human being.

Her thoughts tumble about. Should she abandon her dreams and focus on staying safe? Her mother told her and her siblings each time they procrastinated or strayed from their task, "The longest road out is the shortest road home—effort and time will always pay off in the end." Gertrude decides she must do the job in front of her and stop trying to think that she could ever be a composer.

Gertrude walks slower and slower. Her feet drag in the sand. There is no bounce to her step. Long before the point where she usually turns to walk back to the cottage, she turns and retraces her steps.

She ignores the sea lettuce on the beach. Her eyes don't even look to see if there are fish caught in the shallows. No gear has been brought. She pays no attention to her hungry stomach. She is tired of always thinking about how to find food. Cooking is not fun; it is tedious and boring. She is not preserving food for the winter. She has no idea what to do. Maybe it would be best to go to her family. They will probably not talk to her once they discover her pregnancy, but they would never do anything to hurt her or the baby, so at least she would be able to eat and maybe feel safe again.

Gertrude returns to the cottage, goes inside, and sits at the table. There is no desire to sew and the piles of unfinished uniforms are dismissed. They can just remain unfinished. Her skirts are too tight. Sitting up and bending over are too difficult. At night, there is no position where she is comfortable sleeping. Most nights, she props up with pillows on the settee in front of the fire and naps. Why does it have to be so hard to be pregnant and alone?

Time is just time, and Gertrude does not even know where the time has gone. A knock at the door makes her shout, "Who is it?"

"Eley."

Gertrude pushes with her hands on the tabletop to stand up. She crosses to the door and opens it to find Eley holding a large basket at her side.

"I'm checking up on you. Usually by this time, you are in the big house and running scales. Ain't heard no sound so I come to see if you were all right."

"Fine. I'm fine. I just will not be playing today."

"I see," says Eley. "May I come in and leave a few things for you?"

Gertrude steps back to allow Eley entrance without saying anything to her. Eley bustles in and crosses to put the basket on the table, talking as she unpacks the contents. "Let's see, here are some jars of tomatoes, green beans, and corn. I found some sweet potatoes buried in the backyard that need to be used. And here's some dried beef. Mingo has just outdone himself in getting his huntin' done." Eley glances over at Gertrude, who is sitting back down at the table. "I know you say you ain't playing today, but you got to eat." She squints at Gertrude. "I think something more is bothering you, more than just not playin'."

Gertrude puts her head down on the table and is silent.

"I see. Well, if'n you don't want to talk about it and if'n you aren't going to play, who is gonna tell all those people out on the grass and porch that there is no music today?"

Gertrude raises her head. "What? People are back?"

"Yes'um, they are, lots more than before. News has been travelin' that there is a mighty fine pianist sharing her talents with those of us who can't play."

"I don't know that I can play the pieces I have been writing." Gertrude looks at her hands and flexes her fingers.

"Well, don't you know some tunes from heart? Play songs that will make these folks dance." Eley pauses and looks hard at Gertrude. "And then maybe your sadness will pass and you will feel better about yo'self."

Gertrude looks directly at Elay. "I'm a mess. Look at me."

"Folks aren't lookin' at you; they are listening to you." Eley has finished unloading the basket. "Just put your cloak on, cross over to the big house, and nobody will know you ain't fixed up, looking your best."

Gertrude looks at Eley in her mismatched shirt and blouse. One is striped and the other is gingham with a checkered scarf tied about her shoulders. She has worn leather shoes on her feet and a bandana that doesn't go with any of the other patterns, tied about her hair. Gertrude stands.

"My audience awaits," she says. She takes her cloak down, puts it on, and pulls the hood tight over her hair, which is a blonde mess from the salty ocean breeze. "Shall we?"

Eley sighs. "Yes, let's."

Together, they wend their way through the people on the porch, some of whom move and slide out of the way. All of them are looking at the blue cloak floating around a young woman's face as she hurries through the front door. She goes quickly into the dining room. "Will you open the French doors?" she asks Eley. "Folks might as well hear what I play."

As Eley opens the doors, Gertrude opens the kitchen door to find Captain, Michael, Frances, Mingo, and Lucas all having their tea. "Good day to you," she says. "I'm almost ready to play.

Thank you, Captain, for getting the fire going in the dining room."

"Wasn't me, it was Lucas. He said you might get cold with the door open and the breeze coming in."

Lucas looks over at Captain. "You tell her everything?"

Captain laughs. "As much as she will hear."

"By the way," says Captain as he turns to Lucas, "word came that Richard is wanted on several charges from Savannah to Charleston. The police have moved him to Savannah and will extradite him to Charleston when the Savannah courts are finished with him. Gertrude does not have to file any additional charges against him. He will be out of the area for a long time."

"That's great news!" says Lucas, looking at Gertrude still standing in the doorway.

Gertrude is silent and returns to the dining room. She takes off her cloak, prepares the piano, sits down to play, and pauses before hitting the first note. She remembers playing her recital piece as a warm-up at the pub in Galway. Brahms Rhapsody Op. 119 No. 4 is the piece she now plays.

Outside, the audience applauds when Gertrude finishes. They no longer have to be silent because she knows that they are eavesdropping on her playing. She plays a list of tunes that the band played in the pub next. These tunes are all known by heart. She can play them in her sleep—"The Dawning of the Day," "Down by the Salley Gardens," "Mursheen Durkin," "O'er the Mountain," "The Ferryman," "The Foggy Dew," "The Galway Shawl," "The Last Rose of Summer," "The Moorelough Shore," "Siúil A Rúin (Walk, My Love)," "She Moved Through the Fair," and "Cliffs of Dooneen." Gertrude ends the list with a children's song, "Too-Ra-Loo-Ra-Loo-Ra!"

Finishing softly and then listening to the applause from the people outside, Gertrude does not see the kitchen friends open the door and come into the dining room to applaud. The movement at the door makes her turn to look. They are standing as a group, smiling broadly. Her bow to the group is only with her head. She has no energy to stand and give a formal bow.

Lucas is the first to speak. "This has been fabulous, Gertrude."

Gertrude looks down at her hands. "Another practice over."

The French doors are closed and locked, and the kitchen friends disperse, all but Lucas. As they are cleaning up the kitchen, Lucas is making small conversation, but then suddenly he says, "I learned at Thanksgiving that you come into Savannah at the first of every month."

Gertrude does not look at him; she keeps cleaning.

"Is that so?" he asks.

"Yes, I do come in. There are a few errands I must do." She still does not look at Lucas.

"Why the regularity?" he pursues.

Gertrude stops washing the cups and saucers. "Why do you ask?"

Lucas puts another log in the wood stove and moves the kettle over to the top. "I am a reporter, I ask questions."

"You promised not to write about me."

"And I will keep my promise until you say I can. If I have learned anything from my friendship with Sharon, it is to respect an independent woman."

Gertrude dries the cups and saucers and puts them in the pantry.

Lucas stops her. "Please, let's talk. Have a cup of tea with me."

She looks at him and places two cups and saucers back on the table, then sits down.

Lucas gets the kettle from the stove where the tea has been steeping. He pours the tea into their cups. "So, this is what I know. You live in a cottage to take care of the Fresh Air Home. You sew uniforms for money. You forage for food among the meadows and the seaside. You go into Savannah, where you have a monthly meeting with Sister Mary Joyce." He pauses and looks at Gertrude. "So far, how accurate am I?"

Gertrude nods. "Very."

He takes a sip of tea, then continues. "You are a beautiful young woman with a musical talent. You are offered a scholarship to Brenau to study, but you leave and do not finish. It is a two-year program, and you have only been gone from Savannah for eight months." He stops and takes another sip.

Gertrude does not lift her cup. She remains sitting and just looks at Lucas.

"Then you complain about your feet hurting. You eat little. At breakfast the other morning, I had three griddle cakes and you did not completely finish one, yet your waistline is snug and your face is full."

She sits up a little straighter in her chair.

"The sisters and Mrs. Schultz have found you this hideaway. Not ideal, but convenient and doable. So, I ask myself, why would a young woman with such beauty and talent, live alone on an island during the winter and have to take care of herself?"

Gertrude stands up and crosses to the window. She looks out over the side yard where the garden has been. The soil has not been prepared for the spring planting. Gertrude feels that she needs to get that done. Lucas is silent behind her at the table. Turning to face him, she says, "I had no idea that what I did was of interest to anyone."

"It is to me. Why not tell me the whole story and realize that I, too, can keep the same secrets that Sister Mary Joyce and Mrs. Schultz are keeping?"

Gertrude sits back down across the table from Lucas. "You want to know what has brought me here to Tybee? Okay, I will tell you. I'm pregnant."

36

Telling the entire story to Lucas takes time. Late in the afternoon, after numerous cups of tea, Gertrude finishes. Lucas asks questions along the way, like what happened to the "whiskey man," and what are her feelings now toward Randolph.

"The 'whiskey man' is in Ireland, and that is where I hope he will stay. As to Randolph, I despise him for what he did to me, yet I understand that I allowed myself to be caught up in his flattery and indulgence until it was too late. I take responsibility for what I did, for all the mistakes I have made."

Lucas looks deep into his teacup. "What would you have done differently?"

Gertrude thinks a moment, looking around the kitchen. "I think I would have finished the nursing program here. I only had one semester left, and then I would have gone to Brenau for music. My family would have been more supportive, and I would have had a skill to provide for myself."

"Is that what you want? To be able to take care of yourself?"

"Actually, I want to play and create music."

"So, staying in the music program would help your long-term goals?"

"Exactly. There, I learned about women composers and their difficulties in writing their own music. Even with those difficulties, they have inspired me."

"Help me understand," says Lucas. "You have the time and place to play music and compose here at the Home, so why are you so sad? It seems that the accommodations are good, you are learning how to forage and take care of yourself, and you are getting the medical attention you need. Why is this not working?"

Gertrude stands again but paces about the room this time, "I have been thinking, especially at Thanksgiving, when Sister Mary Joyce talked about gratitude. I am so angry at myself for being duped. I cannot forgive myself for wanting more than I should have out of life. I come from poor Irish roots and had an opportunity to be a nurse. I should be thankful for that, and I wasn't." She stops. "I can only be thankful that I have Sister Mary Joyce and Mrs. Schultz for finding a way to help me survive and to give me time to figure out what the next step might be."

Lucas is silent. Gertrude gives him a strong look, but he is looking down at his hands. The silence extends beyond Gertrude's comfort level. She has grown accustomed to having Lucas around, but now that he knows the truth, what man would stay friends with a woman like her? When Gertrude moves to pick up the cups and saucers from the table and reaches over to take the one in front of Lucas, he extends his hand and holds on to hers.

"Sit, please. There is no hurry to end our conversation. What might be your next step?"

"I take things one day at a time. I have no next step. I always wanted to play music. I never wanted a family, yet here I am pregnant with no husband. There are no next steps in store for me."

"What about your family? Won't they rally around you if you are honest with them?"

"Does yours? Why did you leave France and your family if they were there for you? Were you not honest with them?"

Lucas looks up directly at Gertrude. "That's unfair. You do not know my family."

"Neither do you know mine," Gertrude says. They seem to have reached an impasse. "Aren't you returning to Savannah?"

"I can. There is a late train. We can take a walk on the beach, I know you walk daily and then have dinner."

"Who's cooking?"

"I am," says Lucas.

Gertrude is stunned. "Okay," is all she can manage to say.

They lock up the big house and cross the walkway to the beach. In the twilight, the birds are still sweeping down and hunting for food. Gulls are corralled in large groups within the dunes for the night. The sun is spreading color over the land and the moon has not yet appeared. Iridescent streaks in the tidal waters indicate evidence of oil on the sand. Ocean wave foam is whiter than white, with the water turning a dark indigo behind the foam. Gertrude does not usually venture out on the beach this late in the day and has not seen the deep color changes in the water.

Lucas is silent, which makes it difficult for Gertrude to sort out what he might be thinking. She notices that he usually chatters and gives information, but as they walk down the beach, he is quiet. She looks up at the sky and sees the moon coming up on the horizon. It is a full moon.

"My bandmate in Ireland grew up around gardening with his family, and he knew all the moon cycles and names of the full moons." She glances at Lucas, who looks over where the moon is coming up.

As they both pause to look at the moon, Lucas says, "I wrote an article about how the Euchee natives who lived on Tybee named the moons. The November full moon is called 'Nudadaequa,' the Trading Moon. This was a time to trade and barter. At this time, they also had a Friendship Festival (Ado-huna—new friends made). This festival was when the natives recalled a time before world selfishness and greed; this was a time when all transgressions were forgiven, except for murder. It was also a time when help was given to the needy to help them through the lean winter months."

Gertrude looks at the moon. "All of that makes sense. It is why we should have a Thanksgiving and a season of gratitude and sharing food with others at this time of year."

"Yes, some of the American customs are from the natives, who lived here long before others moved in and took over."

Gertrude could almost see Lucas sitting at a desk as he labored over his article. His memory of these facts made her want to read more and learn about other customs that may be part of the native history. She thinks of Eley and her Gullah heritage. Gertrude has learned about the various foods and ways of gathering food, but there is much more to culture than just food, like when Frances shared the song "Amazing Grace," and then Eley shared another song from her culture, "Lift Every Voice and Sing," one Gertrude had never heard. She asked Mrs. Schultz about the song. Mrs. Schultz did not know, so they sent a note to Mrs. Lynch and found out that it had been written as a poem in 1900 by James Weldon Johnson.

Gertrude stops walking. "It's getting dark, we should turn back." At the cottage, Lucas takes over building a fire. He goes out to the bin and brings in another load of wood. Gertrude watches him out of the corner of her eye as she pulls together various items to begin making dinner for them. She has more venison that Eley has left for her. She has some of the root vegetables that she can put in a pot to make a venison stew. She can make cornbread. When Lucas comes back into the cottage after filling the wood box, Gertrude nods to the items on the counter.

"How about venison stew?"

"Sounds great. I can do that."

"What herbs would you use?" asks Gertrude.

"Thyme, rosemary, and sage."

Gertrude volunteers. "I'll scrape some palmetto roots and cut them up."

They begin working in the kitchen area, with Lucas preparing the venison. He slices the meat and then sears it in a skillet just like Eley taught Gertrude. When the water is hot in the pot on the stove, Lucas adds the meat and takes the vegetables from Gertrude and adds them. Then he snips off the herbs from the windowsill garden and adds them to the pot. Gertrude puts the lid over it all.

"Now we can sit and rest in front of the fire," says Lucas.

"No rest, I need to sew." She moves over to the settee and settles in with the garments that need to be pinned in order to sew on the machine.

Lucas goes over to his jacket and pulls out a small volume from his pocket. He crosses over to the chair nearest the fire to sit. "When I was at Mrs. Schultz's, I saw a copy of Thoreau's *Walden* on a shelf over the writing desk in the parlor. I borrowed it and have it with me. Would you like to hear some of it while you work? A conversation may interrupt your work, but a reading might be soothing."

"You surprise me. Yes, I would love for someone to read to me. It will make the work go faster."

Lucas settles in the chair and positions his body so that the light from the fireplace helps him see the words on the page.

"I was seated by the shore of a small pond, about a mile and a half south of the village of Concord and somewhat higher than it, in the midst of an extensive wood between that town and known to fame, Concord Battle Ground; but I was so low in the woods that the opposite shore, half a mile off, like the rest, covered with wood, was my most distant horizon. For the first week, whenever I looked out on the pond it impressed me like a tarn high up on the side of a mountain, its bottom far above the surface of other lakes, and, as the sun arose, I saw it throwing off its nightly clothing of mist, and here and there by degrees, while the mists, like ghosts, were stealthily withdrawing in every direction into the woods, as at the breaking up of some nocturnal conventicler. The very dew seemed to hang upon the trees later into the day than usual, as on the sides of mountains..."

Gertrude prepares to stand. Lucas pauses his reading. Gertrude is aware that he is watching her and tries hard to shield how difficult it is to get up off the settee. At least now that he knows about her pregnancy, there is no need to try to hide it. She pushes with her hands on the seat and stands, crosses to the stove, and stirs the stew. On her return, she looks at Lucas. "I'm fine, it is just more and more difficult to move with this baby growing inside of me."

Lucas nods and looks down at the book.

"I went to the woods because I wished to live deliberately, to front only the essential facts of life, and see if I could not learn what it had to teach, and not, when I came to die, discover that I had not lived. I did not wish to live what was no life, living is so dear; nor did I wish to practice resignation, unless it was quite necessary. I wanted to live deep and suck out all the marrow of life, to live so sturdily and Spartan-like as to put to rout all that was not life, to cut a broad swath and shave close, to drive life into a corner, and reduce it to its lowest terms, and, if it proved to be mean, why then to get the whole and genuine meanness of it, and publish its meanness to the world; or if it were sublime, to know it by experience, and be able to give a true account of it in my next excursion."

As Gertrude pieces together the uniforms, Lucas reads. Gertrude listens and begins to make comparisons between her location near the beach and Thoreau's near a pond. The beach does change with the wind, birds, and smells. Tybee Island is a different kind of place than Savannah, where she grew up. After being on the island for a while now, Gertrude can distinguish various bird cries, how the weather may be changing from storms out at sea, and how the temperature varies with the sun rising and setting.

However, in the next part of Thoreau's description, Gertrude cannot compare his life in the woods with her life on the island. Thoreau chose isolation. Gertrude only had this one choice: survival and hope for a future. She did not choose to reduce her life to its lowest terms, to have to forage for food, and to learn so many things about her body during pregnancy. None of that was her choice.

After several trips to stir the stew, Gertrude begins to make the cornbread. Lucas pauses and marks the section in the book with a scrap of cloth he found on the chair. Gertrude is aware that he is coming over to the shelf where she is preparing the cornbread to put in the oven.

"Would you like a cup of tea?" he asks.

"That would be lovely."

He moves two cups and saucers from the hanging dresser, gets the kettle from the fireplace, and measures out the tea from the canister where Gertrude keeps it in the pantry. Gertrude observes all that he does. She watches everything even as she prepares the cornbread and stirs the stew. She sees that he knows where everything is. He does not have to ask where the tea canister is, or the pot holder to lift the kettle. His confidence and relaxed nature are soothing to Gertrude. They can be silent and yet still work together in the same room. She never had that feeling with Randolph. He sat and she provided. He asked and she delivered. He got recognized and she was shoved into a corner.

During her growing up years, she never dreamed about getting married. Even when asked, she would say quickly that with practicing the piano and studying to be a nurse, there is no time to think about marriage. And being the fool that she has been with running off with Randolph, her chances of marrying someone like Lucas, who has a job and is secure in what he wants out of life, are nil to none. Her limited choices in life lead her back to the present. She has to survive and get comfortable with being alone for the rest of her life.

Lucas sits at the table and stirs his tea. "I'm getting used to drinking tea. In France, we drank coffee or wine, never tea. But I seem to find myself hanging out with the Irish, and tea is the only beverage I am ever offered."

Gertrude closes the oven door after putting in the cornbread. "Why should there be choices when tea is as good as it gets? Drinking tea is a sacred daily ritual. You scoff, but I do not see you turning away from a good cup of tea." When Lucas smiles, Gertrude notices that his cheeks fill out and make his narrow face fuller. She sits across from him and sips her tea. "Yes, no choice is needed; this is as good as it gets."

"How are you liking Thoreau?"

She pauses with the cup near her lips. "The writing makes me think. I can compare his vision of the woods and pond with mine of the beach and dunes."

"But what about his reasoning for living in solitude?"

"I have thought about that as well. Many of the moments I have lived in solitude have made me feel lonely. My choice was never to sequester myself away from humanity to find myself."

"That's what you think? That solitude is not for you?"

"That's not what I mean. I have found that living alone and having to figure out everything, from how to stay warm, what to eat, and how to earn money, is exhausting and takes away from the energy I want to give to playing the piano and composing." She stands and gets the bowls from the hanging dresser and spoons to set the table. "I had been very despondent over the situation until I found a routine that permitted me to do it all."

"A routine? How so?"

"I walk on the beach in the morning after building up the fire and heating water for tea. On the walk, I forage for sea lettuce, crabs, mussels, or berries to add to the larder. Then I return to the big house to cut out fabric, give Michael a piano lesson, check the house, handle the mail, and listen to Michael practice at odd times during the morning when he has a chance to drop in. I return to the cottage for lunch, leftover soup or nuts and berries, and of course a cup of tea."

"Of course."

"After a nap—sorry, I must have one during the day now. I am not sleeping well and I get so tired. Then I sew pieces I have pinned together on the Singer. If the day is clear, I go to the meadow to see what I can find. Late in the afternoon, I go for another walk on the beach. Sometimes on this walk, depending on the tides, I take a small canvas bag to collect shells I might see. I come back and cook something for dinner, whatever Michael has left me or Eley brings or I have foraged in the meadow or on the shoreline. Then in the evening in front of the fire, I hand-sew any of the uniforms I have made."

"That's why the cottage looks like a factory assembly line."

"Yes, it works for me. Everything has a place and I don't have to rummage around looking for what I need. Mrs. Schultz provided me with a basket full of pins, needles, thread, scissors, and measures. More than enough to keep items at the stations, so when I can work on the uniforms, I don't waste time."

"When do you practice?"

"Ah, that's the problem. By the time I do all of these things, there is no time. I am exhausted from the day, I have interruptions, and I need to go into Savannah for my check-up, on and on and on. That's why I practice on Sunday afternoons. That is my day to play."

"I understand better now," says Lucas. He drinks more of his tea. "But why is it necessary that you go into Savannah monthly for medical checkups with Sister Mary Joyce? Is there something wrong with the pregnancy? Or do you have a medical condition you haven't shared yet?"

Gertrude raises her head and looks at Lucas. Without answering, she stands and goes to the stove to remove the cornbread. The potholders shake as she reaches into the stove and grabs the pan. She leaves the pan on the stovetop next to the stew pot. Lucas is waiting for her to answer. Finally, she turns and faces him. "I have to go in for medical checkups so that Sister Mary Joyce can verify that I have had a healthy pregnancy and have done all I could to have a healthy baby so that she can be adopted."

Lucas's face is stoic. There is no expression that Gertrude can read. She reaches for the bowls.

"Sit down, Gertrude," says Lucas. "I'll serve the stew." He stands and moves toward the stove. Gertrude does not sit. "Seriously, I can do this," Lucas repeats.

Gertrude sits down and takes a large swallow of tea. Her legs hurt. Her back hurts. Sitting down is good.

As Lucas puts the stew in front of her, he puts a pot holder on the table and moves the cornbread between them. "We can be informal, can't we?"

Gertrude smiles, a tired smile, but a smile nevertheless.

After dinner, Lucas insists that Gertrude sit down to rest, and he cleans up the dishes and puts the stew away in the icebox with the leftover cornbread. Then he sits and reads more Thoreau to her. After a short while, Gertrude finds it hard to keep her eyes open. She cannot concentrate on what Lucas has been reading.

"Isn't it time for the late train back to Savannah?" she asks.

Lucas closes the book. "I thought I might stay over in the big house again."

No words come immediately to Gertrude. She is tired and simply nods. "I suggest then that we go over and get you settled." Gertrude puts her sewing away on the chair next to the settee and pushes to stand up. "I'll walk over with you." She can barely stand on her swollen feet.

"If you trust me, I can take the keys and return them in the morning. Just bolt the door to the cottage when I leave and put the lantern on the herb shelf."

"But Richard is in jail. There is no one to threaten me now."

"I know, but I would like to know you are safe by seeing the lantern in the window." He crosses to the door and gets his jacket and the ring of keys. "Goodnight, Gertrude. I hope you sleep better tonight."

With that, Lucas is out the door. Gertrude bolts the door, lights the lantern, and places it on the shelf. All is well, it says, all is well, but Gertrude is not so sure.

37

Gertrude does not sleep well. In a dream, she is asked over and over again, "What have you done with your baby?" The baby is missing, gone. Different people ask her: her mother, her father, her sisters, the nuns at the hospital, the nurses, Sister Mary Joyce, Mrs. Schultz, and then Randolph! She is shoved from one person to another with each asking her, and when all the rounds have been made and the question asked, it starts all over again, ending each time with Randolph.

Gertrude awakes at two in the morning in a sweat. Still on the settee in front of the fireplace, where the fire is just embers, she tosses off the quilt and pushes up to stand. Never having made it to the bedroom after Lucas left, her dress is wrinkled. She goes to the sink. A glass of water calms her down a bit. She looks out the window and up to where Lucas should be sleeping. There is a soft lantern light in the room, evidence that he is still here. It was only a dream. She takes a deep breath.

In the bedroom, the tight clothes come off with relief. In a fresh nightgown, Gertrude balances carefully on the side of the bed, then haphazardly pulls a quilt over her and falls asleep. A solid knock on the front door gets her eyes open. There is light in the sky. She puts on a robe and goes to the door. "Yes, who's there?"

"It's me," says Lucas.

Gertrude unbolts the door. Lucas hands her the key ring. "I knocked softly, but you didn't come, so I knocked harder. I hope you got some sleep. I cannot come in; I must go to catch the train."

"Yes," says Gertrude, "I did sleep."

"Have a good week, and I hope to see you on Sunday."

"Yes, until Sunday."

With that, Lucas turns, puts his hat firmly on his head, and walks quickly toward the lane and the train depot. Gertrude closes and locks the door. She must begin her routine.

December has been busy and the weeks before Christmas go by quickly. Gertrude gets a telegram from Mrs. Schultz asking about her plans for Christmas. It mentions that her mother had dropped by the boarding house and asked about any news. The telegram prompts Gertrude to list the things she should do. First, Mrs. Schultz needs to know that she does not plan to come for Christmas. Second, her mother needs to be contacted, but how should she do that? Through Mrs. Schultz? Through a telegram? Should her mother see her now, the pregnant daughter with no husband, Christmas would be ruined and so would Gertrude. She is not ready to deal with any family dissent, so avoiding the family and maybe even Mrs. Schultz might be the way to go.

On the Monday morning before Christmas, Gertrude knows she must contact Mrs. Schultz. She has no gifts to share, no money to buy gifts, and no time to make anything. Her sewing and her physical discomfort have limited what she can do. In fact, she has even stopped foraging; it is too much to bend over or even kneel. Lucas has missed several Sundays and not sent word as to what might have happened. Her honesty with him has cost her his friendship, she is sure. She should keep her plans for the adoption to herself.

She sends Mrs. Schultz a telegram.

Thank you for the Christmas invitation. I am staying on Tybee Island to finish the uniforms. Please tell my mother if she should ask. Have a merry Christmas. I will see you when I visit in January.

Gertrude

On her way back to the cottage after posting the telegram, she sees Captain.

"Captain," she calls out. He stops and walks toward her. "I will not be practicing again on Sunday. Can you get word to the others?"

"Yes, but are you okay?"

"I'm fine. I just have a lot to do before the end of the year, and I am moving at a much slower pace."

Captain continues to look at Gertrude, which makes her feel uncomfortable. She looks toward the big house. "I need to get some chores finished. Thank you." She turns to go to the cottage.

"If you need anything, let me know."

Gertrude waves her hand over her shoulder as she continues to walk. Back in the cottage, she does not continue the sewing. She does not plan any meals. She has no desire to do any of the chores that should be done. All she wants to do is sit and do nothing. When she puts another log on the fire to take the chill out of the room, she sees *Walden* on the mantle. The book has been there for weeks. She picks it up and sits down on the settee with a quilt over her lap. She is tired but begins to read. All day, her routine changes to reading, napping, waking up to drink some water, then reading some more.

I left the woods for as good a reason as I went there. Perhaps it seemed to me that I had several more lives to live, and could not spare any more time for that one. It is remarkable how easily and insensibly we fall into a particular route, and make a beaten track for ourselves. I had not lived there a week before my feet wore a path from my door to the pond-side; and though it is five or six years since I trod it, it is still quite distinct. It is true, I fear that others may have fallen into it, and so helped to keep it open. The surface of the earth is soft and impressible by the feet of men; and so with the paths which the mind travels. How worn and dusty, then, must be the highways of the world, how deep the ruts of tradition and conformity!

Gertrude has to read the last passage several times. Her established routine, the walks on the beach, and the path to the meadow to forage are all there in her mind. Yet, that is not what Thoreau is talking about when he writes this section. He is not talking about the actual footpath he has worn, though he describes it. Gertrude thinks he is talking about the ruts created in life without experiencing new places, new ideas, and new ways, doing the same thing because that is what is expected, even when it is not the best idea. She is here, alone in a cottage with no future in sight because of these ruts, biding time and trying to survive and hide from those society eyes that keep the ruts in place.

Why does she feel that way? Because she told Randolph that they had to be married in order for her to go with him to Dublin. That rut is a custom of her time and society. Unmarried women do not travel to foreign cities with men who are not their kin or husband. Being a dutiful wife is another tradition she accepted, and it is exactly why she is pregnant now. It was not a traditional marriage of having family and friends come to church and witness the ceremony performed by a priest. It was a civil service that was not even official. In her mind, she was offered a chance to reach her goal of playing the piano professionally and composing music. She took it because of what she had been taught to believe: women need help. Thus, the reason for her despair and depression. There is no hope now for her to live a life of creativity.

Gertrude's guilt about her choices makes her sit silently with her head in her hands. Her body sags on the settee. The weight of all she has been through is now resting on her back, which aches. Her tears slide quietly down her cheeks. A droplet falls onto the page of the open book. Realizing that Mrs. Schultz's book may be damaged, she wipes off the page and clears her eyes to read another passage.

I did not wish to take a cabin passage, but rather to go before the mast and on the deck of the world, for there I could best see the moonlight amid the mountains. I do not wish to go below now. I learned this, at least, by my experiment; that if one advances confidently in the direction of his dreams, and endeavors to live the life which he has imagined, he will meet with a success unexpected in common hours.

Gertrude has to think about this paragraph. This is what she has learned. Women composers have managed to find ways to create their music in spite of society's restrictions. The few who rose to the challenge are remembered. This offers Gertrude a glimmer of hope that she can create her own music, too. However, Clara Schumann's lament about who was she to think that she could compose anything interrupts Gertrude's line of thought. So few women, women who might have been talented and gifted, have had the opportunities to pursue their dreams. Gertrude feels she is one of those women who will never be able to pursue her dream. Like Thoreau, she wishes to live a life that is imagined.

Guilt stops Gertrude's thinking. She feels that there is nothing wrong with wanting to be a professional pianist or to write music. Her guilt comes from how she has handled her desires and dreams. She has lied to family and friends, pushed Randolph into doing something he should not have done, and now hides the part of her that is growing and thriving inside of her. There is a difference between how Thoreau viewed his circumstances and how she can view hers. Thoreau may have had confidence that he could change his world, but she does not. Her world is created by others, not by her. She continues to read.

He will put some things behind, will pass an invisible boundary; new, universal, and more liberal laws will begin to establish themselves around and within him; or the old laws be expanded, and interpreted in his favor in a more liberal sense, and he will live with the license of a higher order of beings. In proportion as he simplifies his life, the laws of the universe will appear less complex, and solitude will not be solitude, nor poverty poverty, nor weakness weakness. If you have built castles in the air, your work need not be lost; that is where they should be. Now put the foundations under them...

Gertrude lifts her head at the end of the last passage. She may not be able to change her circumstances, but she can change how she feels about them. The part that really resonates with her is: "If you have built castles in the air, your work need not be lost; that is where they should be. Now put the foundations under them..."

New thoughts enter her head. Should composing be a goal? Is playing the music that is coming out of her connected to being on an island and paying attention to the natural surroundings? Is that why she must forage and walk on the beach and cook, so that she can learn? If her dreams of playing and composing are to come true, how can she put foundations under these dreams? Her thoughts pause. On the other hand, should the fact that her dreams are not based on reality mean that those dreams need to be changed if anything is to come true? Why can't she accept the fact that she can teach piano and play for friends? Perhaps she should not dream at all. *Walden* is put back on the mantel.

38

———————

On Christmas Eve, Gertrude is alone in the cottage. She has not walked in several days. Michael has left some seaweed and fish for her. She makes a fish stew. No foraging, too tired. Her sleeping has turned into naps on the settee. Christmas Day is spent napping and looking out the cottage windows, wandering from one window to another and languishing there for a while, not really thinking, just standing and looking out at the trees yet not seeing them. There is a warming spell on the island. It would be a good time to take a walk, but instead, she naps.

Two telegrams are left under the door: one from Mrs. Schultz, the other from Sharon. Both wish her a merry Christmas.

The days tumble over each other and she cannot seem to separate one from the other. It's New Year's Eve, and Gertrude is again alone in the cottage.

There is a knock at the door. "Who's there?"

"Eley."

Gertrude opens the door.

"I know you have nothin' going on. You never have nothin' going on. So get your cloak and come with me."

"Eley, I do not feel like traipsing across the island tonight."

"You won't feel any better if you stay here, and at least you'll be around some other folks."

"I really don't want to go out. It will be dark soon and the..."

Eley interrupts. "Have you eaten anything today?"

"Yes, probably, I don't remember," says Gertrude.

"Then that's another reason to come. Get dressed. You're still in your nightgown. We'll get there before dark."

A part of Gertrude wants to be more excited about having something to take her mind off all that has been crowding her brain. Eley is standing with her hands on her hips, waiting for Gertrude to make a decision to come.

"Well, let's go," Eley commands.

Gertrude sees that Eley will not stop until she gets dressed. She changes, dons her cloak, and locks the cottage door.

The two women walk at a slower pace than normal. Gertrude is considerably slower and Eley adjusts her pace to match. No one talks; they just walk. Just as the sun is going down and the color is in the sky, they reach the praise house where Gertrude had found sanctuary on that day she got separated from Hazel and Captain. Inside the praise house are more people than before. There are families with children and elders. As Gertrude and Eley enter, Gertrude is greeted as though these people have known her their entire lives. Not long after they arrive, people begin to form a circle. Eley gets a chair and places it in one corner of the room.

"What is going on?" asks Gertrude.

"We're going to have a ring shout, so you might want to just sit here and watch."

"Why are all these people here? Do they all live on the island?"

"No, some are visitin' kin folks; others live nearby. Tonight is 'watch night,' a tradition that started a long, long time ago, back during the Civil War. It was often called 'Freedom's Eve' because that's when we Black folks come together in our praise houses, churches, and cabins in the masters' lands waiting to hear that the Emancipation Proclamation actually became law. And on the stroke of midnight, January 1, 1863, the enslaved people of the Confederate States were legally free. Everybody prayed, shouted, sang, and fell to their knees thanking God. We remember that day and gather on New Year's Eve to celebrate."

Eley stops talking and moves in to join the circle when two of the deacons step to the front of the praise house. One of the deacons starts, "Who wants to raise a hymn?" Mingo begins singing in a rich bass voice.

"Go down, Moses
Way down in Egypt land
Tell old Pharaoh
To let my people go!
Oh, when Israel was in Egypt land"
The people in the circle join him by singing, "Let my people go!"

Mingo sings, "Oppressed so hard, they could not stand."

The people shift from side to side and sing, "Let my people go!"

Many verses are sung with clapping and singing with Mingo. Gertrude listens and hears the richness of the language and the feelings behind the song lyrics. There are no hymnals or musical instruments. When that song is finished, another songster begins. The call and response continue.

Then a songster begins "Walk, Believer, Walk." A stickman sitting in a chair in the front of the praise house next to the songster starts to beat a simple rhythm on the floor with an upside-down broomstick. The people standing in the circle add to the rhythm with hand clapping and foot tapping and follow the direction of the songster. Slowly, they move in a counter-clockwise direction. The feet shuffle on the floor with the heels down and the back foot close to but never passing the lead foot.

The songster says, "Walk, believer, walk."

And the people answer, "Daniel."

"Walk, I tell you, walk."

"Daniel."

"Walk, I tell you, walk."

"Daniel."

The tempo increases and the songster says, "Shout, believer, shout!"

The circle continues using the shuffle step. "Daniel."

"Shout, believer, shout."

"Daniel."

"On the eagle wing."

As the people respond with "Daniel," they bend their arms at the elbows and flap slightly by rotating the shoulder joints in a parallel motion.

"On the eagle wing," says the songster.

"Daniel," respond the people.

"Fly, I tell you, fly."

"Daniel," and the people add a flying motion. Arms stretch out at full length and are held stiffly in a sailing motion. The right arm goes up and the left arm goes down in the same axis. The dancer does not flap; the dancer soars.

"Rock, I tell you, rock."

"Daniel," and the people do a shuffling step with a rocking motion.

"Fly the other way."

"Daniel," and the circle reverses to clockwise direction.

"Fly back home."

"Daniel," and the circle breaks and people scatter about the praise house. It is the end of that shout.

There are many shouts, other hymns are sung, and testimonials are given as various members of the praise house share their prayers. One man says, "This new year, I want to double my corn field." Another says, "I want to listen more to my head and not my stomach." People laugh because the man saying it has to use suspenders to hold up his pants since his girth is too large to wear a belt comfortably. A woman speaks up, "In this new year, I want to learn how to knit." People murmur and agree that this is a good thing to aspire to.

Toward midnight, the candles are snuffed out and two lanterns are lit. Eley leans over to Gertrude, "The senior deacon is the callman and the other deacon is the watchman."

The people in the praise house get down on their knees. Eley assures Gertrude that she can sit in the chair and be just fine. Gertrude notices that the elders sit in chairs, too, as well as some of the children who are too young to know what kneeling is all about. The watchman goes to the door and opens it slightly. He holds a clock and a lantern.

The callman sings out, "Watchman, watchman, what time is it?"

The watchman looks at the clock. "Five minutes to midnight."

The men repeat this call and response until midnight, when the watchman is asked what time it is. He responds, "It is after the hour of twelve; all is well. Thank God almighty!"

Everyone in the praise house stands and hugs each other. Some begin singing praise songs, others shout. The door is kept wide open and candles are relit. People move out into the yard where a bonfire is blazing. Tables are set up outside with coffee, hot cakes, and other food.

Eley guides Gertrude outside and has Mingo bring out some chairs so they can sit fairly close to the fire to stay warm. Eley goes and puts Hoppin' John and some hot cakes on a plate for Gertrude. When she brings it back, she tells Gertrude, "Eat all of this rice with black eyed peas, we call Hoppin' John, but leave three peas on your plate. I know you're hungry and I piled a pretty big heap on the plate for you, but you gotta leave three peas."

Looking down at the plate, Gertrude shakes her head a bit. "Why three peas?"

"One is for luck, one for fortune, and the other for romance. It goes way back to Africa and is a symbol of good luck."

"Thank you," she tells Eley. "I have not eaten much today."

"Thought so," says Eley. "There's more on the table, don't be bashful."

39

There is a lot of singing and talking, with people dancing and moving about. Finally, Eley comes back over to Gertrude, pulling an empty chair over to sit next to her. "When you are back with your family, what do you do on New Year's Eve?"

A scene emerges in Gertrude's memory. All of her brothers and sisters are sitting on the rug in front of the fireplace in the Savannah house. Her father sits in a chair near them and tells them stories. The children huddle under their mother's "best" quilt and listen. She remembers being told that the Irish changed how the biggest city in America, New York, celebrated New Year's Eve.

In 1888, an Irishman named Patrick Sarsfield Gilmore, born in Galway, decided to add music to the midnight event in New York. Leading a brass band, Gilmore had them perform for the audience waiting for midnight. The band members began the countdown, and then two pistols were fired in the air at midnight, back when the triangle of land at the intersection of Seventh Avenue, Broadway, and Forty-Second Street was known as the Long Acre Square. Then she remembers her father telling them the year before she started the nursing program that the intersection had been renamed Times Square in honor of the New York Times Tower. The New Year's Eve in 1904 was celebrated with a street festival and a fireworks display. Listening to music became part of the way America celebrated New Year's Eve, thanks to an Irishman. That's what Gertrude remembers.

Turning to Eley, Gertrude says, "My father would tell us stories and before midnight we would sing. I'd play and the family sang." She pauses. "We also have our traditions. The first person to enter the house after midnight should be black-haired and male to guarantee the house's luck for the coming year. Black hair is normal in Ireland; my blonde hair stands out like a peacock. I often hid my hair when I was in Dublin because of the stares and comments. I wish I had known how to tie a scarf the way you do to hide my hair."

Eley chuckles. "I hide my hair because it is a mess and unruly, and I have no time to untangle it."

Gertrude continues, "The Irish say *Athbhliain Faoi Mhaise* for Happy New Year. And tomorrow," she corrects herself since it is past midnight, "and today, New Year's Day is the Day of Buttered Bread. *La na gCeapairi.*"

"Buttered bread? I like that," says Eley. "What happens with the bread?"

"The tradition involves a large loaf of bread or a large cake. This is taken outside and thrown against the closed door, symbolizing good luck in the new year with plenty to eat."

"What a waste of bread or cake. And no peas for good luck?"

"No peas. But not to worry, the bread is often gathered and eaten anyway. Our good luck food is bacon and cabbage with potatoes, carrots, and onions."

The two women watch the people gathered in celebration eat, drink, and talk. The children run about, and as the night gets darker, Gertrude is eager to return to the cottage. She is tired and is feeling something different in her abdomen. She needs to rest.

Mingo and Eley walk her back to the cottage. When she opens the door, she stops and sits on the bench. Eley looks at her, then reaches out and feels her brow.

"Your face is flushed. How are you feelin'?"

"Tired. I have a pounding headache."

"Any pain?" Eley motions to Mingo to wait and closes the door.

"No, but I feel like fluid is leaking out," says Gertrude, placing her hand below where the baby bulges.

"Come on over and sit down on the settee where you can stretch out."

Gertrude takes off her cloak and begins to walk to the settee. Eley is behind her but stops her as she gets to the settee. "Hold on just a minute." She dashes into the water closet and comes back with a towel. "Let's put this down first."

"Why," asks Gertrude.

"Because your skirt is blood-stained."

Gertrude grabs her skirt up to take a look. There are blood stains all over the back of the skirt. She unfastens it and steps out, leaving the material heaped on the floor. Just as she gets to the settee, she collapses with Eley holding on to her arm.

"What else is going on?" asks Eley.

"I have a tremendous headache."

Eley goes to the door and opens it enough to say something to Mingo. She comes back to Gertrude. "I think maybe you need to go to the hospital. I have sent Mingo for a cart where we can pull you. How far along are you in your pregnancy?"

"This is the start of my seventh month. The baby is due in March."

There's a knock on the door. Eley picks up the skirt. "Here, put this back on, it's already soiled."

Gertrude half stands and pulls the skirt on. She does not fasten it. Eley takes her arm and together they go to the door and walk outside. Mingo is there with the hand cart that Michael uses to carry off limbs. Eley helps her sit on the cart and then Mingo begins to pull the cart down the path to the lane. The hospital on the island is the military hospital, Fort Screven Hospital, at the north end, not far, but the bumpy roadway and hard wooden cart make it impossible for Gertrude to be calm. She shrieks at the first big bump in the road. Eley walks beside her and begins to sing as they move down the lane.

"Nobody knows the trouble I've seen
Nobody knows my sorrow
Nobody knows the trouble I've seen
Glory, Hallelujah

"Nobody knows the trouble I've seen
Nobody knows but Jesus
Nobody knows the trouble I've seen
Glory, Hallelujah

"Sometimes I'm up
Sometimes I'm down
Oh, yes, Lord
Sometimes I'm almost to the ground
Oh, yes, Lord."

Mingo hums along with her. Gertrude listens. She feels that her troubles are big and begins to cry. Her goal has been to be healthy for her and the baby. That's why the monthly trips to Savannah are needed: to prove that both of them were healthy. Then, in the seventh month, walking across the island and staying up all night to eat and socialize in order to celebrate a new year offers her nothing but more pain. She should have stayed in the cottage tonight. Eley, of all people, should have known better.

Eley leans down toward Gertrude. "It's just around the corner now. How are you doing?"

"How do I know? I'm bleeding. My head is pounding. Why didn't you just let me stay in the cottage like I wanted to?"

"And not celebrate New Year's Eve?"

"Yes, I told you that I didn't want to go, but you insisted."

"I did. I didn't want you being all sad and staying alone."

"And now look at me. I might be losing the baby!" Gertrude cries harder. She doubles over with big sobs in the cart. Eley stands up and keeps on walking next to the cart. Mingo never lessens his stride. Gertrude is facing backward and does not see that they are at the entrance of the hospital. Eley goes inside. As they wait, Mingo keeps humming the song Eley sang. Gertrude attempts to stand up. Mingo goes and takes her arm. Together, they manage to get to the steps of the hospital. Eley comes out with two soldiers. Each soldier takes Gertrude's arms and legs, lifts her up over the steps, and into the hospital. Gertrude sees a gurney that the men place her on. She is wheeled down the hallway and into a room. She is left alone for quite a while. Being alone with her thoughts and not knowing what is happening within her body has her smelling fear again.

Finally, a young woman enters and greets Gertrude. She has street clothes on and hurriedly pulls a white apron over her head and ties it around her waist. She flips her brown hair under her collar and washes her hands at a sink.

"I'm Elizabeth. I'm a midwife. I'll need to ask a few questions and do an examination to see what is going on. I was called because Eley told the hospital staff that you are pregnant."

But before Elizabeth can ask any questions, Gertrude,

almost in a whisper, says, "I am pregnant, I'm bleeding, I have a pounding headache, and I am afraid that I will lose my baby."

Alone in the examining room, Gertrude waits for the midwife to speak. Her attention has been on cleaning Gertrude first. As she works, the midwife explains to Gertrude what she is doing. "I will first palpate your abdomen to determine how the fetus is positioned. I will use both of my hands to feel. Please give me feedback if anything is uncomfortable or if anything hurts."

She takes both of her hands, folded together, and moves them over Gertrude's abdomen. Nothing is hurting as the midwife moves her hands around. "I believe the fetus is right here." She places a hand over a section of Gertrude's abdomen. "Now I will check the fetal movement with a fetoscope and listen for the baby's heartbeat."

Gertrude sees the midwife holding a hollow horn about eight inches long made of wood. She places the wide end against Gertrude's abdomen at the spot where she identified the fetus and listens through the other end. While she listens, she holds onto Gertrude's wrist. "I am feeling your pulse to see if it coincides with the uterine vessels." Gertrude is silent and lies very still on the gurney. "Ah, I hear the baby's heartbeat. It has matched yours. Good." Gertrude lets out a huge breath. Her tears start flowing again. "All is good," says the midwife. "No need to cry." She turns to the sink and fills a glass with water.

"Please drink this. It will help relieve your headache. Don't cry."

"I'm relieved, is all."

"Obviously, you want this baby," says the midwife as she puts away her fetoscope and removes the apron.

"So, if the baby is fine, why am I bleeding?"

"We call it a partial placenta previa, painless bleeding. Though the blood stained your skirt, it is bright red, which indicates that there is no infection. This happens sometimes at this stage of a woman's pregnancy."

"What do I do now?"

"You do what I call 'watchful waiting.' There is no need for you to stay in the hospital, but you must have bed rest for several days until the bleeding totally stops."

"How do I get things done if I have to be on bed rest?"

"Your family or husband will help, surely. Is your husband away? I saw Eley out in the lobby. I think she and her husband brought you into the hospital. You are lucky I am here. I am married to one of the soldiers, so I help out when I am needed on the island. We are to be transferred after the first of the year, which is actually here. This is January first. We leave tomorrow."

Eley comes into the room.

"Well, I see Eley is back. Good to see you."

Eley nods and walks over to Gertrude. "I'm off. Take care," and Elizabeth is out of the examining room.

"I heard what she said," says Eley. "Mingo and I will get you back to the cottage, but you need someone to stay in with you until the bleeding stops, and I can't be there and do what I need to do. What do you want to do?"

After a moment, Gertrude says, "I need to send a telegram to Mrs. Schultz."

Dawn on the island gives a magical lift of color in the sky. Gertrude often sees these dark reds and golds on her beach walks, but now she is seeing them as Mingo pulls her back to the cottage in the cart. At the cottage, Gertrude writes out a telegram to Mrs. Schultz and asks Mingo to take it to the train depot to send and places coins for the cost on top of the paper. Eley, in the meantime, is busily looking in the icebox and talking out loud as she calculates what kind of food Gertrude might need. "You have little to nothing in this house to eat," she says.

Gertrude sits at the table and watches Eley dash around the kitchen area. "I did not feel like foraging."

"I can see that," says Eley. "Well, you do have some dried meat and rice. I can fix you some soup to leave in a pot on the fire. How does that sound?"

"I'm not hungry, remember I ate that whole plate of Hoppin' John, leaving three peas at the praise house. Much good as that has done me. What did you say it would give me: luck, fortune, and romance?"

"That's been hours ago when you ate. You need food to keep up your spirits. And you can't predict a whole year on just the first day. Though I have to admit, it isn't lucky to have the bleeding you have, but it is good that you and the baby will be fine, right?"

Gertrude takes a deep breath. She's no longer sure as to what is good or bad anymore. Things just keep happening to her.

"Now, I'm going to make this soup, and you need to go change and climb into bed."

As Gertrude stands and moves over to the bedroom door, she mutters, "I will change into a nightgown, but I am more comfortable resting on the settee than being in bed."

Eley gives a humph and continues making the soup. When Gertrude returns to sit down, the soup is in the large pot over the fire and a kettle of water for tea is heating there as well. She sits on the settee and tucks the quilt over her legs. "Thank you, Eley. You have been wonderful."

There is another humph from Eley. "That's not what I heard when I was taking you to the hospital."

Gertrude pauses and looks over at Eley. "I'm sorry. I didn't mean those things. I could have stayed at the cottage if I had a mind to, but I didn't. It never was your fault."

"Good to know," says Eley. She comes over to Gertrude's side. "I knew it was the worry that made you say those things." She pats Gertrude on the shoulder. "I am going now but will be back to check on you. There's soup and tea. Do stay off your feet." With that, she is out the door.

Gertrude decides that, since it is early in the day and a holiday, she will not get up to lock the cottage door. She is to stay off her feet.

40

———

Napping on and off on the settee, Gertrude has not gotten up for several hours when there is a knock at the door.

"Who's there?"

"It's me, Mrs. Schultz."

"Please come in. The door is unlocked."

Mrs. Schultz enters, and as Gertrude turns to look, she sees her mother. Gertrude stays seated on the settee as the two women come in and stand over her.

"My dear Gertrude," says her mother, "what did they say at the hospital?"

Gertrude looks at her mother and then at Mrs. Schultz.

"She knows," says Mrs. Schultz. "I wanted her to have a choice of coming with me, so she needed to know. Let's begin with a cup of tea. I see the kettle is over the fire, and we can sit at the table and talk." Mrs. Schultz walks over to the hanging dresser and gets three cups and saucers. "Will you prepare the tea, Mrs. Kelly? I will get the tea leaves from the pantry."

Once everyone is at the table and the tea is steeping, Gertrude tells them what happened at the hospital.

"So, being pregnant is why you have not been to see us?"

As bizarre as the words sound to Gertrude when she hears her mother say them, she nods her head yes. "I expected you to not want to see me or have anything to do with me. I wanted to put off telling you for as long as I could."

"I understand that you were abandoned by Randolph in Dublin."

"That's correct."

"I also understand that there is no easy way for Randolph to be held accountable."

"That's correct."

"And that Mrs. Schultz and the sisters have helped make this living arrangement for you in order for you to save face and give the baby up for adoption when he or she is born."

"That's correct."

"When is the baby due?"

"March."

"I see."

Everyone around the table is quiet. Gertrude does not know where to look. If she looks at Mrs. Schultz, she feels that she is accusing her of letting out her secret. If she looks at her mother, then she is waiting for a response or rebuke. She glances at her mother and sees her stirring her tea after adding sugar. Her hair is greying more than it was when she saw her last. Her small face, much like Gertrude's, has new wrinkles. They drink their tea in silence.

Mrs. Kelly speaks first. "I will need to borrow a skirt and blouse."

Gertrude is confused. "Why?" she asks.

"I didn't pack anything to change into with the hurry and I plan on staying a few days until you get on your feet."

The tears flow freely now. Gertrude can barely see. She looks at her mother. "You are staying?"

"Yes, somebody needs to talk some sense into you and who is better at doing that than your mother?"

To have her mother all to herself is a new experience for Gertrude. The mother and daughter actually talk when having tea or when sewing. Her mother sits with her and helps her with the handwork. Gertrude has all the pieces cut out for the uniforms. Her mother goes upstairs and pulls other pieces down into the main room and places them in the stations that Gertrude has set up. Gertrude notices that her mother does not even have to ask where things might go. She figures it out right away.

Michael, Eley, Mingo, and Captain keep them stocked with fresh meat, fish, and greens. Gertrude is able to show her mother how she cooks seaweed and how to use sea lettuce. In the evenings, they hand-sew in front of the fire after dinner. With the two of them sewing, the uniforms are finishing up quickly, but there are still many to sew on the Singer sewing machine. On the third day of Gertrude's convalescence, she feels better. She stands up and goes over to the Singer to sew. Her mother has not noticed since she is busy at the stove. But then Gertrude hears her mother shout.

"No! Don't you dare!" Mrs. Kelly stands near the table with a spatula in her hand. "You don't need to be treadling. It's not time to do that."

Pausing, Gertrude looks at the pile of cut-out patterns pinned together and ready to sew. "But there are so many still to put together."

"Then I'll do it."

"Do you know how to treadle?"

"Did you know when you first started?"

Gertrude stood and walked over to the stove. "Fine, I'll

cook, you treadle. The instruction book is on the floor near the wall."

Another day goes by with much sewing. Mrs. Kelly is a natural at treadling, and in no time, the pile of pattern pieces is complete. She spends all day sewing and sewing and sewing, stopping only to eat and have a cup of tea with Gertrude at the table.

After dinner that evening, Gertrude cleans off the table and says, "I am feeling so much stronger, and a little exercise will do wonders for my spirits. Before it gets dark, let's take a short, slow walk on the beach."

"That's a good idea. If you feel you are up for it."

They gather their cloaks and lock the cottage door. It is the first time Gertrude has been out of the cottage in days. The sea air feels great on her face as they cross the boardwalk to the ocean. Slogging through the sand, they reach the firmer sand near the water's edge. Gertrude shows her mother how she ties up her skirt so the water from the waves coming onto the beach does not get her hem wet.

As they walk, they are silent. But then Mrs. Kelly begins to talk. "When you were a little girl, all you wanted to do was to play the piano. We had music in the house all the time."

"You taught me."

"Humph," she says. "I sat you down at the piano and showed you the keys."

They walk a little in silence.

Gertrude says, "Thank you for that." She sees her mother grimace. "What?"

"I'm not too sure that teaching you to play was a good thing."

"Why? You think it has taken over my life?"

"Yes."

"You see me on an island foraging for food, sewing

uniforms, maintaining a big house, not playing the piano, and you can still say that?"

"I haven't heard you play in, let's see, a year and a half. I don't know how well you play. I don't have the ear you have."

"You made it clear that you did not want me to play the recital at the Savannah Theatre."

"I wanted you to be a nurse so you could take care of yourself."

"I will finish the program."

"Really? You don't seem to follow through on anything you say you will finish."

Gertrude stops. "Am I taking care of myself after all the bad decisions I have made?"

Her mother shakes her head. "I don't see how barely eating, foraging for food, and being paid for piecework qualify as taking care of yourself. Not to mention getting pregnant."

"Now I see, you are finally getting around to calling out my pregnancy. You don't know the whole story."

"You won't tell me the whole story. You tell me you were abandoned in Dublin. Why?"

Gertrude picks up her pace, and her mother has to increase hers to stay up with her. Gertrude does not answer.

"There, see? You will never tell me the whole story, will you?"

"Let's turn back. It will be dark soon."

They walk in silence back to the cottage. Inside, Gertrude puts another log on the fire and sits down on the settee. Mrs. Kelly goes into the water closet. Gertrude remains staring at the fire. When her mother returns, she sits in the chair near the fire and picks up a uniform to finish the hand sewing.

Clearing her throat, Gertrude speaks up. "Randolph and I were never married."

Mrs. Kelly stops sewing and looks at Gertrude.

"In Dublin, he left a note." Gertrude stands up and goes

into the bedroom. When she returns, she has the note and hands it to her mother. Sitting back down, she waits as her mother reads the note.

"My goodness. And you didn't know this? You didn't know he was married?"

"No."

"This is worse than being abandoned."

"Don't you think I know that? Why would I be here if I didn't know that?"

"Who else knows?"

"Mrs. Schultz, Sister Mary Joyce, oh, and Mrs. Leo Lynch and Lucas. Everyone else has been told that I was abandoned."

"Why Mrs. Lynch and Lucas?"

"Mrs. Lynch needed to know since the Music Club sponsored me to Brenau, and she would not pay me for the piecework if I didn't tell her the whole story. Lucas, being a reporter, figured out things, and to keep him from writing a story about practicing my compositions, I told him the truth."

"Why did you choose this place?"

Gertrude relates the conversation of how the homes in St. Louis were for wayward, younger women and this opportunity came open where Sister Mary Joyce would help her keep healthy until the baby is born."

"And how is that working?" asks Mrs. Kelly.

"I go into Savannah monthly for checkups with Sister Mary Joyce."

"You have been coming into Savannah monthly?"

Gertrude pauses. "Yes."

"And you have never darkened our door?"

"I did not know how you and Papa would take having a daughter who can't seem to follow through on getting things done and became pregnant after living with a married man."

This time, Mrs. Kelly pauses and looks hard at Gertrude. "You're my daughter."

"And you are Irish Catholic with views that make what I have done a major problem."

"How do you know?"

"Because I have grown up in your house and know your teachings."

"Then you must know that a major part of my life has been taking care of all of my children and my husband. My family comes first after my beliefs."

"What does that mean?"

"It means that I will support you in this crisis because I love you."

Gertrude breaks into a sobbing cry. She has been holding back her tears, but now they are released in a torrent of sobs and gasping for breath.

Mrs. Kelly moves over and sits next to Gertrude on the settee, reaching out and holding Gertrude's hand. "What happens to the baby when it is born?"

Sniffing back her tears, Gertrude answers, "Sister Mary Joyce will keep the baby at the hospital until she is adopted."

"She?"

Gertrude half smiles, "I have been told not to think about the baby, not to name her, not to make attachments to her, but she is inside of me and I cannot think of anything else. When the bleeding started, I became fearful that I would lose her."

"But you will lose her when she is born and put up for adoption."

"I know." Gertrude sobs even louder. She feels her mother's arms circle her back and pull her over so that the hug is tender and much needed.

41

———

"When this is done, what will you do?" asks Mrs. Kelly after letting Gertrude cry for a while.

With a handkerchief from her sleeve, Gertrude cleans her face and blows her nose. "I must think about that. The plan is to try to get reinstated into the nursing program. I only have four months and some remedial work to do to finish, if they will accept me. They do not accept a married woman into the boarding house, so to keep my story, I would need a place to live to complete the program. There is a possibility that they will not readmit me to the program because I have a baby and no husband."

"Who makes that decision?"

"The Sisters of Mercy."

"And how much influence does Sister Mary Joyce, the nun who is seeing you monthly, have in this decision?"

Gertrude seems to be studying the fire leaping in giant yellow and red flames in the fireplace for her answer. Then she says, "She knows about the pregnancy, and about the abandonment, and about the non-legal marriage. However, she is also a fighter for women's rights when they have been wronged, according to Mrs. Schultz. I think she will put forth a good word for me if I do a good job here for the Home."

Mrs. Kelly doesn't miss a beat. "Okay, then. Let's finish these uniforms." Mrs. Kelly stands and crosses to pick up the sewn uniforms from the chair across the room. "We need to finish hand-sewing these."

"But what if I don't get into the program? And if I do, how will I have time to earn money to live for four months if I am accepted?"

Mrs. Kelly returns to the settee after placing the uniforms on the floor nearby. "If you get into the program, you will live at home and finish. It might be a bit of a walk early and late, but you can do that. If you don't get into the program, well, there are other skills you have learned here on Tybee that you can draw on?"

"Like foraging for food? I don't think so, and I know I don't want to."

Mrs. Kelly smiles. "You'll figure it out."

After numerous cups of tea and putting more logs on the fire, Gertrude sees that they are almost finished with the uniforms. She and her mother have finished fifty uniforms ready for the children to attend the summer camp. She stands. Her back aches. "I think we need to get some sleep."

Mrs. Kelly stands and walks over to the kitchen window. "Dawn is here already."

"Really?" Gertrude joins her mother in looking out the window. Mrs. Kelly reaches over and puts an arm around Gertrude's back. Gertrude leans her head onto her mother's shoulder. "Thank you."

"You are welcome. And I agree, I need a few hours of sleep."

A loud knock at the door awakens Gertrude as she sleeps on the settee. She slowly stands and walks to the door. "Who is it?"

"Thoreau."

Unbolting the door, she finds Lucas standing on the steps of the cottage. "Come in," she says.

"Are you sure?"

"Of course, my mother is here."

"I won't come in then, but I want to know how you are. Mrs. Schultz came to see me at the newspaper."

"Really, it is fine for you to come in. We worked late into the early morning hours on the uniforms and slept in for a few hours. Mother is still asleep in the bedroom." She opens the door wide and Lucas steps in.

"I have not had a chance to come for a couple of weeks," says Lucas. "With the holidays, there were so many stories that needed to be covered that I was working really late hours and weekends."

"I see."

Gertrude notices that Lucas has not taken off his jacket or removed his hat. He is standing in one spot but is shifting his weight from one foot to another. She has not seen him agitated before. "Would you like a cup of tea?" she asks.

Lucas takes off his hat but holds it in his hand. "I can't stay long. Maybe we can just talk."

"Okay, shall we sit at the table?" Gertrude goes to sit down and Lucas follows.

"Mrs. Schultz said you were in the hospital."

"That's right. Eley and Mingo took me to the Fort Screven Hospital on New Year's Eve, or I should say on New Year's Day. It was after midnight because I ate my Hoppin' John."

Lucas's frown did not lighten the mood. "I got word from Susan Lynch that you were not practicing on Sundays."

"Really? I wonder who could have told her? Oh, I know,

Frances. They are cousins and I am sure they saw each other during the holidays."

"Frances, right. I've not had a chance to talk with her about doing an article. We keep the conversation limited in the kitchen when we are there to hear you play."

"Thank you."

"When did you play?" asks Mrs. Kelly. Gertrude did not hear her come into the room. Lucas stands immediately.

"Hello, Mrs. Kelly. We met at Gertrude's recital in Savannah."

"I remember you. You write for the newspaper."

"That I do."

"Why are you here? Are you still after a story?"

"Mother, Lucas is a friend."

"I did come over to write a story. I had heard that folks were sitting out on the lawn at the Fresh Air Home listening to great piano concerts. So, I came over to hear for myself."

"And did you write the story?" asks Mrs. Kelly.

Lucas's face shows his confusion. Gertrude speaks before he can. "Lucas is going to write about Frances Lynch, the blind piano tuner."

"Yes, that is to be the story."

"I see," says Mrs. Kelly, but Gertrude can tell from her mother's reactions that she did not totally understand. "I'm going to have a cup of tea. Would anyone like to join me?"

Lucas remains standing. "I need to be heading back to Savannah. I just wanted to find out how Gertrude is."

Gertrude stands. "Mother, I will have a cup of tea after I walk Lucas to the door." Gertrude moves to the front door and walks out onto the path. Lucas follows by giving Mrs. Kelly a "good to have seen you" goodbye comment. He steps down to stand in front of Gertrude.

"How are you?"

"I'm fine. I needed some bedrest, so Mother stayed to help out."

"And the baby?"

Gertrude looks at his face carefully. What she sees is an intense gaze into her own face. "The baby is fine, too." She watches as his face relaxes and he puts his hat on.

"Good. Will you be practicing again?"

"I'm not sure. The midwife said I must take it easy."

"I would do what the midwife says, then." Lucas pauses as though he had more to say.

Gertrude waits, and when Lucas says nothing more, she says, "Thank you for coming by, and please give Mrs. Schultz my best when you see her next."

Lucas gives a brief nod of his head, turns, and heads down the path to the lane and the train depot. Gertrude watches as he leaves.

Inside the cottage, her mother has poured two cups of tea. She joins her at the table and they drink their tea silently. When they finish, Mrs. Kelly picks up the two cups and saucers and moves them to the sink. "Lucas seems like a nice enough young man." She turns to face Gertrude. "And I think I need to hear you play."

42

─────────

Mrs. Kelly stays through the day. They take a few naps and then she goes to the market at the train depot to pick up a few provisions. Alone, Gertrude is restless and walks around the cottage, looking at the finished uniforms and at the herbs on the windowsill, remembering how she placed a lantern there for Lucas to see that she was safe. *Walden* resonates with her, more so because Lucas brought the book and introduced it to her. Taking the book off the mantle, she sits down in the chair, not the settee, and flips through the book one more time. She has read all of it, but she rereads the passage where Thoreau suggests that if he simplifies his life, then the laws that have been established and guided his life will appear less complex. That solitude will not be solitude, nor poverty poverty, nor weakness weakness. He suggests that as he changes his life and his viewpoint, these other things change as well. Then she reads:

If you have built castles in the air, your work need not be lost; that is where they should be. Now put the foundations under them...

Gertrude has built castles in the air. Her goal has been to be a concert pianist, but what she discovers in her journey to learn more about being a concert pianist is that in her society, women are only allowed to teach piano. Those who want to play professionally or even to compose are limited by society's ban on women learning to compose unless they have patrons or wealthy families. She has neither. She has been encouraged by teaching Michael to play and watching his desire to improve and to practice even when everything is against him. His parents don't want him to play. He has no piano to practice with except at the Home. And, he has no finances to pay for future lessons. But she has succeeded in teaching Michael the piano basics. She can teach students how to play the piano. Mrs. Schultz has agreed that she could use the parlor to teach students, so that's one thing, should the nursing program not accept her.

How can foundations be put under Gertrude's castles in the air? If she teaches, she will need many students to be able to pay her bills and put food on the table. Living quarters must be found so as not to have to live with her parents, a place with a piano to continue teaching students how to play. Having a family is out of the question with having this baby and giving her up to be adopted. So, what foundations does she need? A job, a place to live, a piano, and access to students who want to learn. All of that will take time and resources that Gertrude does not have. She might as well accept the fact that composing music will be a hobby and not a profession.

Mrs. Kelly is still shopping, so Gertrude picks up some of the uniforms, gets the keys to the big house, and heads over to place the finished uniforms in the dining room. The uniforms are put on the tables in order of size and gender. Gertrude sees that the piano has been left uncovered after her last practice session. Instead of covering the piano, she sits down and runs through the scales. Her piece, the one she has been composing for the last few months, begins to flow from her fingers through the notes on the keyboard. Stumbling through but remembering most of it, Gertrude finishes, pausing with her hands hovering above the keys, and hears clapping. Mrs. Kelly is standing in the doorway with tears running down her cheeks.

"I didn't hear you come in."

"And I had no idea you could play so beautifully." Her mother walks toward Gertrude. "I have always known you were a competent pianist, better than most, but the piece you just played was special."

"Thank you." Gertrude stands and changes the subject. "I brought some of the uniforms over. I need to get the rest of them."

"No, you don't. You still should rest and take it easy. The next time you need to check on the house, bring more over. Let's go back to the cottage. I have provisions sitting on the table. I need to go home. You have improved so much; I feel that you will be fine."

Gertrude locks up the big house. As they cross over to the cottage, Mrs. Kelly reaches out and touches Gertrude's arm. "I have been wrong about many things. I thought I should not have introduced you to the piano, I thought you should not live alone because I did not think you could take care of yourself, and I have been wrong about you playing professionally. You are talented. Who wrote the song you just played?"

"Thank you." Gertrude ducks her head, but answers, "I actually wrote the song, but I cannot do much with it. A woman composer and pianist must have sponsors or patrons who can provide her with an income in order to play and compose. I have neither."

"I'm not so sure," says Mrs. Kelly. "I think you will figure out how to do it sooner or later."

As they enter the cottage, Gertrude thinks about what her mother is saying, and it coincides with Thoreau's quote: "Now put the foundations under them…"

Her mother bought a lot of provisions. There are jars of tomatoes, green beans, and corn. She counts four types of dried beans: black-eyed, field peas, red beans, and butter beans. There are bags of flour, cornmeal, and sugar, with half a dozen eggs, a quart of milk, and canisters of tea, baking powder, salt, pepper, and yeast.

"You did not need to purchase all of this. You don't have the funds for all of these provisions."

"I came prepared to pay nursing and hospital costs. Since there are none, I did have the funds to purchase these." She turns to go into the bedroom. "I need to get my satchel and go to the depot. A train should be leaving soon."

A calmness comes over Gertrude. The worry that has enveloped her for many months has lessened. She has family, friends, and support in ways she had not thought possible. And now she has food and does not have to go foraging.

January days need a new routine. Now that the uniforms are finished and Gertrude has so much food in the pantry supplemented with Michael's buckets of fish and seafood, her walks return to twice daily. These walks are longer, more leisurely walks where she studies the nature around her. In the afternoon, she goes to the big house to give Michael a chance to practice and to give him lessons. To keep herself busy and be present for Michael, she sorts the linens to prepare them for the summer and places them in the various rooms to be put on the beds when time is close. Linens that need mending are saved for those afternoons when Michael is practicing. She did not have to inventory the pantry items because she had used all the food left when she first arrived. Everything on the list that the society members left for her will be needed. Her next task is to inventory the infirmary items and then to verify that the sisters at the hospital might be able to supplement what may be needed.

In the evenings, since sewing is finished, Gertrude returns to the big house and plays the piano. At first, she plays the pub songs she knows by memory. Then she plays her composition, the one developed in the fall on Sunday afternoons. It needs adjustments and fine-tuning. Every evening, long after it is dark, she plays. Somehow, Captain knows and has kept the wood bins full, which is good since the evenings are chilly and the room is cold.

In the first week of February, Gertrude plans to go to Savannah for her checkup. She is up before dawn to catch the first train in order to arrive early in Savannah. Her first stop is the newspaper. As she opens the door, she pauses. Is this the right thing to do? Lucas has not contacted her for a month. He probably does not care that she has finished her original composition. He has his own work to do. Closing the door, Gertrude turns to walk away.

"Gertrude!"

Lucas rushes out the newspaper door.

"Wait!" he calls out.

Quietly, Gertrude stands on the sidewalk. Her face is rigid. She is determined to show no emotion.

"Good morning, Lucas."

"I thought you were coming into the newspaper, but then you didn't. What's going on?"

Gertrude speaks rapidly. "I did not know if you would be in this early, and I need to get to the hospital for my check-up, so I decided not to come in to say hello."

"Okay, well, as it happens, there was a shipwreck late last night and I am headed to St. Joseph's to interview the survivors. I'll walk with you."

As they turn to head toward St. Joseph's, Gertrude starts to speak, but so does Lucas.

"You first," says Lucas.

"I finished the uniforms."

"Good, that has been one of your goals."

"And I finished the composition."

"Ah ha! I thought you might be working on something. When can I hear it?"

"Sunday?"

"Yes, Sunday it is."

"And what were you going to say?"

"Oh, I wanted to ask you about *Walden*. I should return it to Mrs. Schultz if you are finished with it."

"I'm so sorry, I did not bring it."

"Then I'll get it Sunday."

They walk a block in silence.

"Did you read more of it?"

"I read all of it. And I have to say, he has a lot of ideas about solitude."

"And do you, now that you have lived in solitude for all these months?"

Gertrude slows her walk. "I do."

They arrive at the hospital. "And will you share?"

"Yes, later, when we have more time."

With a quick pat on the arm, Lucas leaves her to ask at the front desk where the seamen are in the hospital. Gertrude goes to find Sister Mary Joyce in her office. The conversation with Lucas has not eased her mind.

Slowly, Sister Mary Joyce goes over what to expect during the month before the due date. Several prospective couples are eager to meet Gertrude and verify that everyone is healthy. Gertrude has not thought about having to meet the potential couples who want to adopt her child. Listening to the sister explain all the legal papers that must be signed and endorsed by Gertrude, the hospital, and the prospective parents leaves Gertrude speechless. These papers and the meetings need to be completed before the baby is born.

Gertrude sits on the side of the examining table. She is not ready to let her baby go. There is a need deep inside to see the baby, hold her, and watch her grow. Gertrude does not want to imagine seeing her baby in someone else's home. She has not named her, but she knows her. She doesn't even know what she would name her. What is a good name for a baby that does not have a father and is raised by a single mother?

"I repeat, can you come in within the next two weeks? I will set up the meetings and have the papers prepared for you to sign." Sister Mary Joyce looks at Gertrude and moves over to put her hand on Gertrude's shoulder. "This is what you agreed to, Gertrude, when we set up the stay at the Fresh Air Home. Now is the time to carry it through."

Gertrude nods but remains silent.

"Okay, I will set things up and expect to see you on February 14. Come early and plan on staying the day. I'm sure Mrs. Schultz will want you to rest in the boarding house."

Gertrude nods.

Sister Mary Joyce turns to leave. "Feel free to leave once you are ready. Take your time."

Nothing can fill the emptiness Gertrude feels after Sister Mary Joyce leaves the examining room. Crying will not help. She must steel herself and make this happen. This is what she has been waiting for: to go on with her life, to end her solitude on Tybee Island, to have a future. After dressing to leave, Gertrude does not stop in to see Mrs. Schultz, nor her mother. She goes directly to the train, boards, and returns to Tybee Island and her solitude.

43

No one is in the kitchen when Gertrude goes over to the big house on Sunday, earlier than usual. She wants to practice her composition alone and plays all morning. She hears a knock at the French doors and looks up to see Lucas standing on the porch.

"I knocked at the cottage and the front door, but you did not come. I could hear you play, so I came here."

"Good because I did not hear you knock. Come in." She fastens the door behind him. "I am warmed up. Do you want to sit in here to listen or would you be more comfortable in the kitchen?"

"Is anyone else coming?"

"Yes, Eley, Captain, Frances, and Michael."

"We'll see what they would like, but it might be nice to sit in the dining room and watch you play."

"Then let's at least get the tea water hot."

They cross into the kitchen. Lucas unlocks the back door as Gertrude fills the kettle with water. Then he checks the stove. There is wood ready to light, and he gets the fire going. Gertrude places the kettle on the stove. Not knowing what to do while waiting, she stands and looks out at the garden that has not been prepared for the children to plant and grow vegetables this summer. The soil must be amended, new soil brought in, and the trellises reinforced around the perimeter to keep the rabbits out and lessen the salt air damaging the plants. There is no energy in her to get this done.

Lucas crosses and stands beside her. "What do you see that I don't?"

"I see a garden with children harvesting the vegetables they have grown."

"I can see that. The trellis needs repair. The soil needs to be amended. I can see that happening, but I wanted to ask you something else."

"I'm running out of time to get it all done. What did you want to ask?" The kitchen door opens and Captain and Michael enter, followed by Frances. "Welcome, Lucas and I were talking about how you might like to sit in the dining room today."

"Yes," they all say together and pick up a cup and saucer to head into the dining room. Eley comes in through the back door.

"Good, you haven't started yet. I have been running all day." She sees Captain and Michael carrying their cups and saucers into the dining room. "Good, we'll be able to actually see you playing in the dining room. Frances, I have your cup and saucer, go on in." Eley picks up two sets but stops to look at Gertrude. "How are you doing?"

"Fine. I'm fine."

"Humph, I don't think so, but I will wait until you want to tell me." Eley exits into the dining room.

Reaching out, Gertrude touches Lucas's arm. "What did you want to ask me?"

"Later, we'll talk later." Lucas goes into the dining room.

Gertrude follows with the kettle. She pours the tea and sets the kettle on a trivet on one of the tables. Slowly crossing to the piano and before sitting down, she turns to the seated group and interrupts their tea sipping. "Thank you for coming. I have a new piece for you to hear." Sitting on the bench where she has sat dozens of times, Gertrude stares at the keyboard, then plays.

The composition is finished. Instead of turning to look at her friends, she sits facing the keyboard. The people sitting in the room, who call themselves her friends, are silent. This silence is uncomfortable. As they remain silent, she finally turns and looks at them. Every face has tears. "Well?" Gertrude asks.

Frances speaks first, still dabbing her eyes with her hand-kerchief. "I heard the challenge. There was an idea at the beginning. Then I heard disbelief, like the idea could not be any good. Then I heard grief. But the triumphant conclusion figured it all out."

"Exactly," says Captain, trying not to sniffle.

"I wish I was as articulate as Frances," says Lucas, "but yes, I heard all of that." His sleeve is damp, and he uses it again to wipe his cheek.

"I heard your feelings. I know you have been hol'd up here on this island and needed to confront a lot of things. I just didn't know you knew how to make me feel what you feel," says Eley.

"Can you teach me to play like that?" asks Michael.

Gertrude hears what her friends say and thinks about what has been played. Maybe she can compose, but now what?

"Do you have a title for it?" asks Frances.

"No, I don't," says Gertrude.

Lucas speaks up. "Yes, she has, it is her 'Tybee something.' You wrote it here on the island, right?"

"It sounds like a rhapsody," says Frances. "It has all the parts and the feelings of a rhapsody."

"Yes," says Lucas, "call it 'Tybee Rhapsody.' My, my, what I would give to be able to write about this now."

"Lucas!"

"I know, Gertrude, I promised and will keep my promise, but you have to play this to a larger public," says Lucas.

"I agree," says Frances. "But how?"

Directing his question to Frances, Lucas asks, "Can't we get your cousin, Susan Lynch, to hear this and commit to have the Savannah Music Club sponsor a concert?"

"No!" says Gertrude. "No, that will not happen. Please, enjoy my piece and let it be. At least for now. Please?"

No one seems happy about Gertrude's decision not to ask Susan Lynch, but they all nod and say yes. Captain and Michael say their goodbyes and leave out the back door.

Eley shrugs. "That baby of your'n will like hearing her mama play, but so do the rest of us." She turns and leaves through the kitchen.

Gertrude goes into the kitchen with some of the cups and saucers, leaving Frances and Lucas talking in the dining room. Lucas comes in with the rest of the cups and saucers.

"Where's Frances?"

"She left through the front door." He puts the dishes in the sink. Together they tidy up the kitchen. When they are finished, Gertrude locks up the house and, with Lucas beside her, goes over to the cottage.

"I need to head back to Savannah," says Lucas, "but I want to know what you have planned for the next couple of weeks before the baby is due."

"I'm going to be here," says Gertrude. "Sister Mary Joyce has me scheduled to come to the hospital on February 14 for another exam since the birth date is near."

"I see. How long will that take?"

"She wants me to wait a while at Mrs. Schultz's. There is paperwork to sign and documents to process."

Lucas stands silently next to her with his hat in his hand. "And this is what you want to do?"

Gertrude unlocks the cottage door. As she steps inside, she turns to face Lucas. "I have no choice."

Lucas stuffs his hat on top of his head, turns, and walks in the direction of the train station. Gertrude remembers that he did not ask his question.

44

On February 14, Gertrude boards the train to Savannah much earlier than usual, but Sister Mary Joyce asked her to be there early. She has a small overnight bag with her, just in case the paperwork and meetings take longer than expected.

Arriving in Savannah is uneventful. Gertrude goes straight to Mrs. Schultz's boarding house in hopes of leaving her bag and confirming that she can wait there during the day. Gertrude knocks on the door.

Mrs. Schultz opens it and sees Gertrude. "Come in, dear, come in. I told you to enter when you arrive."

"I know, but it is early, and I had not told you what time I might arrive."

"You are earlier than I had thought you might be, but more than welcome. Here, let me take your bag. Let's put it up in my office. I have a cot in there now in case you need a place to relax. I'll take it up. Meet me in the kitchen and we'll have a cup of tea."

Mrs. Schultz takes the bag and disappears up the steps. Gertrude takes off her cloak and hangs it on the hat tree in the foyer. Before she finishes, Mrs. Schultz is back down the stairs.

"Now, let's have a short visit with a nice cup of tea," Mrs. Schultz says.

In the kitchen, Mrs. Schultz is busy dashing about getting the cups and saucers, lemon, and sugar. Gertrude sits down gently at the table, placing her hands on the wooden surface as she lowers her body down onto the chair. At least it is after breakfast and all the nurses have gone to work at the hospital.

"You have done a good job making the new dress," says Mrs. Schultz, looking carefully at the one Gertrude has on. "I like the lavender color. How did you get it that shade?"

Gertrude looks down at her dress, a loose shift she had made from the upstairs curtains and had dyed using the beautyberries. She had made two and lived in them for the last few months. "Eley showed me how to dye them. We picked beautyberries."

"I like it," says Mrs. Schultz. She finishes bringing everything to the table and sits across from Gertrude. As the tea steeps, she begins. "I know what you must be thinking."

Gertrude looks up at her. "You do? How do you know?" she asks. "What am I thinking? I don't even know, so if you do, please tell me."

Mrs. Schultz pauses, picks up her teacup, and takes a sip. "I understand that I cannot know what you are thinking or feeling," she says. "I only want to ease your mind."

"By telling me that everything will be just fine? That I will be fine? That giving up my baby will solve all my problems and give me a new lease on life?" Gertrude breaks into sobs, harsh sobs that cause Mrs. Schultz to stand and cross over to her.

She kneels next to her and puts an arm around her shoulders. "Gertrude, you did not ask for all of this. You were duped into thinking that someone cared about you. Others do care about you. I do, your mother, Sharon, Sister Mary Joyce, the friends you have made on Tybee Island, and Lucas. All of us care about you. This is a hard decision to make, but we are standing right next to you and support you in your decision."

Tears make it difficult for Gertrude to speak. She puts her face in her hands and leans forward on the table. Mrs. Schultz does not move but continues to hold her. Then there is a knock at the front door.

Mrs. Schultz stands and goes to see who might be at the door.

Gertrude clears her face with a handkerchief stuffed in her sleeve. Her mother always did that, and now she knows why: not all dresses have pockets. She wipes her face and begins to sip her tea.

Mrs. Schultz comes to the kitchen door, pauses, and then crosses to stand next to Gertrude. "This may not be the best time to share this with you, but it is the only time we have."

Gertrude looks up at Mrs. Schultz. "What are you saying?"

"The knock at the door. Mrs. Leo Lynch and Frances Lynch are in the parlor and would like to speak with you."

"Now?" Gertrude's voice goes up an octave.

"Yes, now."

"Oh, Mrs. Schultz, there is no way…"

"Be brave, my dear girl. Remember that you have so much support around you."

Gertrude takes a moment to compose herself. She stands up, pushing on the tabletop. "You are right." She stands and walks with Mrs. Schultz, who leads the way into the parlor.

"Hello, Gertrude," says Mrs. Lynch. "I would have given you notice that we were coming, but Frances is in town only for a short time and insisted that this is what we should do. I do hope this does not find you at an inconvenient time."

Gertrude notices Mrs. Lynch's deep purple gown with green trim. A matching tam hat, purple with a green feather, completes the outfit. *Quite royal*, Gertrude thinks while she folds her hands in front of her homemade lavender duster dress.

"Not at all, Mrs. Lynch. It is good to see you. And you, Frances. What can I do for you?"

Frances is sitting in Mrs. Schultz's chair in the parlor. "You must play your 'Tybee Rhapsody' for Susan," she says.

Gertrude is frozen and quiet.

"Yes, Frances has been telling me all about it and I would like to hear it," she says. "However, you seem to be hesitating. I would like to remind you that you should not feel reluctant to play. I think you remember our conversation."

Gertrude remembers it all too well. She raises her head and slowly looks from Mrs. Lynch to Frances to Mrs. Schultz, who is still standing near the doorway. "Of course."

Gertrude moves to the piano, lifts the keyboard cover, and sits down. The bench needs adjusting to allow for her extended abdomen. She runs a few scales, then puts both hands on her legs. They won't rest easily in her lap. She lowers her head and then places her hands on the keys and begins to play. The notes fall from her heart, exactly how the piece has been dreamed. The sounds of the ocean, of the wind, of the storms all flow from her fingers and onto the keyboard. Feeling her grief, despair, urgency, and elation, the piece is rich in all its natural elements that have led Gertrude to create this composition. At the end of the music, she is elated, not exhausted. She feels good. She feels successful. She feels like she has shared the innermost parts of her and has identified that there is hope.

When Gertrude turns to look at the women in the parlor, Frances has her handkerchief in front of her face. Mrs. Schultz is staring into the fireplace with tears running down her cheeks. Mrs. Lynch still sits on the settee where she had first settled, and says, "My goodness, that is powerful."

"I told you," says Frances through her handkerchief. "So,

can you arrange for Gertrude to play the piece for the Music Club at its meeting next week?"

Gertrude stands. Her pregnancy is pronounced even with the loose duster dress. "I cannot play this piece for the club."

Mrs. Lynch looks at Gertrude. "I agree." Frances starts to say something, but Mrs. Lynch interrupts her. "You cannot see, Frances, but Gertrude is about to have a baby. She cannot play for the club in her condition."

"But the club needs to hear this. They need to know that even though Gertrude did not finish the sponsorship, she is a talented composer and should be sponsored."

Mrs. Lynch stands. "No, Frances, Gertrude cannot play next week. Later perhaps."

"Then let me play it," says Frances. "I have heard it and can learn it before the meeting."

Gertrude looks from one to the other. "I have heard you play; you could play this piece."

"What a great idea," says Mrs. Schultz.

"Wait, please. Let's not get ahead of ourselves. I am confident that Frances could play the piece. However, it cannot be listed under Gertrude's name," Mrs. Lynch says.

All are silent. Frances asks, "Why not?"

"Look at her, she cannot be seen as the composer," says Mrs. Lynch.

Frances twitches her head back and forth, then says, "I wish I could look at her. I hope I will see a beautiful, talented musician who can pull music out of her soul. I will play her 'Tybee Rhapsody.' Okay, Susan?"

With a sigh, Mrs. Lynch agrees.

Gertrude crosses to Frances and pats her on the shoulder. Frances reaches a hand up to hold Gertrude's. "I have business to take care of today at the hospital, and I understand you will be going back to Tybee Island. Shall we meet at the big house tomorrow morning and begin your memory work?"

Frances nods. Gertrude turns to Mrs. Lynch. "Thank you for allowing me to play for you today. It means a lot to me that you made the effort to come. Frances will do a great job." Gertrude turns, leaves the parlor, gets her cloak, and leaves the house. She has an urgent appointment at the hospital and she doesn't want to lose her nerve.

45

Sharing her music with Frances takes over Gertrude's thoughts. Staying the night at Mrs. Schultz's and making small talk with the nurses does not seem like a good idea. When the hospital exam is finished, Gertrude retrieves her bag and returns to Tybee Island with the adoption legal documents to read over. First things first, once in the cottage, she focuses on writing out the parts of her music. It's not for Frances, who cannot see the sheet music, but for Gertrude, who has put so much of her energy into making sure all the notes are down and the music is ready to go. When Frances asks her about different parts, the sheet music will keep both of them on track. After writing out the music, she goes to the big house, sits at the piano, and plays the music over and over until all the notes are right. It is late in the afternoon when she finishes. And rather than leave the sheet music on the piano for the practice with Frances, she takes it with her to the cottage as she prepares for the evening.

She takes a long beach walk after dinner, and then Gertrude sits at the table with the legal adoption documents in front of her to read and sign. Instead, she looks over the sheet music one more time and writes the title boldly at the top, "Tybee Rhapsody." Below it, she writes her name, Gertrude Kelly. Her name needs to be somewhere on something.

The week is full of music. Frances comes every morning and they work on the piece. With the sheet music, Gertrude can help Frances remember what comes next. During the practice, Frances will stop and ask, "What were you thinking when you wrote this section?" She asks about feelings and emotions, not the structure of the piece.

Gertrude answers with short descriptions of wind, rain, thunder, lightning, and ocean waves. She explains how she visualizes an idea, grief, despair, and hope. Frances listens carefully, then plays the section with new and different feelings.

The Savannah Music Club is meeting on Thursday evening at the Savannah Theatre, which was rebuilt after a fire gutted it the previous fall. Frances had gone over earlier to stay with her cousin. Gertrude dresses in her newly washed and ironed duster; nothing else fits. Then, she brushes her hair up and over on the top of her forehead, making a nice neat roll, and tucks the other long blonde curls into side rolls. A hat has been refitted to match the duster with some seashells and a plume of sea oats. Gertrude has grown fond of the sea oats and keeps fresh ones on the table to admire during meals. Clean gloves and added fabric ruffles at the bottom of her skirt complete her outfit. Her swollen feet only feel halfway decent in the wading boots. She added the ruffle to hide the boots.

During the short train ride, Gertrude mentally goes over the music, a habit developed many years ago. It has helped her remember pieces that she can play at a pub all night without any sheet music. As the train stops in Savannah, Gertrude remains sitting. Why should she go and hear someone else play her music? As much as Frances wants to play it like Gertrude would play it, she can't. Her own emotions enter into the piece. There are a few areas where Gertrude likes Frances' interpretation, but there are other places where she has to shrug and leave it alone. She reluctantly gets off the train.

Gertrude is early, really early, and nervous, but she doesn't want to go to Mrs. Schultz's, the hospital, or her parents. A tiredness envelops her. In the square where the theatre is located, there are benches. The short walk from the train depot has made her even more tired. The February sun is hiding behind clouds moving in from the mainland, and the breeze pulling them toward the river is chilly. She pulls her cloak tighter around her, but she cannot put the hood up since a hat completes her ensemble. Her hope is that it will not rain. Just at that moment, a few drops dampen her cheeks. It is still an hour before the meeting, but she goes to the theatre door and finds it unlocked.

This entrance into the theatre is greatly changed from when Gertrude played her recital here. Her recital dress was a black ensemble covered in rhinestones. Her hair was in a high bun decorated with a fabric magnolia blossom made by one of the nurses living in the boarding house. The occasion was festive. The nurses, sisters from the hospital, her family, Mrs. Schultz, and many Savannahians packed into the theatre to hear her play.

Now, no one is to know Gertrude is there. In the theatre, she sits in the back row. Not on the end, but about four seats over, where her view will be clear, but no one can see her. The lights are off in the auditorium, but the lights are shining brightly on stage. A grand piano, ebony black and shiny, is in the middle of the stage where the pianist can see most of the audience. Never having attended a meeting of the Savannah Music Club, Gertrude does not know the order of the program. Mrs. Lynch has not been forthcoming.

Gertrude sits quietly in the back row and waits.

46

The bells in Savannah chime at the quarter till the hour. Gertrude is drowsy and nodding in the dark auditorium but is awakened by the lights being turned on. People are coming in and chatting to each other as they make their way down to the front rows. The music club membership roster has at least a hundred people. The meetings are seen as ways to be seen and to be active in programs produced by the music club.

As the auditorium fills, Gertrude remains in her seat. Mrs. Lynch and Frances enter and walk to the front row, where seats have been saved for them. Mrs. Lynch is in a navy dress with red lace trim and a matching hat. Frances is in a black silk dress for the performance. The members talk and gesture in groups and pairs. Mr. Nickels, president of the club, enters. He's an elegant older man in his fifties wearing his signature gold cuff-links with a large "N" that picks up the light and glitters as he lifts his hand to greet members of the music club. He, too, goes directly to the front. Lights are being turned on and off on stage as the behind-the-scenes people prepare the area for both talking and playing the piano.

The stage is ready. Mr. Nickels stands up and walks up the few steps to the stage. People quiet down. Gertrude sits up straight, but her mind wanders as the program begins and Mr. Nickels talks, and talks, and talks. Then a man moves towards her in the semi-dark and sits down at the seat to her left. She leans toward him. "Lucas, what are you doing here?"

"Thought you might need some company."

"How did you know I would be here?"

"Frances told me."

Gertrude watches as Mrs. Lynch stands with Frances. The two of them step up onto the stage. Mrs. Lynch guides Frances over to the piano. Once Frances is seated and settled, Mrs. Lynch moves back to the center of the stage and announces the next part of the program.

"Ladies and gentlemen, for our meeting tonight, we have the honor of hearing my cousin, Miss Frances Lynch, play a new piece called 'Tybee Rhapsody.' The piece has been written by G.K. Walden. Let's give a warm Music Club welcome to the pianist, Frances Lynch."

Lucas leans closer to Gertrude. "Who thought that name up?"

Gertrude is silent.

Mrs. Lynch walks down the steps and sits in the front row. Frances had been told to count to ten after the introduction to give her cousin time to sit down. Gertrude counts off silently. Then Frances begins to play. The music pours out of the piano and into the corners of the auditorium. Everything Gertrude has put into the notes is now bouncing out to the ears of the audience members. All four parts of the rhapsody are played with excellent skill.

During the last section of the music, Gertrude feels the baby begin to kick and move about. Her hands are on the theatre armrests. Feeling the baby kick, she places her right hand over her abdomen to rub and soften the kicks. As she does, Lucas reaches out and puts his hand over hers on the left armrest. Gertrude glances quickly at Lucas but sees him looking straight ahead with a smile on his face. Her hand remains covered by his.

This is where Michael's definition of hope comes into Gertrude's head. She thinks of Michael then because he so much wants to learn anything to give him hope that his future will be better than his present. She feels that way now. Maybe Lucas can give her hope. He has not said anything, nor has he approached her in any way romantically until now, when he is holding her hand while she is churning with so many emotions. Her music is being played. Hers. Her baby is kicking as though hearing the music. What if? She stops. She is fantasizing. She must put her foundations under her dreams and not the other way around.

Frances ends the piece, and the audience immediately stands to applaud. Frances also stands and takes a small bow. She gestures slightly to the back of the auditorium, but people do not heed her gesture and remain clapping just for Frances.

Gertrude remains in her seat. There is more of the program to hear, but Gertrude wishes to leave. As the members settle back into their seats, Gertrude leans over and whispers to Lucas, "I need to stand." She stands and in the darkened back row of the auditorium, goes out the other end of the row and leaves the theatre. The evening air hits her lungs and she takes a deep breath. Hearing her music makes her want to walk down the aisle and say, "I wrote that. That rhapsody is mine. I composed that while in solitude out on Tybee Island." Instead, alone on the sidewalk at this hour, she has no desire to go back in. She turns to walk to Mrs. Schultz's boarding house. It is much too late to go back to Tybee tonight, yet there is a part of her that does not want to have small talk and be questioned about how she is, what she plans on doing, and what she thinks about her music being played by someone else. There is one more train to Tybee Island tonight.

Gertrude boards the train and sits, but she begins rehashing the meeting at the theatre, going over the music, and feeling Lucas hold her hand while the baby kicks. She thinks about how the paperwork for the adoption has not been finished. It is dark when she arrives on Tybee Island, but knowing the path and knowing that there have not been any recent dangerous incidents in her life, she walks quickly to the cottage.

Too tired to eat, Gertrude changes into her nightgown and prepares to rest on the settee. She puts another log on top of the embers and puts water in the kettle over the fire. Gertrude stares at the flames.

The baby is due in just a few weeks. What should she do? The uniforms are finished, the inventories have been done, but because of the sewing and then the composing, no plans have been made past the last of May, when the Fresh Air Home camp will open and her services will no longer be needed. After the baby comes, there will be two months to rest. Two months. Plans need to be made. She should ask Sister Mary Joyce about the nursing program. However, even if there is a spot for her in the program, that would not start until the fall. She needs to get the word out that piano students will be accepted on Wednesdays at Mrs. Schultz's boarding house.

A job might be found in Savannah to be able to pay her parents for room and board. She did play in the pubs in Dublin, but it is not the same in Savannah, where it would be inappropriate for her to do that and expect to get paying students to take piano lessons from her. There are retail stores on Broughton Street. Her sewing skills might land her a job in helping women choose patterns or fabric to make outfits. Her thinking comes to a halt. Nothing can be done to find a job until the baby comes. Gertrude falls asleep in front of the fire.

47

A knock at the door has Gertrude open her eyes and realize that she has slept through the night. That hasn't happened in a long time. Daylight is streaming through all the windows. She stands and pulls on her robe to go to the door.

"Yes, who's there?"

"Eley."

Gertrude opens the door and steps back to invite Eley into the cottage.

"I heard you were in Savannah, going to get checkups. So, what did the sisters say about when the baby is due?"

"Hello, Eley, I hope you are doing well."

"Yes'm, but I came to check on you." Eley bustles into the cottage and shuts the door.

Gertrude crosses over to the settee and sits down. "I am fine and the baby is fine. The sisters suggest that the baby is due in the next three weeks."

"I see. What's yo plan?"

"My plan? I wait."

"Not by yo'self."

"Why not?"

"'Cause anything can happen and you might need some help. Remember New Year's Day?"

Gertrude nods. "I do remember. But I do not know what else to do, I have never had a baby."

"You need to have someone here to go get help should there be a need."

"Okay, I understand. I will see what I can do."

There is another knock at the door. Eley waves at Gertrude to stay seated and goes to the door. Captain is on the steps.

"Come on in, Captain, Gertrude is sitting right over there."

Captain comes in, holding his hat in his hand. "I heard you were in Savannah getting a check-up and came by to see how you are doing."

Gertrude looks first at Captain and then at Eley. "Who's been sharing my business?"

Before anyone answers, there is another knock at the door. Eley returns to open the door. There on the steps is Michael.

"Come on in. Gertrude is on the settee."

"Michael," says Gertrude, "we might not have a lesson today. I'm feeling a bit tired."

"That's okay, I just came by to check on you."

"You heard that I was in Savannah having a checkup, right?" Gertrude looks at Captain, Eley, and then at Michael. All of them are looking down, out a window, or into space; none of them are looking at Gertrude. There is yet another knock on the door.

"I'll get it," says Eley. Frances and Lucas are on the steps. "Come in. Gertrude is on the settee."

Captain goes over to Frances. "Here, let me guide you over to a chair near Gertrude."

They cross the room, and Frances is seated in the chair near the fireplace. Lucas stands next to Michael.

Gertrude looks at all of them gathered for the first time in the cottage. Each of them has their hands folded in front of them, and all are now looking at her. Gertrude looks at Lucas. "I know. You wanted to see how I am doing."

Lucas nods. "And...I wanted to know why you left without saying anything to me at the music club meeting. I thought you slipped out for just a minute, but you didn't come back. Frances and I came over from Savannah on the morning train."

Gertrude is silent. As she sits there and observes all of her friends, the people who have found ways to make her solitude on Tybee feel like home, she does not know what to say.

Eley speaks up. "The kettle is full of hot water. Who wants a cup of tea?" Everyone speaks up or nods. Captain pulls several of the kitchen chairs over around the fireplace. Lucas is helping Eley with the cups and saucers, and Michael puts another log on the fire.

"I'd help, but from the sounds I hear, I would only get in the way," says Frances.

"Me too," says Gertrude, "and I live here."

The teacups are passed, and one by one, everybody finds a seat. Gertrude slips away into her bedroom and changes out of her gown into one of her comfortable homemade dresses. She comes back into the room and looks at each one of them. Captain, with his military bearing and his large sea-worthy hands, holds the teacup gently in his palm without the saucer. Michael's hands are spotless. No dirt under his nails since his first piano lesson. He does not know what to do with the saucer, so he puts it on the table behind him and holds his cup with both hands like a bowl. Eley has balanced her cup and saucer on her lap and is talking quietly with Frances, who has the cup in one hand and the saucer in the other. Lucas has turned the wooden kitchen chair backward and has straddled the chair so that the cup and saucer can balance on the chair's back rim. He is asking Captain about how the fish camp is gearing up with spring and then summer right around the corner. Gertrude takes a deep breath.

As the group talks, the idea of food comes up. Everyone is hungry. They begin to plan. Captain has some shrimp back at the fish camp that he and Michael had caught earlier. Lucas remembers seeing that the market at the train depot is open and he could get some vegetables. Frances can contribute sausage; they had a lot left over from breakfast. Eley looks in the pantry.

"Gertrude has cornmeal and eggs. I can bake some cornbread. She's got peppers growing on the windowsill. We could have Frogmore stew if Lucas can get some potatoes and corn on the cob at the market."

Suddenly, there is movement in the little cottage. Captain heads to the fish camp for the shrimp. Michael runs to Frances's house to pick up the leftover sausage. Lucas goes to the market. And Eley is tossing pans and skillets onto the stove to begin the cornbread.

Gertrude looks over at Frances. "Now might be a good time to talk about music."

"Yes, I would like that."

"You played 'Tybee Rhapsody' better than I ever imagined. What are your thoughts about the music?"

"When we were learning the piece and I asked you many questions about what you were thinking, your answers were how they sounded to you. Though you told me that it was what you heard in the storm, I was not there and did not hear the same storm."

"But you played the notes like I accented them."

"Yes, but I did not play the notes the way you feel them. Remember, my ears are finely tuned without my sight but not necessarily my emotions. The feeling a musician puts into the notes is the reason we go to hear the person who composed the music. And when someone plays a piece that has been written by someone else, that musician must put his or her own emotion into the piece, their own interpretation.

Immediately, Gertrude thinks about how she plays "Clair de lune." There is no way she can play the music the way Debussy could play it, but it could still be worth hearing. "Are you suggesting that only the composer should play the music?"

"No, I am saying that each musician brings what they know to the music. And since each musician is different, the sound of the music will be different. It can be good, but it is different."

"I see," says Gertrude, and she understands what Frances is saying.

"Now it is my turn. What did you think about when you heard me play your piece?"

A short laugh comes out of Gertrude. "I have to admit I was looking for mistakes."

"See?" says Frances and laughs with Gertrude.

"Creating the music has been an emotional experience for me," says Gertrude. "When I am composing, something takes over my brain and I play a section. When I go back over it, I have no idea where it came from."

"Like something divine?"

"Yes, and mysterious, but there it is," says Gertrude. "Much of the composing is organic. The music flows from the sounds I hear in my head. But then there is an ah-ha moment when I play something and it is just too good for me to have thought of all by myself."

Frances sits back and sips her tea. "I enjoyed playing your 'Tybee Rhapsody,' but I have also enjoyed hearing you play and making friends on the island. Thank you for including me."

"You were a part of this group since the first day you came to tune the piano."

Eley is listening. She interrupts. "Excuse me. Did I hear you say that Frances played your piece?"

"Yes."

"Where and why?"

"She played it at the Savannah Music Club meeting. Why? Come on, Eley, you of all people know why. You were the first to figure it out."

Eley stops what she is doing and, with her hands on her hips, she says, "They wouldn't let you play because you are pregnant?"

"That's right."

"My goodness, they must have not ever heard you play." She starts focusing on baking and turns away from Gertrude and Frances.

Frances gives a wry smile. "That confirms my feeling that if folks will not let you, of all people, play your own music, then blind people like me will never have a chance to make our dreams come true."

"People like you?" asks Gertrude, "I know you probably didn't dream of becoming a piano tuner. What have been your dreams?"

Frances puts the cup gently onto the saucer. "I wanted to write."

"Why don't you?"

"Have you not noticed that I am blind?"

"I have noticed that there seems to be nothing you can't do if you set your mind to it. Do you want to write books?"

"Yes. And now that I have heard your music and played your music, I want to write more than ever."

"Really, why?"

"Your music has reintroduced me to the creative process. You have gotten that process down with your 'Tybee Rhapsody.'"

"I have? I don't know. Please explain."

"Are you familiar with Hawthorne's story, 'The Artist of the Beautiful'?"

"No."

"Before I lost my sight, I read it in my uncle's library, in a collection of Nathaniel Hawthorne's short stories called *Mosses from an Old Manse*. Though the theme of the story is recognizing the beauty of art, what struck me about the story was that Hawthorne was really writing about the four stages of the creative process: the idea, creation, falling short, then succeeding, and giving examples of each throughout the story. And when the end creation is built but then crushed, as it was in Hawthorne's story, it is not a problem because once the creative process is learned, it can be repeated, over and over and over."

The two women are quiet and sip their tea. Gertrude speaks first. "You play the piano so well. Surely you did not play that well when you were fourteen and lost your sight. How did you continue to learn new songs, like the one you shared with me, 'Alice, Where Art Thou Going'?"

"With new music, someone has to read the notes to me or play it until I memorize it. Few people want to spend their time working with a blind woman." She pauses. "I do, however, use some of the money I earn from piano tuning to hire someone to read the notes to me with new sheet music. I just can't resist learning a new piece, like yours. It has been a delight for me to play your music."

Gertrude thinks for a minute, "You could do the same thing with your writing, couldn't you? There is the invention of the typewriter. You could learn to type. I'm sure that you could learn to do that. I have recently read Thoreau's *Walden*, where he writes, 'If you have built castles in the air, your work need not be lost; that is where they should be. Now put the foundations under them...' You need to put the foundations under your dream of being a writer. Learn to type."

Frances pauses, then she says, "I could write a story about birding on Tybee Island."

"I said you could do anything, Frances, but one needs to see the birds to be able to identify them."

"That's where you are wrong. I go to the bird count on Tybee Island every Christmas. I go with some others who help me walk along the paths. But I can hear and identify more birds than the sighted folks can."

"I had no idea," says Gertrude.

"I didn't think you did," says Frances.

Their conversation is interrupted by Captain coming in with the shrimp, Lucas with the potatoes and corn he found that was been canned in a Savannah cannery, and Michael with the sausage. The conversation of who is going to do what takes over the small cottage. Gertrude doesn't even bother offering any help. Eley has the water at full boil for the corn and potatoes. The sausage has been cooked, so it can go into the stew to reheat. Michael is at the sink peeling the shrimp. Lucas opens the jar and hands it off to Eley to put in the pot. Captain washes the potatoes. Dinner is being made without her input. There is a peace about it all that appeals to Gertrude.

48

____

Dinner is loud and busy with passing plates and pouring tea. Attending Gertrude's practice sessions on Sundays has given the six people gathered around her cottage table a chance to know each other. The talk goes from spring preparations—Captain and Michael have work to do at the fishing camp to prepare for summer visitors—to travel. Frances will be visiting her family in New York. Music—there is a rehash of Frances playing for the music club. Food—Eley added peppers to the cornbread to make it hotter. The ocean—changes that the new season will bring, and then to Gertrude and the baby.

Eley is the first to speak up. "Gertrude, who is going to be here with you when the baby starts to come?"

There is silence at the table as each looks at Gertrude, waiting for her answer. She looks back at them, clears her throat, and says, "None of this has been planned. Not the baby, not living here in the cottage on Tybee Island, not getting to know all of you. Therefore, I have not made any plans about what to do when the baby comes."

All five talk at the same time, so that no one person can be understood.

"Wait!" says Gertrude over the top of all the voices. "No sane person can understand what you are saying with everyone talking at once." The voices cease. In the silence, Gertrude looks again at her new friends. "Please, Eley, suggest what I must do."

"I think it will be best, seeing that you already had a rush to the hospital once, that you go to Savannah during these last weeks and wait at your family's home. Your mother seems to be willing to help you get through this," says Eley.

"Or, ask Mrs. Schultz if you can stay at the boarding house," says Lucas. "She already has a cot ready for you in her office, and the house is next door to the hospital."

"There's a different, new midwife at the Fort Screven Hospital," says Frances. "They change frequently when their husbands are transferred. I learned about her at church last week. I met her briefly and she seems eager to help out if anyone needs her."

"Hazel met her too," says Captain.

"But who will be at the cottage to get help?" asks Michael. Every eye is on Gertrude. She looks down at the tea in her cup. There is a strong wish that the tea leaves will tell her what she should do. Finally, she says, "I hear what you say. I will think about my choices and see what I need to do. So, let's finish cleaning up from dinner and then I need to go for a walk."

"You go for a walk," says Eley. "I will do the dishes."

Frances stands and moves over to the sink. "I can dry them if someone will put them away."

Captain stands. "Michael and I need to do some groundwork, so we'll leave y'all to figure out what to do. But let us know." They are out the door before Gertrude can thank them.

Lucas stands. "Too many hands in the dishwater. I'll walk

with you." He reaches out a hand to steady Gertrude as she stands.

"Okay, but just a short walk."

They find the air is crisp with a steady breeze off the ocean. As they pass over the dunes on the boardwalk, Gertrude hears the bird sounds as they fly above the water, looking for food. "I will miss the ocean when I leave Tybee Island," she says out loud.

"Lots of questions as to what you might be doing in the next few months have gone unanswered, so I won't bother asking what you plan on doing when you leave Tybee Island," says Lucas.

Gertrude gives him a quick side glance to see how serious he might be. There is almost a sarcastic tone to what he says. She can't tell. "Actually, I have been thinking about that part."

"Really?"

"Yes. I am prepared to ask Sister Mary Joyce if I can reenter the nursing program. I have only four months to finish the training. If I cannot stay at the boarding house, my mother has encouraged me to stay at home and walk over every day."

"Is finishing the nursing program something you want?"

"It makes logical sense, but I have lost sleep over thinking about what will happen to the baby. Would she be housed at the hospital until new parents are chosen, or would the parents take her away quickly, and I would not be able to see her or care for her?"

Lucas is silent.

Gertrude is walking closest to the ocean waves and looks out over the water. The constant surge of the water reminds her of the heartbeat heard deep inside of her. She also thinks about the feeling washing over her of guilt, loneliness, and abandonment. How will she ever be able to cope with all of those?

They walk in silence.

Finally, Lucas asks, "Will you continue to play the piano?"

Still looking out at the ocean waves, Gertrude answers. "I have no choice. Music seems to be a part of me, as is teaching music now. Though I did not think I would teach, I find that having a student like Michael, who wants to learn and who practices, is a joy. I love hearing him master a song and play it with feeling."

Again, they are silent. Gertrude glances over at Lucas, but he seems content just to walk.

Then he asks, "The nursing program goes through the summer?"

"Yes, it is all year long. The summer months are used as practice. I would use the summer months to brush up on what I may have forgotten from being away and start in the fall with their regular program. And, Mrs. Schultz has agreed to let me have students in the parlor on Wednesdays, if I am not staying at the house, so that I will be there to play songs for the Bible reading."

"You have been thinking about your future after Tybee Island."

"Thanks to Thoreau."

"Thoreau?"

"There's a particular passage that has been resonating with me. Thoreau writes, 'If you have built castles in the air, your work need not be lost; that is where they should be. Now put the foundations under them...' I have my dreams, but now I need to put foundations under them. I need to find a job and be able to take care of myself."

"Your dream is to be a concert pianist. How is the nursing program and teaching piano going to fulfill that dream?"

"The way you ask makes it seem like I will never be a concert pianist or a composer."

"You misunderstand me. I am not asking to contradict, but to understand." He pauses and reaches for Gertrude's hand.

Gertrude stops in the sand. "I don't know how I will do it.

I have botched everything I have tried. But I know I am happiest when I am playing regularly and composing. I don't even know what the foundations look like for a concert pianist. I am groping, looking, and hoping to learn every day."

Lucas still holds her hand and says, "Changes are all around us."

"And you, you ask me all these questions. I know you are not happy doing what you are doing, reporting stories. What will you be doing? You have a future too, you know."

Lucas has them start walking again. He is quiet. Gertrude looks at him. "Well?"

"Yes, I, too, have been thinking about the future. I have been communicating with my family. We have exchanged many letters."

Lucas still holds Gertrude's hand and it is nice. For months, there has been a desire for someone to touch her, hold her, be near her. When Lucas does not continue, Gertrude glances over at him. "What are they saying?"

"My family in France owns several restaurants in Paris."

"You mentioned that before."

"They have opened a third one. We have talked through the letters and they now understand that I do not want to be a chef, like my father and brothers. They know I do not want to be confined in the kitchen or in the restaurant all day. I need my freedom to move about."

Gertrude is silent as they continue to walk. The words "I need my freedom" echo in her ears.

"They have offered to let me purchase all the produce for the restaurants. I could wander around the markets and go out to the farms."

"Are you thinking of going back to France?"

"Yes, I am. They have convinced me that I can be part of the family but work in my own way."

Gertrude pulls her hand from his and tucks her hair under her hood. "When would you leave?"

"I would need to be there in the summer to line up the markets and farms for the restaurants."

"I see." And Gertrude did see. Yet another hope is dashed. He, too, will leave. With her baby due any time and her lack of resources, she should not expect someone like Lucas to hang around and wait until she figures out what her life might look like. Additionally, he has not expressed any desire to be with her outside of getting a story for the newspaper. A little hand-holding is not enough. "I need to rest," she says, turning and walking quickly in the direction of the cottage.

49

Lucas catches up with her. "What just happened?"

"Nothing," she says. "Absolutely nothing."

"We're talking about our futures and you suddenly disengage."

"Our futures? You plan on leaving. I have a limited future and need to find work. And, in case you have missed it, I am having a baby. Our futures?"

Lucas catches her arm to stop her from walking. "Wait, hear me out."

"I have heard enough." She turns and goes into the cottage, leaving Lucas standing in the lane.

Eley and Frances have finished the dishes and are sitting at the table waiting for Gertrude. She closes the cottage door behind her.

"Did Lucas leave?" asks Eley.

Gertrude does not answer. She goes to the settee and looks about the room. The cottage is tidy now that the sewing is finished and the uniforms are neatly stacked in the dining room of the big house. She sits down and awkwardly pulls her feet up on the settee. In front of her, the fire is subsiding in the fireplace. There is nothing else to see. Hope is a fruitless word and should be stricken from her vocabulary. Hope is nothing but a dream; it is not real. Tears begin trickling down her cheeks.

Eley comes to the settee. "Gertrude, what are all these tears about?"

Gertrude continues to cry and does not answer.

There is a knock at the door.

"I'll get it," says Eley to Frances, who has risen from the chair at the table. Eley opens the door to find Lucas on the steps. "I don't think this is a good time for tea."

"I don't want tea. I want to talk with Gertrude."

"That too. Not a good time to talk with her."

Gertrude hears them, but suddenly there is a huge pain going through her. She screams in agony. Eley and Lucas dash inside. Gertrude is holding her stomach and clinching the edge of the settee so tightly that her fingers are turning white from the exertion.

"What's happening?" asks Frances.

Gertrude only grimaces.

Eley grabs Gertrude's arm. "Let's stand up for a minute," she tells Gertrude. And with Lucas on one side and Eley on the other, they bring Gertrude up to a standing position.

"Can someone please talk out loud?" asks Frances.

Eley responds. "I think Gertrude is in labor."

"Oh, my," says Frances. "It's early, isn't it?"

"Not really. She is due in March, according to the sisters at the hospital, but not really knowing when she got pregnant makes it difficult to be accurate, and she can't remember," says Eley.

"Please stop talking about me like I'm not here," mutters Gertrude. "I know I left for Dublin in May."

"Hmph," says Frances, "somebody is better at music than at counting."

Lucas is quietly listening to the women. "So the baby is coming now?"

"Yes, I believe so," says Eley. "Maybe you can go to the hospital and get the midwife to come here. We barely got her up to stand, much less trying to get her to the hospital."

Lucas is out the door. Eley calls out to Frances. "Come take Gertrude's other arm and help me get her into the bedroom."

They maneuver Gertrude onto the bed and pull the quilt up around her shoulders. The February chill hangs in the room.

"Why is this room so cold?" asks Eley.

"I seldom sleep in here. The settee has been more comfortable and the fireplace keeps the front room warmer."

"Well, maybe we ought to leave you on the settee?"

Gertrude screams and curls up on the bed. She yells at Eley, "No, I'm fine."

"Hmph," says Frances. "'I'm fine' screamed at the top of your voice does not work for me."

"I'm fine," says Gertrude in a softer but firm voice. "Is that better?"

"Much better," says Frances and pats Gertrude's arm.

"Well, since I am going to have this baby, ready or not, I need to get ready." Gertrude tries to swing her legs over the edge of the bed to sit up. She has to grab the edge of the bed to raise herself up to a standing position. She sees Eley staring at her. "I need to get a place ready for the baby. We have work to do."

"And what, pray tell, do we need to do?" asks Eley.

"She will need somewhere to sleep. She will need her own little quilt. She will need diapers. We need to prepare!"

Frances says, "I can't help with any..." She is interrupted by another loud scream from Gertrude. "But I can count how long between contractions. Eley, how long should they be?"

"When they remain steady at about five minutes apart is when we need to see about the baby coming," says Eley.

"Okay, I'll begin." Francis takes out a watch from her skirt pocket, holds it gently in her hand, and fingers the back of it.

Eley and Gertrude stop their movement and both stare at what Frances is holding in her hand.

"How does that work?" asks Eley. "You can't see."

"But I can feel," says Frances. "When we traveled to Switzerland last winter, we found this 'touch watch.' Come closer, I'll show you how it works."

Both women stand within inches of Frances and look at the watch.

"Around the edge of the case are pins that correspond to the hours on the watch dial. A revolving hand stops at a point between the pins that corresponds to the hour and approximate minute. With the hand and pins as locators, I can feel the approximate time."

"I'm impressed," says Eley. "You can do a whole lot of things."

Gertrude sees Frances smile for the first time. "It wasn't originally created for the blind to tell time. It was made for people who could afford the watch and wanted to check the time in the dark," says Frances.

"Why would someone want to check the time in the dark?" asks Gertrude.

"Maybe there are no lights and there is an emergency. Maybe they want to be discreet at meetings and end a discussion without pulling out a pocket watch to see the time. I don't know, I just know I don't have to ask people what time it is and can go about my life without depending on others to always have to help me."

Gertrude doubles over and screams with pain.

"That was fifteen minutes," says Frances. "You've still got a ways to go."

"Thanks!" Gertrude screams.

"I'm counting," says Frances.

"Somebody needs to help me with more than counting."

"What do you want to do?" asks Eley.

"We've got to get things ready for the baby. I thought I had time. I don't have time."

"You have fifteen minutes," says Frances.

"Frances!"

"Okay, maybe less. I'm counting."

Gertrude goes into the main room and looks at the leftover fabric from the uniforms. There are pieces big enough that, if she cut them into squares, the cotton material would make nice diapers. "Eley, help me spread the material on the table and square it up. We can cut some diapers." Getrude gets the basket full of sewing supplies and the two of them begin cutting out squares. After another scream from Gertrude, they hear Frances say, "Still fifteen minutes."

There is a knock on the door. Eley goes over quickly to open and sees Lucas there with a woman.

"This is Melinda Maddock. She's the midwife at the hospital," says Lucas.

"Come in. I'm Eley, and Gertrude is there by the table." Eley ushers Melinda in as Lucas hesitantly follows. "This is Frances, who has been keeping track of how long between the contractions," says Eley.

"That's great. How long?" asks Melinda.

"Fifteen minutes," says Frances.

Melinda puts down a bag and takes off her coat. Lucas takes her coat and puts it on a hook in the hallway. "I need to examine you." She looks at Gertrude and then glances over at Lucas, who stumbles about how he needs to go find Captain. He exits quickly from the cottage and shuts the door behind him.

Gertrude suggests that they go into the bedroom.

～

Gertrude feels better with the midwife present. The examination is similar to the one at the hospital on New Year's Day. Melinda goes over everything Gertrude can expect: contractions, waiting, breathing, and finally, the birth and how to take care of the baby. Then Melinda sits in a chair and takes out some knitting from a bag. She is quite thin, and her long fingers clicking through the yarn with the knitting needles indicate an adeptness of taking moments to create something while waiting. Her hair is trimmed above her ears in the new style that many of the younger women are wearing. Gertrude stands up. "I have some preparations to do." Melinda nods and continues to knit.

Entering the main room, Gertrude finds Eley finishing the last of the material for the diapers.

"And that makes one dozen," Eley says as she folds the last one and places it on a pile. "I reckon that will keep you from having to wash every day."

"Thank you. Now we have to figure out where to put the baby to be safe until I can get a crib or something permanent."

"If we had a box, we could pad the sides with some of the material scraps and cut out a couple of little quilts from the ones on the settee," says Eley. "I don't see drawers in the cottage."

"No, there are none upstairs either. There might be some in the big house," says Gertrude. "But wait, I have an idea. The Singer sewing machine came in a crate and with a box. Eley, go check in the closet through the water closet. I put those in there in case I needed them for something. I guess having this baby is something," says Gertrude, but then she grits her teeth and tries to swallow the next scream.

"I don't know which is worse, screaming or trying not to scream," says Frances.

"Obviously, you have not had labor pains," yells Gertrude.

"Obviously," agrees Frances. "But I have had kidney stones. I do know about pain in the abdomen."

Eley and Gertrude stop and look at Frances, who continues. "I may not be able to see visually, but I do see some things mentally. Take, for example, how screaming helps Gertrude cope with her pain. I see that as a way to theatrically demonstrate that something is happening in her body."

Melinda interrupts Frances. She has come to the doorway. "Actually, Gertrude, if you reduce that scream to a moan, your low-toned voice will help move the baby down. Try breathing deeply and releasing the tension when breathing at the next contraction."

Frances turns her head in Melinda's direction. "Well said," she adds.

Gertrude looks at both women and then turns to Eley. "Let's get the sleeping box prepared."

The hours pass as the women prepare the cottage for the baby and walk Gertrude around the main room and down the hallway. She is perfecting the deep breathing. At the next contraction, Frances announces that it is now five minutes between them.

There is a knock at the door. Eley goes and opens the door to find Mrs. Schultz and Gertrude's mother on the steps.

"How is she?" asks Mrs. Schultz.

Before Eley can answer, Mrs. Kelly steps between the women and goes directly to Gertrude. "How long between contractions?"

Frances answers, "Five minutes."

Melinda steps into the room again after hiding out in the bedroom. "She refuses to get in the bed and I have not been able to check her dilation."

"And who are you?" asks Mrs. Kelly.

"Mum, this is Melinda, a midwife from the hospital on the

island." Gertrude bends over with a moan, and Mrs. Kelly takes her arm.

"It's time to be checked," says Mrs. Kelly.

"But I'm not ready," Gertrude says. "I have more to do to get things ready for this baby. How did you know to come?"

"Lucas telegraphed me from the depot on Tybee," says Mrs. Schultz. "I went immediately over to your parents' house and we decided to take the next train. We were lucky that one left soon after we got to the depot."

Mrs. Kelly interrupts. "Ready or not, you need to be checked by the midwife. Come, let's get this over with." She guides Gertrude into the bedroom.

Gertrude remembers the light green scarf she had knitted early on at the cottage. She had hung it on a peg at the door. She calls out to Eley as Melinda and Mrs. Kelly shut the door behind them. "Use the green scarf at the front door to put in the wooden box."

Gertrude angles herself onto the bed. Mrs. Kelly lifts her legs and feet onto the mattress. Melinda has basins of water and clean cloths ready. Gertrude moans loudly.

"Breathe deeply," says Melinda.

Gertrude does and hears her mother singing softly next to her, a song about why they left Ireland, a song Gertrude has listened to her mother sing at home in front of the fire when the children demanded to know why they spoke Irish when no one in their school did but the Irish immigrants. There was always a lot of music in the home as Gertrude grew up. Her mother would sing and play the piano when Gertrude was still learning, and all the family hummed or sang along.

As Melinda begins her examination, Gertrude listens to her mother sing. Now, since she has seen Ireland and experienced Croagh Patrick, she understands better why her mother sings the tune "Slieve Gallion Braes."

"As I went a walking one morning in May
To view your fair valleys and your mountains so gay
I was thinking of your flowers all going to decay
That grow around ye bonny, bonny Slieve Gallion Brae"

Gertrude moans loudly. Her mother stops briefly, but as Gertrude relaxes, her mother continues. And Gertrude, in spite of herself, hums along with her mother.

"Oft times have I wandered with my dog and my gun
And travelled your valleys for joy and for fun
But those days are gone forever and I can no longer
    stray
So farewell unto ye bonny, bonny Slieve Gallion Brae
"Oft times in the evenings and the sun in the west
I roamed hand in hand with the one I love best
But the dreams of youth have vanished and I am far away
So farewell unto ye bonny, bonny Slieve Gallion Brae"

Melinda speaks directly to Gertrude. "I think it is time for you to breathe deeply and then push. I see the crown of the baby's head."

Gertrude cries out in pain, takes a deep breath, and pushes, clamping down hard with her teeth through the exertion. Her mother does not stop singing.

"It is not the want of employment at home
That caused the poor sons of old Ireland to roam
But the rents are getting higher and I can no longer pay
So farewell unto ye bonny, bonny Slieve Gallion Brae"

Gertrude looks over at her mother. "Can you not keep singing? I'm in pain here!"

Mrs. Kelly rubs Gertrude's arm and gently places her hand in Gertrude's. She sings.

> "Farewell to old Erin, a land that is so green
>> To the Parish of Lissen and the cross of Ballinascreen
>> May good fortune shine upon you when I am far away
>> And a long farewell to bonny, bonny Slieve Gallion Brae"

50

Gertrude awakens to an empty room. No one is with her. She feels heavy and so very tired. Then the realization hits her that if she is alone, the baby is gone! She shouts, "Where's my baby?!" The nightmares of her not being able to find her baby are present in her head.

The door opens and in walks Eley. "Why are you yelling?"

"I want to see my baby girl. Where is she? Has someone taken my baby?" Gertrude is in tears and is struggling to get out of bed.

Mrs. Kelly walks in and says, "Whisht, girl, whisht, the baby's right here, she is, see?" Mrs. Kelly holds the baby wrapped in the green knitted scarf. She walks over to Gertrude and hands the baby to her. "See? She's right here."

Gertrude takes a deep breath and gently moves the scarf from around the baby. As she looks down at the smooth and creamy clear face, she sees the dark hair of her Irish ancestors and not her blonde hair. "She's beautiful."

"Aye, as beautiful as you were when you were a wee one as well," says Mrs. Kelly.

Gertrude cannot take her eyes from the baby, studying every feature. Then she asks, "Is Mrs. Schultz still here?"

"Yes, she is having a cup of tea," says Mrs. Kelly.

"Ask Mrs. Schultz to come in. I need to talk with her."

Eley goes into the next room to get Mrs. Schultz. Gertrude props the baby up gently on her lap, and with the help of her mother, she sits up better in the bed with pillows behind her. When Mrs. Schultz comes in, Gertrude is ready for her.

"I have a question for you. What meaning does the name Bridget have?"

Mrs. Schultz looks at the other women gathered around Gertrude and the baby. "Gertrude, Sister Mary Joyce warned you about holding the baby, much less naming the baby. The adoption will go much easier if you do not do this."

"I have no choice, Mrs. Schultz. She is of my blood, and I will find a way to take care of her."

"Can you make a living to support you and the baby?" Mrs. Schultz asks.

"I have learned many things while on Tybee Island. I have learned to cook seafood. I have learned the love of teaching piano to a student. I have learned to accept the community around me that offers help when needed and supports my love of music. I have learned that my family still loves me and stands by me when I am at my lowest. Then I learned that this baby came from me and is mine. I will find a way to take care of both of us. I have not signed the adoption papers, so she is mine." Gertrude pauses, then says, "So is there a Saint Bridget or something?"

Mrs. Schultz smiles. "Yes, Saint Bridget of Kildare helped spread Christianity in Ireland during the fifth century. She was known as 'Mary of the Gael.' The name is associated with strong and determined women."

Gertrude looks down at her baby. "Then her name will be

Bridget. She will be a strong and determined woman and is my bridge to having a life outside my own wants."

There is a gentle knock on the front door. Eley leaves to see who it might be. She returns with Lucas behind her. "I thought since everyone is here around you, it might be okay for Lucas to join us."

"I kinda pushed. Eley didn't want me to come in at first," says Lucas as he crosses over to the bed where Gertrude is holding Bridget.

Gertrude looks at Lucas. "Why are you here? Don't you have to catch a ship to France?"

"Not until June."

"I really do not want to talk with you now."

"But you haven't heard what I have to say."

"I don't want to hear what you have to say. I am done." She begins to cry. She didn't want to cry, but the tears came instantly.

Lucas takes a finger and wipes one of her tears away. "I am not finished," he says.

She sits silently holding her baby, not looking at Lucas.

"To continue where we left off on the beach, yes, I am going back to France. The job sounds like a good way for me to do what I love to do, and that is to be free to move about and create my own work." He reaches over and takes the baby's small hand. "I have one question for you: Are you planning on putting the baby up for adoption?"

"No," Gertrude says quickly. "I will raise this baby. She is mine."

"Thank goodness," says Lucas.

"What? What difference does it make to you?"

"I have always wanted a family. I have for a long time. When I tried to talk Sharon into it, she wanted a career and a partner first. She was the wrong person at the wrong time for me. Now

I'm thinking, if I can talk you into it, I would have a ready-made family."

"What are you saying? Have you thought this through? I am not ready to accept charity."

Lucas laughs. "I am not offering charity. You will have to work for the right to be Mrs. Laurent."

"You can't be serious. I have just had another man's baby. I have no skills or talents that I can offer. And, I am a little tired of having to work for a man and get little in return."

"You can be a really stubborn woman sometimes. You have many skills and talents to offer. You can teach piano in France just as easily as you could teach in Savannah. Music is an international language. Additionally, I have asked my brother to check on music conservatories. Paris has many. You have choices."

"These options are tempting, but you said I would have to work. What type of work?"

"You need to write music."

Gertrude is feeling many things. She is delighted that Lucas is thinking of how to make things work. She has been worried that she might not be able to complete the nursing program and raise Bridget. Even with her family's help, it would be diffi-cult. However, she is not sure that marrying Lucas will solve her problems, much less give her hope for a future in music. She had thought Randolph would help her, and look how that turned out. Plus, Lucas has not said anything about being in love with her.

"I don't know," says Gertrude.

"Are you telling me that you don't have feelings for me? Or are you overwhelmed by all the changes that will happen to you over the next few months?"

Gertrude holds Bridget and looks at how calm the small baby is. "How can everyone be so quiet?" she asks, looking around the room. No one moves or says a word.

Lucas speaks first. "I am in love with you, Gertrude, and with your music." He looks around the room at Mrs. Schultz, Eley, Frances, and Mrs. Kelly. "And with the people who surround you." Then he looks at Bridget. "And now with your baby."

"With my baby?"

"Yes, I want a family. Were you not listening a few minutes ago when I said you were a ready-made family? I have a large family in France. I would love to add to that family with my own children. I could adopt your baby and give her my name before we even leave Savannah. My family in France wants to help raise our children. My sisters are so excited. So, will you marry me?"

Gertrude is silent. More tears trickle silently down her cheeks. She looks into Lucas's eyes. She has wanted to find a way to make everything work: to keep her baby, hope for a future that includes composing her own music, and find a way to eat and live that is better than just surviving. She had hoped that Lucas's holding her hand while listening to her rhapsody being played by Frances was more than just a friendship caring, but he never alluded to anything. She had not even thought that marrying someone would help her solve her dilemma of how to take care of Bridget and earn a living at the same time. Now Lucas is offering her a way forward. She cannot say no to this offer. And she does have feelings for Lucas. That's why she was so angry with him on the beach walk; he was not including her in his future plans.

"Why did you not indicate to me before how you feel? Even on the beach, you were talking about your future, not our future."

"Would you have listened to me or pushed me away? I did not want to take the risk. I have learned that I may have a way of turning off women I care about by being more forceful or having an opinion that does not work with theirs, and I did not want that to happen with you. I was biding my time. I had already worked it out with my family. And I tried to tell you on the beach, but you hastened away."

Gertrude looks at his eyes and believes him. His willingness to not write about her piano concerts, to listen to what she was saying, to be with her when it has been difficult, and to adjust so quickly to her friends, how can she walk away from someone like this? She still remains silent.

Lucas speaks up. "Why would I keep coming over to Tybee Island on my only day off with no guarantee of a story if I did not care about you?"

Gertrude makes no response.

"Who knocked the guy against the house who came to hurt you?"

Gertrude looks up at Lucas. "Thoreau?"

Lucas grins. "So?"

"Yes," she says, "I will marry you."

To kiss her, Lucas has to bend over, and that allows the baby to be in their embrace.

Lucas grins and looks around the room. "Have you seen how beautiful Bridget Laurent is?"

Bridget yawns and lets out a small cry.

Mrs. Kelly takes the baby from Gertrude and goes into the other room singing the Ballyeamon Cradle Song, one she had sung to Gertrude many years earlier.

"Rest tired eyes a while

Sweet is thy baby's smile

Angels are guarding and they watch o'er thee

"Sleep, sleep, grah mo chree

Here on you mamma's knee

Angels are guarding

And they watch o'er thee."

Eley speaks up. "Does this mean that we need to plan a wedding?"

Gertrude smiles up at Lucas. "I want to carry a bouquet of seagrass. What do you think?"

"I think we don't have time to plan a wedding," he says. "The baby is here. We need to plan a concert. The ship will be leaving in June, and we have a lot to do before then. People will want to hear the pianist who has been giving secret concerts on Tybee Island."

"How will they know?" asks Gertrude. "Only my few friends know I have been playing."

"What about all the audiences you have found on the porch this winter? Others will know after I write my final feature for the 'Savannah Morning News.'"

"So, it's all about the story?"

"Yes, but the story must include your music. We can get married at the courthouse, but folks need to hear your 'Tybee Rhapsody.'"

"Why?" Gertrude asks.

"It's music from the deepest part of you, the part I have fallen in love with, the part that gets Thoreau," says Lucas.

Eley pulls her shoulder shawl tighter across her chest. "It pulls my heartstrings," says Eley.

"I have gotten to know the composer," says Frances, "and how this soul-searching music came about. That's special."

"You have a gift," says Mrs. Schultz. "I've said so before. I'll say it again."

Gertrude holds Lucas's hand a little tighter. She thinks about Thoreau's quote that the dream in the air needs a foundation. Her family, friends, and now her love for Lucas are the foundation she needs to make her dream of composing music come true. She had no idea that finding a partner was the hope she needed to put a foundation under her dreams. As she looks around at the people gathered about her and for the first time in many, many months, she is sure that these choices are the right ones.

"I guess we need to plan a concert," says Gertrude.

"I'll go get Captain and Michael," says Eley. "They'll want in on this."

The End

AUTHOR'S COMMENTS

Music has always gotten my attention. When Gertrude stepped into the pages of "The Darkest Midnight in December," I knew I wanted to put more music creativity into the next book. I live not far from Gainesville, Georgia where Brenau is located. I got permission to look at the archives of the program in 1907. I spent many days reading the yearbooks, looking a photographs, and examining relics that commemorated that time period at the school. I walked away with the importance of the program that attracted major musicians from all over Europe to teach but also how the women accepted their role in society and did not push past what was accepted. That's when Gertrude stepped out and became different.

Quotes have always been part of my mantra growing up in rural Georgia. The Thoreau quote at the beginning of this book was hand written on a small piece of paper and taped to the mirror in my dorm room in Boggs Hall at the University of Georgia. It moved as frequently as I did but remained on some mirror so I could see it every day. I needed to stay focused to make my dream come true of becoming a writer. After reading "The Artist of the Beautiful," required in a literature course before graduate school, I incorporated it into teaching feature writing. Though most scholars talk about the art theme of the story, I saw the perfect sketch of the writing process: idea, attempt, disillusionment, retry with success, repeat.

The people I met along my research path included Sheila Dunne, the receptionist at the Irish National Concert Hall in Dublin, who greeted me and then went out of her way to show me the back area of the concert hall that had not been reno-vated to visualize how musicians entered the concert hall in 1906. It's people like Ms. Dunne who help historical fiction writers check facts and make the story come alive. She intro-duced me to the gardens behind the concert hall that online sources had not included.

Other experts include Linda Chafin, Conservation Botanist at the State Botanical Garden of Georgia, who led me to sources for edible plants. Two Georgia women working currently as midwives confirmed and offered information that was difficult to verify through historical records: Christy O'Reily and Julie Gunby. My go-to person for understanding legalese on marriage licenses at the turn of the century was Athen's lawyer Nancee Tomlinson. Dr. Mark Wenthe, instructor in the UGA Department of Linguistics, has an interest in the Gullah dialect and led me to several books to help me understand the Gullah character I was creating and have her speak in ways that make her believable. A loud "Thank You" goes to Sydney Wakeford, for continually making the website better and better.

As always, I thank Sean Polite, who is willing to listen to my ideas and stories over Sunday dinners. He recorded the Book Club Singers and their launch performance of the Wexford carols and got the link prepared to post on the website. Thank you.

Rebekah Boles has gone way beyond being my piano teacher. She has moved up to music inspirational advisor and magician to get music researched and organized for the launch of "The Darkest Midnight in December." I am thankful I have Rebekah in my life.

I do not know how to adequately thank Pam Asberry.

Rebekah had given me her name and contact as someone to talk with and interview as to how a music composer may think. I wanted this to be a woman because the protagonist of this book was a young Irish woman. I may be creative, but I am not a musician.

Pam came over for lunch one Sunday after playing at a church in Atlanta. What I learned blew me away. Classically trained from the age of seven, she earned the Master of Music degree at Southern Illinois University at Carbondale and has over forty years of professional experience as a music educator, adjudicator, performer, recording artist, speaker, author, composer and arranger. A BMI artist, she has released nine solo piano albums to date and was awarded Best New Artist 2018 and Best Holiday Album 2019 by Enlightened Piano Radio. In addition, she is the Print Music Manager and Product Specialist at PianoWorks in Duluth, Georgia, and she maintains a private teaching studio in Lawrenceville, Georgia. Pam's music can be heard on Whisperings Solo Piano Radio, Enlightened Piano Radio, Spotify, Pandora, Apple Music, Sirius XM, and elsewhere. Visit www.pamasberry.com to find out more.

As we talked and I gave her my synopsis of the book, she shared that a Christmas song she put on Pandora had two million spins. That was last year. Now her songs have over three million spins. Then she said, "I would like to write a rhapsody for your book." That rhapsody has been written, and we are cross promoting her "Tybee Rhapsody" with my "Tybee Rhapsody." See the page at the end of the novel to find a way to hear Pam Asberry's "Tybee Rhapsody."

Two other women deserve more than just thanks. My daughter, Jessica, has shown how supportive she is through her kind words after reading my books, sharing my work with others, and offering younger advice in how to manage the social media world I did not grow up in. I thank you and I listen to you. My publisher, Leigh Ebberwein, has been my cheerleader. She has demonstrated through her actions and words that she truly believes in the writers she chooses to publish. Thank you. I am forever grateful.

REFERENCE NOTES

"Best quilts" of immigrants. See Holland, Karen A. (Spring, 2000). Form over function: Irish quilting, 1850-2000. New Hibernia Review, Vol. 4, No. 1, pp. 9-22. Published by University of St. Thomas (Center for Irish Studies). See also:
https://www.antiquequiltdating.com/Early_Irish_Patchwork_Quilts_and_Traditions.html

Blind piano tuners. Wing & Son Pianos. See the following:
https://www.pianoemporium.com/wp-content/uploads/2012/06/WingSonPianoBook-2009-1.pdf
For Piano tuners' history, see the following:
https://www.piano-tuners.org/history/piano-tuner-history.html

Canned corn. L.P. Maggioni and Company (Savannah, GA) began oyster harvesting and canning business in Savannah, Georgia from 1883-1982. L.P. Maggioni and Company first began operation in 1870 after Luigi Paoli Maggioni emigrated from Genoa, Italy to begin a new life in the United States. He and his wife, Natalie Betellini whom he met and married in Jacksonville, Florida settled on the Isle of Hope near Savannah, Georgia and began selling shellfish and other small items. In 1883, they opened an oyster factory on Daufuskie Island and later built an oyster cannery in Beaufort, South Carolina. The company, which started as a retail seafood dealership, peaked in the mid 1900s to include fifteen canneries throughout South Carolina, Georgia and Florida. L.P. Maggioni and Company employed more than 2,500 people and also branched out their oyster business to include shrimp, citrus, and produce as well. https://researchworks.oclc.org/archivegrid/archiveComponent/371153841

Dublin Orchestral Society. Founded in 1898 by Michele Esposito and modelled as a 'professional co-operative orchestra' along the lines of the Società Orchestrale della Scala di Milano, and was funded by a mixture of subscriptions, donations, and ticket sales, and later by grants from Dublin Corporation.

Downey, James Henry (Dr.). Gainesville, GA doctor who built The Downey

Hospital in 1912 located on South Sycamore Street, thought to be the first fully accredited hospital in the state.

Florence Crittenton Services in Kansas. Florence Crittenton, a child who died of scarlet fever before she reached her fifth birthday, lived from 1877-1882. Her father, Charles Crittenton, was so distraught over the death of his daughter that he sought a way to make her name live forever. He opened the Bleeker Street Mission in 1883 in NYC to rescue outcast women and girls.

Foraging in 1906. Foraging for various types of seaweed, which are high in protein and contain Vitamin B12, can flavor soups, thicken sauces, be baked into bread or cakes, or dried and eaten like potato chips. See the following:
https://www.npr.org/sections/thesalt/2017/01/15/508362517/bountiful-beach-buffet-fresh-seaweed-is-making-waves-among-foragers.

The single most illuminating account of the seaweeds in the region in those early days came from a professor of biology at Washington and Lee University, W. D. Hoyt. He collected plants primarily in the region surrounding Beaufort, NC, in the years 1903-1909, but he also visited sites from Ocracoke, NC, through South Carolina to Tybee, GA. See the following: https://api.pageplace.de/preview/DT0400.9780822397984_A35685356/preview-9780822397984_A35685356.pdf

Fresh Air Home on Tybee Fresh Air Home and the Froebel Society
https://freshairhome.weebly.com/history.html

Fr. Angelus Healy. A Capuchin friar (1873-1953) known as the 'Guardian of the Reek,' in honor of his long association with the pilgrimage. The story of the pilgrimage was recounted in the article entitled "A Pilgrimage to Croagh Patrick" written by a cleric who gives his name as E.O.L and was published in the *Irish Monthly* magazine. The article recounts the priest's ascent of the mountain, the weather conditions, and encounters with pilgrims. See the following:
https://pilgrimagemedievalireland.com/tag/collection-of-fr-angelus-healy-ofm-cap-1873-1953/

Galway Hotel near Eyre Park. The Railway Hotel near Eyre Park in the novel, was known as Webb's Hotel built in 1810, then known as the Clanricarde Arms, Kilroy's Hotel, and Murphy's. When it was taken over by Joe Delaney, he changed the name to The Imperial Hotel Galway. Fair days were common events in Eyre Square. Cattle fairs in Galway were originally held at Fairhill but moved to this location towards the end of the 19th century. In addition to the cattle fairs, the Square played host to sheep fairs, horse fairs, pig fairs, turf markets, hay markets, sock markets, etc.

Gilmore, Patrick Sarsfield. In 1888, the Irishman from Galway, decided to add music to the New Year's Eve in Times Square event. At the time, the triangle of land at the intersection of 7th Avenue, Broadway, and 42nd Street was known as the Long Acre. Gilmore brought in his band and performed for the people waiting, led them in a countdown, and fired two pistols in the air at the stroke of midnight. The event became an annual tradition. In 1904 the celebration was expanded with the opening of *The New York Times* whose owner had the Long Acre renamed Times Square in honor of the new Times Tower. That New Year's Eve, the celebration began with a street festival and ended in a fireworks display. At midnight came the cheering of more than 200,000 attendees listening to the music that had become part of the tradition. See the following: https://aoh.com/2020/01/07/the-irish-new-years-eve/

Railway information. Great Southern and Western Railroad, Midland Great Western Railroad. See the following:
https://upload.wikimedia.org/wikipedia/commons/3/3a/Ireland_Rail ways_1906.pdf and
https://attachment.tapatalk-cdn.com/16889/202202/3579887_1c243b0359ad3 fae7e6c188b1e9f9ed2.jpg

Singer Sewing Machine and treadle. See the following:
https://ismacs.net/singer_sewing_machine_company/manuals/singer-sewing-machine-manuals.html

Praise House. A Gullah phrase "pray's house."
https://bdcbcl.wordpress.com/2018/08/13/praise-houses-in-gullah-religion-and-social-practices/

Euchee natives. Tybee's original inhabitants were The Euchee, a native American tribe known to have been fierce and bitter enemies of The Cherokee Nation. When the Cherokee attacked the Euchee city of Chestowee in Eastern Tennessee in 1714, many Euchee migrated to parts of Georgia, including Tybee Island. They were named Tsoyaha, or "Children of the Sun" by neighboring tribal nations. Tybee is the Euchee word meaning Salt.

McCormack, John. A singer (tenor) from Athlone, County Westmeath, Ireland, renowned for his diction and breath control. In 1903, he won the coveted gold medal of the Dublin Feis Ceoil.

In March 1904, McCormack's friend was James Joyce. "I hear you Calling Me" by Harold Harford and Charles Marshall became a 1908 best seller recorded by McCormack. See the following: https://www.youtube.com/watch?v=ZMPdQU_cjB8

Midwives in 1900s. See the following: https://connect.springerpub.com/content/book/978-0-8261-2538-5/part/part01/chapter/ch01

Muir, John. In 39 days, Muir had hiked from Louisville, Kentucky, across the Appalachian Mountains, through Piedmont cotton fields and long-leaf pine forests, and into what he called the "River Country of Georgia." He followed the Savannah River south from Augusta, arriving in Savannah on Oct. 8, 1867, "lonesome and poor," he wrote in his journal. "Went to the meanest looking lodging-house that I could find on account of its cheapness." Events over the next six days had a dramatic impact on what became his life's work. See the following:

https://vault.sierraclub.org/john_muir_exhibit/writings/a_thousand_mile_walk_to_the_gulf/chapter_4.aspx

Muir's environmental, ethical and philosophical beliefs that undergird the American conservation movement took hold at Bonaventure. Ironically, the "father" of the national parks, conscience of the environmental movement, cofounder of the Sierra Club and passionate defender of all things wild owes much of his life's work and reputation to the dead. See the following:

https://savannahmagazine.com/culture/the-road-less-traveled/

Schumann, Clara. "I once believed that I possessed creative talent," (1816-1896). See the following: https://donne-uk.org/did-clara-schumann-believe-women-shouldnt-compose/

Solfege Method. Solfege is a method of ear training. It helps students hear music in their head, freeing them from dependence on a score, instrument or recording. Students learn pitch, harmony and sight reading with this method. An Italian monk, Guido di Arezzo, invented the solfege method back in the eleventh century. He used the "Hymn to St. John the Baptist" and gave spoken or sung syllables to each scale degree in the song. The syllables are the first two letters of the words in the lyrics: do, re, mi, fa, sol, la, ti, do.

St. Nicholas Catholic Church is the oldest medieval Catholic church in Galway. It was founded in 1320 and dedicated to Saint Nicholas of Myra, the patron of seafarers, in recognition of Galway's status as a port.

St. Patrick, Confessio, his spiritual autobiography, and Letter to Corotius. See the following: https://www.confessio.ie/etexts/confessio_english# and https://www.confessio.ie/etexts/epistola_english#

Thoreau, Henry David. See the following
https://www.cusd80.com/cms/lib6/AZ01001175/Centricity/Domain/7314/
    Walden-Excerpt.pdf

Touch watch. Designed for reading in the dark or by the blind. See the following:
https://www.napoleon.org/en/history-of-the-two-empires/objects/tact-watch-
    belonging-to-jerome-bonaparte-king-of-westphalia/

Tybee Island. Tybee became a regional resort when the railroad became a unit of the Central of Georgia in 1890, and then under its direct ownership in 1895. This new affiliation gave the island a direct link to hundreds of towns and cities throughout Georgia and Alabama. To entice people to come to the resort by way of their rail system, the Central of Georgia built an enormous dancing and entertainment pavilion, the Tybrisa, next to Hotel Tybee around 1900. The Strand, built between 1895 and 1923, was a row of private summer cottages that developed along the oceanfront next to Hotel Tybee (between Eleventh and Fourteenth Streets). Each cottage was built in the center of a full oceanfront lot that extended from Butler Avenue to the beach. As the row took shape, a common landscape scheme was adopted by each subsequent addition to the settlement. All cottages were built at a substantial setback from the dunes, which provided a grassy expanse (or strand) between the homes and the beach. A walkway passed in front of the steps of each cottage, connecting the settlement with the resort at Hotel Tybee. This afforded the property owners a spacious and private setting with a somewhat communal aspect when desired. The Back River area was developed early as 1888, although most of the cottages built during this time were destroyed during the devastating hurricanes of 1893 and 1898. A new development, known locally as Colony Row, was begun along the Back River in 1900. Developed between 1900-1915, Colony Row is a concentration of similar, square, two-story cottages built in a row between Inlet Avenue and the mouth if the Back River. Each cottage was situated in the center of a 1.5-acre lot facing the Back River with separate servants' quarters located on the back of the property near Chatham Avenue. A boardwalk ran the length of the bluff in front of the cottages to Inlet Station, where the Central of Georgia turnstile was located. The Back River area was developed as a more secluded alternative to the frenetic bustle of the resort, where families from Savannah and the region returned each season to spend the summer. See the following: https://npgallery.nps.gov/GetAsset/ed481a66-d012-48ab-a265-bb6a711957bd

Watch Night on New Year's Eve. December 31, 1862, enslaved and free African Americans gathered, many in secret, to ring in the new year and await news that the Emancipation Proclamation had taken effect. On September 22, 1862, President Abraham Lincoln issued the executive order that declared enslaved people in the rebelling Confederate States legally free. However, the decree would not take effect until the clock struck midnight at the start of the new year. The occasion, known as Watch Night or "Freedom's Eve," marks when African Americans across the country watched and waited for the news of freedom. Today, Watch Night is an annual New Year's Eve tradition that includes the memory of slavery and freedom, reflections on faith, and celebration of community and strength. See the following: https://nmaahc.si.edu/explore/stories/historical-legacy-watch-night

Notes on Music used in the book

"Alice, Where Art Thou Going," words by William A. Heelan and music by Albert Gumble. It was released by Jerome H. Remick & Company in New York in 1906. https://www.loc.gov/item/jukebox-728520/

"Amazing Grace" published in 1779, written in 1772 by English Anglican clergyman and poet, John Newton, who wrote the words from personal experience; he grew up without any religious conviction, but his life's path was formed by a variety of twists and coincidences that were often put into motion by others' reactions to what they took as his recalcitrant insubordination. He was pressed into service with the Royal Navy, and after leaving the service, he became involved in the Atlantic slave trade. In 1748, a violent storm battered his vessel off the coast of County Donegal, Ireland, so severely that he called out to God for mercy. https://study.com/learn/lesson/amazing-grace-history-origin.html#:~:text=%22Amazing%20Grace%22%20 20lyrics%20are%20based,and%20captained%20a%20slave%20ship.

"As I Roved Out One Morning." Michael Gallagher, Brigid [Tunney]'s brother, Paddy [Tunney]'s Uncle Mick, was born in 1891 and, when recorded, was working as a boot repairer in Belleek. Previously he had been a farmer, and before that lived 33 years in Glasgow. Like his sister, he learned his songs from his parents and grandparents on both sides of the family, as well as from aunts, uncles and others. *The Deluded Lover* was from his aunt, Brigid, in Ballintra, Donegal. The title for this song was provided by the collectors; Michael called it *As I Roved Out.* https://mainlynorfolk.info/june.tabor/songs/asirovedout.html

"Ballyeamon Cradle Song" is a traditional Irish lullaby that was recovered from an old song book by Aine Ui Cheallaigh.

"Billy Boy" may have been written by Hector MacNeill and first published in 1791. https://mainlynorfolk.info/martin.carthy/songs/billyboy.html

"Galway Bay" by Francis A. Fahy. https://www.contemplator.com/ireland/galway.html

"The Last Rose of Summer" is from a poem by Irish poet Thomas Moore, written in 1805 while staying at Jenkinstown Castle in County Kilkenny, Ireland, where he was said to have been inspired by a specimen of Rosa 'Old Blush.' https://www.youtube.com/watch?v=DfLyKWD9Kso

"Lift Every Voice and Sing" often referred to as "The Black National Anthem," was written as a poem by NAACP leader James Weldon Johnson in 1900. His brother, John Rosamond Johnson (1873-1954), composed the music for the lyrics. A choir of 500 schoolchildren at the segregated Stanton School, where James Weldon Johnson was principal, first performed the song in public in Jacksonville, Florida to celebrate President Abraham Lincoln's birthday.
https://www.youtube.com/watch?v=1sghN7ZORkM

"Morrison's Jig" by James Morrison https://www.youtube.com/watch?v=T_UybPKSxJM
First published in 1855 but is thought to be older. Considered a traditional Irish song. Morrison did not compose the jig but rather obtained it from a Dromlacht, County Kerry, accordion player (a member of his band) named Tom Carmody, who knew it as "Stick across the Hob." Carmody in turn had learned it from his father, Maurice.

"Nobody knows the trouble I've seen" originated during slavery but was published in 1867.

"The Rose of Tralee" words by C. Mordaunt Spencer and music by Charles W. Glover. https://roseoftralee.ie/the-story-of-the-rose-of-tralee/

"Slieve Gallion Braes" (*Sliabh Gallion brae*) written by James McGarvey, A Derryman, sometime in the 1800s. https://songoftheisles.com/2013/05/01/sliabh-gallion-braes/

"The Wearing of the Green" is an Irish street ballad lamenting the repression of supporters of the Irish Rebellion of 1798. The best-known lyrics are by Dion Boucicault.
https://www.youtube.com/watch?v=84wg0hq2tuQ

"Wee Falorie Man" has no known author, catalogued here https://www.discogs.com/master/745855-David-Hammond-I-Am-The-Wee-Falorie-Man-Folk-Songs-Of-Ireland?srsltid=AfmBOooJniBFCinA2wPfLFub3oUCbOsVcb5MXGE5KxcvVfKUHAyIrl3q

LISTEN TO THE TYBEE RHAPSODY

"Tybee Rhapsody," music written by Pam Asberry. Access the song by using the QR code here.

The Tybee Rhapsody was performed in Wexford on September 20, 2025, at the St. Iberius Church on Main Street. The solo concert in the 350-year-old church, focused on Pam's adaptations and musical compositions to include the premiere of "Tybee Rhapsody."

"Tybee Rhapsody" music is being cross promoted with the Tybee Rhapsody novel.

MORE FROM LEARA RHODES
"REMEMBERING IRELAND SERIES"

Leaving behind his friends and a thriving business in Galway, Cahey embarks on a journey to New York and struggles to find his way. He quickly discovers he is not alone. He bands with other Irish, Scottish, and French immigrants to build a life away from everything he once loved. Being Irish creates many problems, even in New York. Finding out how severe those problems are could change his life forever. His fear is—can his survival skills and love of horses be enough to become the most sought-after horse trainer at the Vanderbilt American Horse Exchange in 1901?

Set in the early 20th century, a young Irish woman, Sharon McGee, leaves her New York family to start a new life in Savannah, Georgia. Working as an accountant for a shipping firm in Ireland, she stays in a boarding house with other Irish nursing students. While thriving in her career, Sharon faces a romantic dilemma, torn between two very different men. As she discovers the true reason behind her hiring, she must stay true to herself, even if it means facing heartbreak.

COMING SOON
The Next Novel in the "Remembering Ireland Series"
"On the Banks of the River Slaney"

ABOUT THE AUTHOR
LEARA RHODES

Leara Rhodes is the author of Spancil Hill and The Darkest Midnight in December, both recommended by the Celtic Heritage Foundation as books supporting Irish heritage. She was an associate professor of journalism emerita at the Grady College of Journalism and Mass Communication at the University of Georgia for 30 years, teaching newspaper and magazine writing and international communication. She has three academic books and dozens of publications in academic journals and magazines. Upon retiring, she began researching her Irish ancestors but got sidetracked by the characters in her novels.

Leara lives in Athens, Georgia, and spends time in her garden under the oaks, follows several local bands, and participates in the oldest community theatre in the country.

To learn more about Leara, visit Leararhodes.com.